CITY OF BONES

MICHAEL CONNELLY

CITY OF BONES

ORION

First published in Great Britain in 2002 by Orion,
an imprint of the Orion Publishing Group Ltd.

Copyright © Hieronymus, Inc. 2002

The moral right of Michael Connelly to be identified as the author
of this work has been asserted in accordance with the Copyright,
Designs and Patents Act of 1988.

Published by arrangement with Little, Brown and
Company (Inc.), New York, NY, USA

A CIP catalogue record for this book is available
from the British Library.

ISBN 0 75282 140 7 (hardback)
0 75283 869 5 (trade paperback)

Printed in Great Britain by
Clays Ltd, St Ives plc

The Orion Publishing Group Ltd
Orion House
5 Upper Saint Martin's Lane
London, WC2H 9EA

This is for John Houghton,
for the help, the friendship and the stories

CITY OF BONES

1

THE old lady had changed her mind about dying but by then it was too late. She had dug her fingers into the paint and plaster of the nearby wall until most of her fingernails had broken off. Then she had gone for the neck, scrabbling to push the bloodied fingertips up and under the cord. She broke four toes kicking at the walls. She had tried so hard, shown such a desperate will to live, that it made Harry Bosch wonder what had happened before. Where was that determination and will and why had it deserted her until after she had put the extension cord noose around her neck and kicked over the chair? Why had it hidden from her?

These were not official questions that would be raised in his death report. But they were the things Bosch couldn't avoid thinking about as he sat in his car outside the Splendid Age Retirement Home on Sunset Boulevard east of the Hollywood Freeway. It was 4:20 P.M. on the first day of the year. Bosch had drawn holiday call-out duty.

The day more than half over and that duty consisted of two suicide runs — one a gunshot, the other the hanging. Both victims were women. In both cases there was evidence of depression and desperation. Isolation. New Year's Day was always a big day for suicides. While most people greeted the day with a sense of hope and renewal, there were those who saw it as a good day to die, some — like the old lady — not realizing their mistake until it was too late.

Bosch looked up through the windshield and watched as the latest victim's body, on a wheeled stretcher and covered in a green blanket, was loaded into the coroner's blue van. He saw there was one other occupied stretcher in the van and knew it was from the first suicide — a thirty-four-year-old actress who had shot herself while parked at a Hollywood overlook on Mulholland Drive. Bosch and the body crew had followed one case to the other.

Bosch's cell phone chirped and he welcomed the intrusion into his thoughts on small deaths. It was Mankiewicz, the watch sergeant at the Hollywood Division of the Los Angeles Police Department.

"You finished with that yet?"

"I'm about to clear."

"Anything?"

"A changed-my-mind suicide. You got something else?"

"Yeah. And I didn't think I should go out on the radio with it. Must be a slow day for the media — getting more what's-happening calls from reporters than I am getting service calls from citizens. They all want to do something on the first one, the actress on Mulholland. You know, a death-of-a-Hollywood-dream story. And they'd probably jump all over this latest call, too."

"Yeah, what is it?"

"A citizen up in Laurel Canyon. On Wonderland. He just called up and said his dog came back from a run in the woods with a bone in its mouth. The guy says it's human — an arm bone from a kid."

Bosch almost groaned. There were four or five call outs like this a year. Hysteria always followed by simple explanation: animal bones. Through the windshield he saluted the two body movers from the coroner's office as they headed to the front doors of the van.

"I know what you're thinking, Harry. Not another bone run. You've done it a hundred times and it's always the same thing. Coyote, deer, whatever. But listen, this guy with the dog, he's an MD. And he says there's no doubt. It's a humerus. That's the upper arm bone. He says it's a child, Harry. And then, get this. He said . . ."

There was silence while Mankiewicz apparently looked for his notes. Bosch watched the coroner's blue van pull off into traffic. When Mankiewicz came back he was obviously reading.

"The bone's got a fracture clearly visible just above the medial epicondyle, whatever that is."

Bosch's jaw tightened. He felt a slight tickle of electric current go down the back of his neck.

"That's off my notes, I don't know if I am saying it right. The point is, this doctor says it was just a kid, Harry. So could you humor us and go check out this humerus?"

Bosch didn't respond.

"Sorry, had to get that in."

"Yeah, that was funny, Mank. What's the address?"

Mankiewicz gave it to him and told him he had already dispatched a patrol team.

"You were right to keep it off the air. Let's try to keep it that way."

Mankiewicz said he would. Bosch closed his phone and started the car. He glanced over at the entrance to the retirement home before pulling away from the curb. There was nothing about it that looked splendid to him. The woman who had hung herself in the closet of her tiny bedroom had no next of kin, according to the operators of the home. In death, she would be treated the way she had been in life, left alone and forgotten.

Bosch pulled away from the curb and headed toward Laurel Canyon.

2

Bosch listened to the Lakers game on the car radio while he made his way into the canyon and then up Lookout Mountain to Wonderland Avenue. He wasn't a religious follower of professional basketball but wanted to get a sense of the situation in case he needed his partner, Jerry Edgar. Bosch was working alone because Edgar had lucked into a pair of choice seats to the game. Bosch had agreed to handle the call outs and to not bother Edgar unless a homicide or something Bosch couldn't handle alone came up. Bosch was alone also because the third member of his team, Kizmin Rider, had been promoted nearly a year earlier to Robbery-Homicide Division and still had not been replaced.

It was early third quarter, and the game with the Trail Blazers was tied. While Bosch wasn't a hardcore fan he knew enough from Edgar's constant talking about the game and begging to be left free of call-out duty that it was an important matchup with one of the Los Angeles team's top rivals. He decided not to page Edgar until he had gotten to the scene and assessed the situation. He turned the radio off when he started losing the AM station in the canyon.

The drive up was steep. Laurel Canyon was a cut in the

Santa Monica Mountains. The tributary roads ranged up toward the crest of the mountains. Wonderland Avenue dead-ended in a remote spot where the half-million-dollar homes were surrounded by heavily wooded and steep terrain. Bosch instinctively knew that searching for bones in the area would be a logistical nightmare. He pulled to a stop behind a patrol car already at the address Mankiewicz had provided and checked his watch. It was 4:38, and he wrote it down on a fresh page of his legal pad. He figured he had less than an hour of daylight left.

A patrol officer he didn't recognize answered his knock. Her nameplate said Brasher. She led him back through the house to a home office where her partner, a cop whom Bosch recognized and knew was named Edgewood, was talking to a white-haired man who sat behind a cluttered desk. There was a shoe box with the top off on the desk.

Bosch stepped forward and introduced himself. The white-haired man said he was Dr. Paul Guyot, a general practitioner. Leaning forward Bosch could see that the shoe box contained the bone that had drawn them all together. It was dark brown and looked like a gnarled piece of driftwood.

He could also see a dog lying on the floor next to the doctor's desk chair. It was a large dog with a yellow coat.

"So this is it," Bosch said, looking back down into the box.

"Yes, Detective, that's your bone," Guyot said. "And as you can see . . ."

He reached to a shelf behind the desk and pulled down a heavy copy of *Gray's Anatomy*. He opened it to a previously marked spot. Bosch noticed he was wearing latex gloves.

The page showed an illustration of a bone, anterior and posterior views. In the corner of the page was a small sketch of a skeleton with the humerus bone of both arms highlighted.

"The humerus," Guyot said, tapping the page. "And then we have the recovered specimen."

He reached into the shoe box and gently lifted the bone. Holding it above the book's illustration he went through a point-by-point comparison.

"Medial epicondyle, trochlea, greater and lesser tubercle," he said. "It's all there. And I was just telling these two officers, I know my bones even without the book. This bone is human, Detective. There's no doubt."

Bosch looked at Guyot's face. There was a slight quiver, perhaps the first showing of the tremors of Parkinson's.

"Are you retired, Doctor?"

"Yes, but it doesn't mean I don't know a bone when I see —"

"I'm not challenging you, Dr. Guyot." Bosch tried to smile. "You say it is human, I believe it. Okay? I'm just trying to get the lay of the land here. You can put that back into the box now if you want."

Guyot replaced the bone in the shoe box.

"What's your dog's name?"

"Calamity."

Bosch looked down at the dog. It appeared to be sleeping.

"When she was a pup she was a lot of trouble."

Bosch nodded.

"So, if you don't mind telling it again, tell me what happened today."

Guyot reached down and ruffled the dog's collar. The dog looked up at him for a moment and then put its head back down and closed its eyes.

"I took Calamity out for her afternoon walk. Usually when I get up to the circle I take her off the leash and let her run up into the woods. She likes it."

"What kind of dog is she?" Bosch asked.

"Yellow Lab," Brasher answered quickly from behind him.

Bosch turned and looked at her. She realized she had made a mistake by intruding and nodded and stepped back toward the door of the room where her partner was.

"You guys can clear if you have other calls," Bosch said. "I can take it from here."

Edgewood nodded and signaled his partner out.

"Thank you, Doctor," he said as he went.

"Don't mention it."

Bosch thought of something.

"Hey, guys?"

Edgewood and Brasher turned back.

"Let's keep this off the air, okay?"

"You got it," said Brasher, her eyes holding on Bosch's until he looked away.

After the officers left, Bosch looked back at the doctor and noticed that the facial tremor was slightly more pronounced now.

"They didn't believe me at first either," he said.

"It's just that we get a lot of calls like this. But I believe you, Doctor, so why don't you continue with the story?"

Guyot nodded.

"Well, I was up on the circle and I took off the leash. She went up into the woods like she likes to do. She's well trained. When I whistle she comes back. Trouble is, I can't whistle very loud anymore. So if she goes where she can't hear me, then I have to wait, you see."

"What happened today when she found the bone?"

"I whistled and she didn't come back."

"So she was pretty far up there."

"Yes, exactly. I waited. I whistled a few more times, and then finally she came down out of the woods next to Mr. Ulrich's house. She had the bone. In her mouth. At first I thought it was a stick, you see, and that she wanted to play fetch with it. But as she came to me I recognized the shape. I took it from her — had a fight over that —

and then I called you people after I examined it here and was sure."

You people, Bosch thought. It was always said like that, as if the police were another species. The blue species which carried armor that the horrors of the world could not pierce.

"When you called you told the sergeant that the bone had a fracture."

"Absolutely."

Guyot picked up the bone again, handling it gently. He turned it and ran his finger along a vertical striation along the bone's surface.

"That's a break line, Detective. It's a healed fracture."

"Okay."

Bosch pointed to the box, and the doctor returned the bone.

"Doctor, do you mind putting your dog on a leash and taking a walk up to the circle with me?"

"Not at all. I just need to change my shoes."

"I need to change, too. How about if I meet you out front?"

"Right away."

"I'm going to take this now."

Bosch put the top back on the shoe box and then carried it with two hands, making sure not to turn the box or jostle its contents in any way.

Outside, Bosch noticed the patrol car was still in front of the house. The two officers sat inside it, apparently writing out reports. He went to his car and placed the shoe box on the front passenger seat.

Since he had been on call out he had not dressed in a suit. He had on a sport coat with blue jeans and a white oxford shirt. He stripped off his coat, folded it inside out and put it on the backseat. He noticed that the trigger from the weapon he kept holstered on his hip had worn a hole in the lining and the jacket wasn't even a year old. Soon it would work its way into the pocket and then all the way through. More often than not he wore out his coats from the inside.

He took his shirt off next, revealing a white T-shirt beneath. He then opened the trunk to get out the pair of work boots from his crime scene equipment box. As he leaned against the rear bumper and changed his shoes he saw Brasher get out of the patrol car and come back toward him.

"So it looks legit, huh?"

"Think so. Somebody at the ME's office will have to confirm, though."

"You going to go up and look?"

"I'm going to try to. Not much light left, though. Probably be back out here tomorrow."

"By the way, I'm Julia Brasher. I'm new in the division."

"Harry Bosch."

"I know. I've heard of you."

"I deny everything."

She smiled at the line and put her hand out but Bosch was right in the middle of tying one of the boots. He stopped and shook her hand.

"Sorry," she said. "My timing is off today."

"Don't worry about it."

He finished tying the boot and stood up off the bumper.

"When I blurted out the answer in there, about the dog, I immediately realized you were trying to establish a rapport with the doctor. That was wrong. I'm sorry."

Bosch studied her for a moment. She was mid-thirties with dark hair in a tight braid that left a short tail going over the back of her collar. Her eyes were dark brown. He guessed she liked the outdoors. Her skin had an even tan.

"Like I said, don't worry about it."

"You're alone?"

Bosch hesitated.

"My partner's working on something else while I check this out."

He saw the doctor coming out the front door of the house with the dog on a leash. He decided not to get out his crime scene jumpsuit and put it on. He glanced over at Julia Brasher, who was now watching the approaching dog.

"You guys don't have calls?"

"No, it's slow."

Bosch looked down at the MagLite in his equipment box. He looked at her and then reached into the trunk and grabbed an oil rag, which he threw over the flashlight. He took out a roll of yellow crime scene tape and the Polaroid camera, then closed the trunk and turned to Brasher.

"Then do you mind if I borrow your Mag? I, uh, forgot mine."

"No problem."

She slid the flashlight out of the ring on her equipment belt and handed it to him.

The doctor and his dog came up then.

"Ready."

"Okay, Doctor, I want you to take us up to the spot where you let the dog go and we'll see where she goes."

"I'm not sure you'll be able to stay with her."

"I'll worry about that, Doctor."

"This way then."

They walked up the incline toward the small turn-around circle where Wonderland reached a dead end. Brasher made a hand signal to her partner in the car and walked along with them.

"You know, we had a little excitement up this way a few years ago," Guyot said. "A man was followed home from the Hollywood Bowl and then killed in a robbery."

"I remember," Bosch said.

He knew the investigation was still open but didn't mention it. It wasn't his case.

Dr. Guyot walked with a strong step that belied his age and apparent condition. He let the dog set the pace and soon moved several paces ahead of Bosch and Brasher.

"So where were you before?" Bosch asked Brasher.

"What do you mean?"

"You said you were new in Hollywood Division. What about before?"

"Oh. The academy."

He was surprised. He looked over at her, thinking he might need to reassess his age estimate.

She nodded and said, "I know, I'm old."

Bosch got embarrassed.

"No, I wasn't saying that. I just thought that you had been somewhere else. You don't seem like a rookie."

"I didn't go in until I was thirty-four."

"Really? Wow."

"Yeah. Got the bug a little late."

"What were you doing before?"

"Oh, a bunch of different things. Travel mostly. Took me a while to figure out what I wanted to do. And you want to know what I want to do the most?"

Bosch looked at her.

"What?"

"What you do. Homicide."

He didn't know what to say, whether to encourage her or dissuade her.

"Well, good luck," he said.

"I mean, don't you just find it to be the most fulfilling job ever? Look at what you do, you take the most evil people out of the mix."

"The mix?"

"Society."

"Yeah, I guess so. When we get lucky."

They caught up to Dr. Guyot, who had stopped with the dog at the turnaround circle.

"This the place?"

"Yes. I let her go here. She went up through there."

He pointed to an empty and overgrown lot that started level with the street but then quickly rose into a steep incline toward the crest of the hills. There was a large concrete drainage culvert, which explained why the lot had never been built on. It was city property, used to funnel storm water runoff away from the homes on the street. Many of the streets in the canyon were former creek and river beds. When it rained they would return to their original purpose if not for the drainage system.

"Are you going up there?" the doctor asked.

"I'm going to try."

"I'll go with you," Brasher said.

Bosch looked at her and then turned at the sound of a car. It was the patrol car. It pulled up and Edgewood put down the window.

"We got a hot shot, partner. Double D."

He nodded toward the empty passenger seat. Brasher frowned and looked at Bosch.

"I hate domestic disputes."

Bosch smiled. He hated them too, especially when they turned into homicides.

"Sorry about that."

"Well, maybe next time."

She started around the front of the car.

"Here," Bosch said, holding out the MagLite.

"I've got an extra in the car," she said. "You can just get that back to me."

"You sure?"

He was tempted to ask for a phone number but didn't.

"I'm sure. Good luck."

"You too. Be careful."

She smiled at him and then hurried around the front of

the car. She got in and the car pulled away. Bosch turned his attention back to Guyot and the dog.

"An attractive woman," Guyot said.

Bosch ignored it, wondering if the doctor had made the comment based on seeing Bosch's reaction to Brasher. He hoped he hadn't been that obvious.

"Okay, Doctor," he said, "let the dog go and I'll try to keep up."

Guyot unhooked the leash while patting the dog's chest.

"Go get the bone, girl. Get a bone! Go!"

The dog took off into the lot and was gone from sight before Bosch had taken a step. He almost laughed.

"Well, I guess you were right about that, Doc."

He turned to make sure the patrol car was gone and Brasher hadn't seen the dog take off.

"You want me to whistle?"

"Nah. I'll just go in and take a look around, see if I can catch up to her."

He turned the flashlight on.

3

THE woods were dark long before the sun disappeared. The overhead canopy created by a tall stand of Monterey pines blocked out most of the light before it got to the ground. Bosch used the flashlight and made his way up the hillside in the direction in which he had heard the dog moving through the brush. It was slow moving and hard work. The ground contained a foot-thick layer of pine needles that gave way often beneath Bosch's boots as he tried for purchase on the incline. Soon his hands were sticky with sap from grabbing branches to keep himself upright.

It took him nearly ten minutes to go thirty yards up the hillside. Then the ground started to level off and the light got better as the tall trees thinned. Bosch looked around for the dog but didn't see her. He called down to the street, though he could no longer see it or Dr. Guyot.

"Dr. Guyot? Can you hear me?"

"Yes, I hear you."

"Whistle for your dog."

He then heard a three-part whistle. It was distinct but very low, having the same trouble getting through the trees and underbrush as the sunlight had. Bosch tried to repeat it and after a few tries thought he had it right. But the dog didn't come.

Bosch pressed on, staying on the level ground because he believed that if someone was going to bury or abandon a body, then it would be done on even ground as opposed to the steep slope. Following a path of least resistance, he moved into a stand of acacia trees. And here he immediately came upon a spot where the earth had recently been disturbed. It had been overturned, as if a tool or an animal had been randomly rooting in the soil. He used his foot to push some of the dirt and twigs aside and then realized they weren't twigs.

He dropped to his knees and used the light to study the short brown bones scattered over a square foot of dirt. He believed he was looking at the disjointed fingers of a hand. A small hand. A child's hand.

Bosch stood up. He realized that his interest in Julia Brasher had distracted him. He had brought no means with him for collecting the bones. Picking them up and carrying them down the hill would violate every tenet of evidence collection.

The Polaroid camera hung on a shoelace around his neck. He raised it now and took a close-up shot of the bones. He then stepped back and took a wider shot of the spot beneath the acacia trees.

In the distance he heard Dr. Guyot's weak whistle. Bosch went to work with the yellow plastic crime scene tape. He tied a short length of it around the trunk of one of the acacia trees and then strung a boundary around the trees. Thinking about how he would work the case the following morning, he stepped out of the cover of the acacia trees and looked for something to use as an aerial marker. He found a nearby growth of sagebrush. He wrapped the crime scene tape around and over the top of the bush several times.

When he was finished it was almost dark. He took another cursory look around the area but knew that a flashlight search was useless and the ground would need to be exhaustively covered in the morning. Using a small penknife attached to his key chain, he began cutting four-foot lengths of the crime scene tape off the roll.

Making his way back down the hill, he tied the strips off at intervals on tree branches and bushes. He heard voices as he got closer to the street and used them to maintain his direction. At one point on the incline the soft ground suddenly gave way and he fell, tumbling hard into the base of a pine tree. The tree impacted his midsection, tearing his shirt and badly scratching his side.

Bosch didn't move for several seconds. He thought he might have cracked his ribs on the right side. His breathing was difficult and painful. He groaned loudly and slowly pulled himself up on the tree trunk so that he could continue to follow the voices.

He soon came back down into the street where Dr. Guyot was waiting with his dog and another man. The two men looked shocked when they saw the blood on Bosch's shirt.

"Oh my, what happened?" Guyot cried out.

"Nothing. I fell."

"Your shirt is . . . there's blood!"

"Comes with the job."

"Let me look at your chest."

The doctor moved in to look but Bosch held his hands up.

"I'm okay. Who is this?"

The other man answered.

"I'm Victor Ulrich. I live there."

He pointed to the house next to the lot. Bosch nodded.

"I just came out to see what was going on."

"Well, nothing is going on at the moment. But there is a crime scene up there. Or there will be. We probably won't be back to work it until tomorrow morning. But I need both you men to keep clear of it and not to tell anybody about this. All right?"

Both of the neighbors nodded.

"And Doctor, don't let your dog off the leash for a few days. I need to go back down to my car to make a phone call. Mr. Ulrich, I am sure we will want to talk to you tomorrow. Will you be around?"

"Sure. Anytime. I work at home."

"Doing what?"

"Writing."

"Okay. We'll see you tomorrow."

Bosch headed back down the street with Guyot and the dog.

"You really need me to take a look at your injury," Guyot insisted.

"It'll be fine."

Bosch glanced to his left and thought he saw a curtain quickly close behind a window of the house they were passing.

"The way you are holding yourself when you walk — you've damaged a rib," Guyot said. "Maybe you've broken it. Maybe more than one."

Bosch thought of the small, thin bones he had just seen beneath the acacia trees.

"There's nothing you can do for a rib, broken or not," he said.

"I can tape it. You'll breathe a hell of a lot easier. I can also take care of that wound."

Bosch relented.

"Okay, Doc, you get out your black bag. I'm going to get my other shirt."

Inside Guyot's house a few minutes later, the doctor cleaned the deep scratch on the side of Bosch's chest and taped his ribs. It did feel better, but it still hurt. Guyot said he could no longer write a prescription but suggested

Bosch not take anything more powerful than aspirin anyway.

Bosch remembered that he had a prescription bottle with some Vicodin tablets left over from when he'd had a wisdom tooth removed a few months earlier. They would smooth out the pain if he wanted to go that way.

"I'll be fine," Bosch said. "Thanks for fixing me up."

"Don't mention it."

Bosch pulled on his good shirt and watched Guyot as he closed up his first-aid kit. He wondered how long it had been since the doctor had used his skills on a patient.

"How long have you been retired?" he asked.

"Twelve years next month."

"You miss it?"

Guyot turned from the first-aid kit and looked at him. The tremor was gone.

"Every day. I don't miss the actual work — you know, the cases. But it was a job that made a difference. I miss that."

Bosch thought about how Julia Brasher had described homicide work earlier. He nodded that he understood what Guyot was saying.

"You said there was a crime scene up there?" the doctor asked.

"Yes. I found more bones. I've got to make a call, see what we're going to do. Can I borrow your phone? I don't think my cell will work around here."

"No, they never do in the canyon. Use the phone on the desk there and I'll give you some privacy."

He headed out, carrying the first-aid kit with him. Bosch went behind the desk and sat down. The dog was on the ground next to the chair. The animal looked up and seemed startled when she saw Bosch in the master's spot.

"Calamity," he said. "I think you lived up to your name today, girl."

Bosch reached down and rubbed the scruff of the dog's neck. The dog growled and he quickly took his hand away, wondering if it was the dog's training or something about himself that had caused the hostile response.

He picked up the phone and called the home of his supervisor, Lt. Grace Billets. He explained what had happened on Wonderland Avenue and his findings up on the hill.

"Harry, how old do these bones look?" Billets asked.

Bosch looked at the Polaroid he had taken of the small bones he had found in the dirt. It was a bad photo, the flash overexposing it because he was too close.

"I don't know, they look old to me. I'd say we're talking years here."

"Okay, so whatever's there at the scene isn't fresh."

"Maybe freshly uncovered, but no, it's been there."

"That's what I'm saying. So I think we should stick a pin in it and gear up for tomorrow. Whatever is up there on that hill, it's not going anywhere tonight."

"Yeah," Bosch said. "I'm thinking the same thing."

She was silent a moment before speaking.

"These kind of cases, Harry . . ."

"What?"

"They drain the budget, they drain manpower . . . and they're the hardest to close, *if* you can close them."

"Okay, I'll climb back up there and cover the bones up. I'll tell the doctor to keep his dog on a leash."

"Come on, Harry, you know what I mean." She exhaled loudly. "First day of the year and we're going to start in the hole."

Bosch was silent, letting her work through her administrative frustrations. It didn't take long. It was one of the things he liked about her.

"Okay, anything else happen today?"

"Not too much. A couple suicides, that's it so far."

"Okay, when are you going to start tomorrow?"

"I'd like to get out there early. I'll make some calls and see what I can get going. And get the bone the dog found confirmed before we start anything."

"Okay, let me know."

Bosch agreed and hung up the phone. He next called Teresa Corazon, the county medical examiner, at home. Though their relationship outside of work had ended years before and she had moved at least two times since, she had always kept the same number and Bosch knew it by heart. It came in handy now. He explained what he had going and that he needed an official confirmation of the bone as human before he set other things in motion. He also told her that if it was confirmed he would need an archeological team to work the crime scene as soon as possible.

Corazon put him on hold for almost five minutes.

"Okay," she said when she came back on the line. "I couldn't get Kathy Kohl. She's not home."

Bosch knew that Kohl was the staff archeologist. Her real expertise and reason for her inclusion as a full-time employee was retrieving bones from the body dump sites up in the desert of the north county, which was a weekly occurrence. But Bosch knew she would be called in to handle the search for bones off Wonderland Avenue.

"So what do you want me to do? I want to get this confirmed tonight."

"Just hold your horses, Harry. You are always so impatient. You're like a dog with a bone, no pun intended."

"It's a kid, Teresa. Can we be serious?"

"Just come here. I'll look at this bone."

"And what about tomorrow?"

"I'll get things in motion. I left a message for Kathy and as soon as we hang up here I'll call the office and have her paged. She'll head up the dig as soon as the sun is up and we can get in there. Once the bones are recovered, there is a forensic anthropologist at UCLA we have on retainer and I can bring him in if he's in town. And I'll be there myself. Are you satisfied?"

This last part gave Bosch pause.

"Teresa," he finally said, "I want to try to keep this as low profile as I can for as long as I can."

"And what are you implying?"

"That I'm not sure that *the* medical examiner for Los Angeles County needs to be there. And that I haven't seen you at a crime scene without a cameraman in tow for a long time."

"Harry, he is a private videographer, okay? The film he takes is for future use by me and controlled solely by me. It doesn't end up on the six o'clock news."

"Whatever. I just think we need to avoid any complications on this one. It's a child case. You know how they get."

"Just get over here with that bone. I'm leaving in an hour."

She abruptly hung up.

Bosch wished he had been a little more politic with Corazon but was glad he'd made his point. Corazon was a personality, regularly appearing on Court TV and network shows as a forensic expert. She had also taken to having a cameraman follow her so that her cases could be turned into documentaries for broadcast on any of the cop and legal shows on the vast cable and satellite spectrum. He could not and would not let her goals as a celebrity coroner interfere with his goals as an investigator of what might be the homicide of a child.

He decided he'd make the calls to the department's Special Services and K-9 units after he got confirmation on the bone. He got up and left the room, looking for Guyot.

The doctor was in the kitchen, sitting at a small table and writing in a spiral-bound notebook. He looked up at Bosch.

"Just writing a few notes on your treatment. I've kept notes on every patient I've ever treated."

Bosch just nodded, even though he thought it was odd for Guyot to be writing about him.

"I'm going to go, Doctor. We'll be back tomorrow. In force, I'd expect. We might want to use your dog again. Will you be here?"

"I'll be here and be glad to help. How are the ribs?"

"They hurt."

"Only when you breathe, right? That'll last about a week."

"Thanks for taking care of me. You don't need that shoe box back, do you?"

"No, I wouldn't want that back now."

Bosch turned to head toward the front door but then turned back to Guyot.

"Doctor, do you live alone here?"

"I do now. My wife died two years ago. A month before our fiftieth anniversary."

"I'm sorry."

Guyot nodded and said, "My daughter has her own family up in Seattle. I see them on special occasions."

Bosch felt like asking why only on special occasions but didn't. He thanked the man again and left.

Driving out of the canyon and toward Teresa Corazon's place in Hancock Park, he kept his hand on the shoe box so that it would not be jostled or slide off the seat. He felt a deep sense of dread rising from within. He knew it was because fate had certainly not smiled on him this day. He had caught the worst kind of case there was to catch. A child case.

Child cases haunted you. They hollowed you out and scarred you. There was no bulletproof vest thick enough to stop you from being pierced. Child cases left you knowing the world was full of lost light.

4

TERESA Corazon lived in a Mediterranean-style mansion with a stone turnaround circle complete with koi pond in front. Eight years earlier, when Bosch had shared a brief relationship with her, she had lived in a one-bedroom condominium. The riches of television and celebrity had paid for the house and the lifestyle that came with it. She was not even remotely like the woman who used to show up at his house unannounced at midnight with a cheap bottle of red wine from Trader Joe's and a video of her favorite movie to watch. The woman who was unabashedly ambitious but not yet skilled at using her position to enrich herself.

Bosch knew he now served as a reminder of what she had been and what she had lost in order to gain all that she had. It was no wonder their interactions were now few and far between but as tense as a visit to the dentist when they were unavoidable.

He parked on the circle and got out with the shoe box and the Polaroids. He looked into the pond as he came around the car and could see the dark shapes of the fish moving below the surface. He smiled, thinking about the movie *Chinatown* and how often they had watched it the year they were together. He remembered how much she enjoyed the portrayal of the coroner. He wore a black butcher's apron and ate a sandwich while examining a body. Bosch doubted she had the same sense of humor about things anymore.

The light hanging over the heavy wood door to the house went on, and Corazon opened it before he got there. She was wearing black slacks and a cream-colored blouse. She was probably on her way to a New Year's party. She looked past him at the slickback he had been driving.

"Let's make this quick before that car drips oil on my stones."

"Hello to you, too, Teresa."

"That's it?"

She pointed at the shoe box.

"This is it."

He handed her the Polaroids and started taking the lid off the box. It was clear she was not asking him in for a glass of New Year's champagne.

"You want to do this right here?"

"I don't have a lot of time. I thought you'd be here sooner. What moron took these?"

"That would be me."

"I can't tell anything from these. Do you have a glove?"

Bosch pulled a latex glove out of his coat pocket and handed it to her. He took the photos back and put them in an inside pocket of his jacket. She expertly snapped the glove on and reached into the open box. She held the bone up and turned it in the light. He was silent. He could smell her perfume. It was strong as usual, a holdover from her days when she spent most of her time in autopsy suites.

After a five-second examination she put the bone back down in the box.

"Human."

"You sure?"

She looked up at him with a glare as she snapped off the glove.

"It's the humerus. The upper arm. I'd say a child of about ten. You may no longer respect my skills, Harry, but I do still have them."

She dropped the glove into the box on top of the bone. Bosch could roll with all the verbal sparring from her, but it bothered him that she did that with the glove, dropping it on the child's bone like that.

He reached into the box and took the glove out. He remembered something and held the glove back out to her.

"The man whose dog found this said there was a fracture on the bone. A healed fracture. Do you want to take a look and see if you —"

"No. I'm late for an engagement. What you need to know right now is if it is human. You now have that confirmation. Further examination will come later under proper settings at the medical examiner's office. Now, I really have to go. I'll be there tomorrow morning."

Bosch held her eyes for a long moment.

"Sure, Teresa, have a good time tonight."

She broke off the stare and folded her arms across her chest. He carefully put the top back on the shoe box, nodded to her and headed back to his car. He heard the heavy door close behind him.

Thinking of the movie again as he passed the koi pond, he spoke the film's final line quietly to himself.

"Forget it, Jake, it's Chinatown."

He got in the car and drove home, his hand holding the shoe box secure on the seat next to him.

5

By nine o'clock the next morning the end of Wonderland Avenue was a law enforcement encampment. And at its center was Harry Bosch. He directed teams from patrol, K-9, the Scientific Investigation Division, the medical examiner's office and the Special Services unit. A department helicopter circled above and a dozen police academy cadets milled about, waiting for orders.

Earlier, the aerial unit had locked in on the sagebrush Bosch had wrapped in yellow crime scene tape and used it as a base point to determine that Wonderland offered the closest access to the spot where Bosch had found the bones. The Special Services unit then swung into action. Following the trail of crime scene tape up the hillside, the six-man team hammered and strung together a series of wooden ramps and steps with rope guidelines that led up the hillside to the bones. Accessing and exiting the site would now be much easier than it had been for Bosch the evening before.

It was impossible to keep such a nest of police activity quiet. Also by 9 A.M. the neighborhood had become a media encampment. The media trucks were stacked behind the roadblocks set a half block from the turnaround circle. The reporters were gathering into press conference–sized groups. And no fewer than five news helicopters were circling at an altitude above the department's chopper. It all created a background cacophony that had already resulted in numerous complaints from residents on the street to police administrators at Parker Center downtown.

Bosch was getting ready to lead the first group up to the crime scene. He first conferred with Jerry Edgar, who had been apprised of the case the night before.

"All right, we're going to take the ME and SID up first," he said, pronouncing the acronyms as Emmy and Sid. "Then we'll take the cadets and the dogs up. I want you to oversee that part of it."

"No problem. You see your pal the ME's got her damn cameraman with her?"

"Nothing we can do about it at the moment. Let's just hope she gets bored and goes back downtown, where she belongs."

"You know, for all we know, these could be old Indian bones or something."

Bosch shook his head.

"I don't think so. Too shallow."

Bosch walked over to the first group: Teresa Corazon, her videographer and her four-person dig team, which consisted of archeologist Kathy Kohl and three investigators who would do the spadework. The dig team members were dressed in white jumpsuits. Corazon was in an outfit similar to what she was wearing the night before, including shoes with two-inch heels. Also in the group were two criminalists from SID.

Bosch signaled the group into a tighter circle so he could speak privately to them and not be overheard by all the others milling about.

"Okay, we're going to go up and start the documentation and recovery. Once we have all of you in place we'll bring up the dogs and the cadets to search the adjacent areas and possibly expand the crime scene. You guys —"

He stopped to reach his hand up to Corazon's camera-man.

"Turn that off. You can film her but not me."

The man lowered his camera, and Bosch gave Corazon a look and then continued.

"You all know what you are doing so I don't need to brief you. The one thing I do want to say is that it is tough going getting up there. Even with the ramps and the stairs. So be careful. Hold on to the ropes, watch your footing. We don't want anybody hurt. If you have heavy equipment, break it up and make two or three trips. If you still need help I'll have the cadets bring it up. Don't worry about time. Worry about safety. All right, everybody cool?"

He got simultaneous nods from everybody. Bosch signaled Corazon away from the others and into a private conversation.

"You're not dressed right," he said.

"Look, don't you start telling —"

"You want me to take my shirt off so you can see my ribs? The side of my chest looks like blueberry pie because I fell up there last night. Those shoes you've got on aren't going to work. It might look good for the camera but not —"

"I'm fine. I'll take my chances. Anything else?"

Bosch shook his head.

"I warned you," he said. "Let's go."

He headed toward the ramp, and the others followed. Special Services had constructed a wooden gateway to be used as a checkpoint. A patrol officer stood there with a clipboard. He took each person's name and affiliation before they were allowed through.

Bosch led the way. The climbing was easier than the day before but his chest burned with pain as he pulled himself along on the rope guides and negotiated the ramps and steps. He said nothing and tried not to show it.

When he got to the acacia trees he signaled the others to hold back while he went under the crime scene tape to check first. He found the area of overturned earth and the small, brown bones he had seen the night before. They appeared undisturbed.

"Okay, come on in here and have a look."

The group members came under the tape and stood over the bones in a semicircle. The camera started rolling and Corazon now took charge.

"All right, the first thing we're going to do is back out and take photos. Then we're going to set up a grid and Dr. Kohl will supervise the excavation and recovery. If you find anything, photograph it nine ways from Sunday before you collect it."

She turned to one of the investigators.

"Finch, I want you to handle the sketches. Standard grid. Document everything. Don't assume we will be able to rely on photos."

Finch nodded. Corazon turned to Bosch.

"Detective, I think we've got it. The less people in here the better."

Bosch nodded and handed her a two-way radio.

"I'll be around. If you need me use the rover. Cell phones don't work up here. But be careful what you say."

He pointed up at the sky, where the media helicopters were circling.

"Speaking of which," Kohl said, "I think we're going to string a tarp up off these trees so we can have some privacy as well as cut down on the sun glare. Is that okay with you?"

"It's your crime scene now," Bosch said. "Run with it."

He headed back down the ramp with Edgar behind him.

"Harry, this could take days," Edgar said.

"And maybe then some."

"Well, they're not going to give us days. You know that, right?"

"Right."

"I mean, these cases . . . we'll be lucky if we even come up with an ID."

"Right."

Bosch kept moving. When he got down to the street he saw that Lt. Billets was on the scene with her supervisor, Capt. LeValley.

"Jerry, why don't you go get the cadets ready?" Bosch said. "Give them the crime scene one-oh-one speech. I'll be over in a minute."

Bosch joined Billets and LeValley and updated them on what was happening, detailing the morning's activities right down to the neighborhood complaints about noise from the hammers, saws and helicopters.

"We've got to give something to the media," LeValley said. "Media Relations wants to know if you want them to handle it from downtown or you want to take it here."

"I don't want to take it. What does Media Relations know about it?"

"Almost nothing. So you have to call them and they'll work up the press release."

"Captain, I'm kind of busy here. Can I —"

"Make the time, Detective. Keep them off our backs."

When Bosch looked away from the captain to the reporters gathered a half block away at the roadblock, he noticed Julia Brasher showing her badge to a patrol officer and being allowed through. She was in street clothes.

"All right. I'll make the call."

He started down the street to Dr. Guyot's home. He was headed toward Brasher, who smiled at him as she approached.

"I've got your Mag. It's in my car down here. I have to go down to Dr. Guyot's house anyway."

"Oh, don't worry about it. That's not why I'm here."

She changed direction and continued with Bosch. He

looked at her attire: faded blue jeans and a T-shirt from a 5K charity run.

"You're not on the clock, are you?"

"No, I work the three-to-eleven. I just thought you might need a volunteer. I heard about the academy call out."

"You want to go up there and look for bones, huh?"

"I want to learn."

Bosch nodded. They walked up the path to Guyot's door. It opened before they got there and the doctor invited them in. Bosch asked if he could use the phone in his office again and Guyot showed him the way even though he didn't have to. Bosch sat down behind the desk.

"How are the ribs?" the doctor asked.

"Fine."

Brasher raised her eyebrows and Bosch picked up on it.

"Had a little accident when I was up there last night."

"What happened?"

"Oh, I was just sort of minding my own business when a tree trunk suddenly attacked me for no reason."

She grimaced and somehow managed to smile at the same time.

Bosch dialed Media Relations from memory and told an officer about the case in very general terms. At one point he put his hand over the phone and asked Guyot if he wanted his name put in the press release. The doctor declined. A few minutes later Bosch was finished and hung up. He looked at Guyot.

"Once we clear the scene in a few days the reporters will probably stick around. They'll be looking for the dog that found the bone, is my guess. So if you want to stay out of it, keep Calamity off the street or they'll put two and two together."

"Good advice," Guyot said.

"And you might want to call your neighbor, Mr. Ulrich, and tell him not to mention it to any reporters, either."

On the way out of the house Bosch asked Brasher if she wanted her flashlight and she said she didn't want to bother carrying it while she was helping search the hillside.

"Get it to me whenever," she said.

Bosch liked the answer. It meant he would get at least one more chance to see her.

Back at the circle Bosch found Edgar lecturing the academy cadets.

"The golden rule of the crime scene, people, is don't touch anything until it has been studied, photographed and charted."

Bosch walked into the circle.

"Okay, we ready?"

"They're ready," Edgar said. He nodded toward two of the cadets, who were holding metal detectors. "I borrowed those from SID."

Bosch nodded and gave the cadets and Brasher the same safety speech he had given the forensic crew. They then headed up to the crime scene, Bosch introducing Brasher to Edgar and then letting his partner lead the way through the checkpoint. He took up the rear, walking behind Brasher.

"We'll see if you want to be a homicide detective by the end of the day," he said.

"Anything's got to be better than chasing the radio and washing puke out of the back of your car at the end of every shift."

"I remember those days."

Bosch and Edgar spread the twelve cadets and Brasher out in the areas adjacent to the stand of acacia trees and had them begin conducting side-by-side searches. Bosch then went down and brought up the two K-9 teams to supplement the search.

Once things were under way he left Edgar with the cadets and went back to the acacias to see what progress had been made. He found Kohl sitting on an equipment crate and supervising the placement of wooden stakes into the ground so that strings could be used to set the excavation grid.

Bosch had worked one prior case with Kohl and knew she was very thorough and good at what she did. She was in her late thirties with a tennis player's build and tan. Bosch had once run across her at a city park, where she was playing tennis with a twin sister. They had drawn a crowd. It looked like somebody hitting the ball off a mirrored wall.

Kohl's straight blonde hair fell forward and hid her eyes as she looked down at the oversized clipboard on her lap. She was making notations on a piece of paper with a grid already printed on it. Bosch looked over her shoulder at the chart. Kohl was labeling the individual blocks with letters of the alphabet as the corresponding stakes were placed in the ground. At the top of the page she had written "City of Bones."

Bosch reached down and tapped the chart where she had written the caption.

"Why do you call it that?"

She shrugged her shoulders.

"Because we're setting out the streets and the blocks of what will become a city to us," she said, running her fingers over some of the lines on the chart in illustration. "At least while we're working here it will feel like it. Our little city."

Bosch nodded.

"In every murder is the tale of a city," he said.

Kohl looked up at him.

"Who said that?"

"I don't know. Somebody did."

He turned his attention to Corazon, who was squatting over the small bones on the surface of the soil, studying them while the lens of the video camera studied her. He was thinking of something to say about it when his rover was keyed and he took it off his belt.

"Bosch here."

"Edgar. Better come on back over here, Harry. We already have something."

"Right."

Edgar was standing in an almost level spot in the brush about forty yards from the acacia trees. A half dozen of the cadets and Brasher had formed a circle and were looking down at something in the two-foot-high brush. The police chopper was circling in a tighter circle above.

Bosch got to the circle and looked down. It was a child's skull partially submerged in the soil, its hollow eyes staring up at him.

"Nobody touched it," Edgar said. "Brasher here found it."

Bosch glanced at her and the humor she seemed to carry in her eyes and mouth were gone. He looked back at the skull and pulled the radio off his belt.

"Dr. Corazon?" he said into it.

It was a long moment before her voice came back.

"Yes, I'm here. What is it?"

"We are going to have to widen the crime scene."

6

WITH Bosch acting as the general overseeing the small army that worked the expanded crime scene, the day progressed well. The bones came out of the ground and the hillside brush easily, as if they had been impatiently waiting a very long time. By noon, three blocks in the grid were being actively excavated by Kathy Kohl's team, and dozens of bones emerged from the dark soil. Like their archeological counterparts who unearthed the artifacts of the ancients, the dig team used small tools and brushes to bring these bones gently to light. They also used metal detectors and vapor probes. The process was painstaking yet it was moving at an even faster pace than Bosch had hoped for.

The finding of the skull had set this pace and brought a sense of urgency to the entire operation. It was removed from its location first, and the field examination conducted on camera by Teresa Corazon found fracture lines and surgical scarring. The record of surgery assured them they were dealing with relatively contemporary bones. The fractures in and of themselves were not definitive in the indication of homicide, but when added to the evidence that the body had been buried they gave a clear sense that the tale of a murder was unfolding.

By two o'clock, when the hillside crews broke for lunch, almost half of the skeleton had already been recovered from the grid. A small scattering of other bones had been found in the nearby brush by the cadets. Additionally, Kohl's crew had unearthed fragments of deteriorated clothing and a canvas backpack of a size most likely used by a child.

The bones came down the hillside in square wooden boxes with rope handles attached on the sides. By lunch, a forensic anthropologist was examining three boxes of bones in the medical examiner's office. The clothing, most of it rotten and unrecognizable, and the backpack, which had been left unopened, were transported to LAPD's Scientific Investigation Division lab for the same scrutiny.

A metal detector scan of the search grid produced a single coin — a quarter minted in 1975 — found at the same depth as the bones and approximately two inches from the left wing of the pelvis. It was assumed that the quarter had been in the left front pocket of pants that had rotted away along with the body's tissue. To Bosch, the coin gave one of the key parameters of time of death: If the assumption that the coin had been buried with the body was correct, the death could not have happened before 1975.

Patrol had arranged for two construction site lunch wagons to come to the circle to feed the small army working the crime scene. Lunch was late and people were hungry. One truck served hot lunches while the other served sandwiches. Bosch waited at the end of the line for the sandwich truck with Julia Brasher. The line was moving slowly but he didn't mind. They mostly talked about the investigation on the hillside and gossiped about department brass. It was get-to-know-you conversation. Bosch was attracted to her, and the more he heard her talk about her experiences as a rookie and a female in the department, the more he was intrigued by her. She had a mixture of excitement and awe and cynicism about the job that Bosch remembered clearly from his own early days on the job.

When he was about six people from the order window of the lunch truck, Bosch heard someone in the truck asking one of the cadets questions about the investigation.

"Are they bones from a bunch of different people?"

"I don't know, man. We just look for them, that's all."

Bosch studied the man who had asked the question.

"Were they all cut up?"

"Hard to tell."

Bosch broke from his spot with Brasher and walked to the back of the truck. He looked through the open door at the back and saw three men wearing aprons working in the truck. Or appearing to work. They did not notice Bosch watching. Two of the men were making sandwiches and filling orders. The man in the middle, the one who had asked the cadet questions, was moving his arms on the prep counter below the order window. He wasn't making anything, but from outside the truck it would appear he was creating a sandwich. As Bosch watched, he saw the man to the right slice a sandwich in half, put it on a paper plate and slide it to the man in the middle. The middle man then held it out through the window to the cadet who ordered it.

Bosch noticed that while the two real sandwich makers wore jeans and T-shirts beneath their aprons, the man in the middle had on cuffed slacks and a shirt with a button-down collar. Protruding from the back pocket of his pants was a notebook. The long, thin kind that Bosch knew reporters used.

Bosch stuck his head in the door and looked around. On a shelf next to the doorway he saw a sport jacket rolled into a ball. He grabbed it and stepped back away from the door.

He went through the pockets of the jacket and found an LAPD-issued press pass on a neck chain. It had a picture of the middle sandwich maker on it. His name was Victor Frizbe and he worked at the *New Times*.

Holding the jacket to the side of the door, Bosch rapped on the outside of the truck, and when all three men turned to look he signaled Frizbe over. The reporter pointed to his chest with a *Who, me?* look and Bosch nodded. Frizbe came to the door and bent down.

"Yes?"

Bosch reached up and grabbed him by the top bib on the apron and jerked him out of the truck. Frizbe landed on his feet but had to run several steps to stop from falling. As he turned around to protest, Bosch hit him in the chest with the balled-up jacket.

Two patrol officers — they always ate first — were dumping paper plates into a nearby trash can. Bosch signaled them over.

"Take him back to the perimeter. If you see him crossing it again, arrest him."

Each officer took Frizbe by an arm and started marching him down the street to the barricades. Frizbe started protesting, his face growing as red as a Coke can, but the patrol officers ignored everything about him but his arms and marched him toward his humiliation in front of the other reporters. Bosch watched for a moment and then took the press card out of his back pocket and dropped it in the trash can.

He rejoined Brasher in line. Now they were just two cadets away from being served.

"What was that all about?" Brasher asked.

"Health-code violation. Didn't wash his hands."

She started laughing.

"I'm serious. The law's the law as far as I'm concerned."

"God, I hope I get my sandwich before you see a roach or something and close the whole thing down."

"Don't worry, I think I just got rid of the roach."

Ten minutes later, after Bosch lectured the truck owner about smuggling the media into the crime scene, they took their sandwiches and drinks to one of the picnic tables Special Services had set up on the circle. It was a table that had been reserved for the investigative team, but Bosch didn't mind allowing Brasher to sit there. Edgar was there along with Kohl and one of the diggers from her crew. Bosch introduced Brasher to those who didn't know her and mentioned she had taken the initial call on the case and helped him the night before.

"So where's the boss?" Bosch asked Kohl.

"Oh, she already ate. I think she went off to tape an interview with herself or something."

Bosch smiled and nodded.

"I think I'm going to get seconds," Edgar said as he climbed over the bench and left with his plate.

Bosch bit into his BLT and savored its taste. He was starved. He wasn't planning to do anything but eat and rest during the break but Kohl asked if it was all right if she gave him some of her initial conclusions on the excavation.

Bosch had his mouth full. After he swallowed he asked her to wait until his partner came back. They talked in generalities about the condition of the bones and how Kohl believed that the shallow nature of the grave had allowed animals to disinter the remains and scatter the bones — possibly for years.

"We're not going to get them all," she said. "We won't come close. We're going to quickly reach a point where the expense and the effort won't be worth the return."

Edgar returned with another plate of fried chicken. Bosch nodded to Kohl, who looked down at a notepad she had on the table to her left. She checked some of her notations and started talking.

"The things I want you to be mindful of are the grave depth and location terrain. I think these are key things. They're going to have to play somehow into who this child was and what happened to him."

"Him?" Bosch asked.

"The hip spacing and the waistband of the underwear."

She explained that included in the rotten and decomposed clothing was the rubber waistband, which was all that was left of the underwear that had been on the body when it was buried. Decomposition fluids from the body had led to the deterioration of the clothing. But the rubber waistband was largely intact and appeared to have come from a style of underwear made for males.

"Okay," Bosch said. "You were saying about grave depth?"

"Yes, well, we think that the hip assembly and lower spinal column were in undisturbed position when we uncovered them. Going on that, we're talking about a grave that wasn't more than six inches to a foot deep. A grave this shallow reflects speed, panic, a host of things indicative of poor planning. But —" she held up a finger "— by the same token, the location — very remote, very difficult — reflects the opposite. It shows careful planning. So you have some kind of contradiction going on here. The location appears to have been chosen because it was damn hard to get to, yet the burial appears to have been fast and furious. This person was literally just covered with loose topsoil and pine needles. I know pointing all of this out isn't necessarily going to help you catch the bad guy but I want you to see what I'm seeing here. This contradiction."

Bosch nodded.

"It's all good to know. We'll keep it in mind."

"Okay, good. The other contradiction — the smaller

one — is the backpack. Burying it with the body was a mistake. The body decomposes at a much faster rate than the canvas. So if you get identifiers off the bag or its contents, it becomes a mistake made by the bad guy. Again poor planning in the midst of good planning. You're smart detectives, I'm sure you'll figure all this out."

She smiled at Bosch and then studied her pad again, lifting the top page to look beneath it.

"I think that's it. Everything else we talked about up at the site. I think things are going very well up there. By the end of the day we'll have the main grave done. Tomorrow we'll do some sampling in the other grids. But this should probably wrap by tomorrow. Like I said, we're not going to get everything but we should get enough to do what we need to do."

Bosch suddenly thought of Victor Frizbe's question to the cadet at the lunch wagon and realized that the reporter might have been thinking ahead of Bosch.

"Sampling? You think there's more than one body buried up there?"

Kohl shook her head.

"I have no indication of that at all. But we should make sure. We'll do some sampling, sink some gas probes. It's routine. The likelihood — especially in light of the shallow grave — is that this is a singular case, but we should be sure about it. As sure as we can be."

Bosch nodded. He was glad he had eaten most of his sandwich because he was suddenly not hungry. The prospect of mounting an investigation with multiple victims was daunting. He looked at the others at the table.

"That doesn't leave this table. I already caught one reporter sniffing around for a serial killer, we don't want media hysteria here. Even if you tell them what we're doing is routine and just to make sure, it will be the top of the story. All right?"

Everyone nodded, including Brasher. Bosch was about to say something when there was a loud banging from the row of portable toilets on the Special Services trailer on the other side of the circle. Someone was inside one of the phone booth–sized bathrooms pounding on its thin aluminum skin. After a moment Bosch could hear a woman's voice behind the sharp banging. He recognized it and jumped up from the table.

Bosch ran across the circle and up the steps to the truck's platform. He quickly determined which toilet the banging was coming from and went to the door. The exterior hasp — used for securing the toilet for transport — had been closed over the loop and a chicken bone had been used to secure it.

"Hold on, hold on," Bosch yelled.

He tried to pull the bone out but it was too greasy and slipped from his grip. The pounding and screaming continued. Bosch looked around for a tool of some kind but didn't see anything. Finally, he took his pistol out of his holster, checked the safety and used the butt of the weapon to hammer the bone through the hasp, careful all the time to aim the barrel of the gun at a downward angle.

When the bone finally popped out he put the gun away and flipped the hasp open. The door burst outward and Teresa Corazon charged out, almost knocking him over. He grabbed her to maintain his balance but she roughly pushed him away.

"You did that!"

"What? No, I didn't! I was over there the whole —"

"I want to know who did it!"

Bosch lowered his voice. He knew everyone in the encampment was probably looking at them. The media down the street as well.

"Look, Teresa, calm down. It was a joke, okay? Whoever did it did it as a joke. I know you don't like confined spaces but they didn't know that. Somebody just wanted to ease the tension around here a little bit, and you just happened to be —"

"It's because they're jealous, that's why."

"What?"

"Of who I am, what I've done."

Bosch was nonplussed by that.

"Whatever."

She headed for the stairs, then abruptly turned around and came back to him.

"I'm leaving, you happy now?"

Bosch shook his head.

"Happy? That has nothing to do with anything here. I'm trying to conduct an investigation, and if you want to know the truth, not having the distraction of you and your cameraman around might be a help."

"Then you've got it. And you know that phone number you called me on the other night?"

Bosch nodded. "Yeah, what about —"

"Burn it."

She walked down the steps, angrily hooked a finger at her cameraman and headed toward her official car. Bosch watched her go.

When he got back to the picnic table, only Brasher and Edgar remained. His partner had reduced his second order of fried chicken to bones. He sat with a satisfied smirk on his face.

Bosch dropped the bone he had knocked out of the hasp onto Edgar's plate.

"That went over real well," he said.

He gave Edgar a look that told him he knew he had been the one who did it. But Edgar revealed nothing.

"The bigger the ego the harder they fall," Edgar said. "I wonder if her cameraman got any of that action on tape."

"You know, it would have been good to keep her as an

ally," Bosch said. "To just put up with her so that she was on our side when we needed her."

Edgar picked up his plate and struggled to slide his large body out of the picnic table.

"I'll see you up on the hill," he said.

Bosch looked at Brasher. She raised her eyebrows.

"You mean he was the one who did it?"

Bosch didn't answer.

7

THE work in the city of bones lasted only two days. As Kohl had predicted, the majority of the pieces of the skeleton had been located and removed from the spot beneath the acacia trees by the end of the first day. Other bones had been found nearby in the brush in a scatter pattern indicative of disinterment over time by foraging animals. On Friday the searchers and diggers returned, but a daylong search of the hillside by fresh cadets and further excavation of the main squares of the grid found no more bones. Vapor probes and sample digs in all the remaining squares of the grid turned up no bones or other indications that other bodies had been buried beneath the acacia trees.

Kohl estimated that sixty percent of the skeleton had been collected. On her recommendation and with Teresa Corazon's approval the excavation and search were suspended pending further developments at dusk on Friday.

Bosch had not objected to this. He knew they were facing limited returns for a large amount of effort and he deferred to the experts. He was also anxious to proceed with the investigation and identification of the bones — elements which were largely stalled as he and Edgar had worked exclusively on Wonderland Avenue during the two days, supervising the collection of evidence, canvassing the neighborhood and putting together the initial reports on the case. It was all necessary work but Bosch wanted to move on.

On Saturday morning he and Edgar met in the lobby of the medical examiner's office and told the receptionist they had an appointment with Dr. William Golliher, the forensic anthropologist on retainer from UCLA.

"He's waiting for you in suite A," the receptionist said after making a call to confirm. "You know which way that is?"

Bosch nodded and they were buzzed through the gate. They took an elevator down to the basement level and were immediately greeted by the smell of the autopsy floor when they stepped out. It was a mixture of chemicals and decay that was unique in the world. Edgar immediately took a paper breathing mask out of a wall dispenser and put it on. Bosch didn't bother.

"You really ought to, Harry," Edgar said as they walked down the hall. "Do you know that all smells are particulate?"

Bosch looked at him.

"Thanks for that, Jerry."

They had to stop in the hallway as a gurney was pushed out of an autopsy suite. There was a body on it, wrapped in plastic.

"Harry, you ever notice that they wrap 'em up the same way they do the burritos at Taco Bell?"

Bosch nodded at the man pushing the gurney.

"That's why I don't eat burritos."

"Really?"

Bosch moved on down the hall without answering.

Suite A was an autopsy room reserved for Teresa Corazon for the infrequent times she actually left her administrative duties as chief medical examiner and performed an autopsy. Because the case had initially garnered her hands-on attention she had apparently authorized Golliher to use her suite. Corazon had not returned to the crime scene on Wonderland Avenue after the portable toilet incident.

They pushed through the double doors of the suite and were met by a man in blue jeans and a Hawaiian shirt.

"Please call me Bill," Golliher said. "I guess it's been a long two days."

"Say that again," Edgar said.

Golliher nodded in a friendly manner. He was about fifty with dark hair and eyes and an easy manner. He gestured toward the autopsy table that was in the center of the room. The bones that had been collected from beneath the acacia trees were now spread across the stainless steel surface.

"Well, let me tell you what's been going on in here," Golliher said. "As the team in the field has been collecting the evidence, I've been here examining the pieces, doing the radiograph work and generally trying to put the puzzle of all of this together."

Bosch stepped over to the stainless steel table. The bones were laid out in place so as to form a partial skeleton. The most obvious pieces missing were the bones of the left arm and leg and the lower jaw. It was presumed that these were the pieces that had long ago been taken and scattered distantly by animals that had rooted in the shallow grave.

Each of the bones was marked, the larger pieces with stickers and the smaller ones with string tags. Bosch knew that notations on these markers were codes by which the location of each bone had been charted on the grid Kohl had drawn on the first day of the excavation.

"Bones can tell us much about how a person lived and died," Golliher said somberly. "In cases of child abuse, the bones do not lie. The bones become our final evidence."

Bosch looked back at him and realized his eyes were not dark. They actually were blue but they were deeply set and seemed haunted in some way. He was staring past Bosch at the bones on the table. After a moment he broke from this reverie and looked at Bosch.

"Let me start by saying that we are learning quite a bit from the recovered artifacts," the anthropologist said. "But I have to tell you guys, I've consulted on a lot of cases but this one blows me away. I was looking at these bones and taking notes and I looked down and my notebook was smeared. I was crying, man. I was crying and I didn't even know it at first."

He looked back at the outstretched bones with a look of tenderness and pity. Bosch knew that the anthropologist saw the person who was once there.

"This one is bad, guys. Real bad."

"Then give us what you've got so we can go out there and do our job," Bosch said in a voice that sounded like a reverent whisper.

Golliher nodded and reached back to a nearby counter for a spiral notebook.

"Okay," Golliher said. "Let's start with the basics. Some of this you may already know but I'm just going to go over all of my findings, if you don't mind."

"We don't mind," Bosch said.

"Good. Then here it is. What you have here are the remains of a young male Caucasoid. Comparisons to the indices of Maresh growth standards put the age at approximately ten years old. However, as we will soon discuss, this child was the victim of severe and prolonged physical abuse. Histologically, victims of chronic abuse often suffer from what is called growth disruption. This abuse-related stunting serves to skew age estimation. What you often get is a skeleton that looks younger than it is. So what I am saying is that this boy looks ten but is probably twelve or thirteen."

Bosch looked over at Edgar. He was standing with his

arms folded tightly across his chest, as if bracing for what he knew was ahead. Bosch took a notebook out of his jacket pocket and started writing notes in shorthand.

· "Time of death," Golliher said. "This is tough. Radiological testing is far from exact in this regard. We have the coin which gives us the early marker of nineteen seventy-five. That helps us. What I am estimating is that this kid has been in the ground anywhere from twenty to twenty-five years. I'm comfortable with that and there is some surgical evidence we can talk about in a few minutes that adds support to that estimation."

"So we've got a ten- to thirteen-year-old kid killed twenty to twenty-five years ago," Edgar summarized, a note of frustration in his voice.

"I know I am giving you a wide set of parameters, Detective," Golliher said. "But at the moment it's the best the science can do for you."

"Not your fault, Doc."

Bosch wrote it all down. Despite the wide spread of the estimation, it was still vitally important to set a time frame for the investigation. Golliher's estimation put the time of death into the late seventies to early eighties. Bosch momentarily thought of Laurel Canyon in that time frame. It had been a rustic, funky enclave, part bohemian and part upscale, with cocaine dealers and users, porno purveyors and burned out rock-and-roll hedonists on almost every street. Could the murder of a child have been part of that mix?

"Cause of death," Golliher said. "Tell you what, let's get to cause of death last. I want to start with the extremities and the torso, give you guys an idea of what this boy endured in his short lifetime."

His eyes locked on Bosch's for a moment before returning to the bones. Bosch breathed in deeply, producing a sharp pain from his damaged ribs. He knew his fear from the moment he had looked down at the small bones on the hillside was now going to be realized. He instinctively knew all along that it would come to this. That a story of horror would emerge from the overturned soil.

He started scribbling on the pad, running the ballpoint deep into the paper, as Golliher continued.

"First of all, we only have maybe sixty percent of the bones here," he said. "But even still, we have incontrovertible evidence of tremendous skeletal trauma and chronic abuse. I don't know what your level of anthropological expertise is but I'm going to assume much of this will be new to you. I'm going to give you the basics. Bones heal themselves, gentlemen. And it is through the study of bone regeneration that we can establish a history of abuse. On these bones there are multiple lesions in different stages of healing. There are fractures old and new. We only have two of the four extremities but both of these show multiple instances of trauma. In short, this boy spent pretty much most of his life either healing or being hurt."

Bosch looked down at the pad and pen clutched tightly in his hands. His hands were turning white.

"You will be getting a written report from me by Monday, but for now, if you want a number, I will tell you that I found forty-four distinct locations indicating separate trauma in various stages of healing. And these were just his bones, Detectives. It doesn't cover the damage that could have been inflicted on vital organs and the tissue. But it is without a doubt that this boy lived probably day in and day out with a lot of pain."

Bosch wrote the number down on the pad. It seemed like a meaningless gesture.

"Primarily, the injuries I have catalogued can be noted on the artifacts by subperiosteal lesions," Golliher said. "These lesions are thin layers of new bone that grow beneath the surface in the area of trauma or bleeding."

"Subperi — how do you spell that?" Bosch asked.

"What does it matter? It will be in the report."

Bosch nodded.

"Take a look at this," Golliher said.

Golliher went to the X-ray box on the wall and flipped on the light. There was already film on the box. It showed an X-ray of a long thin bone. He ran his finger along the stem of the bone, pointing out a slight demarcation of color.

"This is the one femur that was collected," he said. "The upper thigh. This line here, where the color changes, is one of the lesions. This means that this area — the boy's upper leg — had suffered a pretty strong blow in the weeks before his death. A crushing blow. It did not break the bone but it damaged it. This kind of injury would no doubt have caused surface bruising and I think affected the boy's walk. What I am telling you is that it could not have gone unnoticed."

Bosch moved forward to study the X-ray. Edgar stayed back. When he was finished Golliher removed the X-ray and put up three more, covering the entire light box.

"We also have periosteal shearing on both of the limbs present. This is the stripping of the bone's surface, primarily seen in child abuse cases when the limb is struck violently by the adult hand or other instrument. Recovery patterns on these bones show that this particular type of trauma occurred repeatedly and over years to this child."

Golliher paused to look at his notes, then he glanced at the bones on the table. He picked up the upper arm bone and held it up while he referred to his notes and spoke. Bosch noticed he wore no gloves.

"The humerus," Golliher said. "The right humerus shows two separate and healed fractures. The breaks are longitudinal. This tells us the fractures are the result of the twisting of the arm with great force. It happened to him once and then it happened again."

He put the bone down and picked up one of the lower arm bones.

"The ulna shows a healed latitudinal fracture. The break caused a slight deviation in the attitude of the bone. This was because the bone was allowed to heal in place after the injury."

"You mean it wasn't set?" Edgar asked. "He wasn't taken to a doctor or an emergency room?"

"Exactly. This kind of injury, though commonly accidental and treated every day in every emergency room, can also be a defensive injury. You hold your arm up to ward off an attack and take the blow across the forearm. The fracture occurs. Because of the lack of indication of medical attention paid to this injury, my supposition is that this was not an accidental injury and was part of the abuse pattern."

Golliher gently returned the bone to its spot and then leaned over the examination table to look down at the rib cage. Many of the rib bones had been detached and were lying separated on the table.

"The ribs," Golliher said. "Nearly two dozen fractures in various stages of healing. A healed fracture on rib twelve I believe may date to when the boy was only two or three. Rib nine shows a callus indicative of trauma only a few weeks old at the time of death. The fractures are primarily consolidated near the angles. In infants this is indicative of violent shaking. In older children this is usually indicative of blows to the back."

Bosch thought of the pain he was in, of how he had been unable to sleep well because of the injury to his ribs. He thought of a young boy living with that kind of pain year in and year out.

"I gotta go wash my face," he suddenly said. "You can continue."

He walked to the door, shoving his notebook and pen

into Edgar's hands. In the hallway he turned right. He knew the layout of the autopsy floor and knew there were rest rooms around the next turn of the corridor.

He entered the rest room and went right to an open stall. He felt nauseous and waited but nothing happened. After a long moment it passed.

Bosch came out of the stall just as the door opened from the hallway and Teresa Corazon's cameraman walked in. They looked warily at each other for a moment.

"Get out of here," Bosch said. "Come back later."

The man silently turned and walked out.

Bosch walked to the sink and looked at himself in the mirror. His face was red. He bent down and used his hands to cup cold water against his face and eyes. He thought about baptisms and second chances. Of renewal. He raised his face until he was looking at himself again.

I'm going to get this guy.

He almost said it out loud.

When Bosch returned to suite A all eyes were on him. Edgar gave him his notebook and pen back and Golliher asked if he was all right.

"Yeah, fine," he said.

"If it is any help to you," Golliher said, "I have consulted on cases all over the world. Chile, Kosovo, even the World Trade Center. And this case . . ."

He shook his head.

"It's hard to comprehend," he added. "It's one of those where you have to think that maybe the boy was better off leaving this world. That is, if you believe in a God and a better place than this."

Bosch walked over to a counter and pulled a paper towel out of a dispenser. He started wiping his face again.

"And what if you don't?"

Golliher walked over to him.

"Well, you see, this is why you must believe," he said. "If

this boy did not go from this world to a higher plane, to something better, then . . . then I think we're all lost."

"Did that work for you when you were picking through the bones at the World Trade Center?"

Bosch immediately regretted saying something so harsh. But Golliher seemed unfazed. He spoke before Bosch could apologize.

"Yes, it did," he said. "My faith was not shaken by the horror or the unfairness of so much death. In many ways it became stronger. It brought me through it."

Bosch nodded and threw the towel into a trash can with a foot-pedal device for opening it. It closed with an echoing slam when he took his foot off the pedal.

"What about cause of death?" he said, getting back to the case.

"We can jump ahead, Detective," Golliher said. "All injuries, discussed and not discussed here, will be outlined in my report."

He went back to the table and picked up the skull. He brought it over to Bosch, holding it in one hand close to his chest.

"In the skull we have the bad — and possibly the good," Golliher said. "The skull exhibits three distinct cranial fractures showing mixed stages of healing. Here is the first."

He pointed to an area at the lower rear of the skull.

"This fracture is small and healed. You can see here that the lesions are completely consolidated. Then, next we have this more traumatic injury on the right parietal extending to the frontal. This injury required surgery, most likely for a subdural hematoma."

He outlined the injury area with a finger, circling the forward top of the skull. He then pointed to five small and smooth holes which were linked by a circular pattern on the skull.

"This is a trephine pattern. A trephine is a medical saw

used to open the skull for surgery or to relieve pressure from brain swelling. In this case it was probably swelling due to the hematoma. Now the fracture itself and the surgical scar show the beginning of bridging across the lesions. New bone. I would say this injury and subsequent surgery occurred approximately six months prior to the boy's death."

"It's not the injury causing death?" Bosch asked.

"No. This is."

Golliher turned the skull one more time and showed them another fracture. This one in the lower left rear of the skull.

"Tight spider web fracture with no bridging, no consolidation. This injury occurred at the time of death. The tightness of the fracture indicates a blow with tremendous force from a very hard object. A baseball bat, perhaps. Something like that."

Bosch nodded and stared down at the skull. Golliher had turned it so that its hollow eyes were focused on Bosch.

"There are other injuries to the head, but not of a fatal nature. The nose bones and the zygomatic process show new bone formation following trauma."

Golliher returned to the autopsy table and gently placed the skull down.

"I don't think I need to summarize for you, Detectives, but in short, somebody beat the shit out of this boy on a regular basis. Eventually, they went too far. It will all be in the report to you."

He turned from the autopsy table and looked at them.

"There is a glimmer of light in all of this, you know. Something that might help you."

"The surgery," Bosch said.

"Exactly. Opening a skull is a very serious operation. There will be records somewhere. There had to be follow-up. The roundel is held back in place with metal clips after surgery. There were none found with the skull. I would assume they were removed in a second procedure. Again, there will be records. The surgical scar also helps us date the bones. The trephine holes are too large by today's standards. By the mid-eighties the tools were more advanced than this. Sleeker. The perforations were smaller. I hope this all helps you."

Bosch nodded and said, "What about the teeth? Anything there?"

"We are missing the lower mandible," Golliher said. "On the upper teeth present there is no indication of any dental work despite indication of ante-mortem decay. This in itself is a clue. I think it puts this boy in the lower levels of social classification. He didn't go to the dentist."

Edgar had pulled his mask down around his neck. His expression was pained.

"When this kid was in the hospital with the hematoma, why wouldn't he tell the doctors what was happening to him? What about his teachers, his friends?"

"You know the answers to that as well as me, Detective," Golliher said. "Children are reliant on their parents. They are scared of them and they love them, don't want to lose them. Sometimes there is no explanation for why they don't cry out for help."

"What about all these fractures and such? Why didn't the doctors see it and do something?"

"That's the irony of what I do. I see the history and tragedy so clearly. But with a living patient it might not be apparent. If the parents came in with a plausible explanation for the boy's injury, what reason would a doctor have to X-ray an arm or a leg or a chest? None. And so the nightmare goes unnoticed."

Unsatisfied, Edgar shook his head and walked to the far corner of the room.

"Anything else, Doctor?" Bosch asked.

Golliher checked his notes and then folded his arms.

"That's it on a scientific level — you'll get the report. On a purely personal level, I hope you find the person who did this. They will deserve whatever they get, and then some."

Bosch nodded.

"We'll get him," Edgar said. "Don't you worry about that."

They walked out of the building and got into Bosch's car. Bosch just sat there for a moment before starting the engine. Finally, he hit the steering wheel hard with the heel of his palm, sending a shock down the injured side of his chest.

"You know it doesn't make me believe in God like him," Edgar said. "Makes me believe in aliens, little green men from outer space."

Bosch looked over at him. Edgar was leaning his head against the side window, looking down at the floor of the car.

"How so?"

"Because a human couldn't have done this to his own kid. A spaceship must've come down and abducted the kid and done all that stuff to him. Only explanation."

"Yeah, I wish that was on the checklist, Jerry. Then we could all just go home."

Bosch put the car into drive.

"I need a drink."

He started driving out of the lot.

"Not me, man," Edgar said. "I just want to go see my kid and hug him until this gets better."

They didn't speak again until they got over to Parker Center.

8

Bosch and Edgar rode the elevator to the fifth floor and went into the SID lab, where they had a meeting set up with Antoine Jesper, the lead criminalist assigned to the bones case. Jesper met them at the security fence and took them back. He was a young black man with gray eyes and smooth skin. He wore a white lab coat that swayed and flapped with his long strides and always moving arms.

"This way, guys," he said. "I don't have a lot but what I got is yours."

He took them through the main lab, where only a handful of other criminalists were working, and into the drying room, a large climate-controlled space where clothing and other material evidence from cases were spread on stainless steel drying tables and examined. It was the only place that could rival the autopsy floor of the medical examiner's office in the stench of decay.

Jesper led them to two tables where Bosch saw the open backpack and several pieces of clothing blackened with soil and fungus. There was also a plastic sandwich bag filled with an unrecognizable lump of black decay.

"Water and mud got into the backpack," Jesper said. "Leached in over time, I guess."

Jesper took a pen out of the pocket of his lab coat and

extended it into a pointer. He used it to help illustrate his commentary.

"We've got your basic backpack containing three sets of clothes and what was probably a sandwich or some kind of food item. More specifically, three T-shirts, three underwear, three sets of socks. And the food item. There was also an envelope, or what was left of an envelope. You don't see that here because documents has it. But don't get your hopes up, guys. It was in worse shape than that sandwich — *if* it was a sandwich."

Bosch nodded. He made a list of the contents in his notebook.

"Any identifiers?" he asked.

Jesper shook his head.

"No personal identifiers on the clothing or in the bag," he said. "But two things to note. First, this shirt here has a brand-name identifier. 'Solid Surf.' Says it across the chest. You can't see it now but I picked it up with the black light. Might help, might not. If you are not familiar with the term 'Solid Surf,' I can tell you that it is a skateboarding reference."

"Got it," Bosch said.

"Next is the outside flap of the bag."

He used his pointer to flip over the flap.

"Cleaned this up a little bit and came up with this."

Bosch leaned over the table to look. The bag was made of blue canvas. On the flap was a clear demarcation of color forming a large letter B at the center.

"It looks like there was some kind of adhesive applicate at one time on the bag," Jesper said. "It's gone now and I don't really know if that occurred before or after this thing was put in the ground. My guess is before. It looks like it was peeled off."

Bosch stepped back from the table and wrote a few lines in his notebook. He then looked at Jesper.

"Okay, Antoine, good stuff. Anything else?"

"Not on this stuff."

"Then let's go to documents."

Jesper led the way again through the central lab and then into a sub-lab where he had to enter a combination into a door lock to enter.

The documents lab contained two rows of desks that were all empty. Each desk had a horizontal light box and a magnifying glass mounted on a pivot. Jesper went to the middle desk in the second row. The nameplate on the desk said Bernadette Fornier. Bosch knew her. They had worked a case previously in which a suicide note had been forged. He knew she did good work.

Jesper picked up a plastic evidence pouch that was sitting in the middle of the desk. He unzipped it and removed two plastic viewing sleeves. One contained an unfolded envelope that was brown and smeared with black fungus. The other contained a deteriorated rectangular piece of paper that was broken into three parts along the folds and was also grossly discolored by decay and fungus.

"This is what happens when stuff gets wet, man," Jesper said. "It took Bernie all day just to unfold the envelope and separate the letter. As you can see, it came apart at the folds. And as far as whether we'll ever be able to tell what was in the letter, it doesn't look good."

Bosch turned on the light box and put the plastic sleeves down on it. He swung the magnifier over and studied the envelope and the letter it had once contained. There was nothing remotely readable on either document. One thing he noted was that it looked like there was no stamp on the envelope.

"Damn," he said.

He flipped the sleeves over and kept looking. Edgar came over next to him as if to confirm the obvious.

"Woulda been nice," he said.

"What will she do now?" Bosch asked Jesper.

"Well, she'll probably try some dyes, some different lights. Try to get something that reacts with the ink, brings it up. But she wasn't too optimistic yesterday. So like I said, I wouldn't be getting my hopes up about it."

Bosch nodded and turned off the light.

9

NEAR the back entrance to the Hollywood Division station was a bench with large sand-filled ashtrays on either side. It was called the Code 7, after the radio call for out-of-service or on break. At 11:15 P.M. on Saturday night Bosch was the only occupant on the Code 7 bench. He wasn't smoking, though he wished he was. He was waiting. The bench was dimly lit by the lights over the station's back door and had a view of the parking lot jointly shared by the station and the firehouse on the back end of the city complex.

Bosch watched as the patrol units came in from the three-to-eleven shift and the officers went into the station to change out of uniforms, shower and call it a night, if they could. He looked down at the MagLite he held in his hands and rubbed his thumb over the end cap and felt the scratchings where Julia Brasher had etched her badge number.

He hefted the light and then flipped it in his hand, feeling its weight. He flashed on what Golliher had said about the weapon that had killed the boy. He could add flashlight to the list.

Bosch watched a patrol car come into the lot and park by the motor pool garage. A cop he recognized as Julia Brasher's partner, Edgewood, emerged from the passenger side and headed into the station carrying the car's shotgun.

Bosch waited and watched, suddenly unsure of his plan and wondering if he could abandon it and get into the station without being seen.

Before he decided on a move Brasher got out of the driver's side and headed toward the station door. She walked with her head down, the posture of someone tired and beat from a long day. Bosch knew the feeling. He also thought something might be wrong. It was a subtle thing, but the way Edgewood had gone in and left her behind told Bosch something was off. Since Brasher was a rookie, Edgewood was her training officer, even though he was at least five years younger than her. Maybe it was just an awkward situation because of age and gender. Or maybe it was something else.

Brasher didn't notice Bosch on the bench. She was almost to the station door before he spoke.

"Hey, you forgot to wash the puke out of the back seat."

She looked back while continuing to walk until she saw it was him. She stopped then and walked over to the bench.

"I brought you something," Bosch said.

He held out the flashlight. She smiled tiredly as she took it.

"Thank you, Harry. You didn't have to wait here to —"

"I wanted to."

There was an awkward silence for a moment.

"Were you working the case tonight?" she asked.

"More or less. Started the paperwork. And we sort of got the autopsy earlier today. If you could call it an autopsy."

"I can tell by your face it was bad."

Bosch nodded. He felt strange. He was still sitting and she was still standing.

"I can tell by the way you look that you had a tough one, too."

"Aren't they all?"

Before Bosch could say anything two cops, fresh from

showers and in street clothes, came out of the station and headed toward their personal cars.

"Cheer up, Julia," one of them said. "We'll see you over there."

"Okay, Kiko," she said back.

She turned and looked back down at Bosch. She smiled.

"Some people from the shift are getting together over at Boardner's," she said. "You want to come?"

"Um . . ."

"That's okay. I just thought maybe you could use a drink or something."

"I could. I need one. Actually, that's why I was waiting here for you. I just don't know if I want to get into a group thing at a bar."

"Well, what were you thinking, then?"

Bosch checked his watch. It was now eleven-thirty.

"Depending on how long you take in the locker room, we could probably catch the last martini call at Musso's."

She smiled broadly now.

"I love that place. Give me fifteen minutes."

She headed toward the station door without waiting for a reply from him.

"I'll be here," he called after her.

10

Musso and Frank's was an institution that had been serving martinis to the denizens of Hollywood — both famous and infamous — for a century. The front room was all red leather booths and quiet conversation with ancient waiters in red half-coats moving slowly about. The back room contained the long bar, where most nights it was standing room only while patrons vied for the attention of bartenders who could have been the fathers of the waiters. As Bosch and Brasher came into the bar two patrons slipped off their stools to leave. Bosch and Brasher quickly moved in, beating two black-clad studio types to the choice spots. A bartender who recognized Bosch came over and they both ordered vodka martinis, slightly dirty.

Bosch was already feeling at ease with her. They had spent lunch together at the crime scene picnic tables the last two days and she had never been far from his sight during the hillside searches. They had ridden over to Musso's together in his car and it seemed like a third or fourth date already. They small-talked about the division and the details Bosch was willing to part with about his case. By the time the bartender put down their martini glasses along with the sidecar carafes, he was ready to forget about bones and blood and baseball bats for a while.

They clinked glasses and Brasher said, "To life."

"Yeah," Bosch said. "Getting through another day."

"Just barely."

Bosch knew that now was the time to talk to her about what was troubling her. If she didn't want to talk, he wouldn't press it.

"That guy you called Kiko in the back lot, why'd he tell you to cheer up?"

She slumped a little and didn't answer at first.

"If you don't want to talk about —"

"No, it's not that. It's more like I don't want to *think* about it."

"I know the feeling. Forget I asked."

"No, it's okay. My partner's going to write me up and since I'm on probation, it could cost me."

"Write you up for what?"

"Crossing the tube."

It was a tactical expression, meaning to walk in front of the barrel of a shotgun or other weapon held by a fellow officer.

"What happened? I mean, if you want to talk about it."

She shrugged and they both took long drinks from their glasses.

"Oh, it was a domestic — I hate domestics — and the guy locked himself in the bedroom with a gun. We didn't know if he was going to use it on himself, his wife or us. We waited for backup and then we were going to go in."

She took another drink. Bosch watched her. Her inner turmoil showed clearly in her eyes.

"Edgewood had shotgun. Kiko had the kick. Fennel, Kiko's partner, and I had the door. So we did the deed. Kiko's big. He opened the door with one kick. Fennel and I went in. The guy was passed out on the bed. Seemed like no problem but Edgewood had a big problem with me. He said I crossed the tube."

"Did you?"

"I don't think so. But if I did, then so did Fennel, and he didn't say jack to him."

"You're the rookie. You're the one on probation."

"Yeah, and I'm getting tired of it, that's for sure. I mean, how did you make it through, Harry? Right now you've got a job that makes a difference. What I do, just chasing the radio all day and night, going from dirtbag to dirtbag, it's like spitting on a house fire. We're not making any headway out there and on top of that I've got this uptight male asshole telling me every two minutes how I fucked up."

Bosch knew what she was feeling. Every cop in a uniform went through it. You wade through the cesspool every day and soon it seems that that is all there is. An abyss. It was why he could never go back to working patrol. Patrol was a Band-Aid on a bullet hole.

"Did you think it would be different? When you were in the academy, I mean."

"I don't know what I thought. I just don't know if I can make it through to a point where I think I'm making any difference."

"I think you can. The first couple years are tough. But you dig in and you start seeing the long view. You pick your battles and you pick your path. You'll do all right."

He didn't feel confident giving her the rah-rah speech. He had gone through long stretches of indecision about himself and his choices. Telling her to stick it out made him feel a little false.

"Let's talk about something else," she said.

"Fine with me," he said.

He took a long drink from his glass, trying to think of how to turn the conversation in another direction. He put his glass down, turned and smiled at her.

"So there you were, hiking in the Andes and you said to yourself, 'Gee, I wanna be a cop.'"

She laughed, seemingly shaking off the blues of her earlier comments.

"Not quite like that. And I've never been in the Andes."

"Well, what about the rich, full life you lived before putting on the badge? You said you were a world traveler."

"Never made it to South America."

"Is that where the Andes are? All this time I thought
they were in Florida."

She laughed again and Bosch felt good about success-
fully changing the subject. He liked looking at her teeth
when she laughed. They were just a little bit crooked and
in a way that made them perfect.

"So seriously, what did you do?"

She turned in the stool so they were shoulder to shoulder, looking at each other in the mirror behind all the col-
ored bottles lined along the back wall of the bar.

"Oh, I was a lawyer for a while — not a defense lawyer,
so don't get excited. Civil law. Then I realized that was
bullshit and quit and just started traveling. I worked along
the way. I made pottery in Venice, Italy. I was a horse guide
in the Swiss Alps for a while. I was cook on a day-trip tourist
boat in Hawaii. I did other things and I just saw a lot of the
world — except for the Andes. Then I came home."

"To L.A.?"

"Born and raised. You?"

"Same. Queen of Angels."

"Cedars."

She held out her glass and they clinked.

"To the few, the proud, the brave," she said.

Bosch finished off his glass and poured in the contents of
his sidecar. He was way ahead of Brasher but didn't care.
He was feeling relaxed. It was good to forget about things
for a while. It was good to be with somebody not directly
related to the case.

"Born at Cedars, huh?" he asked. "Where'd you grow up?"

"Don't laugh. Bel Air."

"Bel Air? I guess somebody's daddy isn't too happy about her joining the cops."

"Especially since his was the law firm she walked out of one day and wasn't heard from for two years."

Bosch smiled and raised his glass. She clicked hers off it.

"Brave girl."

After they put their glasses down, she said, "Let's stop all the questions."

"Okay," Bosch said. "And do what?"

"Just take me home, Harry. To your place."

He paused for a moment, looking at her shiny blue eyes. Things were moving lightning fast, greased on the smooth runners of alcohol. But that was often the way it was between cops, between people who felt they were part of a closed society, who lived by their instincts and went to work each day knowing that how they made their living could kill them.

"Yeah," he finally said, "I was just thinking the same thing."

He leaned over and kissed her on the mouth.

11

JULIA Brasher stood in the living room of Bosch's house and looked at the CDs stored in the racks next to the stereo.

"I love jazz."

Bosch was in the kitchen. He smiled when he heard her say it. He finished pouring the two martinis out of a shaker and came out to the living room and handed her a glass.

"Who do you like?"

"Ummm, lately Bill Evans."

Bosch nodded, went to the rack and came up with *Kind of Blue*. He loaded it into the stereo.

"Bill and Miles," he said. "Not to mention Coltrane and a few other guys. Nothing better."

As the music began he picked up his martini and she came over and tapped it with her glass. Rather than drink, they kissed each other. She started laughing halfway through the kiss.

"What?" he said.

"Nothing. I'm just feeling reckless. And happy."

"Yeah, me too."

"I think it was you giving me the flashlight."

Bosch was puzzled.

"What do you mean?"

"You know, it's so phallic."

The look on Bosch's face made her laugh again and she spilled some of her drink on the floor.

Later, when she was lying face down on his bed, Bosch was tracing the outline of the flaming sun tattooed on the small of her back and thinking about how comfortable and yet strange she felt to him. He knew almost nothing about her. Like the tattoo, there seemed to be a surprise from every angle of view he had on her.

"What are you thinking about?" she asked.

"Nothing. Just wondering about the guy who got to put this on your back. I wish it had been me, I guess."

"How come?"

"Because there will always be a piece of him with you."

She turned on her side, revealing her breasts and her smile. Her hair was out of its braid and down around her shoulders. He liked that, too. She reached up and pulled him down into a long kiss. Then she said, "That's the nicest thing that's been said to me in a long time."

He put his head down on her pillow. He could smell the sweet scent of perfume and sex and sweat.

"You don't have any pictures on your walls," she said. "Photos, I mean."

He shrugged his shoulders.

She turned over so her back was to him. He reached under her arm and cupped one of her breasts and pulled her back into him.

"Can you stay till the morning?" he asked.

"Well . . . my husband will probably wonder where I am, but I guess I could call him."

Bosch froze. Then she started laughing.

"Don't scare me like that."

"Well, you never even asked me if I was involved with anyone."

"You didn't ask me."

"You were obvious. The lone detective type." And then

in a deep male voice: "Just the facts, ma'am. No time for dames. Murder is my business. I have a job to do and I am —"

He ran his thumb down her side, over the indentations of her ribs. She cut off her words with laughter.

"You lent me your flashlight," he said. "I didn't think an 'involved' woman would have done that."

"And I've got news for you, tough guy. I saw the Mag in your trunk. In the box before you covered it up. You weren't fooling anybody."

Bosch rolled back on the other pillow, embarrassed. He could feel his face getting red. He brought his hands up to hide it.

"Oh, God . . . Mr. Obvious."

She rolled over to him and peeled back his hands. She kissed him on the chin.

"I thought it was nice. Kinda made my day and gave me something to maybe look forward to."

She turned his hands back and looked at the scarring across the knuckles. They were old marks and not very noticeable anymore.

"Hey, what is this?"

"Just scars."

"I know that. From what?"

"I had tattoos. I took them off. It was a long time ago."

"How come?"

"They made me take them off when I went into the army."

She started to laugh.

"Why, what did it say, Fuck the army or something?"

"No, nothing like that."

"Then what? Come on, I want to know."

"It said H-O-L-D on one hand and F-A-S-T on the other."

"Hold fast? What does 'hold fast' mean?"

"Well, it's kind of a long story . . ."

"I have time. My husband doesn't mind."

She smiled.

"Come on, I want to know."

"It's not a big deal. When I was a kid, one of the times I ran away I ended up down in San Pedro. Down around the fishing docks. And a lot of those guys down there, the fishermen, the tuna guys, I saw they had this on their hands. Hold fast. And I asked one of them about it and he told me it was like their motto, their philosophy. It's like when they were out there in those boats, way out there for weeks, and the waves got huge and it got scary, you just had to grab on and hold fast."

Bosch made two fists and held them up.

"Hold fast to life . . . to everything that you have."

"So you had it done. How old were you?"

"I don't know, sixteen, thereabouts."

He nodded and then he smiled.

"What I didn't know was that those tuna guys got it from some navy guys. So a year later I go waltzing into the army with 'Hold Fast' on my hands and the first thing my sergeant told me was to get rid of it. He wasn't going to have any squid tattoo on one of his guys' hands."

She grabbed his hands and looked closely at the knuckles.

"This doesn't look like laser work."

Bosch shook his head.

"They didn't have lasers back then."

"So what did you do?"

"My sergeant, his name was Rosser, took me out of the barracks and over to the back of the administration building. There was a brick wall. He made me punch it. Until every one of my knuckles was cut up. Then after they were scabbed up in about a week he made me do it again."

"Jesus fucking Christ, that's barbaric."

"No, that's the army."

He smiled at the memory. It wasn't as bad as it sounded. He looked down at his hands. The music stopped and he got up and walked through the house naked to change it. When he came back to the bedroom, she recognized the music.

"Clifford Brown?"

He nodded and came toward the bed. He didn't think he had ever known a woman who could identify jazz music like that.

"Stand there."

"What?"

"Let me look at you. Tell me about those other scars."

The room was dimly lit by a light from the bathroom but Bosch became conscious of his nakedness. He was in good shape but he was more than fifteen years older than her. He wondered if she had ever been with a man so old.

"Harry, you look great. You totally turn me on, okay? What about the other scars?"

He touched the thick rope of skin above his left hip.

"This? This was a knife."

"Where'd that happen?"

"A tunnel."

"And your shoulder?"

"Bullet."

"Where?"

He smiled.

"A tunnel."

"Ouch, stay out of tunnels."

"I try."

He got into the bed and pulled the sheet up. She touched his shoulder, running her thumb over the thick skin of the scar.

"Right in the bone," she said.

"Yeah, I got lucky. No permanent damage. It aches in the winter and when it rains, that's about it."

"What did it feel like? Being shot, I mean."

Bosch shrugged his shoulders.

"It hurt like hell and then everything sort of went numb."

"How long were you down?"

"About three months."

"You didn't get a disability out?"

"It was offered. I declined."

"How come?"

"I don't know. I like the job, I guess. And I thought that if I stuck with it, someday I'd meet this beautiful young cop who'd be impressed by all my scars."

She jammed him in the ribs and the pain made him grimace.

"Oh, poor baby," she said in a mocking voice.

"That hurt."

She touched the tattoo on his shoulder.

"What's that supposed to be, Mickey Mouse on acid?"

"Sort of. It's a tunnel rat."

Her face lost all trace of humor.

"What's the matter?"

"You were in Vietnam," she said, putting things together. "I've been in those tunnels."

"What do you mean?"

"When I was on the road. I spent six weeks in Vietnam. The tunnels, they're like a tourist thing now. You pay your money and you can go down into them. It must've been . . . what you had to do must've been so frightening."

"It was more scary afterward. Thinking about it."

"They have them roped off so they can sort of control where you go. But nobody really watches you. So I went under the rope and went further in. It got so dark in there, Harry."

Bosch studied her eyes.

"And did you see it?" he asked quietly. "The lost light?"

She held his eyes for a moment and nodded.

"I saw it. My eyes adjusted and there was light. Almost like a whisper. But it was enough for me to find my way."

"Lost light. We called it lost light. We never knew where it came from. But it was down there. Like smoke hanging in the dark. Some people said it wasn't light, that it was the ghosts of everybody who died in those things. From both sides."

They spoke no more after that. They held each other and soon she was asleep.

Bosch realized he had not thought about the case for more than three hours. At first this made him feel guilty but then he let it go and soon he too was asleep. He dreamed he was moving through a tunnel. But he wasn't crawling. It was as if he were underwater and moving like an eel through the labyrinth. He came to a dead end and there was a boy sitting against the curve of the tunnel's wall. He had his knees up and his face down, buried in his folded arms.

"Come with me," Bosch said.

The boy peeked his eyes over one arm and looked up at Bosch. A single bubble of air rose from his mouth. He then looked past Bosch as if something was coming up behind him. Bosch turned around but there was only the darkness of the tunnel behind him.

When he looked back at the boy, he was gone.

12

LATE Sunday morning Bosch drove Brasher to the Hollywood station so she could get her car and he could resume work on the case. She was off duty Sundays and Mondays. They made plans to meet at her house in Venice that night for dinner. There were other officers in the parking lot when Bosch dropped her next to her car. Bosch knew that word would get around quickly that it appeared they had spent the night together.

"I'm sorry," he said. "I should have thought it out better last night."

"I don't really care, Harry. I'll see you tonight."

"Hey, look, you should care. Cops can be brutal."

She made a face.

"Oh, police brutality, yeah, I've heard of it."

"I'm serious. It's also against regs. On my part. I'm a D-three. Supervisor level."

She looked at him a moment.

"Well, that's your call, then. I'll see you tonight. I hope."

She got out and closed the door. Bosch drove on to his assigned parking slot and went into the detective bureau, trying not to think of the complications he might have just invited into his life.

It was deserted in the squad room, which was what he was hoping for. He wanted time alone with the case. There was still a lot of office work to do but he also wanted to step back and think about all the evidence and information that had been accumulated since the discovery of the bones.

The first thing to do was put together a list of what needed to be done. The murder book — the blue binder containing all written reports pertaining to the case — had to be completed. He had to draw up search warrants seeking medical records of brain surgeries at local hospitals. He had to run routine computer checks on all the residents living in the vicinity of the crime scene on Wonderland. He also had to read through all the call-in tips spawned by the media coverage of the bones on the hill and start gathering missing person and runaway reports that might match the victim.

He knew it was more than a day's work if he labored by himself but decided to keep with his decision to allow Edgar the day off. His partner, the father of a thirteen-year-old boy, had been greatly upset by Golliher's report the day before and Bosch wanted him to take a break. The days ahead would likely be long and just as emotionally upsetting.

Once Bosch had his list together he took his cup out of a drawer and went back to the watch office to get coffee. The smallest he had on him was a five-dollar bill but he put it in the coffee fund basket without taking any change. He figured he'd be drinking more than his share through the day.

"You know what they say?" someone said behind him as he was filling the cup.

Bosch turned. It was Mankiewicz, the watch sergeant.

"About what?"

"Fishing off the company dock."

"I don't know. What do they say?"

"I don't know either. That's why I was asking you."

Mankiewicz smiled and moved toward the machine to warm up his cup.

So already it was starting to get around, Bosch thought. Gossip and innuendo — especially anything with a sexual tone — moved through a police station like a fire racing up a hill in August.

"Well, let me know when you find out," Bosch said as he started for the door of the watch office. "Could be useful to know."

"Will do. Oh, and one other thing, Harry."

Bosch turned, ready for another shot from Mankiewicz. "What?"

"Just stop fooling around and wrap up your case. I'm tired of my guys having to take all the calls."

There was a facetious tone in his voice. In his humor and sarcasm was a legitimate complaint about his officers on the desk being tied up by the tip calls.

"Yeah, I know. Any good ones today?"

"Not that I could tell, but you'll get to slog through the reports and use your investigative wiles to decide that."

"Wiles?"

"Yes, wiles. Like Wile E. Coyote. Oh, and CNN must've had a slow morning and picked up the story — good video, all you brave guys on the hill with your makeshift stairs and little boxes of bones. So now we're getting the long-distance calls. Topeka and Providence so far this morning. It's not going to end until you clear it, Harry. We're all counting on you back here."

Again there was a smile — and a message — behind what he was saying.

"All right, I'll use all my wiles. I promise, Mank."

"That's what we're counting on."

Back at the table Bosch sipped his coffee and let the details of the case move through his mind. There were anomalies, contradictions. There were the conflicts between

location choice and method of burial noticed by Kathy
Kohl. But the conclusions made by Golliher added even
more to the list of questions. Golliher saw it as a child abuse
case. But the backpack full of clothes was an indication that
the victim, the boy, was possibly a runaway.

Bosch had spoken to Edgar about it the day before when
they returned to the station from the SID lab. His partner
was not as sure of the conflict as Bosch but offered a theory
that perhaps the boy was the victim of child abuse both at
the hands of his parents and then an unrelated killer. He
rightfully pointed out that many victims of abuse run away
only to be drawn into another form of abusive relationship.
Bosch knew the theory was legitimate but tried not to let
himself go down that road because he knew it was even
more depressing than the scenario Golliher had spun.

His direct line rang and Bosch answered, expecting it
to be Edgar or Lt. Billets checking in. It was a reporter
from the *L.A. Times* named Josh Meyer. Bosch barely knew
him and was sure he'd never given him the direct line.
He didn't let on that he was annoyed, however. Though
tempted to tell the reporter that the police were running
down leads extending as far as Topeka and Providence, he
simply said there was no further update on the investigation since Friday's briefing from the Media Relations office.

After he hung up he finished his first cup of coffee and
got down to work. The part of an investigation Bosch
enjoyed the least was the computer work. Whenever possible he gave it to his partners to handle. So he decided to
put the computer runs at the end of his list and started with
a quick look through the accumulated tip sheets from the
watch office.

There were about three dozen more sheets since he had
last looked through the pile on Friday. None contained
enough information to be helpful or worth pursuing at the
moment. Each was from a parent or sibling or friend of

someone who had disappeared. All of them permanently forlorn and seeking some kind of closure to the most pressing mystery of their lives.

He thought of something and rolled his chair over to one of the old IBM Selectrics. He inserted a sheet of paper and typed out four questions.

Do you know if your missing loved one underwent any kind of surgical procedure in the months before his disappearance?
If so, what hospital was he treated at?
What was the injury?
What was the name of his physician?

He rolled the page out and took it to the watch office. He gave it to Mankiewicz to be used as a template of questions to be asked of all callers about the bones.

"That wily enough for you?" Bosch asked.

"No, but it's a start."

While he was there Bosch took a plastic cup and filled it with coffee and then came back to the bureau and dumped it into his cup. He made a note to ask Lt. Billets on Monday to procure some help in contacting all the callers of the last few days to ask the same medical questions. He then thought of Julia Brasher. He knew she was off on Mondays and would volunteer if needed. But he quickly dismissed it, knowing that by Monday the whole station would know about them and bringing her into the case would make matters worse.

He started the search warrants next. It was a matter of routine in homicide work to need medical records in the course of an investigation. Most often these records came from physicians and dentists. But hospitals were not unusual. Bosch kept a file with search warrant templates for hospitals as well as a listing of all twenty-nine hospitals in the Los Angeles area and the attorneys who handled legal filings at each location. Having all of this handy allowed him to draw up twenty-nine search warrants in a little over an hour. The warrants sought the records of all male patients under the age of sixteen who underwent brain surgery entailing the use of a trephine drill between 1975 and 1985.

After printing out the requests he put them in his brief-case. While normally it was proper on a weekend to fax a search warrant to a judge's home for approval and signa-ture, it would certainly not be acceptable to fax twenty-nine requests to a judge on a Sunday afternoon. Besides, the hospital lawyers would not be available on a Sunday anyway. Bosch's plan was to take the warrants to a judge first thing Monday morning, then divide them with Edgar and hand-deliver them to the hospitals, thereby being able to push the urgency of the matter with the lawyers in per-son. Even if things went according to plan, Bosch didn't expect to start receiving returns of records from the hospi-tals until mid-week or later.

Bosch next typed out a daily case summary as well as a recap of the anthropological information from Golliher. He put these in the murder book and then typed up an evi-dence report detailing the preliminary SID findings on the backpack.

When he was finished Bosch leaned back and thought about the unreadable letter that had been found in the backpack. He did not anticipate that the documents section would have any success with it. It would forever be the mystery shrouded in the mystery of the case. He gulped the last of his second cup of coffee and opened the murder book to the page containing a copy of the crime scene sketch and chart. He studied the chart and noted that the backpack had been found right next to the spot Kohl had marked as the probable original location of the body.

Bosch wasn't sure what it all meant but instinctively he

knew that the questions he now had about the case should be kept foremost in his mind as new evidence and details continued to be gathered. They would be the screen through which everything would be sifted.

He put the report into the murder book and then finished the updating of the paperwork by bringing the investigator's log — an hour-by-hour time chart with small entry blocks — up to date. He then put the murder book in his briefcase.

Bosch took his coffee cup to the sink in the rest room and washed it out. He then returned it to its drawer, picked up his briefcase and headed out the back door to his car.

13

THE basement of Parker Center, the headquarters of the Los Angeles Police Department, serves as the record archives for every case the department has taken a report on in the modern era. Until the mid-nineties records were kept on paper for a period of eight years and then transferred to microfiche for permanent storage. The department now used computers for permanent storage and was also moving backward, putting older files into digital storage banks. But the process was slow and had not gone further back than the late eighties.

Bosch arrived at the counter in archives at one o'clock. He had two containers of coffee with him and two roast beef sandwiches from Philippe's in a paper bag. He looked at the clerk and smiled.

"Believe it or not I need to see the fiche on missing person reports, nineteen seventy-five to 'eighty-five."

The clerk, an old guy with a basement pallor, whistled and said, "Look out, Christine, here they come."

Bosch smiled and nodded and didn't know what the man was talking about. There appeared to be no one else behind the counter.

"The good news is they break up," the clerk said. "I

mean, I think it's good news. You looking for adult or juvy records?"

"Juveniles."

"Then that cuts it up a bit."

"Thanks."

"Don't mention it."

The clerk disappeared from the counter and Bosch waited. In four minutes the man came back with ten small envelopes containing microfiche sheets for the years Bosch requested. Altogether the stack was at least four inches thick.

Bosch went to a microfiche reader and copier, set out a sandwich and the two coffees and took the second sandwich back to the counter. The clerk refused the first offer but then took the sandwich when Bosch said it was from Philippe's.

Bosch went back to the machine and started fiche-ing, wading first into the year 1985. He was looking for missing person and runaway reports of young males in the age range of the victim. Once he got proficient with the machine he was able to move quickly through the reports. He would scan first for the "closed" stamp that indicated the missing individual had returned home or been located. If there was no stamp his eyes would immediately go to the age and sex boxes on the form. If they fit the profile of his victim, he'd read the summary and then push the photocopy button on the machine to get a hard copy to take with him.

The microfiche also contained records of missing person reports forwarded to the LAPD by outside agencies seeking people believed to have gone to Los Angeles.

Despite his speed at the task, it took Bosch more than three hours to go through all the reports for the ten years he had requested. He had hard copies of more than three hundred reports in the tray to the side of the machine when he was finished. And he had no idea whether his effort had been worth the time or not.

Bosch rubbed his eyes and pinched the bridge of his nose. He had a headache from staring at the machine's screen and reading tale after tale of parental anguish and juvenile angst. He looked over and realized he hadn't eaten his sandwich.

He returned the stack of microfiche envelopes to the clerk and decided to do the computer work in Parker Center rather than drive back to Hollywood. From Parker Center he could jump on the 10 Freeway and shoot out to Venice for dinner at Julia Brasher's house. It would be easier.

The squad room of the Robbery-Homicide Division was empty except for the two on-call detectives who were sitting in front of a television watching a football game. One of them was Bosch's former partner, Kizmin Rider. The other Bosch didn't recognize. Rider stood up smiling when she saw it was Bosch.

"Harry, what are you doing here?" she asked.

"Working a case. I want to use a computer, that all right?"

"That bone thing?"

He nodded.

"I heard about it on the news. Harry, this is Rick Thornton, my partner."

Bosch shook his hand and introduced himself.

"I hope she makes you look as good as she did me."

Thornton just nodded and smiled and Rider looked embarrassed.

"Come on over to my desk," she said. "You can use my computer."

She showed him the way and let him sit in her seat.

"We're just twiddling our thumbs here. Nothing happening. I don't even like football."

"Don't complain about the slow days. Didn't anybody ever tell you that?"

"Yeah, my old partner. Only thing he ever said that made any sense."

"I bet."

"Anything I can do to help?"

"I'm just running the names — the usual."

He opened his briefcase and took out the murder book. He opened it to a page where he had listed the names, addresses and birth dates of residents on Wonderland Avenue who had been interviewed during the neighborhood canvas. It was a matter of routine and due diligence to run the name of every person investigators came across in an investigation.

"You want a coffee or something?" Rider asked.

"Nah, I'm fine. Thanks, Kiz."

He nodded in the direction of Thornton, who had his back to them and was on the other side of the room.

"How are things going?"

She shrugged her shoulders.

"Every now and then he lets me do some real detective work," she said in a whisper.

"Well, you can always come back to Hollywood," he whispered back with a smile.

He started typing in the commands for entering the National Crime Index Computer. Immediately, Rider made a sound of derision.

"Harry, you're still typing with two fingers?"

"It's all I know, Kiz. I've been doing it this way for almost thirty years. You expect me to suddenly know how to type with ten fingers? I'm still not fluent in Spanish and don't know how to dance, either. You've only been gone a year."

"Just get up, dinosaur. Let me do it. You'll be here all night."

Bosch raised his hands in surrender and stood up. She sat down and went to work. Behind her back Bosch secretly smiled.

"Just like old times," he said.

"Don't remind me. I always get the shit work. And stop smiling."

She hadn't looked up from her typing. Her fingers were a blur above the keyboard. Bosch watched in awe.

"Hey, it's not like I planned this. I didn't know you were going to be here."

"Yeah, like Tom Sawyer didn't know he had to paint a fence."

"What?"

"Never mind. Tell me about the boot."

Bosch was stunned.

"What?"

"Is that all you can say? You heard me. The rookie you're, uh . . . seeing."

"How the hell do you know about it already?"

"I'm a highly skilled gatherer of information. And I still have sources in Hollywood."

Bosch stepped away from her cubicle and shook his head.

"Well, is she nice? That's all I wanted to know. I don't want to pry."

Bosch came back.

"Yes, she's nice. I hardly know her. You seem to know more about her and me *than* me."

"You havin' dinner with her tonight?"

"Yeah, I'm having dinner with her."

"Hey, Harry?"

Rider's voice had lost any note of humor.

"What?"

"You got a pretty good hit here."

Bosch leaned down and looked at the screen. After digesting the information he said, "I don't think I'm going to make it to dinner tonight."

14

Bosch pulled to a stop in front of the house and studied the darkened windows and porch.

"Figures," Edgar said. "The guy ain't even going to be home. Probably already in the wind."

Edgar was annoyed with Bosch, who had called him in from home. The way he figured it, the bones had been in the ground twenty years, what was the harm of waiting until Monday morning to talk to this guy? But Bosch said he was going by himself if Edgar didn't come in.

Edgar came in.

"No, he's home," Bosch said.

"How d'you know?"

"I just know."

He looked at his watch and wrote the time and address down on a page in his small notebook. It occurred to him then that the house they were at was the one where he had seen the curtain pulled closed behind a window on the evening of the first call out.

"Let's go," he said. "You talked to him the first time, so you take the lead. I'll jump in when it feels right."

They got out and walked up the driveway to the house. The man they were visiting was named Nicholas Trent. He lived alone in the house, which was across the street and two houses down from the hillside where the bones had been found. Trent was fifty-seven years old. He had told Edgar during his initial canvas of the neighborhood that he was a set decorator for a studio in Burbank. He was unmarried and had no children. He knew nothing about the bones on the hill and could offer no clues or suggestions that were helpful.

Edgar knocked hard on the front door and they waited.

"Mr. Trent, it's the police," he said loudly. "Detective Edgar. Answer your door, please."

He had raised his fist to hit the door again when the porch light went on. The door was then opened and a white man with a shaved scalp stood in the darkness within. The light from the porch slashed across his face.

"Mr. Trent? It's Detective Edgar. This is my partner, Detective Bosch. We have a few follow-up questions for you. If you don't mind."

Bosch nodded but didn't offer his hand. Trent said nothing and Edgar forced the issue by putting his hand against the door and pushing it open.

"All right if we come in?" he asked, already halfway across the threshold.

"No, it's not all right," Trent said quickly.

Edgar stopped and put a puzzled look on his face.

"Sir, we just have a few more questions we'd like to ask."

"Yeah, and that's bullshit!"

"Excuse me?"

"We all know what is going on here. I talked to my attorney already. Your act is just that, an act. A bad one."

Bosch could see they were not going to get anywhere with the trick-or-treat strategy. He stepped up and pulled Edgar back by the arm. Once his partner had cleared the threshold he looked at Trent.

"Mr. Trent, if you knew we'd be back, then you knew we'd find out about your past. Why didn't you tell Detective Edgar about it before? It could have saved us some time. Instead, it gives us suspicion. You can understand that, I'm sure."

"Because the past is the past. I didn't bring it up. I buried the past. Leave it that way."

"Not when there are bones buried in it," Edgar said in an accusatory tone.

Bosch looked back at Edgar and gave him a look that said use some finesse.

"See?" Trent said. "This is why I am saying, 'Go away.' I have nothing to tell you people. Nothing. I don't know anything about it."

"Mr. Trent, you molested a nine-year-old boy," Bosch said.

"The year was nineteen sixty-six and I was punished for it. Severely. It's the past. I've been a perfect citizen ever since. I had nothing to do with those bones up there."

Bosch waited a moment and then spoke in a calm and quieter tone.

"If that is the truth, then let us come in and ask our questions. The sooner we clear you, the sooner we move on to other possibilities. But you have to understand something here. The bones of a young boy were found about a hundred yards from the home of a man who molested a young boy in nineteen sixty-six. I don't care what kind of citizen he's been since then, we need to ask him some questions. And we *will* ask those questions. We have no choice. Whether we do it in your home right now or with your lawyer at the station with all of the news cameras waiting outside, that's going to be your choice."

He paused. Trent looked at him with scared eyes.

"So you can understand our situation, Mr. Trent, and we can certainly understand yours. We are willing to move quickly and discreetly but we can't without your cooperation."

Trent shook his head as though he knew that no matter what he did now, his life as he knew it was in jeopardy and probably permanently altered. He finally stepped back and signaled Bosch and Edgar in.

Trent was barefoot and wearing baggy black shorts that showed off thin ivory legs with no hair on them. He wore a flowing silk shirt over his thin upper body. He had the same build as a ladder, all hard angles. He led them to a living room cluttered with antiques. He sat down in the center of a couch. Bosch and Edgar took the two leather club chairs opposite. Bosch decided to keep the lead. He didn't like the way Edgar had handled the door.

"To be cautious and careful, I am going to read you your constitutional rights," he said. "Then I'll ask you to sign a waiver form. This protects you as well as us. I am also going to record our conversation so that nobody ends up putting words in anybody else's mouth. If you want a copy of the tape I will make it available."

Trent shrugged and Bosch took it as reluctant agreement. When Bosch had the form signed he slipped it into his briefcase and took out a small recorder. Once he started it and identified those present as well as the time and date, he nodded to Edgar to assume the lead again. This was because Bosch thought that observations of Trent and his surroundings were going to be more important than his answers now.

"Mr. Trent, how long have you lived in this house?"

"Since nineteen eighty-four."

He then laughed.

"What is funny about that?" Edgar asked.

"Nineteen eighty-four. Don't you get it? George Orwell? Big Brother?"

He gestured toward Bosch and Edgar as the front men of Big Brother. Edgar apparently didn't follow the statement and continued with the interview.

"Rent or own?"

"Own. Uh, at first I rented, then I bought the house in 'eighty-seven from the landlord."

"Okay, and you are a set designer in the entertainment industry?"

"Set decorator. There is a difference."

"What is the difference?"

"The designer plans and supervises the construction of the set. The decorator then goes in and puts in the details. The little character strokes. The characters' belongings or tools. Like that."

"How long have you done this?"

"Twenty-six years."

"Did you bury that boy up on the hillside?"

Trent stood up indignantly.

"Absolutely not. I've never even set foot on that hill. And you people are making a big mistake if you waste your time on me when the true killer of that poor soul is still out there somewhere."

Bosch leaned forward in his chair.

"Sit down, Mr. Trent," he said.

The fervent way in which Trent delivered the denial made Bosch instinctively think he was either innocent or one of the better actors he had come across on the job. Trent slowly sat down on the couch again.

"You're a smart guy," Bosch said, deciding to jump in. "You know exactly what we're doing here. We have to bag you or clear you. It's that simple. So why don't you help us out? Instead of dancing around with us, why don't you tell us how to clear you?"

Trent raised his hands wide.

"I don't know how! I don't know anything about the case! How can I help you when I don't know the first thing about it?"

"Well, right off the bat, you can let us take a look around

here. If I can start to get comfortable with you, Mr. Trent, then maybe I can start seeing it from your side of things. But right now . . . like I said, I've got you with your record and I've got bones across the street."

Bosch held up his two hands as if he was holding those two things in them.

"It doesn't look that good from where I'm looking at things."

Trent stood up and threw one hand out in a gesture toward the interior of the house.

"Fine! Be my guest. Look around to your heart's content. You won't find a thing because I had nothing to do with it. Nothing!"

Bosch looked at Edgar and nodded, the signal being that he should keep Trent occupied while Bosch took a look around.

"Thank you, Mr. Trent," Bosch said as he stood up.

As he headed into a hallway that led to the rear of the house, he heard Edgar asking if Trent had ever seen any unusual activity on the hillside where the bones had been found.

"I just remember kids used to play up —"

He stopped, apparently when he realized that any mention he made of kids would only further suspicion about him. Bosch glanced back to make sure the red light of the recorder was still on.

"Did you like watching the kids play up there in the woods, Mr. Trent?" Edgar asked.

Bosch stayed in the hallway, out of sight but listening to Trent's answer.

"No, I couldn't see them if they were up in the woods. On occasion I would be driving up or walking my dog — when he was alive — and I would see the kids climbing up there. The girl across the street. The Fosters next door. All the kids around here. It's a city-owned right-of-way — the only undeveloped land in the neighborhood. So they went up there to play. Some of the neighbors thought the older ones went up there to smoke cigarettes, and the concern was they would set the whole hillside on fire."

"How long ago are you talking about?"

"Like when I first moved here. I didn't get involved. The neighbors who had been here took care of it."

Bosch moved down the hall. It was a small house, not much bigger than his own. The hallway ended at a conjunction of three doors. Bedrooms on the right and left and a linen closet in the middle. He checked the closet first, found nothing unusual, and then moved into the bedroom on the right. It was Trent's bedroom. It was neatly kept but the tops of the twin bureaus and bed tables were cluttered with knickknacks that Bosch assumed Trent used on the job in helping to turn sets into real places for the camera.

He looked in the closet. There were several shoe boxes on the upper shelf. Bosch started opening them and found they contained old, worn-out shoes. It was apparently Trent's habit of buying new shoes and putting his old ones in the box, then shelving them. Bosch guessed that these, too, became part of his work inventory. He opened one box and found a pair of work boots. He noticed that dirt had dried hard in some of the treads. He thought about the dark soil where the bones had been found. Samples of it had been collected.

He put the boots back and made a mental note of it for the search warrant. His current search was just a cursory look around. If they moved to the next step with Trent and he became a full-fledged suspect, then they would come back with a search warrant and literally tear the place apart looking for evidence tying him to the bones. The work boots might be a good place to start. He was already on tape saying he had never been up on that hillside. If the dirt in the treads matched the soil samples from the excavation, then they'd have Trent caught in a lie. Most of what sparring with suspects was about was the locking in of a story. It was then that the investigator looked for the lies.

There was nothing else in the closet that warranted Bosch's attention. Same with the bedroom or the attached bathroom. Bosch, of course, knew that if Trent was the killer, he'd had many years to cover his tracks. He would also have had the last three days — since Edgar first questioned him during the canvas — to double-check his trail and be ready.

The other bedroom was used as an office and a storage room for his work. On the walls hung framed one sheets advertising the films Bosch assumed Trent had worked on. Bosch had seen some of them on television but rarely went to theaters to see movies. He noticed that one of the frames held the one sheet for a film called *The Art of the Cape*. Years before, Bosch had investigated the murder of that film's producer. He had heard that after that, the one sheets from the movie had become collector items in underground Hollywood.

When he was finished looking around the rear of the house, Bosch went through a kitchen door into the garage. There were two bays, one containing Trent's minivan. The other was stacked with boxes with markings on them corresponding to rooms in a house. At first Bosch was shocked at the thought that Trent had still not completely unpacked after moving in nearly twenty years before. Then he realized the boxes were work related and used in the process of set decoration.

When he turned around he was looking at an entire wall hung with the heads of wild game, their black marble eyes staring at him. Bosch felt a nerve tickle run down his spine. All of his life he had hated seeing things like that. He wasn't sure why.

He spent another few minutes in the garage, mostly

going through a box in the stack that was marked "boy's room 9–12." It contained toys, airplane models, a skateboard, and a football. He took the skateboard out for a few moments and studied it, all the while thinking about the shirt from the backpack with "Solid Surf" printed on it. After a while he put the skateboard back in the box and closed it.

There was a side door to the garage that led to a path that went to the backyard. A pool took up most of the level ground before the yard rose into the steep, wooded hillside. It was too dark to see much and Bosch decided he would have to do the exterior look during daylight hours.

Twenty minutes after he left to begin the search Bosch returned to the living room empty-handed. Trent looked up at him expectantly.

"Satisfied?"

"I'm satisfied for now, Mr. Trent. I appreciate your —"

"You see? It never ends. 'Satisfied for now.' You people will never let it go, will you? I mean, if I was a drug dealer or a bank robber, my debt would be cleared and you people would leave me alone. But because I touched a boy almost forty years ago I am guilty for life."

"I think you did more than touch him," Edgar said. "But we'll get the records. Don't worry."

Trent put his face in his hands and mumbled something about it being a mistake to have cooperated. Bosch looked at Edgar, who nodded that he was finished and ready to go. Bosch stepped over and picked up his recorder. He slid it into the breast pocket of his jacket but didn't turn it off. He'd learned a valuable lesson on a case the year before — sometimes the most important and telling things are said after an interview is supposedly over.

"Mr. Trent, thank you for your cooperation. We're going to go. But we might need to talk to you tomorrow. Are you working tomorrow?"

"God, no, don't call me at work! I need this job and you'll ruin it. You'll ruin everything."

He gave Bosch his pager number. Bosch wrote it down and headed toward the front door. He looked back at Edgar.

"Did you ask him about trips? He's not planning to go anywhere, is he?"

Edgar looked at Trent.

"Mr. Trent, you work on movies, you know how the dialogue goes. You call us if you plan to go out of town. If you don't and we have to find you . . . you're not going to like it very much."

Trent spoke in a flat-line monotone, his eyes focused forward, somewhere far away.

"I'm not going anywhere at all. Now please leave. Just leave me alone."

They walked out the door and Trent closed it hard behind them. At the bottom of the driveway was a large bougainvillea bush in full bloom. It blocked Bosch's view of the left side of the street until he got there.

A bright light suddenly flashed on and in Bosch's face. A reporter with a cameraman in tow moved in on the two detectives. Bosch was blinded for a few moments until his eyes started to adjust.

"Hi, detectives. Judy Surtain, Channel Four news. Is there a break in the bones case?"

"No comment," Edgar barked. "No comment and turn that damn light off."

Bosch finally saw her in the glare of the light. He recognized her from TV and from the gathering at the roadblock earlier in the week. He also recognized that a "no comment" was not the way to leave this situation. He needed to diffuse it and keep the media away from Trent.

"No," he said. "No breakthrough. We're just following routine procedures."

Surtain shoved the microphone she was carrying toward Bosch's face.

"Why are you out here in the neighborhood again?"

"We're just finishing the routine canvas of the residents here. I hadn't had a chance to talk to the resident here before. We just finished up, that's all."

He was talking with a bored tone in his voice. He hoped she was buying it.

"Sorry," he added. "No big story tonight."

"Well, was this neighbor or any of the neighbors helpful to the investigation?"

"Well, everyone here has been very cooperative with us but as far as investigative leads go it has been difficult. Most of these people weren't even living in the neighborhood when the bones were buried. That makes it tough."

Bosch gestured toward Trent's house.

"This gentleman, for example. We just found out that he didn't buy his home here until nineteen eighty-seven and we're pretty sure those bones were already up there by then."

"So then it's back to the drawing board?"

"Sort of. And that's really all I can tell you. Good night."

He pushed past her toward his car. A few moments later Surtain was on him at the car door. Without her cameraman.

"Detective, we need to get your name."

Bosch opened his wallet and took out a business card. The one with the general station number printed on it. He gave it to her and said good night again.

"Look, if there is anything you can tell me, you know, off the record, I would protect you," Surtain said. "You know, off camera like this, whatever you want to do."

"No, there is nothing," Bosch said as he opened the door. "Have a good night."

Edgar cursed the moment the doors of the car were closed.

"How the hell did she know we were here?"

"Probably a neighbor," Bosch said. "She was out here the whole two days of the dig. She's a celebrity. She made nice with the residents. Made friends. Plus, we're sitting in a goddamn Shamu. Might as well have called a press conference."

Bosch thought of the inanity of trying to do detective work in a car painted black and white. Under a program designed to make cops more visible on the street, the department had assigned detectives in the divisions to black-and-whites that didn't carry the emergency lights on top but were just as noticeable.

They watched as the reporter and her cameraman went to Trent's door.

"She's going to try to talk to him," Edgar said.

Bosch quickly went into his briefcase and got out his cell phone. He was about to dial Trent's number and tell him not to answer when he realized he couldn't get a cell signal.

"Goddammit," he said.

"Too late anyway," Edgar said. "Let's just hope he plays it smart."

Bosch could see Trent at his front door, totally bathed in the white light from the camera. He said a few words and then made a waving gesture and closed the door.

"Good," Edgar said.

Bosch started the car, turned it around and headed back through the canyon to the station.

"So what's next?" Edgar asked.

"We have to pull the records on his conviction, see what it was about."

"I'll do that first thing."

"No. First thing I want to deliver the search warrants to the hospitals. Whether Trent fits our picture or not, we need to ID the kid in order to connect him to Trent. Let's meet at Van Nuys Courthouse at eight. We get them signed and then split 'em up."

Bosch had picked Van Nuys court because Edgar lived nearby and they could separate and go from there in the morning after the warrants had been approved by a judge.

"What about a warrant on Trent's place?" Edgar said. "You see anything while you were looking around?"

"Not much. He's got a skateboard in a box in the garage. You know, with his work stuff. For putting on a set. I was thinking of our victim's shirt when I saw that. And there were some work boots with dirt in the treads. It might match the samples from the hill. But I'm not counting on a search coming through for us. The guy has had twenty years to make sure he's clear. *If* he's the guy."

"You don't think so?"

Bosch shook his head.

"Timing's wrong. 'Eighty-four is on the late side. The far edge of our window."

"I thought we were looking at 'seventy-five to 'eighty-five."

"We are. In general. But you heard Golliher — twenty to twenty-five years ago. That's early eighties on the high side. I don't know about 'eighty-four being early eighties."

"Well, maybe he moved to that house *because* of the body. He buried the kid there before and wanted to be close by so he moves into the neighborhood. I mean, Harry, these are sick fucks, these guys."

Bosch nodded.

"There's that. But I just wasn't getting the vibe from the guy. I believed him."

"Harry, your mojo's been wrong before."

"Oh, yeah . . ."

"I think it's him. He's the guy. Hear how he said, 'just because I touched a boy.' Probably to him, sodomizing a nine-year-old is reaching out and touching somebody."

Edgar was being reactionary but Bosch didn't call him on it. He was a father; Bosch wasn't.

"We'll get the records and we'll see. We also have to go to the Hall to check the reverses, see who was on that street back then."

The reverses were phone books that listed residents by address instead of by name. A collection of the books for every year was kept in the Hall of Records. They would allow the detectives to determine who was living on the street during the 1975 to 1985 range they were looking at as the boy's time of death.

"That's going to be a lot of fun," Edgar said.

"Oh, yeah," Bosch said. "I can't wait."

They drove in silence the rest of the way. Bosch became depressed. He was disappointed with himself for how he had run the investigation so far. The bones were discovered Wednesday, and the full investigation took off on Thursday. He knew he should have run the names — a basic part of the investigation — sooner than Sunday. By delaying it he had given Trent the advantage. He'd had three days to expect and prepare for their questions. He had even been briefed by an attorney. He could have even been practicing his responses and looks in a mirror. Bosch knew what his internal lie detector said. But he also knew that a good actor could beat it.

15

Bosch drank a beer on the back porch with the sliding door open so he could hear Clifford Brown on the stereo. Almost fifty years before, the trumpet player made a handful of recordings and then checked out in a car crash. Bosch thought about all the music that had been lost. He thought about young bones in the ground and what had been lost. And then he thought about himself and what he had lost. Somehow the jazz and the beer and the grayness he was feeling about the case had all mixed together in his mind. He felt on edge, like he was missing something that was right in front of him. For a detective it was just about the worst feeling in the world.

At 11 P.M. he came inside and turned the music down so he could watch the news on Channel 4. Judy Surtain's report was the third story after the first break. The anchor said, "New developments in the Laurel Canyon bone case. We go to Judy Surtain at the scene."

"Ah, shit," Bosch said, not liking the sound of the introduction.

The program cut to a live shot of Surtain on Wonderland Avenue, standing on the street in front of a house Bosch recognized as Trent's.

"I'm here on Wonderland Avenue in Laurel Canyon, where four days ago a dog brought home a bone that authorities say was human. The dog's find led to the discovery of more bones belonging to a young boy who investigators believe was murdered and then buried more than twenty years ago."

Bosch's phone started ringing. He picked it up off the arm of the TV chair and answered it.

"Hold on," he said and then held the phone down by his side while he watched the news report.

Surtain said, "Tonight the lead investigators on the case returned to the neighborhood to speak to one resident who lives less than one hundred yards from the place where the boy was buried. That resident is Nicholas Trent, a fifty-seven-year-old Hollywood set decorator."

The program cut to tape of Bosch being questioned by Surtain that night. But it was used as visual filler while Surtain continued her report in a voice-over dub.

"Investigators declined to comment on their questioning of Trent, but Channel Four news has learned —"

Bosch sat down heavily on the chair and braced himself.

"— that Trent was once convicted of molesting a young boy."

The sound was then brought up on the street interview just as Bosch said, "That's really all I can tell you."

The next jump was to video of Trent standing in his doorway and waving the camera off and closing the door.

"Trent declined comment on his status in the case. But neighbors in the normally quiet hillside neighborhood expressed shock upon learning of Trent's background."

As the report shifted to a taped interview of a resident Bosch recognized as Victor Ulrich, Bosch hit the mute button on the TV remote and brought the phone up. It was Edgar.

"You watching this shit?" he asked.

"Oh, yeah."

"We look like shit. We look like we told her. They used your quote out of context, Harry. We're going to be fucked by this."

"Well, you didn't tell her, right?"

"Harry, you think I'd tell some —"

"No, I don't. I was confirming. You didn't tell her, right?"

"Right."

"And neither did I. So, yeah, we're going to take some shit but we're clear on it."

"Well, who else knew? I doubt Trent was the one who told her. About a million people now know he's a child molester."

Bosch realized the only people who knew were Kiz, who had gotten the records flag while doing the computer work, and Julia Brasher, whom Bosch told while he was making his excuse for missing dinner. Suddenly a vision of Surtain standing at the roadblock on Wonderland came to him. Brasher had volunteered her help during both days of the hillside search and excavation. It was entirely possible that she had connected with Surtain in some way. Was she the reporter's source, the leak?

"There didn't have to be a leak," Bosch said to Edgar. "All she needed was Trent's name. She could have gotten any cop she knew to run it on the box for her. Or she could have looked it up on the sexual offenders CD. It's public record. Hold on."

He had gotten a call-waiting beep on the phone. He switched over and learned it was Lt. Billets calling. He told her to hold while he got off the other line. He clicked over.

"Jerry, it's Bullets. I gotta call you back."

"It's still me," Billets said.

"Oh, sorry. Hold on."

He tried again and this time made the switch back. He told Edgar he'd call him back if Billets said anything he needed to know right away.

"Otherwise, go with the plan," he added. "See you at Van Nuys at eight."

He switched back over to Billets.

"Bullets?" she said. "Is that what you guys call me?"

"What?"

"You said 'Bullets.' When you thought I was Edgar you called me 'Bullets.' "

"You mean just now?"

"Yes, just now."

"I don't know. I don't know what you're talking about. You mean when I was switching over to —"

"Never mind, it doesn't matter. I assume you saw Channel Four?"

"Yeah, I saw it. And all I can tell you is that it wasn't me and it wasn't Edgar. That woman got a tip that we were out there and we 'no comment'-ed our way out of there. How she came up with his —"

"Harry, you didn't 'no comment' your way out of there. They have you on tape, your mouth moving, and then I hear you say, 'that's all I can say.' If you say 'that's all,' that means you gave her something."

Bosch shook his head, even though he was on the phone.

"I didn't give her shit. I just bullshitted my way by. I told her we were just finishing up the routine canvas of the neighborhood and I hadn't talked to Trent before."

"Was that true?"

"Not really, but I wasn't going to say we were there because the guy's a child molester. Look, she didn't know about Trent when we were there. If she did, she would have asked me. She found out later, and how I don't know. That's what Jerry and I were just talking about."

There was silence for a moment before Billets continued.

"Well, you better have your shit together on this tomorrow because I want a written explanation from you that I can send up the line. Before that report on Four was even over I got a call from Captain LeValley and she said she had already gotten a call from Deputy Chief Irving."

"Yeah, yeah, typical. Right on down the food chain."

"Look, you know that leaking the criminal record of a citizen is against departmental policy, whether that citizen is the target of an investigation or not. I just hope you have your story straight on this. I don't need to tell you that there are people in the department just waiting for you to make a mistake they can sink their teeth into."

"Look, I'm not trying to downplay the leak. It was wrong and it was bad. But I'm trying to solve a murder here, Lieutenant, and now I've got a whole new obstacle to overcome. And that's what's typical. There is always something thrown in the way."

"Then you should be more careful next time."

"Careful of what? What did I do wrong? I'm following leads where they go."

Bosch immediately regretted the explosion of frustration and anger. Of those people in the department waiting for his self-destruction, Billets certainly wasn't on the list. She was only the messenger here. In the same moment, he realized his anger was also self-directed because he knew Billets was right. He should have handled Surtain differently.

"Look, I'm sorry," he said in a low, even tone. "It's just the case. It's got its hooks, you know?"

"I think I do," Billets answered just as quietly. "And speaking of the case, what exactly is going on? This whole thing with Trent came out of left field for me. I thought you were going to keep me up to date."

"It all came up today. Late. I was just going to fill you in in the morning. I didn't know Channel Four would be doing it for me. And doing it for LeValley and Irving as well."

"Never mind them for now. Tell me about Trent."

16

I⊤ was well after midnight by the time Bosch got to Venice. Parking on the little streets near the canals was nonexistent. He drove around looking for ten minutes and ended up parking in the lot by the library out on Venice Boulevard and then walking back in.

Not all of the dreamers drawn to Los Angeles came to make movies. Venice was the century-old dream of a man named Abbot Kinney. Before Hollywood and the film industry barely had a pulse, Kinney came to the marshlands along the Pacific. He envisioned a place built on a network of canals with arched bridges and a town center of Italian architecture. It would be a place emphasizing cultural and artistic learning. And he would call it Venice of America.

But like most of the dreamers who come to Los Angeles his vision was not uniformly shared or realized. Most financiers and investigators were cynical and passed on the opportunity to build Venice, putting their money into projects of less grand design. Venice of America was dubbed "Kinney's Folly."

But a century later many of the canals and the arched bridges reflected in their waters remained while the financiers and doomsayers and their projects were long swept away by time. Bosch liked the idea of Kinney's Folly out-lasting them all.

Bosch had not been to the canals in many years, though for a short period in his life after returning from Vietnam he had lived there in a bungalow with three other men he knew from overseas. In the years since, many of the bunga-lows had been erased and modern two- and three-story homes costing a million dollars or more had replaced them.

Julia Brasher lived in a house at the corner of the How-land and Eastern canals. Bosch expected it to be one of the new structures. He guessed she probably used her law-firm money to buy it or even build it. But as he came to the address he saw that he was wrong. Her house was a small bungalow made of white clapboard with an open front porch overlooking the joining of the two canals.

Bosch saw lights on behind the windows of her house. It was late but not that late. If she worked the three-to-eleven shift, then it was unlikely she was used to going to bed be-fore two.

He stepped up onto the porch but hesitated before knocking on the door. Until the doubts of the last hour had crept in, he had gotten only good feelings about Brasher and their fledgling relationship. He knew he now had to be careful. There could be nothing wrong and yet he could spoil everything if he misstepped here.

Finally, he raised his arm and knocked. Brasher answered right away.

"I was wondering if you were going to knock or stand out there all night."

"You knew I was standing here?"

"The porch is old. It creaks. I heard it."

"Well, I got here and then figured it was too late. I should have called first."

"Just come in. Is anything wrong?"

Bosch came in and looked around. He didn't answer the question.

The living room had an unmistakable beach flavor to it, right down to the bamboo-and-rattan furniture and the surfboard leaning in one corner. The only deviation was her equipment belt and holster hanging on a wall rack near the door. It was a rookie mistake leaving it out like that, but Bosch assumed she was proud of her new career choice and wanted to remind friends outside the cop world of it.

"Sit down," she said. "I have some wine open. Would you like a glass?"

Bosch thought a moment about whether mixing wine with the beer he'd had an hour earlier would lead to a headache the next day when he knew he'd have to be focused.

"It's red."

"Uh, I'll take just a little bit."

"Got to be sharp tomorrow, huh?"

"I guess."

She went into the kitchen while he sat down on the couch. He looked around the room and now saw a mounted fish with a long sharp point hanging over the white brick fireplace. The fish was a brilliant blue shading to black with a white and yellow underside. Mounted fish didn't bother him the way the heads of mounted game did but he still didn't like the eye of the fish always watching.

"You catch this thing?" he called out.

"Yeah. Off Cabo. Took me three and a half hours to bring it in."

She then appeared with two glasses of wine.

"On fifty-pound test line," she said. "That was a workout."

"What is it?"

"Black marlin."

She toasted the fish with her glass and then toasted Bosch.

"Hold fast."

Bosch looked at her.

"That's my new toast," she said. "Hold fast. It seems to cover everything."

She sat down on the chair closest to Bosch. Behind her was the surfboard. It was white with a rainbow design in a border running along the edges. It was a short board.

"So you surf the wild waves, too."

She glanced back at the board and then at Bosch and smiled.

"I try to. Picked it up in Hawaii."

"You know John Burrows?"

She shook her head.

"Lot of surfers in Hawaii. What beach does he surf?"

"No, I mean here. He's a cop. He works Homicide out of Pacific Division. Lives on a walk street by the beach. Not too far from here. He surfs. On his board it says 'To Protect and Surf.'"

She laughed.

"That's cool. I like that. I'll have to get that put on my board."

Bosch nodded.

"John Burrows, huh? I'll have to look him up."

She said it with just a touch of teasing in her voice.

Bosch smiled and said, "And maybe not."

He liked the way she kidded him like that. It all felt good to Bosch, which made him feel all the more out of sorts because of his reason for being there. He looked at his wine glass.

"I've been fishing all day and didn't catch a thing," he said. "Microfiche mostly."

"I saw you on the news tonight," she said. "Are you trying to put the squeeze on that guy, the child molester?"

Bosch sipped his wine to give himself time to think. She had opened the door. He now just had to step through very carefully.

"What do you mean?" he asked.

"Well, giving that reporter his criminal background. I figured you must be making some kind of play. You know, turning up the heat on him. To make him talk or something. It seems kind of risky."

"Why?"

"Well, first of all, trusting a reporter is always risky. I know that from back when I was a lawyer and got burned. And second . . . and second, you never know how people are going to react when their secrets are no longer secrets."

Bosch studied her for a moment and then shook his head.

"I didn't give it to her," he said. "Somebody else did."

He studied her eyes for any kind of tell. There was nothing.

"There's going to be trouble over it," he added.

She raised her eyebrows in surprise. Still no tell.

"Why? If you didn't give her the information, why would there . . ."

She stopped and now Bosch could see her put it together. He saw the disappointment fill her eyes.

"Oh, Harry . . ."

He tried to back out through the door.

"What? Don't worry about it. I'll be fine."

"It wasn't me, Harry. Is that what you're here about? To see if I'm the leak or the source or whatever you'd call it?"

She abruptly put her wine glass down on the coffee table. Red wine lapped over the edge and onto the table. She didn't do anything about it. Bosch knew there was no use trying to avoid the collision. He had screwed up.

"Look, only four people knew . . ."

"And I was one of them. So you thought you'd come here undercover and find out if it was me."

She waited for a response. Finally, all Bosch could do was nod.

"Well, it wasn't me. And I think you should go now."

Bosch nodded and put down his glass. He stood up.

"Look, I'm sorry. I screwed it up. I thought the best way to not mess anything up, you know, between you and me, was to . . ."

He made a helpless gesture with his hands as he headed to the door.

"Was to do the undercover thing," he continued. "I just didn't want to mess it up, that's all. But I had to know. I think if you were me you would've felt the same way about it."

He opened the door and looked back at her.

"I'm sorry, Julia. Thanks for the wine."

He turned to go.

"Harry."

He turned back. She came to him and reached up and grabbed the lapels of his jacket with both hands. She slowly pulled him forward and then pushed him backward, as if roughing up a suspect in slow motion. Her eyes dropped to his chest as her mind worked and she came to a decision.

She stopped shaking him but kept her grasp on his jacket.

"I can get over it," she said. "I think."

She looked up to his eyes and pulled him forward. She kissed him hard on the mouth for a long time and then pushed him back. She let go.

"I hope. Call me tomorrow."

Bosch nodded and stepped through the door. She closed it.

Bosch went down the porch to the sidewalk next to the canal. He looked at the reflection of the lights of all the houses on the water. An arched footbridge, lighted by the moon and nothing else, crossed the canal twenty yards away, its reflection perfect on the water. He turned and walked back up the steps to the porch. He hesitated at the door again and soon Brasher opened it.

"The porch creaks, remember?"

He nodded and she waited. He wasn't sure how to say what he wanted to say. Finally, he just began.

"One time when I was in one of those tunnels we were talking about last night I came up head-on with some guy. He was VC. Black pajamas, greased face. We sort of looked at each other for a split second and I guess instincts took over. We both raised up and fired at the same time. Simultaneous. And then we fucking ran in opposite directions. Both of us scared shitless, screaming in the dark."

He paused as he thought about the story, seeing it more than remembering it.

"Anyway, I thought he had to have hit me. It was almost point-blank, too close to miss. I thought my gun had backfired and jammed or something. The kick had felt wrong. When I got up top the first thing I did was check myself. No blood, no pain. I took all of my clothes off and checked myself. Nothing. He had missed. Point-blank and somehow the guy had missed."

She stepped over the door's threshold and leaned against the front wall beneath the porch light. She didn't say anything and he pressed on.

"Anyway, then I checked my forty-five for a jam and I found out why he hadn't hit me. The guy's bullet was in the barrel of my gun. With mine. We had pointed at each other and his shot went right up the barrel of my gun. What were the chances of that? A million to one? A billion?"

As he spoke he held his empty hand out as a gun pointing at her. His hand was extended directly in front of his chest. The bullet that day in the tunnel had been meant for his heart.

"I guess I just want you to know that I know how lucky I was with you tonight."

He nodded and then turned and went down the steps.

17

Death investigation is a pursuit with countless dead ends, obstacles and colossal chunks of wasted time and effort. Bosch knew this every day of his existence as a cop but was reminded of it once again when he got to the homicide table shortly before noon Monday and found his morning's time and effort had most likely been wasted while a brand-new obstacle awaited him.

The homicide squad had the area at the rear corner of the detective bureau. The squad consisted of three teams of three. Each team had a table consisting of the three detectives' desks pushed together, two facing each other, the third along one side. Sitting at Bosch's table, in the slot left vacant by Kiz Rider's departure, was a young woman in a business suit. She had dark hair and even darker eyes. They were eyes sharp enough to peel a walnut and they held on Bosch his whole way through the squad room.

"Can I help you?" he asked when he got to the table.

"Harry Bosch?"

"That's me."

"Detective Carol Bradley, IAD. I need to take a statement from you."

Bosch looked around. There were several people in

the squad room trying to act busy while surreptitiously watching.

"Statement about what?"

"Deputy Chief Irving asked our division to determine if the criminal record of Nicholas Trent was improperly divulged to the media."

Bosch still hadn't sat down. He put his hands on the top of his chair and stood behind it. He shook his head.

"I think it's pretty safe to assume it was improperly divulged."

"Then I need to find out who did it."

Bosch nodded.

"I'm trying to run an investigation here and all anybody cares about is —"

"Look, I know you think it's bullshit. And I may think it's bullshit. But I've got the order. So let's go into one of the rooms and put your story on tape. It won't take long. And then you can go back to your investigation."

Bosch put his briefcase on the table and opened it. He took out his tape recorder. He had remembered it while driving around all morning delivering search warrants at the local hospitals.

"Speaking of tape, why don't you take this into one of the rooms and listen to it first? I had it on last night. It should end my involvement in this pretty quick."

She hesitantly took the recorder, and Bosch pointed to the hallway that led to the three interview rooms.

"I'm still going to need to —"

"Fine. Listen to the tape, then we'll talk."

"Your partner, too."

"He should be in anytime now."

Bradley went down the hall with the recorder. Bosch finally sat down and didn't bother to look at any of the other detectives.

It wasn't even noon but he felt exhausted. He had spent the morning waiting for a judge in Van Nuys to sign the search warrants for medical records and then driving across the city delivering them to the legal offices of nineteen different hospitals. Edgar had taken ten of the warrants and headed off on his own. With fewer to deliver, he was then going downtown to conduct record searches on Nicholas Trent's criminal background and to check the reverse directories and property records for Wonderland Avenue.

Bosch noticed that waiting for him was a stack of phone messages and the latest batch of call-in tips from the front desk. He took the phone messages first. Nine out of twelve of them were from reporters, all no doubt wanting to follow up on Channel 4's report on Trent the night before and then rebroadcast during the morning news program. The other three were from Trent's lawyer, Edward Morton. He had called three times between 8 and 9:30 A.M.

Bosch didn't know Morton but expected he was calling to complain about Trent's record being given to the media. He normally wasn't quick to return calls to lawyers but decided it would be best to get the confrontation over with and to assure Morton that the leak had not come from the investigators on the case. Even though he doubted that Morton would believe anything he said, he picked up the phone and called back. A secretary told him that Morton had gone to a court hearing but was due to check in at any moment. Bosch said he would be waiting for him to call again.

After hanging up Bosch dropped the pink slips with the reporters' numbers on them into the trash can next to his spot at the table. He started going through the call-in sheets and quickly noticed that the desk officers were now asking the questions he had typed out the morning before and given to Mankiewicz.

On the eleventh report in the pile he came across a direct hit. A woman named Sheila Delacroix had called at 8:41 A.M. that morning and said she had seen the Channel 4 report that morning. She said her younger brother Arthur Delacroix disappeared in 1980 in Los Angeles. He was twelve years old at the time and was never heard from since.

In answer to the medical questions, she responded that her brother had been injured during a fall from a skateboard a few months before his disappearance. He suffered a brain injury that required hospitalization and neurosurgery. She did not remember the exact medical details but was sure the hospital was Queen of Angels. She could not recall the name of any of the doctors who treated her brother. Other than an address and call-back number for Sheila Delacroix, that was all the information on the report.

Bosch circled the word "skateboard" on the sheet. He opened his briefcase and got out a business card Bill Golliher had given him. He called the first number and got a machine at the anthropologist's office at UCLA. He called the second and got Golliher while he was eating lunch in Westwood Village.

"Got a quick question. The injury that required surgery on the skull."

"The hematoma."

"Right. Could that have been caused by a fall from a skateboard?"

There was silence and Bosch let Golliher think. The clerk who took the calls to the general lines in the squad room came up to the homicide table and shot Bosch a peace sign. Bosch covered his receiver.

"Who is it?"

"Kiz Rider."

"Tell her to hold."

He uncovered the receiver.

"Doc, you there?"

"Yes, I'm just thinking. It might be possible, depending on what it was he hit. But a fall just to the ground, I would say it's not likely. You had a tight fracture pattern, which indicates a small area of surface-to-surface contact. Also, the location is high up on the cranium. It's not the back of the head, which you would normally associate with fall injuries."

Bosch felt some of the wind going out of his sails. He had thought he might have an ID on the victim.

"Is this a particular person you are talking about?" Golliher asked.

"Yeah, we just got a tip."

"Are there X-rays, surgical records?"

"I'm working on it."

"Well, I'd like to see them to make a comparison."

"As soon as I get them. What about the other injuries? Could they be from skateboarding?"

"Of course some of them could be from that," Golliher said. "But I would say not all. The ribs, the twist fractures — also, some of these injuries dated to very early childhood, Detective. There aren't many three-year-olds on skateboards, I would think."

Bosch nodded and tried to think if there was anything else to ask.

"Detective, you do know that in abuse cases the reported cause of injury and the true cause are not often the same?"

"I understand. Whoever brought the kid into the emergency room wouldn't volunteer he hit him with a flashlight or whatever."

"Right. There would be a story. The child would adhere to it."

"Skateboard accident."

"It's possible."

"Okay, Doc, I gotta go. I'll get you the X-rays as soon as I get them. Thanks."

He punched line two on the phone.

"Kiz?"

"Harry, hi, how're you doing?"

"Busy. What's up?"

"I feel awful, Harry. I think I fucked up."

Bosch leaned back in his chair. He would have never guessed it was her.

"Channel Four?"

"Yeah. I, uh . . . yesterday after you left Parker and my partner stopped watching the football game, he asked what was up with you being in there. So I told him. I'm still trying to establish the relationship, Harry, you know? I told him I ran the names for you and there was a hit. One of the neighbors had a molestation record. That's all I told him, Harry. I swear."

Bosch breathed out heavily. He actually felt better. His instinct about Rider had been right on. She was not the leak. She had simply trusted someone she should have been able to trust.

"Kiz, I got IAD sitting up here waiting to talk to me about this. How do you know Thornton gave it to Channel Four?"

"I saw the report on TV this morning when I was getting ready. I know Thornton knows that reporter. Surtain. Thornton and I worked a case a few months ago — an insurance murder on the Westside. It got some media play and he was feeding her stuff off the record. I saw them together. Then yesterday, after I told him about the hit, he said he had to go to the can. He picked the sports page up and went down the hall. But he didn't go to the can. We got a call out and I went down and banged on the door to tell him we were rolling. He didn't answer. I didn't really think anything about it until I saw the news today. I think he didn't go to the can because he went into another office or down to the lobby to use a phone to call her."

"Well, it explains a lot."

"I'm really sorry, Harry. That TV report didn't make you look good at all. I'm going to talk to IAD."

"Just hold on to that, Kiz. For now. I'll let you know if I need you to talk to IAD. But what are *you* going to do?"

"Get a new partner. I can't work with this guy."

"Be careful. You start jumping partners and pretty soon you'll be all alone."

"I'd rather work alone than with some asshole I can't trust."

"There's that."

"What about you? The offer still stand?"

"What, I'm an asshole you can trust?"

"You know what I mean."

"The offer stands. All you have to do is —"

"Hey, Harry, I gotta go. Here he comes."

"Okay, bye."

Bosch hung up and rubbed his mouth with his hand as he thought about what to do about Thornton. He could tell Kiz's story to Carol Bradley. But there was still too much room in it for error. He wouldn't feel comfortable going to IAD with it unless he was sure. The actual idea of going to IAD about anything repulsed him, but in this instance someone was harming Bosch's investigation.

And that was something he could not let pass.

After a few minutes he came up with a plan and checked his watch. It was ten minutes before noon. He called Kiz Rider back.

"It's Harry. Is he there?"

"Yeah, why?"

"Repeat after me, in a sort of excited voice. 'You did, Harry? Great! Who was he?'"

"You did, Harry? That's great! Who was he?"

"Okay, now you're listening, listening, listening. Now say, 'How did a ten-year-old get here from New Orleans?'"

"How did a ten-year-old get all the way here from New Orleans?"

"Perfect. Now hang up and don't say anything. If Thornton asks you, tell him we ID'd the kid through dental records. He was a ten-year-old runaway from New Orleans last seen in nineteen seventy-five. His parents are on a plane heading here now. And the chief is going to have a press conference about it all today at four."

"Okay, Harry, good luck."

"You, too."

Bosch hung up and looked up. Edgar was standing across the table from him. He had heard the last part of the conversation and his eyebrows were up.

"No, it's all bullshit," Bosch said. "I'm setting up the leak. And that reporter."

"The leak? Who is the leak?"

"Kiz's new partner. We think."

Edgar slid into his chair and just nodded.

"But we do have a possible ID on the bones," Bosch said.

He told Edgar about the call-in sheet on Arthur Delacroix and his subsequent conversations with Bill Golliher.

"Nineteen eighty? That's not going to work with Trent. I checked the reverses and property records. He wasn't on that street until 'eighty-four. Like he said last night."

"Something tells me he isn't our guy."

Bosch thought about the skateboard again. It wasn't enough to alter his gut feeling.

"Tell that to Channel Four."

Bosch's phone rang. It was Rider.

"He just went to the can."

"You tell him about the press conference?"

"I told him everything. He kept asking questions, the dipshit."

"Well, if he tells her that everybody will have it at four, she'll go out with the exclusive on the noon news. I'm going to go watch."

"Let me know."

He hung up and checked his watch. He still had a few minutes. He looked at Edgar.

"By the way, IAD is in one of the rooms back there. We're under investigation."

Edgar's jaw dropped. Like most cops, he resented Internal Affairs because even when you did a good and honest job, the IAD could still be on you for any number of things. It was like the Internal Revenue Service, the way just seeing a letter with the IRS return address in the corner was enough to pull your guts into a knot.

"Relax. It's about the Channel Four thing. We should be clear of it in a few minutes. Come with me."

They went into Lt. Billets's office, where there was a small television on a stand. She was doing paperwork at her desk.

"You mind if we check out Channel Four's noon report?" Bosch asked.

"Be my guest. I'm sure Captain LeValley and Chief Irving are going to be watching as well."

The news program opened with a report on a sixteen-car pileup in the morning fog on the Santa Monica Freeway. It wasn't that significant a story — no one was killed — but they had good video, so it led the program. But the "dog bone" case had moved up to second billing. The anchor said they were going to Judy Surtain with another exclusive report.

The program cut to Surtain sitting at a desk in the Channel 4 newsroom.

"Channel Four has learned that the bones found in Laurel Canyon have been identified as those of a ten-year-old runaway from New Orleans."

Bosch looked at Edgar and then at Billets, who was rising from her seat with an expression of surprise on her face. Bosch put out his hand as if to signal her to wait a moment.

"The parents of the boy, who reported him missing more than twenty-five years ago, are en route to Los Angeles to meet with police. The remains were identified through dental records. Later today, the chief of police is expected to hold a press conference where he will identify the boy and discuss the investigation. As reported by Channel Four last night, police are focusing on —"

Bosch turned the TV off.

"Harry, Jerry, what's going on?" Billets asked immediately.

"All of that was bogus. I was smoking out the leak."

"Who?"

"Kiz's new partner. A guy named Rick Thornton."

Bosch explained what Rider had explained to him earlier. He then outlined the scam he had just pulled.

"Where's the IAD detective?" Billets asked.

"One of the interview rooms. She's listening to a tape I had of me and the reporter last night."

"A tape? Why didn't you tell me about it last night?"

"I forgot about it last night."

"All right, I'll take it from here. You feel Kiz is clean on this?"

Bosch nodded.

"She has to trust her partner enough to tell him anything. He took that trust and gave it to Channel Four. I don't know what he's getting in return but it doesn't matter. He's fucking with my case."

"All right, Harry, I said I would handle it. You go back to the case. Anything new I should know about?"

"We've got a possible ID — this one legit — that we'll be running down today."

"What about Trent?"

"We're letting that sit until we find out if this is the kid. If it is, the timing is wrong. The kid disappeared in nineteen eighty. Trent didn't move into the neighborhood until four years later."

"Great. Meantime, we've taken his buried secret and put it on TV. Last I heard from patrol, the media was camped in his driveway."

Bosch nodded.

"Talk to Thornton about it," he said.

"Oh, we will."

She sat down behind her desk and picked up the phone. It was their cue to leave. On the way back to the table Bosch asked Edgar if he had pulled the file on Trent's conviction.

"Yeah, I got it. It was a weak case. Nowadays the DA probably wouldn't have even filed on it."

They went to their respective spots at the table and Bosch saw that he had missed a callback from Trent's lawyer. He reached for the phone but then waited until Edgar finished his report.

"The guy worked as a teacher at an elementary school in Santa Monica. He was caught by another teacher in a stall in the bathroom holding an eight-year-old's penis while he urinated. He said he was teaching the kid how to aim it, that the kid kept pissing on the floor. What it came down to is the kid's story was all over the place but didn't back his. And the parents said the boy already knew how to aim by the time he was four. Trent was convicted and got a two plus one. He served fifteen months of it up at Wayside."

Bosch thought about all of this. His hand was still on the phone.

"It's a long ass jump from that to beating a kid to death with a baseball bat."

"Yeah, Harry, I'm beginning to like your mojo better all the time."

"I wish I did."

He picked up the phone and punched in the number for Trent's attorney, Edward Morton. He was transferred to the lawyer's cell phone. He was on his way to lunch.

"Hello?"

"Detective Bosch."

"Bosch, yes, I want to know where he is."

"Who?"

"Don't play this game, Detective. I've called every holding jail in the county. I want to be able to speak to my client. Right now."

"I'm assuming you are speaking about Nicholas Trent. Have you tried his job?"

"Home and work, no answer. Pager, too. If you people have him, he's entitled to representation. And I am entitled to know. I'm telling you now, if you fuck with me on this, I will go right to a judge. And the media."

"We don't have your man, counselor. I haven't seen him since last night."

"Yes, he called me after you left. Then again after watching the news. You people fucked him over — you should be ashamed of yourself."

Bosch's face burned with the rebuke but he didn't respond to it. If he didn't personally deserve it, then the department did. He'd take the bullet for now.

"Do you think he ran, Mr. Morton?"

"Why run if you are innocent?"

"I don't know. Ask O.J."

A horrible thought suddenly shot into Bosch's gut. He stood up, the phone still pressed to his ear.

"Where are you now, Mr. Morton?"

"Sunset heading west. Near Book Soup."

"Turn around and come back. Meet me at Trent's house."

"I have a lunch. I'm not going —"

"Meet me at Trent's house. I'm leaving now."

He put the phone in its cradle and told Edgar it was time to go. He'd explain on the way.

18

THERE was a small gathering of television reporters in the street in front of Nicholas Trent's house. Bosch parked behind the Channel 2 van and he and Edgar got out. Bosch didn't know what Edward Morton looked like but didn't see anyone in the group who looked like an attorney. After more than twenty-five years on the job, he had unerring instincts that allowed him to identify lawyers and reporters. Over the top of the car, Bosch spoke to Edgar before the reporters could hear them.

"If we have to go in, we'll do it around back — without the audience."

"I gotya."

They walked up to the driveway and were immediately accosted by the media crews, who turned on cameras and threw questions that went unanswered. Bosch noticed that Judy Surtain of Channel 4 was not among the reporters.

"Are you here to arrest Trent?"

"Can you tell us about the boy from New Orleans?"

"What about the press conference? Media Relations doesn't know anything about a press conference."

"Is Trent a suspect or not?"

Once Bosch was through the crowd and on Trent's driveway, he suddenly turned back and faced the cameras.

He hesitated a moment as if composing his thoughts. What he really was doing was giving them time to focus and get ready. He didn't want anyone to miss this.

"There is no press conference scheduled," Bosch said. "There has been no identification of the bones yet. The man who lives in this house was questioned last night as was every resident of this neighborhood. At no time was he called a suspect by the investigators on this case. Information leaked to the media by someone outside of the investigation and then broadcast without being checked first with the actual investigators has been completely wrong and damaging to the ongoing investigation. That's it. That's all I'm going to say. When there is some real and accurate information to report, we will give it to you through Media Relations."

He turned back around and headed up the driveway to the house with Edgar. The reporters threw more questions at them but Bosch gave no indication of even hearing them.

At the front door Edgar knocked sharply and called out to Trent, telling him it was the police. After a few moments he knocked again and made the same announcement. They waited again and nothing happened.

"The back?" Edgar asked.

"Yeah, or the garage has a door on the side."

They walked across the driveway and started heading down the side of the house. The reporters yelled more questions. Bosch guessed they were so used to throwing questions that were not answered at people that it simply became natural for them to do it and natural for them to know they would not be answered. Like a dog barking in the backyard long after the master has left for work.

They passed the side door to the garage, and Bosch noted that he was correct in remembering that there was only a single key lock on the knob. They continued into the backyard. There was a kitchen door with a dead bolt and a key lock on the knob. There was also a sliding door, which would be easy to pop open. Edgar stepped over to it but looked down through the glass to the interior sliding track and saw that there was a wooden dowel in place that would prevent the door from being opened from the outside.

"This won't work, Harry," he said.

Bosch had a small pouch containing a set of lock picks in his pocket. He didn't want to have to work the dead bolt on the kitchen door.

"Let's do the garage, unless . . ."

He walked over to the kitchen door and tried it. It was unlocked and he opened the door. In that moment he knew they would find Trent dead inside. Trent would be the helpful suicide. The one who leaves the door open so people don't have to break in.

"Shit."

Edgar came over, pulling his gun from its holster.

"You're not going to need that," Bosch said.

He stepped into the house and they moved through the kitchen.

"Mr. Trent?" Edgar yelled. "Police! Police in the house! Are you here, Mr. Trent?"

"Take the front," Bosch said.

They split up and Bosch went down the short hallway to the rear bedrooms. He found Trent in the walk-in shower of the master bath. He had taken two wire hangers and fashioned a noose which he had attached to the stem pipe of the shower. He had then leaned back against the tiled wall and dropped his weight and asphyxiated himself. He was still dressed in the clothes he had worn the night before. His bare feet were on the floor tiles. There were no indications at all that Trent had had second thoughts about killing himself. Being that it was not a suspension hanging, he could have stopped his death at any time. He didn't.

Bosch would have to leave it for the coroner's people but

he judged by the darkening of the body's tongue, which was distended from the mouth, that Trent had been dead at least twelve hours. That would put his death in the vicinity of the very early morning, not long after Channel 4 had first announced his hidden past to the world and labeled him a suspect in the bones case.

"Harry?"

Bosch nearly jumped. He turned around and looked at Edgar.

"Don't do that to me, man. What?"

Edgar was staring at the body as he spoke.

"He left a three-page note out on the coffee table."

Bosch stepped out of the shower and pushed past Edgar. He headed toward the living room, taking a pair of latex gloves from his pocket and blowing into them to expand the rubber before snapping them on.

"Did you read the whole thing?"

"Yeah, he says he didn't do the kid. He says he's killing himself because the police and reporters have destroyed him and he can't go on. Like that. There's some weird stuff, too."

Bosch went into the living room. Edgar was a few steps behind him. Bosch saw three handwritten pages spread side by side on the coffee table. He sat down on the couch in front of them.

"This how they were?"

"Yup. I didn't touch them."

Bosch started reading the pages. What he presumed were Trent's last words were a rambling denial of the murder of the boy on the hillside and a purging of anger over what had been done to him.

Now EVERYBODY will know! You people have ruined me, KILLED me. The blood is on you, not on me! I didn't do it, I didn't do it, no, no, NO! I never hurt anyone. Never, never, never.

Not a soul on this earth. I love the children. LOVE!!!! No, it was you who hurt me. You. But it is I who can't live with the pain of what you have ruthlessly caused. I can't.

It was repetitive and almost as if someone had written down an extemporaneous diatribe rather than sat down with pen and paper and wrote out their thoughts. The middle of the second page was blocked off and inside the box were names under a heading of "Those Found Responsible." The list started with Judy Surtain, included the anchor on the Channel 4 nightly news, and listed Bosch, Edgar and three names Bosch didn't recognize. Calvin Stumbo, Max Rebner and Alicia Felzer.

"Stumbo was the cop and Rebner was the DA on the first case," Edgar said. "In the sixties."

Bosch nodded.

"And Felzer?"

"Don't know that one."

The pen with which the pages were apparently written was on the table next to the last page. Bosch didn't touch it because he planned to have it checked for Trent's fingerprints.

As he continued to read, Bosch noticed that each page was signed at the bottom with Trent's signature. At the end of the last page, Trent made an odd plea that Bosch didn't readily understand.

My one regret is for my children. Who will care for my children? They need food and clothes. I have some money. The money goes to them. Whatever I have. This is my last will and testament signed by me. Give the money to the children. Have Morton give the money and don't charge me anything. Do it for the children.

"His children?" Bosch asked.

"Yeah, I know," Edgar said. "Weird."

"What are you doing here? Where is Nicholas?"

They looked at the doorway from the kitchen to the living room. A short man in a suit who Bosch guessed was a lawyer and had to be Morton stood there. Bosch stood up.

"He's dead. It looks like a suicide."

"Where?"

"Master bath, but I wouldn't —"

Morton was already gone, heading to the bathroom. Bosch called after him.

"Don't touch anything."

He nodded to Edgar to follow and make sure. Bosch sat back down and looked at the pages again. He wondered how long it took Trent to decide that killing himself was all that he had left and then to labor over the three-page note. It was the longest suicide note he had ever encountered.

Morton came back into the living room, Edgar just behind him. His face was ashen and his eyes held on the floor.

"I tried to tell you not to go back there," Bosch said.

The lawyer's eyes came up and fixed on Bosch. They filled with anger, which seemed to restore some color to Morton's face.

"Are you people happy now? You completely destroyed him. Give a man's secret to the vultures, they put it on the air and this is what you get."

He gestured with a hand in the direction of the bathroom.

"Mr. Morton, you've got your facts wrong, but essentially it looks like that's what happened. In fact, you'd probably be surprised by how much I agree with you."

"Now that he's dead, that must be very easy for you to say. Is that a note? Did he leave a note?"

Bosch got up and gestured for him to take his spot on the couch in front of the three pages.

"Just don't touch the pages."

Morton sat down, unfolded a pair of reading glasses and started studying the pages.

Bosch walked over to Edgar and said in a low voice, "I'm going to use the phone in the kitchen to make the calls."

Edgar nodded.

"Better get Media Relations on it. The shit is going to hit that fan."

"Yeah."

Bosch picked up the wall phone in the kitchen and saw it had a redial button. He pushed it and waited. He recognized the voice that answered as Morton's. It was an answering machine. Morton said he wasn't home and to leave a message.

Bosch called Lt. Billets's direct line. She answered right away and Bosch could tell she was eating.

"Well, I hate to break this to you while you're eating, but we're up here at Trent's place. It looks like he killed himself."

There was silence for a long moment and then she asked Bosch if he was sure.

"I'm sure he's dead and I'm pretty sure he did it himself. Hung himself with a couple of wire hangers in the shower. There's a three-page note here. He denies anything to do with the bones. He blames his death on Channel Four and the police mostly — me and Edgar in particular. You're the first one I've called."

"Well, we all know it wasn't you who —"

"That's okay, Lieutenant, I don't need the absolution. What do you want me to do here?"

"You handle the routine call outs. I'll call Chief Irving's office and tell him what has transpired. This is going to get hot."

"Yes. What about Media Relations? There's already a gang of reporters out on the street."

"I'll call them."

"Did you do anything about Thornton yet?"

"Already in the pipeline. The woman from IAD, Bradley, is running with it. With this latest thing, I'd bet Thornton not only leaked his way out of a job, but they might want to go after him with a charge of some kind."

Bosch nodded. Thornton deserved it. He still had no second thoughts about the scam he had devised.

"All right, well, we'll be here. For a while, at least."

"Let me know if you find anything there that connects him to the bones."

Bosch thought of the boots with the dirt in the treads and the skateboard.

"You got it," he said.

Bosch clicked off the call and then immediately made calls to the coroner's office and SID.

In the living room Morton had finished reading the note.

"Mr. Morton, when was the last time you talked to Mr. Trent?" Bosch asked.

"Last night. He called me at home after the news on Channel Four. His boss had seen it and called him."

Bosch nodded. That accounted for the last call.

"You know his boss's name?"

Morton pointed to the middle page on the table.

"Right here on the list. Alicia Felzer. She told him she was going to seek his termination. The studio makes movies for children. She couldn't have him on a set with a child. You see? The leaking of his record to the media destroyed this man. You recklessly took a man's existence and —"

"Let me ask the questions, Mr. Morton. You can save your outrage for when you go outside and talk to the reporters yourself, which I know you'll do. What about that last page? He mentions the children. His children. What does that mean?"

"I have no idea. He obviously was emotionally distraught when he wrote this. It may mean nothing."

Bosch remained standing, studying the attorney.

"Why did he call you last night?"

"Why do you think? To tell me you had been here, that it was all over the news, that his boss had seen it and wanted to fire him."

"Did he say whether he buried that boy up there on the hill?"

Morton put on the best indignant look he could muster.

"He certainly said that he did not have a thing to do with it. He believed he was being persecuted for a past mistake, a very distant mistake, and I'd say he was correct about that."

Bosch nodded.

"Okay, Mr. Morton, you can leave now."

"What are you talking about? I'm not going to —"

"This house is now a crime scene. We are investigating your client's death to confirm or deny it was by his own hand. You are no longer welcome here. Jerry?"

Edgar stepped over to the couch and waved Morton up.

"Come on. Time to go out there and get your face on TV. It'll be good for business, right?"

Morton stood up and left in a huff. Bosch walked over to the front windows and pulled the curtain back a few inches. When Morton came down the side of the house to the driveway, he immediately walked to the center of the knot of reporters and started talking angrily. Bosch couldn't hear what was said. He didn't need to.

When Edgar came back into the room, Bosch told him to call the watch office and get a patrol car up to Wonderland for crowd control. He had a feeling that the media mob, like a virus replicating itself, was going to start growing bigger and hungrier by the minute.

19

THEY found Nicholas Trent's children when they searched his home following the removal of his body. Filling the entire two drawers of a small desk in the living room, a desk Bosch had not searched the night before, were files, photographs and financial records, including several thick bank envelopes containing canceled checks. Trent had been sending small amounts of money on a monthly basis to a number of charitable organizations that fed and clothed children. From Appalachia to the Brazilian rain forest to Kosovo, Trent had been sending checks for years. Bosch found no check for an amount higher than twelve dollars. He found dozens and dozens of photographs of the children he was supposedly helping as well as small handwritten notes from them.

Bosch had seen any number of public-service ads for the charities on late-night television. He had always been suspicious. Not about whether a few dollars could keep a child from going hungry and unclothed, but about whether the few dollars would actually get to them. He wondered if the photos Trent kept in the drawers of his desk were the same stock shots sent to everybody who contributed. He wondered if the thank-you notes in childish printing were fake.

"Man," Edgar said as he surveyed the contents of the desk. "This guy, it's like I think he was paying a penance or something, sending all his cash to these outfits."

"Yeah, a penance for what?"

"We may never know."

Edgar went back to searching the second bedroom. Bosch studied some of the photos he had spread on the top of the desk. There were boys and girls, none looking older than ten, though this was hard to estimate because they all had the hollow and ancient eyes of children who have been through war and famine and indifference. He picked up one shot of a young white boy and turned it over. The information said the boy had been orphaned during the fighting in Kosovo. He had been injured in the mortar blast that killed his parents. His name was Milos Fidor and he was ten years old.

Bosch had been orphaned at age eleven. He looked into the boy's eyes and saw his own.

At 4 P.M. they locked Trent's home and took three boxes of seized materials to the car. A small group of reporters lingered outside during the whole afternoon, despite word from Media Relations that all information on the day's events would be distributed through Parker Center.

The reporters approached them with questions but Bosch quickly said that he was not allowed to comment on the investigation. They put the boxes in the trunk and drove off, heading downtown, where a meeting had been called by Deputy Chief Irvin Irving.

Bosch was uncomfortable with himself as he drove. He was ill at ease because Trent's suicide — and he had no doubts now that it was — had served to deflect the forward movement of the investigation of the boy's death. Bosch had spent half the day going through Trent's belongings when what he had wanted to be doing was nailing down the ID of the boy, running out the lead he had received in the call-in reports.

"What's the matter, Harry?" Edgar asked at one point on the drive.

"What?"

"I don't know. You're acting all morose. I know that's probably your natural disposition, but you usually don't show it so much."

Edgar smiled but didn't get one in return from Bosch.

"I'm just thinking about things. This guy might be alive today if we had handled things differently."

"Come on, Harry. You mean like if we didn't investigate him? There was no way. We did our job and things ran their course. Nothing we could do. If anybody's responsible it's Thornton, and he's gonna get his due. But if you ask me, the world's better off without somebody like Trent in it anyway. My conscience is clear, man. Crystal clear."

"Good for you."

Bosch thought about his decision to give Edgar the day off on Sunday. If he hadn't done that, Edgar might have been the one to make the computer runs on the names. Kiz Rider would've been out of the loop and the information would have never gotten to Thornton.

He sighed. Everything always seemed to work on a domino theory. If, then, if, then, if, then.

"What's your gut say on this guy?" he asked Edgar.

"You mean, like did he do the boy on the hill?"

Bosch nodded.

"I don't know," Edgar said. "Have to see what the lab says about the dirt and the sister says about the skateboard. If it is the sister and we get an ID."

Bosch didn't say anything. But he always felt uncomfortable about relying on lab reports in determining which way to go with an investigation.

"What about you, Har?"

Bosch thought of the photos of all the children Trent thought he was caring for. His act of contrition. His chance at redemption.

"I'm thinking we're spinning our wheels," he said. "He isn't the guy."

20

DEPUTY Chief Irvin Irving sat behind his desk in his spacious office on the sixth floor of Parker Center. Also seated in the room were Lt. Grace Billets, Bosch and Edgar and an officer from the Media Relations unit named Sergio Medina. Irving's adjutant, a female lieutenant named Simonton, stood in the open doorway of the office in case she was needed.

Irving had a glass-topped desk. There was nothing on it except for two pieces of paper with printing on them that Bosch could not read from his spot in front of Irving's desk and to the left.

"Now then," Irving began. "What do we know as fact about Mr. Trent? We know he was a pedophile with a criminal record of abusing a child. We know that he lived a stone's throw from the burial site of a murdered child. And we know that he committed suicide on the evening he was questioned by investigators in regard to the first two points just stated."

Irving picked up one of the pages on his desk and studied it without sharing its contents with the room. Finally, he spoke.

"I have here a press release that states those same three facts and goes on to say, 'Mr. Trent is the subject of an ongoing investigation. Determination of whether he was responsible for the death of the victim found buried near his home is pending lab work and follow-up investigation.'"

He looked at the page silently again and then finally put it down.

"Nice and succinct. But it will do little to quell the thirst of the media for this story. Or to help us avert another troubling situation for this department."

Bosch cleared his throat. Irving seemed to ignore it at first but then spoke without looking at the detective.

"Yes, Detective Bosch?"

"Well, it sort of seems as though you're not satisfied with that. The problem is, what is on that press release is exactly where we stand. I'd love to tell you I think the guy did the kid on the hill. I'd love to tell you I *know* he did it. But we are a long way from that and, if anything, I think we're going to end up concluding the opposite."

"Based on what?" Irving snapped.

It was becoming clear to Bosch what the purpose of the meeting was. He guessed that the second page on Irving's desk was the press release the deputy chief wanted to put out. It probably pinned everything on Trent and called his suicide the result of his knowing he would be found out. This would allow the department to handle Thornton, the leaker, quietly outside of the magnifying glass of the press. It would spare the department the humiliation of acknowledging that a leak of confidential information from one of its officers caused a possibly innocent man to kill himself. It would also allow them to close the case of the boy on the hill.

Bosch understood that everyone sitting in the room knew that closing a case of this nature was the longest of long shots. The case had drawn growing media attention, and Trent with his suicide had now presented them with a way out. Suspicions could be cast on the dead pedophile, and the department could call it a day and move on to the next case — hopefully one with a better chance of being solved.

Bosch could understand this but not accept it. He had seen the bones. He had heard Golliher run down the litany of injuries. In that autopsy suite Bosch had resolved to find the killer and close the case. The expediency of department politics and image management would be second to that.

He reached into his coat pocket and pulled out his notebook. He opened it to a page with a folded corner and looked at it as if he was studying a page full of notes. But there was only one notation on the page, written on Saturday in the autopsy suite.

44 separate indications of trauma

His eyes held on the number he had written until Irving spoke again.

"Detective Bosch? I asked, 'Based on what?' "

Bosch looked up and closed the notebook.

"Based on the timing — we don't think Trent moved into that neighborhood until after that boy was in the ground — and on the analysis of the bones. This kid was physically abused over a long period of time — from when he was a small child. It doesn't add up to Trent."

"Analysis of both the timing and the bones will not be conclusive," Irving said. "No matter what they tell us, there is still a possibility — no matter how slim — that Nicholas Trent was the perpetrator of this crime."

"A very slim possibility."

"What about the search of Trent's home today?"

"We took some old work boots with dried mud in the treads. It will be compared to soil samples taken where the bones were found. But they'll be just as inconclusive. Even

if they match up, Trent could have picked up the dirt hiking behind his house. It's all part of the same sediment, geo-
logically speaking."

"What else?"

"Not much. We've got a skateboard."

"A skateboard?"

Bosch explained about the call-in tip he had not had
time to follow up on because of the suicide. As he told it, he
could see Irving warming to the possibility that a skateboard in Trent's possession could be linked to the bones on
the hill.

"I want that to be your priority," he said. "I want that
nailed down and I want to know it the moment you do."

Bosch only nodded.

"Yes, sir," Billets threw in.

Irving went silent and studied the two pages on his desk.
Finally, he picked up the one he had not read from — the
page Bosch guessed was the loaded press release — and
turned at his desk. He slid it into a shredder, which whined
loudly as it destroyed the document. He then turned back
to his desk and picked up the remaining document.

"Officer Medina, you may put this out to the press."

He handed the document to Medina, who stood up to
receive it. Irving checked his watch.

"Just in time for the six o'clock news," he said.

"Sir?" Medina said.

"Yes?"

"Uh, there have been many inquiries about the erro-
neous reports on Channel Four. Should we —"

"Say it is against policy to comment on any internal
investigation. You may also add that the department will
not condone or accept the leaking of confidential information to the media. That is all, Officer Medina."

Medina looked like he had another question to ask but
knew better. He nodded and left the office.

Irving nodded to his adjutant and she closed the office door, remaining in the anteroom outside. The deputy chief then turned his head, looking from Billets to Edgar to Bosch.

"We have a delicate situation here," he said. "Are we clear on how we are proceeding?"

"Yes," Billets and Edgar said in unison.

Bosch said nothing. Irving looked at him.

"Detective, do you have something to say?"

Bosch thought a moment before answering.

"I just want to say that I am going to find out who killed that boy and put him up in that hole. If it's Trent, fine. Good. But if it's not him, I'm going to keep going."

Irving saw something on his desk. Something small like a hair or other near-microscopic particle. Something Bosch couldn't see. Irving picked it up with two fingers and dropped it into the trash can behind him. As he brushed his fingers together over the shredder, Bosch looked on and wondered if the demonstration was some sort of threat directed at him.

"Not every case is solved, Detective, not every case is solvable," he said. "At some point our duties may require us to move on to more pressing matters."

"Are you giving me a deadline?"

"No, Detective. I am saying I understand you. And I just hope you understand me."

"What's going to happen with Thornton?"

"It's under internal review. I can't discuss it with you at this time."

Bosch shook his head in frustration.

"Watch yourself, Detective Bosch," Irving said curtly. "I've shown a lot of patience with you. On this case and others before it."

"What Thornton did jammed up this case. He should —"

"If he is responsible he will be dealt with accordingly. But keep in mind he was not operating in a vacuum. He needed to get the information in order to leak it. The investigation is ongoing."

Bosch stared at Irving. The message was clear. Kiz Rider could go down with Thornton if Bosch didn't fall into step with Irving's march.

"You read me, Detective?"

"I read you. Loud and clear."

21

BEFORE taking Edgar back to Hollywood Division and then heading out to Venice, Bosch got the evidence box containing the skateboard out of the trunk and took it back inside Parker Center to the SID lab. At the counter he asked for Antoine Jesper. While he waited, he studied the skateboard. It appeared to be made out of laminated plywood. It had a lacquered finish to which several decals had been applied, most notably a skull and crossbones located in the middle of the top surface of the board.

When Jesper came to the counter, Bosch presented him with the evidence box.

"I want to know who made this, when it was made and where it was sold," he said. "It's priority one. I got the sixth floor riding my back on this case."

"No problem. I can tell you the make right now. It's a Boney board. They don't make 'em anymore. He sold out and moved, I think, to Hawaii."

"How do you know all of that?"

"'Cause when I was a kid I was a boarder and this was what I wanted but never had the dough for. Pretty ironic, huh?"

"What is?"

"A Boney board and the case. You know, bones."

Bosch nodded.

"Whatever. I want whatever you can get me by tomorrow."

"Um, I can try. I can't prom —"

"Tomorrow, Antoine. The sixth floor, remember? I'll be talking to you tomorrow."

Jesper nodded.

"Give me the morning, at least."

"You got it. Anything happening with documents?"

Jesper shook his head.

"Nothing yet. She tried the dyes and nothing came up. I don't think you should count on anything there, Harry."

"All right, Antoine."

Bosch left him there holding the box.

On the way back to Hollywood he let Edgar drive while he pulled the tip sheet out of his briefcase and called Sheila Delacroix on his cell phone. She answered promptly and Bosch introduced himself and said her call had been referred to him.

"Was it Arthur?" she asked urgently.

"We don't know, ma'am. That's why I'm calling."

"Oh."

"Will it be possible for me and my partner to come see you tomorrow morning to talk about Arthur and get some information? It will help us to be better able to determine if the remains are those of your brother."

"I understand. Um, yes. You can come here, if that is convenient."

"Where is there, ma'am?"

"Oh. My home. Off Wilshire in the Miracle Mile."

Bosch looked at the address on the call-in sheet.

"On Orange Grove."

"Yes, that's correct."

"Is eight-thirty too early for you?"

"That would be fine, Officer. If I can help I would like

to. It just bothers me to think that that man lived there all those years after doing something like this. Even if the victim wasn't my brother."

Bosch decided it wasn't worth telling her that Trent was probably completely innocent in terms of the bone case. There were too many people in the world who believed everything they saw on television.

Instead, Bosch gave her his cell phone number and told her to call it if something came up and eight-thirty the next morning turned out to be a bad time for her.

"It won't be a bad time," she said. "I want to help. If it's Arthur, I want to know. Part of me wants it to be him so I know it is over. But the other part wants it to be somebody else. That way I can keep thinking he is out there someplace. Maybe with a family of his own now."

"I understand," Bosch said. "We'll see you in the morning."

22

I⊤ was a brutal drive to Venice and Bosch arrived more than a half hour late. His lateness was then compounded by his fruitless search for a parking space before he went back to the library lot in defeat. His delay was no bother to Julia Brasher, who was in the critical stage of putting things together in the kitchen. She instructed him to go to the stereo and put on some music, then pour himself a glass of wine from the bottle that was already open on the coffee table. She did not make a move to touch him or kiss him, but her manner was completely warm. He thought things seemed good, that maybe he had gotten past the gaffe of the night before.

He chose a CD of live recordings of the Bill Evans Trio at the Village Vanguard in New York. He had the CD at home and knew it would make for quiet dinner music. He poured himself a glass of red wine and casually walked around the living room, looking at the things she had on display.

The mantel of the white brick fireplace was crowded with small framed photos he hadn't gotten a chance to look at the night before. Some were propped on stands and displayed more prominently than others. Not all were of people. Some photos were of places he assumed she had visited in her travels. There was a ground shot of a live volcano billowing smoke and spewing molten debris in the air. There was an underwater shot of the gaping mouth and jagged teeth of a shark. The killer fish appeared to be launching itself right at the camera — and whoever was behind it. At the edge of the photo Bosch could see one of the iron bars of the cage the photographer — who he assumed was Brasher — had been protected by.

There was a photo of Brasher with two Aboriginal men on either side of her standing somewhere, Bosch assumed, in the Australian outback. And there were several other photos of her with what appeared to be fellow backpackers in other locations of exotic or rugged terrain that Bosch could not readily identify. In none of the photos in which Julia was a subject was she looking at the camera. Her eyes were always staring off in the distance or at one of the other individuals posed with her.

In the last position on the mantel, as if hidden behind the other photos, was a small gold-framed shot of a much younger Julia Brasher with a slightly older man. Bosch reached behind the photos and lifted it out so he could see it better. The couple was sitting at a restaurant or perhaps a wedding reception. Julia wore a beige gown with a low-cut neckline. The man wore a tuxedo.

"You know, this man is a god in Japan," Julia called from the kitchen.

Bosch put the framed photo back in its place and walked to the kitchen. Her hair was down and he couldn't decide which way he liked it best.

"Bill Evans?"

"Yeah. It seems like they have whole channels of the radio dedicated to playing his music."

"Don't tell me, you spent some time in Japan, too."

"About two months. It's a fascinating place."

It looked to Bosch like she was making a risotto with chicken and asparagus in it.

"Smells good."

"Thank you. I hope it is."

"So what do you think you were running from?"

She looked up at him from her work at the stove. A hand held a stirring spoon steady.

"What?"

"You know, all the travel. Leaving Daddy's law firm to go swim with sharks and dive into volcanoes. Was it the old man or the law firm the old man ran?"

"Some people would look at it as maybe I was running toward something."

"The guy in the tuxedo?"

"Harry, take your gun off. Leave your badge at the door. I always do."

"Sorry."

She went back to work at the stove and Bosch came up behind her. He put his hands on her shoulders and pushed his thumbs into the indentations of her upper spine. She offered no resistance. Soon he felt her muscles begin to relax. He noticed her empty wine glass on the counter.

"I'll go get the wine."

He came back with his glass and the bottle. He refilled her glass and she picked it up and clicked it off the side of his.

"Whether to something or away from something, here's to running," she said. "Just running."

"What happened to 'Hold fast'?"

"There's that, too."

"Here's to forgiveness and reconciliation."

They clicked glasses again. He came around behind her and started working her neck again.

"You know, I thought about your story all last night after you left," she said.

"My story?"

"About the bullet and the tunnel."

"And?"

She shrugged her shoulders.

"Nothing. It's just amazing, that's all."

"You know, after that day, I wasn't afraid anymore when I was down in the darkness. I just knew that I was going to make it through. I can't explain why, I just knew. Which, of course, was stupid, because there are no guarantees of that — back then and there or anywhere else. It made me sort of reckless."

He held his hands steady for a moment.

"It's not good to be too reckless," he said. "You cross the tube too often, you'll eventually get burned."

"Hmm. Are you lecturing me, Harry? You want to be my training officer now?"

"No. I checked my gun and my badge at the door, remember?"

"Okay, then."

She turned around, his hands still on her neck, and kissed him. Then she pulled back away.

"You know, the great thing about this risotto is that it can keep in the oven as long as we need it to."

Bosch smiled.

Later on, after they had made love, Bosch got up from her bed and went out to the living room.

"Where are you going?" she called after him.

When he didn't answer she called out to him to turn the oven up. He came back into the room carrying the gold-framed photo. He got into the bed and turned on the light on the bed table. It was a low-wattage bulb beneath a heavy lamp shade. The room still was cast in shadow.

"Harry, what are you doing?" Julia said in a tone that warned he was treading close to her heart. "Did you turn the oven up?"

"Yeah, three-fifty. Tell me about this guy."

"Why?"

"I just want to know."

"It's a private story."

"I know. But you can tell me."

She tried to take the photo away but he held it out of her reach.

"Is he the one? Did he break your heart and send you running?"

"Harry. I thought you took your badge off."

"I did. And my clothes, everything."

She smiled.

"Well, I'm not telling you anything."

She was on her back, head propped on a pillow. Bosch put the picture on the bed table and then turned back and moved in next to her. Under the sheet he put his arm across her body and pulled her tightly to him.

"Look, you want to trade scars again? I got my heart broken twice by the same woman. And you know what? I kept her picture on a shelf in my living room for a long time. Then on New Year's Day I decided it had been a long enough time. I put her picture away. Then I got called out to work and I met you."

She looked at him, her eyes moving slightly back and forth as she seemed to be searching his face for something, maybe the slightest hint of insincerity.

"Yes," she finally said. "He broke my heart. Okay?"

"No, not okay. Who is the creep?"

She started laughing.

"Harry, you're my knight in tarnished armor, aren't you?"

She pulled herself up into a sitting position, the sheet falling away from her breasts. She folded her arms across them.

"He was in the firm. I really fell for him — right down

the old elevator shaft. And then . . . then he decided it was over. And he decided to betray me and to tell secret things to my father."

"What things?"

She shook her head.

"Things I will never tell a man again."

"Where was that picture taken?"

"Oh, at a firm function — probably the New Year's banquet, I don't remember. They have a lot of them."

Bosch had become angled behind her. He leaned down and kissed her back, just above the tattoo.

"I couldn't be there anymore while he was there. So I quit. I said I wanted to travel. My father thought it was a midlife crisis because I had turned thirty. I just let him think it. But then I had to do what I said I wanted to do — travel. I went to Australia first. It was the farthest place I could think of."

Bosch pulled himself up and stacked two pillows behind his back. He then pulled her back against his chest. He kissed the top of her head and kept his nose in her hair.

"I had a lot of money from the firm," she said. "I didn't have to worry. I just kept traveling, going wherever I wanted, working odd jobs when I felt like it. I didn't come home for almost four years. And when I did, that's when I joined the academy. I was walking along the boardwalk and saw the little Venice community service office. I went in and picked up a pamphlet. It all happened pretty fast after that."

"Your history shows impulsive and possibly reckless decision-making processes. How did that get by the screeners?"

She gently elbowed him in the side, setting off a flare of pain from his ribs. He tensed.

"Oh, Harry, sorry. I forgot."

"Yeah, sure."

She laughed.

"I guess all you old guys know that the department's been pushing big time for what they term 'mature' women cadets the last few years. To smooth off all the hard testosterone edges of the department."

She rocked her hips back against Bosch's genitals to underline the point.

"And speaking of testosterone," she said, "you never told me how it went with old bullet head himself today."

Bosch groaned but didn't answer.

"You know," she said, "Irving came to address our class one day on the moral responsibilities that come with carrying the badge. And everybody sitting there knew the guy probably makes more backroom deals up there on the sixth floor than there are days in the year. The guy's the classic fixer. You could practically cut the irony in the auditorium with a knife."

Her use of the word "irony" made Bosch flash on what Antoine Jesper had said about coupling the bones found on the hill with the bones on the skateboard. He felt his body tensing as thoughts of the case started encroaching on what had been an oasis of respite from the investigation.

She sensed his tightness.

"What is it?"

"Nothing."

"You got all tense all of a sudden."

"The case, I guess."

She was quiet a moment.

"I think it's kind of amazing," she then said. "Those bones being up there all of these years and then coming up out of the ground. Like a ghost or something."

"It's a city of bones. And all of them are waiting to come up."

He paused.

"I don't want to talk about Irving or the bones or the case or anything else right now."

"Then what do you want?"

He didn't answer. She turned to face him and started pushing him down off the pillows until he was flat on his back.

"How about a mature woman to smooth off all the hard edges again?"

It was impossible for Bosch not to smile.

23

BEFORE dawn Bosch was on the road. He left Julia Brasher sleeping in her bed and started on his way to his home, after first stopping at Abbot's Habit for a coffee to go. Venice was like a ghost town, with the tendrils of the morning fog moving across the streets. But as he got closer to Hollywood the lights of cars on the streets multiplied and Bosch was reminded that the city of bones was a twenty-four-hour city.

At home he showered and put on fresh clothes. He then climbed back into his car and went down the hill to Hollywood Division. It was 7:30 when he got there. Surprisingly, a number of detectives were already in place, chasing paperwork and cases. Edgar wasn't among them. Bosch put his briefcase down and walked to the watch office to get coffee and to see if any citizen had brought in doughnuts. Almost every day a John Q who still kept the faith brought in doughnuts for the division. A little way of saying there were still those out there who knew or at least understood the difficulties of the job. Every day in every division cops put on the badge and tried to do their best in a place where the populace didn't understand them, didn't particularly like them and in many instances outright despised them. Bosch always thought it was amazing how far a box of doughnuts could go in undoing that.

He poured a cup and dropped a dollar in the basket. He took a sugar doughnut out of a box on the counter that had already been decimated by the patrol guys. No wonder. They were from Bob's Donuts in the farmers' market. He noticed Mankiewicz sitting at his desk, his dark eyebrows forming a deep V as he studied what looked like a deployment chart.

"Hey, Mank, I think we pulled a grade A lead off the call-in sheets. Thought you'd want to know."

Mankiewicz answered without looking up.

"Good. Let me know when my guys can give it a rest. We're going to be short on the desk the next few days."

Bosch knew this meant he was juggling personnel. When there weren't enough uniforms to put in cars — due to vacations, court appearances or sick-outs — the watch sergeant always pulled people off the desk and put them on wheels.

"You got it."

Edgar still wasn't at the table when Bosch got back to the detective squad room. Bosch put his coffee and doughnut down next to one of the Selectrics and went to get a search warrant application out of a community file drawer. For the next fifteen minutes he typed out an addendum to the search warrant he had already delivered to the records custodian at Queen of Angels. It asked for all records from the care of Arthur Delacroix circa 1975 to 1985.

When he was finished he took it to the fax machine and sent it to the office of Judge John A. Houghton, who had signed all the hospital search warrants the day before. He added a note requesting that the judge review the addendum application as soon as possible because it might lead to the positive identification of the bones and therefore swing the investigation into focus.

Bosch returned to the table and from a drawer pulled out the stack of missing person reports he had gathered while fiche-ing in the archives. He started looking through them quickly, glancing only at the box reserved for the name of the missing individual. In ten minutes he was finished. There had been no report in the stack about Arthur Delacroix. He didn't know what this meant but he planned to ask the boy's sister about it.

It was now eight o'clock and Bosch was ready to leave to visit the sister. But still no Edgar. Bosch ate the remainder of his doughnut and decided to give his partner ten minutes to show before he would leave on his own. He had worked with Edgar for more than ten years and still was bothered by his partner's lack of punctuality. It was one thing to be late for dinner. It was another to be late for a case. He had always taken Edgar's tardiness as a lack of commitment to their mission as homicide investigators.

His direct line rang and Bosch answered it with an annoyed rasp, expecting it to be Edgar announcing he was running late. But it wasn't Edgar. It was Julia Brasher.

"So, you just leave a woman high and dry in bed, huh?"

Bosch smiled and his frustration with Edgar quickly drained away.

"I got a busy day here," he said. "I had to get going."

"I know but you could've said good-bye."

Bosch saw Edgar making his way through the squad room. He wanted to get going before Edgar started his coffee, doughnut and sports-page ritual.

"Well, I'm saying good-bye now, okay? I'm in the middle of something here and I gotta run."

"Harry . . ."

"What?"

"I thought you were going to hang up on me or something."

"I'm not, but I gotta go. Look, come by before you go up for roll call, okay? I'll probably be back by then."

"All right. I'll see you."

Bosch hung up and stood up just as Edgar got to the homicide table and dropped the folded sports page at his spot.

"You ready?"

"Yeah, I was just going to get —"

"Let's go. I don't want to keep the lady waiting. And she'll probably have coffee there."

On the way out Bosch checked the incoming tray on the fax machine. His search warrant addendum had been signed and returned by Judge Houghton.

"We're in business," Bosch said to Edgar, showing him the warrant as they walked to the car. "See? You come in early, you get stuff done."

"What's that supposed to mean? Is that a crack on me?"

"It means what it means, I guess."

"I just want some coffee."

24

SHEILA Delacroix lived in a part of the city called the Miracle Mile. It was a neighborhood south of Wilshire that wasn't quite up to the standards of nearby Hancock Park but was lined with nicely kept homes and duplexes with modest stylistic adjustments to promote individuality.

Delacroix's home was the second floor of a duplex with pseudo–Beaux Arts styling. She invited the detectives into her home in a friendly manner, but when the first question Edgar asked was about coffee, she said it was against her religion. She offered tea, and Edgar reluctantly accepted. Bosch passed. He wondered which religion outlawed coffee.

They took seats in the living room while the woman made Edgar his tea in the kitchen. She called out to them, saying she only had an hour and then had to leave for work.

"What is it you do?" Bosch asked as she came out with a mug of hot tea, the tag from the tea bag looped over the side. She put it down on a coaster on a side table next to Edgar. She was a tall woman. She was slightly overweight with blonde hair cut short. Bosch thought she wore too much makeup.

"I'm a casting agent," she said as she took a seat on the couch. "Mostly independent films, some episodic television. I'm actually casting a cop show this week."

Bosch watched Edgar sip some tea and make a face. He then held the mug so he could read the tea bag tag.

"It's a blend," Delacroix said. "Strawberry and Darjeeling. Do you like it?"

Edgar put the mug down on its coaster.

"It's fine."

"Ms. Delacroix? If you're in the entertainment business, did you by any chance know Nicholas Trent?"

"Please, just call me Sheila. Now, that name, Nicholas Trent. It sounds familiar but I can't quite place it. Is he an actor or is he in casting?"

"Neither. He's the man who lived up on Wonderland. He was a set designer — I mean, decorator."

"Oh, the one on TV, the man who killed himself. Oh, no wonder it was familiar."

"So you didn't know him from the business, then?"

"No, not at all."

"Okay, well I shouldn't have asked that. We're out of order here. Let's just start with your brother. Tell us about Arthur. Do you have a picture we can look at?"

"Yes," she said, as she stood up and walked behind his chair. "Here he is."

She went to a waist-high cabinet Bosch hadn't noticed behind him. There were framed photos on it displayed in much the same way he had seen the photos on Julia Brasher's mantel. Delacroix chose one and turned around and handed it to Bosch.

The frame contained a photo of a boy and a girl sitting on a set of stairs Bosch recognized as the stairs they had climbed before knocking on her door. The boy was much smaller than the girl. Both were smiling at the camera and had the smiles of children who have been told to smile — a lot of teeth but not a legitimately turned-up mouth.

Bosch handed the photo to Edgar and looked at Delacroix, who had returned to the couch.

"Those stairs . . . was that taken here?"

"Yes, this is the home we grew up in."

"When he disappeared, it was from here?"

"Yes."

"Are any of his belongings still here in the house?"

Delacroix smiled sadly and shook her head.

"No, it's all gone. I gave his things to the charity rummage sale at church. That was a long time ago."

"What church is that?"

"The Wilshire Church of Nature."

Bosch just nodded.

"They're the ones who don't let you have coffee?" Edgar asked.

"Nothing with caffeine."

Edgar put the framed photo down next to his tea.

"Do you have any other photos of him?" he asked.

"Of course, I have a box of old photos."

"Can we look at those? You know, while we talk."

Delacroix's eyebrows came together in confusion.

"Sheila," Bosch said. "We found some clothing with the remains. We would like to look at the photos to see if any of it matches. It will help the investigation."

She nodded.

"I see. Well, then I'll be right back. I just need to go to the closet in the hallway."

"Do you need help?"

"No, I can manage."

After she was gone Edgar leaned over to Bosch and whispered, "This Church of Nature tea tastes like piss water."

Bosch whispered back, "How would you know what piss water tastes like?"

The skin around Edgar's eyes drew tight with embarrassment as he realized he had walked into that one. Before he could muster a response Sheila Delacroix came back into the room carrying an old shoe box. She put it down on the coffee table and removed the lid. The box was filled with loose photographs.

"These aren't in any order or anything. But he should be in a lot of them."

Bosch nodded to Edgar, who reached into the box for the first stack of photos.

"While my partner looks through these, why don't you tell me about your brother and when he disappeared?"

Sheila nodded and composed her thoughts before beginning.

"May fourth, nineteen eighty. He didn't come home from school. That's it. That's all. We thought he had run away. You said you found clothes with the remains. Well, my father looked in his drawers and said that Arthur had taken clothes. That was what made us think he had run away."

Bosch wrote a few notes down in a notebook he had pulled from his coat pocket.

"You mentioned that he had been injured a few months before on a skateboard."

"Yes, he hit his head and they had to operate."

"When he disappeared, did he take his skateboard?"

She thought about this for a long moment.

"It was so long ago . . . all I know is that he loved that board. So I think he probably took it. But I just remember the clothes. My father found some of his clothes missing."

"Did you report him missing?"

"I was sixteen years old at the time, so I didn't do anything. My father talked to the police though. I'm sure of it."

"I couldn't find any record of Arthur being reported missing. Are you sure he reported him missing?"

"I drove with him to the police station."

"Was it Wilshire Division?"

"I would assume but I don't really remember."

"Sheila, where is your father? Is he still alive?"

"He's alive. He lives in the Valley. But he's not well these days."

"Where in the Valley?"

"Van Nuys. In the Manchester Trailer Park."

There was silence while Bosch wrote the information down. He had been to the Manchester Trailer Park before on investigations. It wasn't a pleasant place to live.

"He drinks . . ."

Bosch looked at her.

"Ever since Arthur . . ."

Bosch nodded that he understood. Edgar leaned forward and handed him a photograph. It was a yellowed 3 × 5. It showed a young boy, his arms raised in an effort to maintain balance, gliding on the sidewalk on a skateboard. The angle of the photograph showed little of the skateboard other than its profile. Bosch could not tell if it carried a bone design on it or not.

"Can't see much there," he said as he started to hand the photo back.

"No, the clothes — the shirt."

Bosch looked at the photo again. Edgar was right. The boy in the photo wore a gray T-shirt with SOLID SURF printed across the chest.

Bosch showed the photo to Sheila.

"This is your brother, right?"

She leaned forward to look at the photo.

"Yes, definitely."

"That shirt he is wearing, do you remember if it is one of the pieces of clothing your father found missing?"

Delacroix shook her head.

"I can't remember. It's been — I just remember that he liked that shirt a lot."

Bosch nodded and gave the photo back to Edgar. It wasn't the kind of solid confirmation they could get from

X-rays and bone comparison but it was one more notch. Bosch was feeling more and more sure that they were about to identify the bones. He watched Edgar put the photo in a short stack of pictures he intended to borrow from Sheila's collection.

Bosch checked his watch and looked back at Sheila.

"What about your mother?"

Sheila immediately shook her head.

"Nope, she was long gone by the time all of this happened."

"You mean she died?"

"I mean she took a bus the minute the going got tough. You see, Arthur was a difficult child. Right from the beginning. He needed a lot of attention and it fell to my mother. After a while she couldn't take it any longer. One night she went out to get some medicine at the drugstore and she never came back. We found little notes from her under our pillows."

Bosch dropped his eyes to his notebook. It was hard to hear this story and keep looking at Sheila Delacroix.

"How old were you? How old was your brother?"

"I was six, so that would make Artie two."

Bosch nodded.

"Did you keep the note from her?"

"No. There was no need. I didn't need a reminder of how she supposedly loved us but not enough to stay with us."

"What about Arthur? Did he keep his?"

"Well, he was only two, so my father kept it for him. He gave it to him when he was older. He may have kept it, I don't know. Because he never really knew her, he was always very interested in what she was like. He asked me a lot of questions about her. There were no photos of her. My father had gotten rid of them all so he wouldn't have any reminders."

"Do you know what happened to her? Or if she's still alive?"

"I haven't the faintest idea. And to tell you the truth, I don't care if she is alive or not."

"What is her name?"

"Christine Dorsett Delacroix. Dorsett was her maiden name."

"Do you know her birth date or Social Security number?"

Sheila shook her head.

"Do you have your own birth certificate handy here?"

"It's somewhere in my records. I could go look for it."

She started to get up.

"No, wait, we can look for that at the end. I'd like to keep talking here."

"Okay."

"Um, after your mother was gone, did your father remarry?"

"No, he never did. He lives alone now."

"Did he ever have a girlfriend, someone who might have stayed in the house?"

She looked at Bosch with eyes that seemed almost lifeless.

"No," she said. "Never."

Bosch decided to move on to an area of discussion that would be less difficult for her.

"What school did your brother go to?"

"At the end he was going to The Brethren."

Bosch didn't say anything. He wrote the name of the school down on his pad and then a large letter *B* beneath it. He circled the letter, thinking about the backpack. Sheila continued unbidden.

"It was a private school for troubled boys. My dad paid to send him there. It's off of Crescent Heights near Pico. It's still there."

"Why did he go there? I mean, why was he considered troubled?"

"Because he got kicked out of his other schools for fighting mostly."

"Fighting?" Edgar said.

"That's right."

Edgar picked the top photograph off of his keeper file and studied it for a moment.

"This boy looks like he was as light as smoke. Was he the one starting these fights?"

"Most times. He had trouble getting along. All he wanted to do was be on his skateboard. I think that by today's standards he would be diagnosed as having attention deficit disorder or something similar. He just wanted to be by himself all the time."

"Did he get hurt in these fights?" Bosch asked.

"Sometimes. Black and blue mostly."

"Broken bones?"

"Not that I remember. Just schoolyard fights."

Bosch felt agitated. The information they were getting could point them in many different directions. He had hoped a clear-cut path might emerge from the interview.

"You said your father searched the drawers in your brother's room and found clothes missing."

"That's right. Not a lot. Just a few things."

"Any idea what was missing specifically?"

She shook her head.

"I can't remember."

"What did he take the clothes in? Like a suitcase or something?"

"I think he took his schoolbag. Took out the books and put in some clothes."

"Do you remember what that looked like?"

"No. Just a backpack. Everybody had to use the same

thing at The Brethren. I still see kids walking on Pico with them, the backpacks with the *B* on the back."

Bosch glanced at Edgar and then back at Delacroix.

"Let's go back to the skateboard. Are you sure he took it with him?"

She paused to think about this, then slowly nodded.

"Yes, I'm pretty sure he took it with him."

Bosch decided to cut off the interview and concentrate on completing the identification. Once they confirmed the bones came from Arthur Delacroix, then they could come back to his sister.

He thought about Golliher's take on the injuries to the bones. Chronic abuse. Could it all have been injuries from schoolyard fights and skateboarding? He knew he needed to approach the issue of child abuse but did not feel the time was appropriate. He also didn't want to tip his hand to the daughter so that she could turn around and possibly tell the father. What Bosch wanted was to back out and come back in later when he felt he had a tighter grasp on the case and a solid investigative plan to go with.

"Okay, we're going to wrap things up here pretty quickly, Sheila. Just a few more questions. Did Arthur have some friends? Maybe a best friend, someone he might confide in?"

She shook her head.

"Not really. He mostly was by himself."

Bosch nodded and was about to close his notebook when she continued.

"There was one boy he'd go boarding with. His name was Johnny Stokes. He was from somewhere down near Pico. He was bigger and a little bit older than Arthur but they were in the same class at The Brethren. My father was pretty sure he smoked pot. So we didn't like Arthur being friends with him."

"By 'we,' you mean your dad and you?"

"Yes, my father. He was upset about it."

"Did either of you talk to Johnny Stokes after Arthur went missing?"

"Yes, that night when he didn't come home my father called Johnny Stokes, but he said he hadn't seen Artie. The next day when Dad went to the school to ask about him, he told me he talked to Johnny again about Artie."

"And what did he say?"

"That he hadn't seen him."

Bosch wrote down the friend's name in his notebook and underlined it.

"Any other friends you can think of?"

"No, not really."

"What's your father's name?"

"Samuel. Are you going to talk to him?"

"Most likely."

Her eyes dropped to the hands clasped in her lap.

"Is that a problem if we talk to him?"

"Not really. He's just not well. If those bones turn out to be Arthur . . . I was thinking it would be better if he didn't ever know."

"We'll keep that in mind when we talk to him. But we won't do it until we have a positive identification."

"But if you talk to him, then he'll know."

"It may be unavoidable, Sheila."

Edgar handed Bosch another photo. It showed Arthur standing next to a tall blond man who looked faintly familiar to Bosch. He showed the photo to Sheila.

"Is this your father?"

"Yes, it's him."

"He looks familiar. Was he ever —"

"He's an actor. Was, actually. He was on some television shows in the sixties and a few things after that, some movie parts."

"Not enough to make a living?"

"No, he always had to work other jobs. So we could live."

Bosch nodded and handed the photo back to Edgar but Sheila reached across the coffee table and intercepted it.

"I don't want that one to leave, please. I don't have many photos of my father."

"Fine," Bosch said. "Could we go look for the birth certificate now?"

"I'll go look. You can stay here."

She got up and left the room again, and Edgar took the opportunity to show Bosch some of the other photos he had taken to keep during the investigation.

"It's him, Harry," he whispered. "I got no doubt."

He showed him a photo of Arthur Delacroix that had apparently been taken for school. His hair was combed neatly and he wore a blue blazer and tie. Bosch studied the boy's eyes. They reminded him of the photo of the boy from Kosovo he had found in Nicholas Trent's house. The boy with the thousand-yard stare.

"I found it."

Sheila Delacroix came into the room carrying an envelope and unfolding a yellowed document. Bosch looked at it for a moment and then copied down the names, birth dates and Social Security numbers of her parents.

"Thanks," he said. "You and Arthur had the same parents, right?"

"Of course."

"Okay, Sheila, thank you. We're going to go. We'll call you as soon as we know something for sure."

He stood up and so did Edgar.

"All right if we borrow these photos?" Edgar asked. "I will personally see that you get them back."

"Okay, if you need them."

They headed to the door and she opened it. While still on the threshold Bosch asked her one last question.

"Sheila, have you always lived here?"

She nodded.

"All my life. I've stayed here in case he comes back, you know? In case he doesn't know where to start and comes here."

She smiled but not in any way that imparted humor. Bosch nodded and stepped outside behind Edgar.

25

Bosch walked up to the museum ticket window and told the woman sitting behind it his name and that he had an appointment with Dr. William Golliher in the anthropology lab. She picked up a phone and made a call. A few minutes later she rapped on the glass with her wedding band until it drew the attention of a nearby security guard. He came over and the woman instructed him to escort Bosch to the lab. He did not have to pay the admission.

The guard said nothing as they walked through the dimly lit museum, past the mammoth display and the wall of wolf skulls. Bosch had never been inside the museum, though he had gone to the La Brea Tar Pits often on field trips when he was a child. The museum was built after that, to house and display all of the finds that bubbled up out of the earth in the tar pits.

When Bosch had called Golliher's cell phone after receiving the medical records on Arthur Delacroix, the anthropologist said he was already working on another case and couldn't get downtown to the medical examiner's office until the next day. Bosch had said he couldn't wait. Golliher said he did have copies of the X-rays and photographs from the Wonderland case with him. If Bosch could come to him, he could make the comparisons and give an unofficial response.

Bosch took the compromise and headed to the tar pits while Edgar remained at Hollywood Division working the computer to see if he could locate Arthur and Sheila Delacroix's mother as well as run down Arthur's friend Johnny Stokes.

Now Bosch was curious as to what the new case was that Golliher was working. The tar pits were an ancient black hole where animals had gone to their death for centuries. In a grim chain reaction, animals caught in the miasma became prey for other animals, who in turn were mired and slowly pulled down. In some form of natural equilibrium the bones now came back up out of the blackness and were collected for study by modern man. All of this took place right next to one of the busiest streets in Los Angeles, a constant reminder of the crushing passage of time.

Bosch was led through two doors and into the crowded lab where the bones were identified, classified, dated and cleaned. There appeared to be boxes of bones everywhere on every flat surface. A half dozen people in white lab coats worked at stations, cleaning and examining the bones.

Golliher was the only one not in a lab coat. He had on another Hawaiian shirt, this one with parrots on it, and was working at a table in the far corner. As Bosch approached, he saw there were two wooden bone boxes on the worktable in front of him. In one of the boxes was a skull.

"Detective Bosch, how are you?"

"Doing okay. What's this?"

"This, as I'm sure you can tell, is a human skull. It and some other human bones were collected two days ago from asphalt that was actually excavated thirty years ago to make room for this museum. They've asked me to take a look before they make the announcement."

"I don't understand. Is it . . . old or . . . from thirty years ago?"

"Oh, it's quite old. It was carbon-dated to nine thousand years ago, actually."

Bosch nodded. The skull and the bones in the other box looked like mahogany.

"Take a look," Golliher said and he lifted the skull out of the box.

He turned it so that the rear of the skull faced Bosch. He moved his finger in a circle around a star fracture near the top of the skull.

"Look familiar?"

"Blunt-force fracture?"

"Exactly. Much like your case. Just goes to show you."

He gently replaced the skull in the wooden box.

"Show me what?"

"Things don't change that much. This woman — at least we think it was a woman — was murdered nine thousand years ago, her body probably thrown into the tar pit as a means of covering the crime. Human nature, it doesn't change."

Bosch stared at the skull.

"She's not the first."

Bosch looked up at Golliher.

"In nineteen fourteen the bones — a more complete skeleton, actually — of another woman were found in the tar. She had the same star fracture in the same spot on her skull. Her bones were carbon-dated as nine thousand years old. Same time frame as her."

He nodded to the skull in the box.

"So, what are you saying, Doc, that there was a serial killer here nine thousand years ago?"

"It's impossible to know that, Detective Bosch. All we have are the bones."

Bosch looked down at the skull again. He thought about what Julia Brasher had said about his job, about his taking evil out of the world. What she didn't know was a truth he had known for too long. That true evil could never be taken out of the world. At best he was wading into the dark waters of the abyss with two leaking buckets in his hands.

"But you have other things on your mind, don't you?" Golliher said, interrupting Bosch's thoughts. "Do you have the hospital records?"

Bosch brought his briefcase up onto the worktable and opened it. He handed Golliher a file. Then, from his pocket he pulled the stack of photos he and Edgar had borrowed from Sheila Delacroix.

"I don't know if these help," he said. "But this is the kid."

Golliher picked up the photos. He went through them quickly, stopping at the posed close-up of Arthur Delacroix in a jacket and tie. He went over to a chair where a backpack was slung over the armrest. He pulled out his own file and came back to the worktable. He opened the file and took out an 8 × 10 photo of the skull from Wonderland Avenue. For a long moment he held the photos of Arthur Delacroix and the skull side by side and studied them.

Finally, he said, "The malar and superciliary ridge formation look similar."

"I'm not an anthropologist, Doc."

Golliher put the photos down on the table. He then explained by running his finger across the left eyebrow of the boy and then down around the outside of his eye.

"The brow ridge and the exterior orbit," he said. "It's wider than usual on the recovered specimen. Looking at this photo of the boy, we see his facial structure is in line with what we see here."

Bosch nodded.

"Let's look at the X-rays," Golliher said. "There's a box back here."

Golliher gathered the files and led Bosch to another worktable, where there was a light box built into the surface. He opened the hospital file, picked up the X-rays and began reading the patient history report.

Bosch had already read the document. The hospital reported that the boy was brought into the emergency room at 5:40 P.M. on February 11, 1980, by his father, who said he was found in a dazed and unresponsive state following a fall from a skateboard in which he struck his head. Neurosurgery was performed in order to relieve pressure inside the skull caused by swelling of the brain. The boy remained in the hospital under observation for ten days and was then released to his father. Two weeks later he was readmitted for follow-up surgery to remove the clips that had been used to hold his skull together following the neurosurgery.

There was no report anywhere in the file of the boy complaining about being mistreated by his father or anyone else. While recovering from the initial surgery he was routinely interviewed by an on-site social worker. Her report was less than half a page. It reported that the boy said he had hurt himself while skateboarding. There was no follow-up questioning or referral to juvenile authorities or the police.

Golliher shook his head while he finished his scan of the document.

"What is it?" Bosch asked.

"It's nothing. And that's the problem. No investigation. They took the boy at his word. His father was probably sitting right there in the room with him when he was interviewed. You know how hard it would have been for him to tell the truth? So they just patched him up and sent him right back to the person who was hurting him."

"Hey, Doc, you're getting a little bit ahead of us. Let's get the ID, if it's there, and then we'll figure out who was hurting the kid."

"Fine. It's your case. It's just that I've seen this a hundred times."

Golliher dropped the reports and picked up the X-rays. Bosch watched him with a bemused smile on his face. It seemed that Golliher was annoyed because Bosch had not jumped to the same conclusions he had with the same speed he had.

Golliher put two X-rays down on the light box. He then went to his own file and brought out X-rays he had taken of the Wonderland skull. He flipped the box's light on and three X-rays glowed before them. Golliher pointed to the X-ray he had taken from his own file.

"This is a radiological X-ray I took to look inside the bone of the skull. But we can use it here for comparison purposes. Tomorrow when I get back to the medical examiner's office I will use the skull itself."

Golliher leaned over the light box and reached for a small glass eyepiece that was stored on a nearby shelf. He held one end to his eye and pressed the other against one of the X-rays. After a few moments he moved to one of the hospital X-rays and pressed the eyepiece to the same location on the skull. He went back and forth numerous times, making comparison after comparison.

When he was finished, Golliher straightened up, leaned back against the next worktable and folded his arms.

"Queen of Angels was a government-subsidized hospital. Money was always tight. They should have taken more than two pictures of this kid's head. If they had, they might have seen some of his other injuries."

"Okay. But they didn't."

"Yeah, they didn't. But based on what they did do and

what we've got here, I was able to make several comparison points on the roundel, the fracture pattern and along the squamous suture. There is no doubt in my mind."

He gestured toward the X-rays still glowing on the light box.

"Meet Arthur Delacroix."

Bosch nodded.

"Okay."

Golliher stepped over to the light box and started collecting the X-rays.

"How sure are you?"

"Like I said, there's no doubt. I'll look at the skull tomorrow when I'm downtown, but I can tell you now, it's him. It's a match."

"So, if we get somebody and go into court with it, there aren't going to be any surprises, right?"

Golliher looked at Bosch.

"No surprises. These findings can't be challenged. As you know, the challenge lies in the interpretation of the injuries. I look at this boy and see something horribly, horribly wrong. And I will testify to that. Gladly. But then you have these official records."

He gestured dismissively to the open file of hospital records.

"They say skateboard. That's where the fight will be."

Bosch nodded. Golliher put the two X-rays back into the file and closed it. Bosch put it back in his briefcase.

"Well, Doctor, thanks for taking the time to see me here. I think —"

"Detective Bosch?"

"Yes?"

"The other day you seemed very uncomfortable when I mentioned the necessity of faith in what we do. Basically, you changed the subject."

"Not really a subject I feel comfortable talking about."

"I would think that in your line of work it would be paramount to have a healthy spirituality."

"I don't know. My partner likes blaming aliens from outer space for everything that's wrong. I guess that's healthy, too."

"You're avoiding the question."

Bosch grew annoyed and the feeling quickly slipped toward anger.

"What is the question, Doc? Why do you care so much about me and what I believe or don't believe?"

"Because it is important to me. I study bones. The framework of life. And I have come to believe that there is something more than blood and tissue and bone. There is something else that holds us together. I have something inside, that you'll never see on any X-ray, that holds me together and keeps me going. And so, when I meet someone who carries a void in the place where I carry my faith, I get scared for him."

Bosch looked at him for a long moment.

"You're wrong about me. I have faith and I have a mission. Call it blue religion, call it whatever you like. It's the belief that this won't just go by. That those bones came out of the ground for a reason. That they came out of the ground for me to find, and for me to do something about. And that's what holds me together and keeps me going. And it won't show up on any X-ray either. Okay?"

He stared at Golliher, waiting for a reply. But the anthropologist said nothing.

"I gotta go, Doctor," Bosch finally said. "Thanks for your help. You've made things very clear for me."

He left him there, surrounded by the dark bones the city had been built on.

26

EDGAR was not at his spot at the homicide table when Bosch got back to the squad room.

"Harry?"

Bosch looked up and saw Lt. Billets standing in the doorway to her office. Through the glass window Bosch could see Edgar in there sitting in front of her desk. Bosch put his briefcase down and headed over.

"What's up?" he said as he entered the office.

"No, that's my question," Billets said as she closed the door. "Do we have an ID?"

She went around behind her desk and sat down as Bosch took the seat next to Edgar.

"Yes, we have an ID. Arthur Delacroix, disappeared May fourth, nineteen eighty."

"The ME is sure of this?"

"Their bone guy says there is no doubt."

"How close are we on time of death?"

"Pretty close. The bone guy said before we knew anything that the fatal impact to the skull came about three months after the kid had the earlier skull fracture and surgery. We got the records on that surgery today. February eleven, nineteen eighty at Queen of Angels. You add three months and we're almost right on the button — Arthur

Delacroix disappeared May fourth, according to his sister. The point is, Arthur Delacroix was dead four years before Nicholas Trent moved into that neighborhood. I think that puts him in the clear."

Billets reluctantly nodded.

"I've had Irving's office and Media Relations on my ass all day about this," she said. "They're not going to like it when I call them back with this."

"That's too bad," Bosch said. "That's the way the case shakes out."

"Okay, so Trent wasn't in the neighborhood in nineteen eighty. Do we have anything yet on where he was?"

Bosch blew out his breath and shook his head.

"You're not going to let this go, are you? We need to concentrate on the kid."

"I'm not letting go because they're not. Irving called me himself this morning. He was very clear without having to say the words. If it turns out an innocent man killed himself because a cop leaked information to the media that held him up to public ridicule, then it's one more black eye for the department. Haven't we had enough humiliation in the last ten years?"

Bosch smiled without a hint of humor.

"You sound just like him, Lieutenant. That's really good."

It was the wrong thing to say. He could see that it hurt her.

"Yeah, well, maybe I sound like him because I agree with him, for once. This department has had nothing but scandal after scandal. Like most of the decent cops around here, I for one am sick of it."

"Good. So am I. But the solution is not to bend things to fit our needs. This is a homicide case."

"I know that, Harry. I'm not saying bend anything. I'm saying we have to be sure."

"We're sure. I'm sure."

They were silent for a long moment, everyone's eyes avoiding the others'.

"What about Kiz?" Edgar finally asked.

Bosch sneered.

"Irving won't do a thing to Kiz," he said. "He knows it will make him look even worse if he touches her. Besides, she's probably the best cop they got down there on the third floor."

"You're always so sure, Harry," Billets said. "It must be nice."

"Well, I'm sure about this."

He stood up.

"And I'd like to get back to it. We've got stuff happening."

"I know all about it. Jerry was just telling me. But sit down and let's get back to this for one minute, okay?"

Bosch sat back down.

"I can't just talk to Irving the way I let you talk to me," Billets said. "This is what I am going to do. I am going to update him on the ID and everything else. I am going to say you are pursuing the case as is. I will then invite him to assign IAD to the background investigation of Trent. In other words, if he remains unconvinced by the circumstances of the ID, then he can have IAD or whoever he can find run the background on Trent to see where he was in nineteen eighty."

Bosch just looked at her, giving no indication of approval or disapproval of her plan.

"Can we go now?"

"Yes, you can go."

When they got back to the homicide table and sat down Edgar asked Bosch why he hadn't mentioned the theory that maybe Trent moved into the neighborhood because he knew the bones were up on the hillside.

"Because your 'sick fuck' theory is too farfetched to go beyond this table for the time being. If that gets to Irving, next thing you know it's in a press release and is the official line. Now, did you get anything on the box or not?"

"Yeah, I got stuff."

"What?"

"First of all, I confirmed Samuel Delacroix's address at the Manchester Trailer Park. So he's there when we want to go see him. In the last ten years he's had two DUIs. He drives on a restricted license at the moment. I also ran his Social and came up with a hit — he works for the city."

Bosch's face showed his surprise.

"Doing what?"

"He works part-time at a driving range at the municipal golf course right next to the trailer park. I made a call to Parks and Recs — discreetly. Delacroix drives the cart that collects all the balls. You know, out on the range. The guy everybody tries to hit when he's out there. I guess he comes over from the trailer park and does it a couple times a day."

"Okay."

"Next, Christine Dorsett Delacroix, the name of the mother on Sheila's birth certificate. I ran her Social and got her now listed as a Christine Dorsett Waters. Address is in Palm Springs. Must've gone there to re-invent herself. New name, new life, whatever."

Bosch nodded.

"You pull the divorce?"

"Got it. She filed on Samuel Delacroix in 'seventy-three. The boy would've been about five at the time. Cited mental and physical abuse. Details of what that abuse consisted of were not included. It never went to trial, so the details never came out."

"He didn't contest it?"

"It looks like a deal was made. He got custody of the two

kids and didn't contest. Nice and clean. The file's about twelve pages thick. I've seen some that are twelve inches. My own, for example."

"If Arthur was five . . . some of those injuries predate that, according to the anthropologist."

Edgar shook his head.

"The extract says the marriage had ended three years prior and they were living separately. So it looks like she split when the boy was about two — like Sheila said. Harry, you usually don't refer to the vic by name."

"Yeah, so?"

"Just pointing it out."

"Thank you. Anything else in the file?"

"That's about it. I got copies if you want it."

"Okay, what about the skateboard friend?"

"Got him, too. Still alive, still local. But there's a problem. I ran all the usual data banks and came up with three John Stokes in L.A. that fall into the right age range. Two are in the Valley, both clean. The third's a player. Multiple arrests for petty theft, auto theft, burglary and possession going back to a full juvy jacket. Five years ago he finally ran out of second chances and got sent to Corcoran to iron out a nickel. Did two and a half to parole."

"You talk to his agent? Is Stokes still on the line?"

"Talked to his agent, yes. No, Stokes isn't on the hook. He cleared parole two months ago. The agent doesn't know where he is."

"Damn."

"Yeah, but I got him to pull a look at the client bio. It has Stokes growing up mostly in Mid-Wilshire. In and out of foster homes. In and out of trouble. He's gotta be our guy."

"The agent think he's still in L.A.?"

"Yeah, he thinks so. We just gotta find him. I already had patrol go by his last known — he moved out of there as soon as he cleared parole."

"So he's in the wind. Beautiful."

Edgar nodded.

"We have to put him on the box," Bosch said. "Start with —"

"Did it," Edgar said. "I also typed up a roll-call notice and gave it to Mankiewicz a while ago. He promised to get it read at all calls. I'm having a batch of visor photos made, too."

"Good."

Bosch was impressed. Getting photos of Stokes to clip to the sun visors of every patrol car was the sort of extra step Edgar usually didn't bother to make.

"We'll get him, Harry. I'm not sure what good he'll do us, but we'll get him."

"He could be a key witness. If Arthur — I mean, the vic — ever told him his father was beating him, then we've got something."

Bosch looked at his watch. It was almost two. He wanted to keep things moving, keep the investigation focused and urgent. For him the most difficult time was waiting. Whether it was for lab results or other cops to make moves, it was always when he became most agitated.

"What do you have going tonight?" he asked Edgar.

"Tonight? Nothing much."

"You got your kid tonight?"

"No, Thursdays. Why?"

"I'm thinking about going out to the Springs."

"Now?"

"Yeah, talk to the ex-wife."

He saw Edgar check his watch. He knew that even if they left that moment, they still wouldn't get back until late.

"It's all right. I can go by myself. Just give me the address."

"Nah, I'm going with you."

"You sure? You don't have to. I just don't like waitin' around for something to happen, you know?"

"Yeah, Harry, I know."

Edgar stood up and took his jacket off the back of his chair.

"Then I'll go tell Bullets," Bosch said.

27

Hey were more than halfway across the desert to Palm Springs before either one of them spoke.

"Harry," Edgar said, "you're not talking."

"I know," Bosch said.

The one thing they had always had as partners was the ability to share long silences. Whenever Edgar felt the need to break the silence, Bosch knew there was something on his mind he wanted to talk about.

"What is it, J. Edgar?"

"Nothing."

"The case?"

"No, man, nothing. I'm cool."

"All right, then."

They were passing a windmill farm. The air was dead. None of the blades were turning.

"Did your parents stay together?" Bosch asked.

"Yeah, all the way," Edgar said, then he laughed. "I think they wished sometimes they didn't but, yeah, they stuck it out. That's how it goes, I guess. The strong survive."

Bosch nodded. They were both divorced but rarely talked about their failed marriages.

"Harry, I heard about you and the boot. It's getting around."

Bosch nodded. This is what Edgar had wanted to bring up. Rookies in the department were often called "boots." The origin of the term was obscure. One school of thought was that it referred to boot camp, another that it was a sarcastic reference to rookies being the new boots of the fascist empire.

"All I'm saying, man, is be careful with that. You got rank on her, okay?"

"Yeah, I know. I'll figure something out."

"From what I hear and have seen, she's worth the risk. But you still gotta be careful."

Bosch didn't say anything. After a few minutes they passed a road sign that said Palm Springs was coming up in nine miles. It was nearing dusk. Bosch was hoping to knock on the door where Christine Waters lived before it got dark.

"Harry, you going to take the lead on this, when we get there?"

"Yeah, I'll take it. You can be the indignant one."

"That will be easy."

Once they crossed the city boundary into Palm Springs they picked up a map at a gas station and made their way through the town until they found Frank Sinatra Boulevard and took it up toward the mountains. Bosch pulled the car up to the gate house of a place called Mountaingate Estates. Their map showed the street Christine Waters lived on was within Mountaingate.

A uniformed rent-a-cop stepped out of the gate house, eying the slickback they were in and smiling.

"You guys are a little ways off the beat," he said.

Bosch nodded and tried to give a pleasant smile. But it only made him look like he had something sour in his mouth.

"Something like that," he said.

"What's up?"

"We're going to talk to Christine Waters, three-twelve Deep Waters Drive."

"Mrs. Waters know you're coming?"

"Not unless she's a psychic or you tell her."

"That's my job. Hold on a second."

He returned to the gate house and Bosch saw him pick up a phone.

"Looks like Christine Delacroix seriously traded up," Edgar said.

He was looking through the windshield at some of the homes that were visible from their position. They were all huge with manicured lawns big enough to play touch football on.

The guard came out, put both hands on the window sill of the car and leaned down to look in at Bosch.

"She wants to know what it's about."

"Tell her we'll discuss it with her at her house. Privately. Tell her we have a court order."

The guard shrugged his shoulders in a have-it-your-way gesture and went back inside. Bosch watched him speaking on the phone for a few more moments. After he hung up, the gate started to open slowly. The guard stood in the open doorway and waved them in. But not without the last word.

"You know that tough-guy stuff probably works real well for you in L.A. Out here in the desert it's just —"

Bosch didn't hear the rest. He drove through the gate while putting the window up.

They found Deep Waters Drive at the far extreme of the development. The homes here looked to be a couple million dollars more opulent than those built near the entrance to Mountaingate.

"Who would name a street in the desert Deep Waters Drive?" Edgar mused.

"Maybe somebody named Waters."

It dawned on Edgar then.

"Damn. You think? Then she really has traded up."

The address Edgar came up with for Christine Waters corresponded with a mansion of contemporary Spanish design that sat at the end of a cul-de-sac at the terminus of Mountaingate Estates. It was most definitely the development's premier lot. The house was positioned on a promontory that afforded it a view of all the other homes in the development as well as a sweeping view of the golf course that surrounded it.

The property had its own gated drive but the gate was open. Bosch wondered if it always stood open or had been opened for them.

"This is going to be interesting," Edgar said as they pulled into a parking circle made of interlocking paving stones.

"Just remember," Bosch said, "people can change their addresses but they can't change who they are."

"Right. Homicide one-oh-one."

They got out and walked under the portico that led to the double-wide front door. It was opened before they got to it by a woman in a black-and-white maid's uniform. In a thick Spanish accent the woman told them that Mrs. Waters was waiting in the living room.

The living room was the size and had the feel of a small cathedral, with a twenty-five-foot ceiling with exposed roof beams. High on the wall facing the east were three large stained-glass windows, a triptych depicting a sunrise, a garden and a moonrise. The opposite wall had six side-by-side sliding doors with a view of a golf course putting green. The room had two distinct groupings of furniture, as if to accommodate two separate gatherings at the same time.

Sitting in the middle of a cream-colored couch in the first grouping was a woman with blonde hair and a tight face. Her pale blue eyes followed the men as they entered and took in the size of the room.

"Mrs. Waters?" Bosch said. "I am Detective Bosch and this is Detective Edgar. We're from the Los Angeles Police Department."

He held out his hand and she took it but didn't shake it. She just held it for a moment and then moved on to Edgar's outstretched hand. Bosch knew from the birth certificate that she was fifty-six years old. But she looked close to a decade younger, her smooth tan face a testament to the wonders of modern medical science.

"Please have a seat," she said. "I can't tell you how embarrassed I am to have that car sitting in front of my house. I guess discretion is not the better part of valor when it comes to the LAPD."

Bosch smiled.

"Well, Mrs. Waters, we're kind of embarrassed about it, too, but that's what the bosses tell us to drive. So that's what we drive."

"What is this about? The guard at the gate said you have a court order. May I see it?"

Bosch sat down on a couch directly opposite her and across a black coffee table with gold designs inlaid on it.

"Uh, he must have misunderstood me," he said. "I told him we could get a court order, if you refused to see us."

"I'm sure he did," she replied, the tone of her voice letting them know she didn't believe Bosch at all. "What do you want to see me about?"

"We need to ask you about your husband."

"My husband has been dead for five years. Besides that, he rarely went to Los Angeles. What could he possibly —"

"Your first husband, Mrs. Waters. Samuel Delacroix. We need to talk to you about your children as well."

Bosch saw a wariness immediately enter her eyes.

"I . . . I haven't seen or spoken to them in years. Almost thirty years."

"You mean since you went out for medicine for the boy and forgot to come back home?" Edgar asked.

The woman looked at him as though he had slapped her. Bosch had hoped Edgar was going to use a little more finesse when he acted indignant with her.

"Who told you that?"

"Mrs. Waters," Bosch said. "I want to ask questions first and then we can get to yours."

"I don't understand this. How did you find me? What are you doing? Why are you here?"

Her voice rose with emotion from question to question. A life she had put aside thirty years before was suddenly intruding into the carefully ordered life she now had.

"We are homicide investigators, ma'am. We are working on a case that may involve your husband. We —"

"He's *not* my husband. I divorced him twenty-five years ago, at least. This is crazy, you coming here to ask about a man I don't even know anymore, that I didn't even know was still alive. I think you should leave. I want you to leave."

She stood up and extended her hand in the direction they had come in.

Bosch glanced at Edgar and then back at the woman. Her anger had turned the tan on her sculptured face uneven. There were blotches beginning to form, the tell of plastic surgery.

"Mrs. Waters, sit down," Bosch said sternly. "Please try to relax."

"Relax? Do you know who I am? My husband built this place. The houses, the golf course, everything. You can't just come in here like this. I could pick up the phone and have the chief of police on the line in two —"

"Your son is dead, lady," Edgar snapped. "The one you

left behind thirty years ago. So sit down and let us ask you our questions."

She dropped back onto the couch as if her feet had been kicked out from beneath her. Her mouth opened and then closed. Her eyes were no longer on them, they were on some distant memory.

"Arthur . . ."

"That's right," Edgar said. "Arthur. Glad you at least remember it."

They watched her in silence for a few moments. All the years and all the distance wasn't enough. She was hurt by the news. Hurt bad. Bosch had seen it before. The past had a way of coming back up out of the ground. Always right below your feet.

Bosch took his notebook out of his pocket and opened it to a blank page. He wrote "Cool it" on it and handed the notebook to Edgar.

"Jerry, why don't you take some notes? I think Mrs. Waters wants to cooperate with us."

His speaking drew Christine Waters out of her blue reverie. She looked at Bosch.

"What happened? Was it Sam?"

"We don't know. That's why we're here. Arthur has been dead a long time. His remains were found just last week."

She slowly brought one of her hands to her mouth in a fist. She lightly started bumping it against her lips.

"How long?"

"He had been buried for twenty years. It was a call from your daughter that helped us identify him."

"Sheila."

It was as if she had not spoken the name in so long she had to try it out to see if it still worked.

"Mrs. Waters, Arthur disappeared in nineteen eighty. Did you know about that?"

She shook her head.

"I was gone. I left almost ten years before that."

"And you had no contact with your family at all?"

"I thought . . ."

She didn't finish. Bosch waited.

"Mrs. Waters?"

"I couldn't take them with me. I was young and couldn't handle . . . the responsibility. I ran away. I admit that. I ran away. I thought that it would be best for them to not hear from me, to not even know about me."

Bosch nodded in a way he hoped conveyed that he understood and agreed with her thinking at the time. It didn't matter that he did not. It didn't matter that his own mother had faced the same hardship of having a child too soon and under difficult circumstances but had clung to and protected him with a fierceness that inspired his life.

"You wrote them letters before you left? Your children, I mean."

"How did you know that?"

"Sheila told us. What did you say in the letter to Arthur?"

"I just . . . I just told him I loved him and I'd always think about him, but I couldn't be with him. I can't really remember everything I said. Is it important?"

Bosch shrugged his shoulders.

"I don't know. Your son had a letter with him. It might have been the one from you. It's deteriorated. We probably won't ever know. In the divorce petition you filed a few years after leaving home, you cited physical abuse as a cause of action. I need you to tell us about that. What was the physical abuse?"

She shook her head again, this time in a dismissive way, as if the question was annoying or stupid.

"What do you think? Sam liked to bat me around. He'd get drunk and it was like walking on eggshells. Anything could set him off, the baby crying, Sheila talking too loud. And I was always the target."

"He would hit you?"

"Yes, he would hit me. He'd become a monster. It was one of the reasons I had to leave."

"But you left the kids with the monster," Edgar said.

This time she didn't react as if struck. She fixed her pale eyes on Edgar with a deathly look that made Edgar turn his indignant eyes away. She spoke very calmly to him.

"Who are you to judge anyone? I had to survive and I could not take them with me. If I had tried none of us would have survived."

"I'm sure they understood that," Edgar said.

The woman stood up again.

"I don't think I am going to talk to you anymore. I'm sure you can find your way out."

She headed toward the arched doorway at the far end of the room.

"Mrs. Waters," Bosch said. "If you don't talk to us now, we will go get that court order."

"Fine," she said without looking back. "Do it. I'll have one of my attorneys handle it."

"And it will become public record at the courthouse in town."

It was a gamble but Bosch thought it might stop her. He guessed that her life in Palm Springs was built squarely atop her secrets. And that she wouldn't want anybody going down into the basement. The social gossips might, like Edgar, have a hard time viewing her actions and motives the way she did. Deep inside, she had a hard time herself, even after so many years.

She stopped under the archway, composed herself and came back to the couch. Looking at Bosch, she said, "I will only talk to you. I want him to leave."

Bosch shook his head.

"He's my partner. It's our case. He stays, Mrs. Waters."

"I will still answer questions from you only."

"Fine. Please sit down."

She did so, this time sitting on the side of the couch far-thest from Edgar and closest to Bosch.

"I know you want to help us find your son's killer. We'll try to be as fast as we can here."

She nodded once.

"Just tell us about your ex-husband."

"The whole sordid story?" she asked rhetorically. "I'll give you the short version. I met him in an acting class. I was eighteen. He was seven years older, had already done some film work and to top it off was very, very handsome. You could say I quickly fell under his spell. And I was pregnant before I was nineteen."

Bosch checked Edgar to see if he was writing any of this down. Edgar caught the look and started writing.

"We got married and Sheila was born. I didn't pursue a career. I have to admit I wasn't that dedicated. Acting just seemed like something to do at the time. I had the looks but soon I found out every girl in Hollywood had the looks. I was happy to stay at home."

"How did your husband do at it?"

"At first, very well. He got a recurring role on *First Infantry*. Did you ever watch it?"

Bosch nodded. It was a World War II television drama that ran in the mid to late sixties, until public sentiment over the Vietnam War and war in general led to declining ratings and it was cancelled. The show followed an army platoon as it moved behind German lines each week. Bosch had liked the show as a kid and always tried to watch it, whether he was in a foster home or the youth hall.

"Sam was one of the Germans. His blond hair and Aryan looks. He was on it the last two years. Right up until I got pregnant with Arthur."

She let some silence punctuate that.

"Then the show got cancelled because of that stupid war in Vietnam. It got cancelled and Sam had trouble finding work. He was typecast as this German. He really started drinking then. And hitting me. He'd spend his days going to casting calls and getting nothing. He'd then spend his nights drinking and being angry at me."

"Why you?"

"Because I was the one who had gotten pregnant. First with Sheila and then with Arthur. Neither was planned and it all added up to too much pressure on him. He took it out on whoever was close."

"He assaulted you."

"Assaulted? It sounds so clinical. But yes, he assaulted me. Many times."

"Did you ever see him strike the children?"

It was the key question they had come to ask. Everything else was window dressing.

"Not specifically," she said. "When I was carrying Arthur he hit me once. In the stomach. It broke my water. I went into labor about six weeks before my due date. Arthur didn't even weigh five pounds when he was born."

Bosch waited. She was talking in a way that hinted she would say more as long as he gave her the space. He looked out through the sliding door behind her at the golf course. There was a deep sand trap guarding a putting green. A man in a red shirt and plaid pants was in the trap, flailing with a club at an unseen ball. Sprays of sand were flying up out of the trap onto the green. But no ball.

In the distance three other golfers were getting out of two carts parked on the other side of the green. The lip of the sand trap shielded them from view of the man in the red shirt. As Bosch watched, the man checked up and down the fairway for witnesses, then reached down and grabbed his ball. He threw it up onto the green, giving it the nice arc of a perfectly hit shot. He then climbed out of the trap, holding his club with both hands still locked in their grip, a posture that suggested he had just hit the ball.

Finally, Christine Waters began to talk again and Bosch looked back at her.

"Arthur only weighed five pounds when he was born. He was small right up through that first year and very sickly. We never talked about it but I think we both knew that what Sam had done had hurt that boy. He just wasn't right."

"Aside from that incident when he struck you, you never saw him strike Arthur or Sheila?"

"He might have spanked Sheila. I don't really remember. He never hit the children. I mean, he had me there to hit."

Bosch nodded, the unspoken conclusion being that once she was gone, who knows who became the target? Bosch thought of the bones laid out on the autopsy table and all the injuries Dr. Golliher had catalogued.

"Is my hus — is Sam under arrest?"

Bosch looked at her.

"No. We're in the fact-finding stage here. The indication from your son's remains is that there is a history of chronic physical abuse. We're just trying to figure things out."

"And Sheila? Was she . . . ?"

"We haven't specifically asked her. We will. Mrs. Waters, when you were struck by your husband, was it always with his hand?"

"Sometimes he would hit me with things. A shoe once, I remember. He held me on the floor and hit me with it. And once he threw his briefcase at me. It hit me in the side."

She shook her head.

"What?"

"Nothing. Just that briefcase. He carried it with him to all his auditions. Like he was so important and had so much going on. And all he ever had in it were a few head shots and a flask."

Bitterness burned in her voice, even after so many years.

"Did you ever go to a hospital or an emergency room? Is there any physical record of the abuse?"

She shook her head.

"He never hurt me enough that I had to go. Except when I had Arthur, and then I lied. I said I fell and my water broke. You see, Detective, it wasn't something I wanted the world to know about."

Bosch nodded.

"When you left, was that planned? Or did you just go?"

She didn't answer for a long moment as she watched the memory first on her inside screen.

"I wrote the letters to my children long before I left. I carried them in my purse and waited for the right time. On the night I left, I put them under their pillows and left with my purse and only the clothes I was wearing. And my car that my father had given us when we got married. That was it. I'd had enough. I told him we needed medicine for Arthur. He had been drinking. He told me to go out and get it."

"And you never went back."

"Never. About a year later, before I came out to the Springs, I drove by the house at night. Saw the lights on. I didn't stop."

Bosch nodded. He couldn't think of anything else to ask. While the woman's memory of that early time in her life was good, what she was remembering wasn't going to help make a case against her ex-husband for a murder committed ten years after she had last seen him. Maybe Bosch had known that all along — that she wouldn't be a vital part of the case. Maybe he had just wanted to take the measure of a woman who had abandoned her children, leaving them with a man she believed was a monster.

"What does she look like?"

Bosch was momentarily taken aback by her question.

"My daughter."

"Um, she's blonde like you. A little taller, heavier. No children, not married."

"When will Arthur be buried?"

"I don't know. You would have to call the medical examiner's office. Or you could probably check with Sheila to see if . . ."

He stopped. He couldn't get involved in mending the thirty-year gaps in people's lives.

"I think we're finished here, Mrs. Waters. We appreciate your cooperation."

"Definitely," Edgar said, the sarcasm in his tone making its mark.

"You came all this way to ask so few questions."

"I think that's because you have so few answers," Edgar said.

They walked to the door and she followed a few paces behind. Outside, under the portico, Bosch looked back at the woman standing in the open doorway. They held each other's eyes for a moment. He tried to think of something to say. But he had nothing for her. She closed the door.

28

THEY pulled into the station lot shortly before eleven. It had been a sixteen-hour day that had netted very little in terms of evidence that could carry a case toward prosecution. Still, Bosch was satisfied. They had the identification and that was the center of the wheel. All things would come from that.

Edgar said good night and went straight to his car without going inside the station. Bosch wanted to check with the watch sergeant to see if anything had come up with Johnny Stokes. He also wanted to check for messages and knew that if he hung around until eleven he might see Julia Brasher when she got off shift. He wanted to talk to her.

The station was quiet. The midnight shift cops were up in roll call. The incoming and outgoing watch sergeants would be up there as well. Bosch went down the hallway to the detective bureau. The lights were out, which was in violation of an order from the Office of the Chief of Police. The chief had mandated that the lights in Parker Center and every division station should never be off. His goal was to let the public know that the fight against crime never slept. The result was that the lights glowed brightly every night in empty police offices across the city.

Bosch flicked on the row of lights over the homicide

table and went to his spot. There were a number of pink phone message slips and he looked through these, but all were from reporters or related to other cases he had pending. He tossed the reporters' messages in the trash can and put the others in his top drawer to follow up on the next day.

There were two department dispatch envelopes waiting on the desk for him. The first contained Golliher's report and Bosch put it aside for reading later. He picked up the second envelope and saw it was from SID. He realized he had forgotten to call Antoine Jesper about the skateboard.

He was about to open the envelope when he noticed it had been dropped on top of a folded piece of paper on his calendar blotter. He unfolded it and read the short message. He knew it was from Julia, though she had not signed it.

Where are you, tough guy?

He had forgotten that he had told her to come by the squad room before she started her shift. He smiled at the note but felt bad about forgetting. He also thought once more about Edgar's admonishment to be careful with the relationship.

He refolded the page and put it in his drawer. He wondered how Julia would react to what he wanted to talk about. He was dead tired from the long hours but didn't want to wait until the next day.

The dispatch envelope from SID contained a one-page evidence analysis report from Jesper. Bosch read the report quickly. Jesper had confirmed that the board was made by Boneyard Boards Inc., a Huntington Beach manufacturer. The model was called a "Boney Board." The particular model at hand was made from February 1978 until June 1986, when design variations created a slight change in the board's nose.

Before Bosch could get excited by the implications of a match between the board and the time frame of the case, he read the last paragraph of the report, which put any match in doubt.

The trucks (wheel assemblies) are of a design first implemented by Boneyard in May 1984. The graphite wheels also indicate a later manufacture. Graphite wheels did not become common-place in the industry until the mid-80s. However, because trucks and wheels are interchangeable and often are traded out or re-placed by boarders, it is impossible to determine the exact date of manufacture of the skateboard in evidence. Best estimate pending additional evidence is manufacture between February 1978 and June 1986.

Bosch slid the report back into the dispatch envelope and dropped it on the desk. The report was inconclusive but to Bosch the factors Jesper had outlined leaned toward the skateboard not having been Arthur Delacroix's. In his mind the report tilted toward clearing rather than impli-cating Nicholas Trent in the boy's death. In the morning he would type up a report with his conclusions and give it to Lt. Billets to send up the chain to Deputy Chief Irving's office.

As if to punctuate the end of this line of investigation, the sound of the back door to the station banging open echoed down the hallway. Several loud male voices fol-lowed, all heading out into the night. Roll call was over and fresh troops were taking the field, their voices full of us-versus-them bravado.

The police chief's wishes notwithstanding, Bosch flicked off the light and headed back down the hallway to the watch office. There were two sergeants in the small office. Lenkov was going off duty, while Renshaw was just start-ing her shift. They both registered surprise at Bosch's appearance so late at night but then didn't ask him what he was doing in the station.

"So," Bosch said, "anything on my guy, Johnny Stokes?"

"Nothing yet," Lenkov said. "But we're looking. We're putting it out at all roll calls and we've got the pictures in the cars now. So . . ."

"You'll let me know."

"We'll let you know."

Renshaw nodded her agreement.

Bosch thought about asking if Julia Brasher had come in to end her shift yet but thought better of it. He thanked them and stepped back into the hallway. The conversation had felt odd, like they couldn't wait for him to get out of there. He sensed it was because of the word getting around about him and Julia. Maybe they knew she was coming off of shift and wanted to avoid seeing them together. As supervisors they would then be witnesses to what was an infraction of department policy. As minor and rarely enforced as the rule was, things would be better all the way around if they didn't see the infraction and then have to look the other way.

Bosch walked out the back door and into the parking lot. He had no idea whether Julia was in the station locker room, still out on patrol or had come and gone already. Mid-shifts were fluid. You didn't come in until the watch sergeant sent your replacement out.

He found her car in the parking lot and knew he hadn't missed her. He walked back toward the station to sit down on the Code 7 bench. But when he got to it, Julia was already sitting there. Her hair was slightly wet from the locker room shower. She wore faded blue jeans and a long-sleeved pullover with a high neck.

"I heard you were in the house," she said. "I checked and saw the light out and thought maybe I'd missed you."

"Just don't tell the chief about the lights."

She smiled and Bosch sat down next to her. He wanted to touch her but didn't.

"Or us," he said.

She nodded.

"Yeah. A lot of people know, don't they?"

"Yeah. I wanted to talk to you about that. Can you get a drink?"

"Sure."

"Let's walk over to the Cat and Fiddle. I'm tired of driving today."

Rather than walk through the station together and out the front door, they took the long way through the parking lot and around the station. They walked two blocks up to Sunset and then another two down to the pub. Along the way Bosch apologized for missing her in the squad room before her shift and explained he had driven to Palm Springs. She was very quiet as they walked, mostly just nodding her head at his explanations. They didn't talk about the issue at hand until they reached the pub and slid into one of the booths by the fireplace.

They both ordered pints of Guinness and then Julia folded her arms on the table and fixed Bosch with a hard stare.

"Okay, Harry, I've got my drink coming. You can give it to me. But I have to warn you, if you are going to say you want to just be friends, well, I already have enough friends."

Bosch couldn't help but break into a broad smile. He loved her boldness, her directness. He started shaking his head.

"Nah, I don't want to be your friend, Julia. Not at all."

He reached across the table and squeezed her forearm. Instinctively, he glanced around the pub to make sure no

212 / MICHAEL CONNELLY

one from the cop shop had wandered over for an after-shift drink. He didn't recognize anyone and looked back at Julia.

"What I want is to be with you. Just like we've been."

"Good. So do I."

"But we have to be careful. You haven't been around the department long enough. I have and I know how things get around, and so it's my fault. We should've never left your car in the station lot that first night."

"Oh, fuck 'em if they can't take a joke."

"No, it's —"

He waited while the barmaid put their beers down on little paper coasters with the Guinness seal on them.

"It's not like that, Julia," he said when they were alone again. "If we're going to keep going, we need to be more careful. We have to go underground. No more meeting at the bench, no more notes, no more anything like that. We can't even go here anymore because cops come here. We have to be totally underground. We meet outside the division, we talk outside the division."

"You make it sound like we're a couple of spies or something."

Bosch picked up his glass, clicked it off hers and drank deeply from it. It tasted so good after such a long day. He immediately had to stifle a yawn, which Julia caught and repeated.

"Spies? That's not too far off. You forget, I've been in this department more than twenty-five years. You're just a boot, a baby. I've got more enemies inside the wire than you've got arrests under your belt. Some of these people would take any opportunity to put me down if they could. It sounds like I'm just worrying about myself here, but the thing is if they need to go after a rookie to get to me, they'll do it in a heartbeat. I mean that. A heartbeat."

She turtled her head down and looked both ways.

"Okay, Harry — I mean, Secret Agent double-oh-forty-five."

Bosch smiled and shook his head.

"Yeah, yeah, you think it's all a joke. Wait until you get your first IAD jacket. Then you'll see the light."

"Come on, I don't think it's a joke. I'm just having fun."

They both drank from their beers, and Bosch leaned back and tried to relax. The heat from the fireplace felt good. The walk over had been brisk. He looked at Julia and she was smiling like she knew a secret about him.

"What?"

"Nothing. You just get so worked up."

"I'm trying to protect you, that's all. I'm plus-twenty-five, so it doesn't matter as much to me."

"What does that mean? I've heard people say that — 'plus-twenty-five' — like they're untouchable or something."

Bosch shook his head.

"Nobody's untouchable. But after you hit twenty-five years in, you top out on the pension scale. So it doesn't matter if you quit at twenty-five years or thirty-five years, you get the same pension. So 'plus-twenty-five' means you have some fuck-you room. You don't like what they're doing to you, you can always pull the pin and say have a nice day. Because you're not in it for the check and the bennies anymore."

The waitress came back to the table and put down a basket of popcorn. Julia let some time go by and then leaned across the table, her chin almost over the mouth of her pint.

"Then what are you in it for?"

Bosch shrugged his shoulders and looked down at his glass.

"The job, I guess. . . . Nothing big, nothing heroic. Just the chance to maybe make things right every now and then in a fucked-up world."

He used his thumb to draw patterns on the frosted glass. He continued speaking without taking his eyes off the glass.

"This case, for example . . ."

"What about it?"

"If we can just figure it out and put it together . . . we can maybe make up a little bit for what happened to that kid. I don't know, I think it might mean something, something really small, to the world."

He thought about the skull Golliher had held up to him that morning. A murder victim buried in tar for 9,000 years. A city of bones, and all of them waiting to come up out of the ground. For what? Maybe nobody cares anymore.

"I don't know," he said. "Maybe it doesn't mean anything in the long run. Suicide terrorists hit New York and three thousand people are dead before they've finished their first cup of coffee. What does one little set of bones buried in the past matter?"

She smiled sweetly and shook her head.

"Don't go existential on me, Harry. The important thing is that it means something to you. And if it means something to you, then it is important to do what you can. No matter what happens in the world, there will always be the need for heroes. I hope someday I get a chance to be one."

"Maybe."

He nodded and kept his eyes from hers. He played some more with his glass.

"Do you remember that commercial that used to be on TV, where there's this old lady who's on the ground or something and she says, 'I've fallen and I can't get up,' and everybody used to make fun of it?"

"I remember. They sell T-shirts that say that on Venice Beach."

"Yeah, well . . . sometimes I feel like that. I mean, plus twenty-five. You can't go the distance without screwing up from time to time. You fall down, Julia, and sometimes you feel like you can't get up."

He nodded to himself.

"But then you get lucky and a case comes along and you say to yourself, this is the one. You just feel it. This is the one I can get back up with."

"It's called redemption, Harry. What's that song say, 'Everybody wants a shot at it'?"

"Something like that. Yeah."

"And maybe this case is your shot?"

"Yeah, I think it is. I hope so."

"Then here's to redemption."

She picked up her glass for a toast.

"Hold fast," he said.

She banged it off of his. Some of her beer sloshed into his almost empty glass.

"Sorry. I need to practice that."

"It's okay. I needed a refill."

He raised his glass and drained it. He put it back down and wiped his mouth with the back of his hand.

"So are you coming home with me tonight?" he asked.

She shook her head.

"No, not with you."

He frowned and started to wonder if his directness had offended her.

"I'm *following* you home tonight," she said. "Remember? Can't leave the car at the division. Everything's got to be top secret, hush-hush, eyes only from now on."

He smiled. The beer and her smile were like magic on him.

"You got me there."

"I hope in more ways than one."

29

Bosch came in late to the meeting in Lt. Billets's office. Edgar was already there, a rarity, as well as Medina from Media Relations. Billets pointed him to a seat with a pencil she was holding, then picked up her phone and punched in a number.

"This is Lieutenant Billets," she said when her call was answered. "You can tell Chief Irving that we are all here now and ready to begin."

Bosch looked at Edgar and raised his eyebrows. The deputy chief was still keeping his hand directly in the case.

Billets hung up and said, "He's going to call back and I'll put him on the speaker."

"To listen or to tell?" Bosch asked.

"Who knows?"

"While we're waiting," Medina said, "I've started getting a few calls about a BOLO you guys put out. A man named John Stokes? How do you want me to handle that? Is he a new suspect?"

Bosch was annoyed. He knew the Be on the Lookout flier distributed at roll calls would eventually leak to the media. He didn't anticipate it happening so quickly.

"No, he's not a suspect at all," he said to Medina. "And if

the reporters screw that up like they did Trent, we'll never find him. He's just somebody we want to talk to. He was an acquaintance of the victim. Many years ago."

"Then you have the victim's ID?"

Before Bosch could answer, the phone buzzed. Billets answered and put Deputy Chief Irving on the speaker.

"Chief, we have Detectives Bosch and Edgar here, along with Officer Medina from Media Relations."

"Very good," Irving's voice boomed from the phone's speaker. "Where are we at?"

Billets started tapping a button on the phone to turn down the volume.

"Uh, Harry, why don't you take that?" she said.

Bosch reached into his inside coat pocket and took out his notebook. He took his time about it. He liked the idea of Irving sitting behind his spotless glass desk in his office at Parker Center, waiting for voices over the phone. He opened the notebook to a page full of jottings he had made that morning while eating breakfast with Julia.

"Detective, are you there?" Irving said.

"Uh, yes, sir, I'm right here. I was just going through some notes here. Um, the main thing is we have made a positive identification of the victim. His name is Arthur Delacroix. He disappeared from his home in the Miracle Mile area on May fourth, nineteen eighty. He was twelve years old."

He stopped there, anticipating questions. He noticed that Medina was writing the name down.

"I'm not sure we want to put that out yet," Bosch said.

"Why is that?" Irving asked. "Are you saying the identification is not positive?"

"No, we're positive on it, Chief. It's just that if we put the name out, we might be telegraphing which way we're moving here."

"Which is?"

"Well, we are very confident that Nicholas Trent was clear on this. So we are looking elsewhere. The autopsy — the injuries to the bones — indicate chronic child abuse, dating to early childhood. The mother was out of the picture, so we are looking at the father now. We haven't approached him yet. We're gathering string. If we were to announce that we have an ID and the father saw it, we would be putting him on notice before we need to."

"If he buried the kid there, then he already is on notice."

"To a degree. But he knows if we can't come up with a legit ID we'll never link it to him. The lack of an ID is what keeps him safe. And it gives us time to look at him."

"Understood," Irving said.

They sat in silence for a few moments, Bosch expecting Irving to say something else. But he didn't. Bosch looked at Billets and spread his hands in a what-gives gesture. She shrugged her shoulders.

"So then . . . ," Bosch began, "we're not putting it out, right?"

Silence. Then:

"I think that is the prudent course to follow," Irving said.

Medina tore the page he had written on out of his notebook, crumpled it and tossed it into a trash can in the corner.

"Is there anything we *can* put out?" he asked.

"Yes," Bosch said quickly. "We can clear Trent."

"Negative," Irving said just as quickly. "We do that at the end. When and if you make a case, then we will clean up the rest."

Bosch looked at Edgar and then at Billets.

"Chief," he said. "If we do it that way, we could be hurting our case."

"How so?"

"It's an old case. The older the case, the longer the shot. We can't take chances. If we don't go out there and tell them Trent is clear, we'll be giving the guy we eventually take down a defense. He'll be able to point at Trent and say he was a child molester, he did it."

"But he will be able to do that, whether we clear Trent now or later."

Bosch nodded.

"True. But I am looking at it from the standpoint of testifying at trial. I want to be able to say we checked Trent out and quickly dismissed him. I don't want some lawyer asking me why, if we so quickly dismissed him, we waited a week or two weeks to announce it. Chief, it will look like we were hiding something. It's going to be subtle but it will have an impact. People on juries look for any reason not to trust cops in general and the LAPD in par —"

"Okay, Detective, you have made your point. My decision still stands. There will be no announcement on Trent. Not at this time, not until we have a solid suspect we can come forward with."

Bosch shook his head and slumped a bit in his seat.

"What else?" Irving said. "I have a briefing with the chief in two minutes."

Bosch looked at Billets and shook his head again. He had nothing else he wanted to share. Billets spoke up.

"Chief, at this time I think that's pretty much where we stand."

"When do you plan to approach the father, Detectives?"

Bosch poked his chin at Edgar.

"Uh, Chief, Detective Edgar here. We are still looking for a witness that could be important to talk to before approaching the father. That would be a boyhood friend of the victim. We're thinking he might have knowledge of the abuse the boy suffered. We're planning to give it the day. We believe he's here in Hollywood and we have a lot of eyes out there on the —"

"Yes, that is fine, Detective. We will reconvene this conversation tomorrow morning."

"Yes, Chief," Billets said. "At nine-thirty again?"

There was no answer. Irving was already gone.

30

Bosch and Edgar spent the rest of the morning updating reports and the murder book and calling hospitals all over the city to cancel the records searches they had requested by warrant on Monday morning. But by noon Bosch had had enough of the office work and said he had to get out of the station.

"Where you want to go?" Edgar asked.

"I'm tired of waiting around," Bosch said. "Let's go take a look at him."

They used Edgar's personal car because it was unmarked and there were no undercover units left in the motor pool. They took the 101 up into the Valley and then the 405 north before exiting in Van Nuys. The Manchester Trailer Park was on Sepulveda near Victory. They drove by it once before coming back and driving in.

There was no gate house, just a yellow-striped speed bump. The park road circled the property, and Sam Delacroix's trailer was at the rear of the tract, where it bumped up against a twenty-foot-high sound-retention wall next to the freeway. The wall was designed to knock down the nonstop roar of the freeway. All it did was redirect and change its tone, but it was still there.

The trailer was a single-wide with rust stains dripping

down the aluminum skin from most of the steel rivet seams. There was an awning with a picnic table and a charcoal grill beneath it. A clothesline ran from one of the awning's support poles to a corner of the next trailer in line. Near the back of the narrow yard an aluminum storage shed about the size of an outhouse was pushed up against the sound wall.

The windows and door of the trailer were closed. There was no vehicle in the lone parking spot. Edgar kept the car going by at an even five miles an hour.

"Looks like nobody's home."

"Let's try the driving range," Bosch said. "If he's over there, maybe you can hit a bucket of balls or something."

"Always like to practice."

The range had few customers when they got there but it looked like it had been a busy morning. Golf balls littered the entire range, which was three hundred yards deep, extending to the same sound wall that backed the trailer park. At the far end of the property, netting was erected on high utility poles to protect the freeway drivers from long balls. A small tractor with ball harvesters attached at the rear was slowly traversing the far end of the range, its driver secured in a safety cage.

Bosch watched for a few moments alone until Edgar came up with a half bucket of balls and his golf bag, which had been in the trunk of his car.

"I guess that's him," Edgar said.

"Yeah."

Bosch went over to a bench and sat down to watch his partner hit some balls from a little square of rubber grass. Edgar had taken off his tie and jacket. He didn't look that much out of place. Hitting balls a few green squares down from him were two men wearing suit pants and button-down shirts, obviously using their lunch break from the office to fine-tune their game.

Edgar propped his bag on a wooden stand and chose one of the irons. He put on a glove, which he had taken from the bag, took a few warm-up swings and then started striking balls. The first few were grounders that made him curse. Then he started getting some air underneath them and he seemed pleased with himself.

Bosch was amused. He had never played golf a single time in his life and couldn't understand the draw it had for many men — in fact, most of the detectives in the squad room played religiously, and there was a whole network of police tournaments around the state. He enjoyed watching Edgar get worked up even though hitting range balls didn't count.

"Take a shot at him," he instructed after he thought Edgar was fully warmed up and ready.

"Harry," Edgar said. "I know you don't play but I got news for you. In golf you hit the ball at the pin — the flag. No moving targets in golf."

"Then how come the ex-presidents are always hitting people?"

"Because they're allowed to."

"Come on, you said everybody tries to hit the guy in the tractor. Take a shot."

"Everybody but the serious golfers."

But he angled his body so that Bosch could tell he was going to take a shot at the tractor as it came to the end of a crossing and was making the U-turn to go back the other way. Judging by the yardage markers, the tractor was a hundred forty yards out.

Edgar swung but the ball was another grounder.

"Dammit! See, Harry? This could hurt my game."

Bosch started laughing.

"What are you laughing at?"

"It's just a game, man. Take another shot."

"Forget it. It's childish."

"Take the shot."

Edgar didn't say anything. He angled his body again, taking aim at the tractor, which was now in the middle of the range. He swung and hit the ball, sending it screaming down the middle but a good twenty feet over the tractor.

"Nice shot," Bosch said. "Unless you were aiming for the tractor."

Edgar gave him a look but didn't say anything. For the next five minutes he hit ball after ball at the range tractor but never came closer to it than ten yards. Bosch never said anything but Edgar's frustrations increased until he turned and angrily said, "You want to try?"

Bosch feigned confusion.

"Oh, you're still trying to hit him? I didn't realize."

"Come on, let's go."

"You still have half your balls there."

"I don't care. This will set my game back a month."

"That's all?"

Edgar angrily shoved the club he had been using into his bag and gave Bosch his dead-eye look. It was all Bosch could do not to burst into laughter.

"Come on, Jerry, I want to get a look at the guy. Can't you hit a few more? It looks like he's gotta be done soon."

Edgar looked out at the range. The tractor was now near the fifty-yard markers. Assuming he had started back at the sound wall, he would be finished soon. There weren't enough new balls out there — just Edgar's and the two business guys' — to warrant going back over the entire range.

Edgar silently relented. He took out one of his woods and went back to the green square of fake grass. He hit a beautiful shot that almost carried to the sound wall.

"Tiger Woods, kiss my ass," he said.

The next shot he put into the real grass ten feet from the tee.

"Shit."

"When you play for real, do you hit off that fake grass?"

"No, Harry, you don't. This is practice."

"Oh, so in practice you don't re-create the actual playing situation."

"Something like that."

The tractor pulled off the range and up to a shed behind the concession stand where Edgar had paid for his bucket of balls. The cage door opened and a man in his early sixties got out. He started pulling wire-mesh baskets full of balls out of the harvester and carrying them into the shed. Bosch told Edgar to keep hitting balls so that they wouldn't be obvious. Bosch nonchalantly walked toward the concession stand and bought another half bucket of balls. This put him no more than twenty feet from the man who had been driving the tractor.

It was Samuel Delacroix. Bosch recognized him from a driver's license photo Edgar had pulled and shown him. The man who once played a blond, blue-eyed Aryan soldier and had put a spell on an eighteen-year-old girl was now about as distinguished as a ham sandwich. He was still blond but it obviously came from a bottle and he was bald to the crown of his head. He had day-old whiskers that shone white in the sun. His nose was swollen by time and alcohol and pinched by a pair of ill-fitting glasses. He carried a beer paunch that would've been a ticket to a discharge in anybody's army.

"Two-fifty."

Bosch looked at the woman behind the cash register.

"For the balls."

"Right."

He paid her and picked up the bucket by the handle. He took a last glance at Delacroix, who suddenly looked over at Bosch at the same time. Their eyes locked for a moment and Bosch casually looked away. He headed back toward Edgar. That was when his cell phone started to chirp.

He quickly handed the bucket to Edgar and pulled the phone out of his back pocket. It was Mankiewicz, the day-shift watch sergeant.

"Hey, Bosch, what are you doing?"

"Just hitting some balls."

"Figures. You guys fuck off while we do all the work."

"You found my guy?"

"We think so."

"Where?"

"He's working at the Washateria. You know, picking up some tips, loose change."

The Washateria was a car wash on La Brea. It employed day laborers to vacuum and wipe down cars. They worked mostly for tips and what they could steal out of the cars without getting caught.

"Who spotted him?"

"Couple guys from vice. They're eighty percent sure. They want to know if you want them to make the move or do you want to be on scene."

"Tell them to sit tight and that we're on the way. And you know what, Mank? We think this guy's a rabbit. You got a unit we can use as an extra backup in case he runs?"

"Um . . ."

There was silence and Bosch guessed that Mankiewicz was checking his deployment chart.

"Well, you're in luck. I got a couple three-elevens start-ing early. They should be out of roll call in fifteen. That work for you?"

"Perfect. Tell them to meet us in the parking lot of the Checkers at La Brea and Sunset. Have the vice guys meet us there, too."

Bosch signaled to Edgar that they were going to roll.

"Uh, one thing," Mankiewicz said.

"What's that?"

"On the backup, one of them's Brasher. Is that going to be a problem?"

Bosch was silent a moment. He wanted to tell Mankie-wicz to put somebody else on it but knew it was not his place to. If he tried to influence deployment or anything else based on his relationship with Brasher, then he could leave himself open to criticism and the possibility of án IAD investigation.

"No, no problem."

"Look, I wouldn't do it but she's green. She's made a few mistakes and needs this kind of experience."

"I said no problem."

31

THEY planned the takedown of Johnny Stokes on the hood of Edgar's car. The vice guys, Eyman and Leiby, drew the layout of the Washateria on a legal pad and circled the spot where they had spotted Stokes working under the waxing canopy. The car wash was surrounded on three sides by concrete walls and other structures. The area fronting La Brea was almost fifty yards, with a five-foot retention wall running the border except for entry and exit lanes at each corner of the property. If Stokes decided to run, he could go to the retention wall and climb it, but it was more likely that he would go for one of the open lanes.

The plan was simple. Eyman and Leiby would cover the car wash entrance, and Brasher and her partner, Edgewood, would cover the exit. Bosch and Edgar would drive Edgar's car in as customers and make the move on Stokes. They switched their radios to a tactical unit and worked out a code; red meant Stokes had rabbitted, and green meant he had been taken peaceably.

"Remember something," Bosch said. "Almost every wiper, rubber, soaper and vacuum guy on that lot is probably running from something — even if it's just *la migra*. So even if we take Stokes without a problem, the others may rumble. Cops showing up at a car wash is like yelling fire in a theater. Everybody scatters till they see who's the one who's it."

Everybody nodded and Bosch looked pointedly at Brasher, the rookie. In keeping with the plan agreed to the night before, they made no showing of knowing each other as anything other than fellow cops. But now he wanted to make sure she understood just how fluid a takedown like this could become.

"You got that, boot?" he said.

She smiled.

"Yeah, I got it."

"All right, then let's concentrate. Let's go."

He thought he saw the smile stay on Brasher's face as she and Edgewood walked to their patrol car.

He and Edgar walked to Edgar's Lexus. Bosch stopped when he got to it and realized that it looked like it had just been washed and waxed.

"Shit."

"What can I say, Harry? I take care of my car."

Bosch looked around. Behind the fast-food restaurant was an open Dumpster in a concrete alcove that had recently been washed down. There was a puddle of black water pooling on the pavement.

"Drive through that puddle a couple times," he said. "Get it on your car."

"Harry, I'm not going to get that shit on my car."

"Come on, your car has to look like it needs to be washed or it might be a tell. You said yourself, the guy's a rabbit. Let's not give him a reason."

"But we're not actually going to get the car washed. I splash that shit on there, it stays there."

"Tell you what, Jerry. If we get this guy, I'll have Eyman and Leiby drive him in while you get your car washed. I'll even pay for it."

"Shit."

"Come on, just drive through the puddle. We're wasting time."

After messing up Edgar's car they made the drive to the car wash in silence. As they came up on it, Bosch could see the vice car parked at the curb a few car lengths from the car wash entrance. Further down the block past the car wash, the patrol unit was stopped in a lane of parked cars. Bosch went to his rover.

"Okay, everybody set?"

He got two return clicks on the mike from the vice guys. Brasher responded by voice.

"All ready."

"Okay. We're going in."

Edgar pulled into the car wash and drove into the service lane, where customers delivered their cars to the vacuum station and ordered the kind of wash or wax they wanted. Bosch's eyes immediately started moving among the workers, all of whom were dressed in identical orange jumpsuits and baseball caps. It slowed the identification process but Bosch soon saw the blue wax canopy and picked out Johnny Stokes.

"He's there," he said to Edgar. "On the black Beemer."

Bosch knew that once they stepped out of the car most of the cons on the lot would be able to identify them as cops. In the same way Bosch could spot a con ninety-eight percent of the time, they in turn could spot a cop. He would have to move swiftly in on Stokes.

He looked over at Edgar.

"Ready?"

"Let's do it."

They cracked the doors at the same time. Bosch got out and turned toward Stokes, who was twenty-five yards away with his back turned. He was crouched down and spraying something on the wheels of a black BMW. Bosch heard Edgar tell someone to skip the vacuum and that he'd be right back.

Bosch and Edgar had covered half the distance to their target when they were made by other workers on the lot. From somewhere behind him, Bosch heard a voice call out, "Five-oh, five-oh, five-oh."

Immediately alerted, Stokes stood up and started turning. Bosch started running.

He was fifteen feet from Stokes when the ex-con realized he was the target. His obvious escape was to his left and then out through the car wash entrance but the BMW was blocking him. He made a move to his right but then seemed to stop when he realized it was a dead end.

"No, no!" Bosch called out. "We just want to talk, we just want to talk."

Stokes visibly slumped. Bosch moved directly toward him while Edgar moved out to the right in case the ex-con decided to make a break.

Bosch slowed and opened his hands wide as he got close. One hand held his rover.

"LAPD. We just want to ask you a few questions, nothing else."

"Man, about what?"

"About —"

Stokes suddenly raised his arm and sprayed Bosch in the face with the tire cleaner. He then bolted to his right, seemingly toward the dead end, where the high rear wall of the car wash joined the side wall of a three-story apartment building.

Bosch instinctively brought his hands up to his eyes. He heard Edgar yell at Stokes and then the scuffling sound of his shoes on concrete as he gave chase. Bosch couldn't open his eyes. He put his mouth to the radio and yelled, "Red! Red! Red! He's heading toward the back corner."

He then dropped the radio to the concrete, using his shoe to break its fall. He used the sleeves of his jacket to wipe at his burning eyes. He finally could open them for brief moments at a time. He spotted a hose coiled on a faucet near the rear of the BMW. He made his way to it, turned it on and doused his face and eyes, not caring how wet his clothes got. His eyes felt like they had been dropped in boiling water.

After a few moments the water eased the burning sensation and he dropped the hose without turning it off and went back to get the radio. His vision was blurred at the edges but he could see well enough to get moving. As he bent down for the radio he heard laughter from some of the other men in orange jumpsuits.

Bosch ignored it. He switched the rover to the Hollywood patrol channel and spoke into it.

"Hollywood units, officers in pursuit of assault suspect, La Brea and Santa Monica. Suspect white male, thirty-five YOA, dark hair, orange jumpsuit. Suspect in the vicinity of Hollywood Washateria."

He couldn't remember the exact address of the car wash but wasn't worried. Every cop on patrol would know it. He switched the rover to the department's main communication channel and requested that a paramedic unit respond as well to treat an injured officer. He had no idea what had been sprayed into his eyes. They were beginning to feel better but he didn't want to take a chance on long-term injury.

Lastly, he switched back to the tactical channel and asked for the others' locations. Only Edgar came back up on the radio.

"There was a hole in the back corner. He went through to the alley. He's in one of these apartment complexes on the north side of the car wash."

"Where are the others?"

Edgar's return was broken up. He was moving into a radio void.

"They're back . . . spread out. I think . . . garage. You . . . ight, Harry?"

"I'll make it. Backup's on the way."

He didn't know if Edgar had heard that. He put the rover in his pocket and hustled to the back corner of the car wash lot, where he found the hole Stokes had slipped through. Behind a two-high pallet of fifty-five-gallon drums of liquid soap, the concrete wall was broken in. It appeared that at one time a car in the alley on the other side had struck the wall, creating the hole. Intentionally done or not, it was probably a well-known escape hatch for every wanted man who worked at the car wash.

Bosch crouched down and slipped through, momentarily catching his jacket on a rusty piece of rebar protruding from the broken wall. On the other side he got up in an alley that ran behind rows of apartment buildings on either side for the length of the block.

The patrol car was stopped at an angle forty yards down the alley. It was empty, both doors open. Bosch could hear the sound of the main communications channel playing over the dash radio. Further down, at the end of the block, the vice car was parked across the alley.

He quickly moved down the alley toward the patrol car, looking and listening for anything. When he got to the car he pulled the rover out again and tried to raise someone on tactical. He got no response.

He saw the patrol car was parked in front of a ramp that dipped down into an underground garage beneath the largest of the apartment complexes on the alley. Remembering auto theft was in Edgar's recitation of Stokes's criminal record, Bosch suddenly knew that Stokes would go for the garage. His only way out was to get a car.

He trotted down the garage ramp into the dark.

The garage was huge and appeared to follow the imprint of the building above. There were three parking lanes and a ramp leading to an even lower level. Bosch saw no one. The only sound he heard was a dripping from the overhead pipes. He moved swiftly down the middle lane, drawing his weapon for the first time. Stokes had already fashioned a weapon out of a spray bottle. There was no telling what he might find in the garage to also use as a weapon.

As he moved, Bosch checked the few vehicles in the garage — everyone was at work, he guessed — for signs of break-in. He saw nothing. He was raising the rover to his mouth when he heard the sound of running footsteps echo up the ramp from the lower level of the garage. He quickly moved to the ramp and descended, careful to keep the rubber soles of his shoes as quiet as he could.

The lower garage was even darker, with less natural light finding its way down. As the incline leveled, his eyes adjusted. He saw no one, but the ramp structure blocked his view of half of the space. As he began his way around the ramp he suddenly heard a high and taut voice coming from the far end. It was Brasher's.

"Right there! Right there! Don't move!"

Bosch followed the sound, moving in tight to the side of the ramp and holding his weapon up. His training told him to call out, to alert the other officer to his presence. But he knew that if Brasher was alone with Stokes his calling might distract her and give Stokes another chance to break or make a move on her.

As he cut beneath the underside of the ramp, Bosch saw them at the far wall, no more than fifty feet away. Brasher had Stokes up against the wall, legs and arms spread. She held him there with one hand pressed against his back. Her flashlight was on the ground next to her right foot, its beam lighting the wall on which Stokes leaned.

It was perfect. Bosch felt relief flood his body and almost immediately he understood it was relief that she had not been hurt. He came out of the semi-crouch he was in and started toward them, lowering his weapon.

He was directly behind them. After he had taken only a few steps he saw Brasher take her hand off Stokes and step back from him, glancing to either side as she did it. This immediately registered with Bosch as the wrong thing to do. It was completely out of training. It would allow Stokes to make another run if he wanted to.

Things seemed to slow down then. Bosch started to yell to her but the garage suddenly filled with the flash and shattering blast of a gunshot. Brasher went down, Stokes remained up. The blast echo reverberated through the concrete structure, obscuring its origin.

All Bosch could think was, where is the gun?

He raised his weapon while lowering his body into a combat crouch. He started to turn his head to look for the gun. But he saw Stokes start turning from the wall. He then saw Brasher's arm rising up from the ground, her gun pointed at Stokes's turning body.

Bosch aimed his Glock at Stokes.

"Freeze!" he yelled. "Freeze! Freeze! Freeze!"

In a second he was on them.

"Don't shoot, man," Stokes yelled. "Don't shoot!"

Bosch kept his eyes unwavering on Stokes. They still burned and needed relief but he knew even one blink now could be a fatal mistake.

"Down! Get on the ground. Now!"

Stokes dropped onto his stomach and spread his arms at ninety-degree angles to his body. Bosch stepped over him and with a move performed a thousand times before quickly cuffed his wrists behind his back.

He then holstered his weapon and turned to Brasher. Her eyes were wide and moving in a back-and-forth pattern. Blood had spattered onto her neck and had already soaked the front of her uniform shirt. He knelt over her and ripped open her shirt. Still, there was so much blood it took him a moment to find the wound. The bullet had entered her left shoulder, just an inch or so from the Velcro shoulder strap of her Kevlar vest.

The blood was flowing freely from the wound, and Bosch could see Brasher's face was losing color quickly. Her lips were moving but not making any sound. He looked around for something and saw a car wash rag poking out of Stokes's back pocket. He yanked it out and pressed it down on the wound. Brasher moaned in pain.

"Julia, this is going to hurt but I have to stop the bleeding."

With one hand he stripped off his tie and pushed it under her shoulder and then over the top. He tied a knot that was just tight enough to keep the rag compress in place.

"Okay, hang on, Julia."

He grabbed his rover off the ground and quickly switched the frequency knob to the main channel.

"CDC, officer down, lower-level garage at the La Brea Park apartments, La Brea and Santa Monica. We need paramedics right NOW! Suspect in custody. Confirm CDC."

He waited for what seemed to be an interminable time before a CDC dispatcher came on the air to say he was breaking up and needed to repeat his call. Bosch clicked the call button and yelled, "Where's my paramedics? Officer DOWN!"

He switched to tactical.

"Edgar, Edgewood, we're in the lower level of the garage. Brasher is down. I've got Stokes controlled. Repeat, Brasher is down."

He dropped the radio and yelled Edgar's name as loud as he could. He took off his jacket and balled it together.

"Man, I didn't do it," Stokes yelled. "I don't know what —"

"Shut up! Shut the fuck up!"

Bosch put his jacket under Brasher's head. Her teeth were clenched in pain, her chin jutting upward. Her lips were almost white.

"Paramedics are coming, Julia. I called 'em before this even went down. I must be psychic or something. You just gotta hold on, Julia. Hold on."

She opened her mouth, though it looked like a terrible struggle. But before she could say anything Stokes yelled out again in a voice now tinged with fear bordering on hysteria.

"I did not do that, man. Don't let them kill me, man. I didn't DO it!"

Bosch leaned over, putting his weight on Stokes's back. He bent down and spoke in a loud voice directly into his ear.

"Shut the fuck up or I'll kill you myself!"

He turned his attention back to Brasher. Her eyes were still open. Tears were going down her cheeks.

"Julia, just a few more minutes. You've got to hang on."

He pulled the gun out of her right hand and put it on the ground, far away from Stokes. He then held her hand in both of his.

"What happened? What the hell happened?"

She opened and then closed her mouth again. Bosch could hear running feet on the ramp. He heard Edgar call his name.

"Over here!"

In a moment both Edgar and Edgewood were there.

"Julia!" Edgewood cried out. "Oh, shit!"

Without a moment's hesitation Edgewood stepped forward and delivered a vicious kick to Stokes's side.

"You motherfucker!"

He readied himself to do it again when Bosch yelled.

"No! Get back! Get away from him!"

Edgar grabbed Edgewood and pulled him away from Stokes, who had let out a hurt animal cry at the impact of the kick and was now murmuring and moaning in fear.

"Take Edgewood up and get the paramedics down here," Bosch said to Edgar. "The rovers aren't for shit down here."

Both of them seemed frozen.

"Go! Now!"

As if on cue, the sound of sirens could be heard in the distance.

"You want to help her? Go get them!"

Edgar turned Edgewood around and they both ran back toward the ramp.

Bosch turned back to Brasher. Her face was now the color of death. She was going into shock. Bosch didn't understand. It was a shoulder wound. He suddenly wondered if he had heard two shots. Had the blast and echo obscured a second shot? He checked her body again but found nothing. He didn't want to turn her to check her back for fear of causing more damage. But there was no blood coming from beneath her.

"Come on, hang in there, Julia. You can do it. You hear that? The paramedics are just about here. Just hang in there."

She opened her mouth again, jutted her chin and started to speak.

"He . . . he grabbed . . . he went for . . ."

She clenched her teeth and rocked her head back and forth on his coat. She tried to talk again.

"It wasn't . . . I'm not . . ."

Bosch leaned his face close to hers and lowered his voice to an urgent whisper.

"Shhhh, shhhh. Don't talk. Just stay alive. Concentrate, Julia. Hold fast. Stay alive. Please, stay alive."

He could feel the garage rumble with noise and vibration. In a moment red lights were bouncing off the walls and then a paramedic truck was pulling up next to them. A patrol cruiser was behind it and other uniformed officers, as well as Eyman and Leiby, were running down the ramp and flooding the garage.

"Oh God, oh please," Stokes mumbled. "Don't let it happen . . ."

The first paramedic reached them and the first thing he did was put a hand on Bosch's shoulder and gently push him back. Bosch went willingly, realizing he was only complicating things now. As he moved backward away from Brasher, her right hand suddenly grasped his forearm and pulled him back toward her. Her voice was now as thin as paper.

"Harry, don't let them —"

The paramedic put a breathing mask over her face and her words were lost.

"Officer, please get back," the paramedic said firmly.

As Bosch crawled backward on hands and knees he reached over and gripped Brasher's ankle for a moment and squeezed it.

"Julia, you'll be all right."

"Julia?" said the second paramedic as he crouched next to her with a large equipment case.

"Julia."

"Okay, Julia," the paramedic said. "I'm Eddie and that there's Charlie. We're going to fix you up here. Like your buddy just said, you're going to be all right. But you gotta be tough for us. You gotta want it, Julia. You gotta fight."

She said something that was garbled through the mask. Just one word but Bosch thought he recognized it. *Numb.*

The paramedics started stabilizing procedures, the one called Eddie talking to her all the while. Bosch got up and moved over to Stokes. He pulled him up into a standing position and pushed him away from the rescue scene.

"My ribs are broken," Stokes complained. "I need the paramedics."

"Trust me, Stokes, there's nothing they can do about it. So just shut the fuck up."

Two uniforms came up to them. Bosch recognized them from the other night when they had told Julia they would meet her at Boardner's. Her friends.

"We'll take him to the station for you."

Bosch pushed Stokes past them without hesitation.

"No, I got him."

"You need to stay here for OIS, Detective Bosch."

They were right. The Officer Involved Shooting team would soon descend on the scene and Bosch would be questioned as a primary witness. But he wasn't putting Stokes into any hands he did not explicitly trust.

He walked Stokes up the ramp toward the light.

"Listen, Stokes, you want to live?"

The younger man didn't answer. He was walking with his upper body hunched forward because of the injury to his ribs. Bosch tapped him lightly in the spot Edgewood had kicked him. Stokes groaned loudly.

"Are you listening?" Bosch asked. "Do you want to stay alive?"

"Yes! I want to stay alive."

"Then you listen to me. I'm going to put you in a room and you don't talk to anybody but me. You understand that?"

"I understand. Just don't let them hurt me. I didn't do anything. I don't know what happened, man. She said get against the wall and I did what I was told. I swear to God all I did was —"

"Shut up!" Bosch ordered.

More cops were coming down the ramp and he just wanted to get Stokes out of there.

When they got to daylight, Bosch saw Edgar standing on the sidewalk talking on his cell phone and using his other hand to signal a transport ambulance into the parking garage. Bosch pushed Stokes toward him. As they approached, Edgar closed the phone.

"I just talked to the lieutenant. She's on the way."

"Great. Where's your car?"

"Still at the car wash."

"Go get it. We're taking Stokes to the division."

"Harry, we can't just leave the scene of a —"

"You saw what Edgewood did. We need to get this shit-bag to a place of safety. Go get your car. If we get any shit for it, I'll take it."

"You got it."

Edgar started running in the direction of the car wash.

Bosch saw a utility pole near the corner of the apartment building. He walked Stokes to it and recuffed him with his arms around it.

"Wait here," he said.

He then stepped away and ran a hand through his hair.

"What the hell happened back there?"

He didn't realize he had spoken out loud until Stokes started answering the question, stammering about him not doing anything wrong.

"Shut up," Bosch said. "I wasn't talking to you."

32

Bosch and Edgar walked Stokes through the squad room and down the short hallway leading to the interview rooms. They took him into room 3 and cuffed him to the steel ring bolted to the middle of the table.

"We'll be back," Bosch said.

"Hey, man, don't leave me in here," Stokes began. "They'll come in here, man."

"Nobody's coming in but me," Bosch said. "Just sit tight."

They left the room and locked it. Bosch went to the homicide table. The squad room was completely empty. When a cop went down in the division everybody responded. It was part of keeping the faith in the blue religion. If it was you who went down, you'd want everybody coming. So you responded in kind.

Bosch needed a smoke, he needed time to think and he needed some answers. His mind was crowded with thoughts about Julia and her condition. But he knew it was out of his hands and the best way to control his thoughts was to concentrate on something still in his hands.

He knew he had little time before the OIS detail would pick up the trail and come for him and Stokes. He picked up the phone and called the watch office. Mankiewicz answered. He was probably the last cop in the station.

"What's the latest?" Bosch asked. "How is she?"

"I don't know. I hear it's bad. Where are you?"

"In the squad. I've got the guy here."

"Harry, what are you doing? OIS is all over this. You should be at the scene. Both of you."

"Let's just say I was fearful of a deteriorating situation. Listen, let me know the minute you hear something about Julia, okay?"

"You got it."

Bosch was about to hang up when he remembered something.

"And Mank, listen. Your guy Edgewood tried to kick the shit out of the suspect. He was cuffed and on the ground at the time. He's probably got four or five broken ribs."

Bosch waited. Mankiewicz didn't say anything.

"Your choice. I can go formal with it or I can let you take care of it your way."

"I'll take care of it."

"All right. Remember, let me know what you know."

He hung up and looked at Edgar, who nodded his approval on the way Bosch was handling the Edgewood matter.

"What about Stokes?" Edgar said. "Harry, what the fuck happened in that garage?"

"I'm not sure. Listen, I'm going to go in there and talk to him about Arthur Delacroix, see what I can get before OIS storms the place and takes him away. When they get here, see if you can stall them."

"Yeah, and this Saturday I'm planning to kick Tiger Woods's ass on Riviera."

"Yeah, I know."

Bosch went into the rear hallway and was about to enter room 3 when he realized he had not gotten his recorder back from Detective Bradley of IAD. He wanted to record his interview with Stokes. He walked past the door to room 3 and stepped into the adjoining video room. He turned on the room 3 camera and auxiliary recorder and then went back to room 3.

Bosch sat across from Stokes. The life appeared drained from the younger man's eyes. Less than an hour before he had been waxing a BMW, picking up a few bucks. Now he was looking at a return to prison — if he was lucky. He knew cop blood in the water brought out the blue sharks. Many were the suspects who were shot trying to escape or inexplicably hung themselves in rooms just like this. Or so it was explained to the reporters.

"Do yourself a big favor," Bosch said. "Calm the fuck down and don't do anything stupid. Don't do anything with these people that gets you killed. You understand me?"

Stokes nodded.

Bosch saw the package of Marlboros in the breast pocket of Stokes's jumpsuit. He reached across the table, causing Stokes to flinch.

"Relax."

He took the pack of cigarettes and fired one up with a match from a book slipped behind the cellophane. From the corner of the room he pulled a small trash can next to his chair and dropped in the match.

"If I wanted to hurt you I would've done it in the garage. Thanks for the smoke."

Bosch savored the smoke. It had been at least two months since he'd had a cigarette.

"Can I have one?" Stokes asked.

"No, you don't deserve one. You don't deserve shit. But I'm going to make a little deal with you here."

Stokes raised his eyes to Bosch's.

"You know that little kick in the ribs you got back there? I'll trade you. You forget about it and take it like a man and I'll forget about you spraying me in the face with that shit."

"My ribs are broke, man."

"My eyes still burn, man. That was a commercial cleaning chemical. The DA will be able to get assault on a police officer out of that faster than you can say five to ten in Corcoran. You remember being in the Cork, don't you?"

Bosch let that sink in for a long moment.

"So do we have a deal?"

Stokes nodded but said, "What difference is it going to make? They're going to say I shot her. I —"

"But I know you didn't."

Bosch saw a glimmer of hope returning to Stokes's eyes.

"And I will tell them exactly what I saw."

"Okay."

Stokes's voice was barely a whisper.

"So let's start at the start. Why'd you run?"

Stokes shook his head.

"Because it's what I do, man. I run. I'm a convict and you're the Man. I run."

Bosch realized that in all of the confusion and haste, nobody had searched Stokes. He told him to stand up, which could only be accomplished by Stokes leaning over the table because of his shackled wrists. Bosch moved around behind him and started checking his pockets.

"You got any needles?"

"No, man, no needles."

"Good, I don't want to get stuck. I get stuck and all deals are off."

As he searched he held the cigarette in his lips. The smoke stung his already burning eyes. Bosch took out a wallet, a set of keys and roll of cash totaling $27 in ones. Stokes's tips for the day. There was nothing else. If Stokes had been carrying drugs for sale or personal use, he had tossed them while trying to make his escape.

"They'll be out there with dogs," Bosch said. "If you

tossed a stash, they'll find it and there won't be anything I can do about it."

"I didn't toss anything. If they find something, they planted it."

"Yeah. Just like O.J."

Bosch sat back down.

"What was the first thing I said to you? I said, 'I just want to talk.' It was the truth. All of this . . ."

Bosch made a sweeping gesture with his hands.

"It could have all been avoided if you had just listened."

"Cops never want to talk. They always want something more."

Bosch nodded. He had never been surprised by how accurate the street knowledge of ex-convicts was.

"Tell me about Arthur Delacroix."

Confusion tightened Stokes's eyes.

"What? Who?"

"Arthur Delacroix. Your skateboard buddy. From the Miracle Mile days. Remember?"

"Jesus, man, that was —"

"A long time ago. I know. That's why I'm asking."

"What about him? He's long gone, man."

"Tell me about him. Tell me about when he disappeared."

Stokes looked down at his cuffed hands and slowly shook his head.

"That was a long time ago. I can't remember that."

"Try. Why did he disappear?"

"I don't know. He just couldn't take no more of the shit and ran away."

"Did he tell you he was running away?"

"No, man, he just left. One day he was just gone. And I never saw him again."

"What shit?"

"What do you mean?"

"You said he couldn't take any more of the shit and ran away. That shit. What are you talking about?"

"Oh, you know, like all the shit in his life."

"Did he have trouble at home?"

Stokes laughed. He mocked Bosch in an imitation.

"'Did he have trouble at home?' Like, who didn't, man?"

"Was he abused — physically abused — at home? is what I mean."

Again, laughter.

"Who wasn't? My old man, he'd rather take a shot at me than talk to me about anything. When I was twelve he hit me from across the room with a full can of beer. Just because I ate a taco he wanted. They took me away from him for that."

"You know, that's a real shame, but we're talking about Arthur Delacroix here. Did he ever tell you his father hit him?"

"He didn't have to, man. I saw the bruises. The guy always had a black eye is what I remember."

"That was from skateboarding. He fell a lot."

Stokes shook his head.

"Fuck that, man. Artie was the best. That's all he did. He was too good to get hurt."

Bosch's feet were flat on the floor. He could tell by the sudden vibrations through his soles that there were people in the squad room now. He reached over and pushed the button lock on the doorknob.

"You remember when he was in the hospital? He'd hurt his head. Did he tell you that it was from a skateboarding accident?"

Stokes knitted his brow and looked down. Bosch had jogged loose a direct memory. He could tell.

"I remember he had a shaved head and stitches like a fucking zipper. I can't remember what he —"

Someone tried the door from the outside and then there was a harsh banging on the door. A muffled voice came through.

"Detective Bosch, this is Lieutenant Gilmore, OIS. Open the door."

Stokes suddenly reared back, panic filling his eyes.

"No! Don't let them —"

"Shut up!"

Bosch leaned across the table, grabbed Stokes by the collar and pulled him forward.

"Listen to me, this is important."

There was another knock on the door.

"Are you saying that Arthur never told you his father hurt him?"

"Look, man, take care of me here and I'll say whatever the fuck you want me to say. Okay? His father was an asshole. You want me to say Artie told me his father beat him with the goddamn broomstick, I'll say it. You want it to be a baseball bat? Fine, I'll say —"

"I don't want you to say anything but the truth, goddammit. Did he ever tell you that or not?"

The door came open. They had gotten a key from the drawer at the front desk. Two men in suits came in. Gilmore, whom Bosch recognized, and another OIS detective Bosch didn't recognize.

"All right, this is over," Gilmore announced. "Bosch, what the fuck are you doing?"

"Did he?" Bosch said to Stokes.

The other OIS detective took keys from his pocket and started taking the cuffs off of Stokes's wrists.

"I didn't do anything," Stokes started to protest. "I didn't —"

"Did he ever tell you?" Bosch yelled.

"Get him out of here," Gilmore barked to the other detective. "Put him in another room."

The detective physically lifted Stokes from his seat and half carried, half pushed him out of the room. Bosch's cuffs remained on the table. Bosch stared blankly at them, thinking of the answers Stokes had given him and feeling a terrible weight on his chest from the knowledge that the whole thing had been a dead end. Stokes added nothing to the case. Julia had been shot and it was for nothing.

He finally looked up at Gilmore, who closed the door and then turned to face Bosch.

"Now, like I said, what the fuck were you doing, Bosch?"

33

GILMORE twiddled a pencil in his fingers, drumming the eraser on the table. Bosch never trusted an investigator who took notes in pencil. But that's what the Officer Involved Shooting team was all about, making stories and facts fit the picture the department wanted to present to the public. It was a pencil squad. To get it right often meant using the pencil and eraser, never ink, never a tape recorder.

"So we're going to go over this again," he said. "Tell me once more, what did Officer Brasher do?"

Bosch looked past him. He had been moved to the suspect's chair in the interview room. He was facing the mirror — the one-way glass behind which he was sure there were at least a half dozen people, probably including Deputy Chief Irving. He wondered if anybody had noticed that the video had been running. If they had, it would have immediately been shut off.

"Somehow she shot herself."

"And you saw this."

"Not exactly. I saw it from the rear. Her back was to me."

"Then how do you know she shot herself?"

"Because there was no one else there but her, me and

Stokes. I didn't shoot her and Stokes didn't shoot her. She shot herself."

"During the struggle with Stokes."

Bosch shook his head.

"No, there was no struggle at the moment of the shooting. I don't know what happened before I got there, but at the moment of the shooting Stokes had both hands flat on the wall and his back to her when the gun went off. Officer Brasher had her hand on his back, holding him in place. I saw her step back from him and drop her hand. I didn't see the gun but I then heard the shot and saw the flash originate in front of her. And she went down."

Gilmore drummed his pencil loudly on the table.

"That's probably messing up the recording," Bosch said. "Oh, that's right, you guys never put anything on tape."

"Never mind that. Then what happened?"

"I started moving toward them at the wall. Stokes started to turn to see what had happened. From the ground Officer Brasher raised her right arm and took aim with her weapon at Stokes."

"But she didn't fire, did she?"

"No. I yelled 'Freeze!' to Stokes and she did not fire and he did not move. I then moved to the scene and put Stokes on the ground. I handcuffed him. I then used the radio to call for help and tried to tend to Officer Brasher's wound as best I could."

Gilmore was also chewing gum in a loud way that annoyed Bosch. He worked it for several chews before speaking.

"See, what I'm not getting here is why would she shoot herself?"

"You'll have to ask her that. I'm only telling you what I saw."

"Yeah, but I'm asking you. You were there. What do you think?"

Bosch waited a long moment. Things had happened so fast. He had put off thinking about the garage by concentrating on Stokes. Now the images of what he had seen kept replaying in his mind. He finally shrugged.

"I don't know."

"I'll tell you what, let's go your way with it for a minute. Let's assume she was re-holstering her weapon — which would have been against procedures, but let's assume it for the sake of argument. She's reholstering so she can cuff the guy. Her holster is on her right hip and the entry wound is on the left shoulder. How does that happen?"

Bosch thought about Brasher's questioning him a few nights earlier about the scar on his left shoulder. About being shot and what it had felt like. He felt the room closing in, getting tight on him. He started sweating.

"I don't know," he said.

"You don't know very much, do you, Bosch?"

"I only know what I saw. I told you what I saw."

Bosch wished they hadn't taken away Stokes's pack of cigarettes.

"What was your relationship with Officer Brasher?"

Bosch looked down at the table.

"What do you mean?"

"From what I hear you were fucking her. That's what I mean."

"What's it have to do with anything?"

"I don't know. Maybe you tell me."

Bosch didn't answer. He worked hard not to show the fury building inside.

"Well, first off, this relationship of yours was a violation of department policy," Gilmore said. "You know that, don't you?"

"She's in patrol. I'm in detective services."

"You think that matters? That doesn't matter. You're a D-three. That's supervisor level. She's a grunt and a rookie no less. If this was the military you'd get a dishonorable just for starters. Maybe even some custody time."

"But this is the LAPD. So what's it get me, a promotion?"

That was the first offensive move Bosch had made. It was a warning to Gilmore to go another way. It was a veiled reference to several well-known and not so well-known dalliances between high-ranking officers and members of the rank and file. It was known that the police union, which represented the rank and file to the level of sergeant, was waiting with the goods ready to challenge any disciplinary action taken under the department's so-called sexual harassment policy.

"I don't need any smart remarks from you," Gilmore said. "I'm trying to conduct an investigation here."

He followed this with an extended drum roll while he looked at the few notes he had written on his pad. What he was doing, Bosch knew, was conducting a reverse investigation. Start with a conclusion and then gather only the facts that support it.

"How are your eyes?" Gilmore finally asked without looking up.

"One of them still stings like a son of a bitch. They feel like poached eggs."

"Now, you say that Stokes hit you in the face with a shot from his bottle of cleaner."

"Correct."

"And it momentarily blinded you."

"Correct."

Now Gilmore stood up and started pacing in the small space behind his chair.

"How long between the moment you were blinded and when you were down in that dark garage and supposedly saw her shoot herself?"

Bosch thought for a moment.

"Well, I used a hose to wash my eyes, then I followed the pursuit. I would say not more than five minutes. But not too much less."

"So you went from blind man to eagle scout — able to see everything — inside of five minutes."

"I wouldn't characterize it like that but you have the time right."

"Well, at least I got something right. Thank you."

"No problem, Lieutenant."

"So you're saying you didn't see the struggle for control of Officer Brasher's gun before the shot occurred. Is that correct?"

He had his hands clasped behind his back, the pencil between two fingers like a cigarette. Bosch leaned across the table. He understood the game of semantics Gilmore was playing.

"Don't play with the words, Lieutenant. There was no struggle. I saw no struggle because there was no struggle. If there had been a struggle I would have seen it. Is that clear enough for you?"

Gilmore didn't respond. He kept pacing.

"Look," Bosch said, "why don't you just go do a GSR test on Stokes? His hands, his jumpsuit. You won't find anything. That should end this pretty quick."

Gilmore came back to his chair and leaned down on it. He looked at Bosch and shook his head.

"You know, Detective, I would love to do that. Normally in a situation like this, first thing we'd do is look for gunshot residue. The problem is, you broke the box. You took it upon yourself to take Stokes out of the crime scene and bring him back here. The chain of evidence was broken, you understand that? He could've washed himself, changed his clothes, I don't know what else, because you took it upon yourself to take him from the crime scene."

Bosch was ready for that.

"I felt there was a safety issue there. My partner will back me on that. So will Stokes. And he was never out of my custody and control until you came busting in here."

"That doesn't change the fact that you thought your case was more important than us getting the facts about a shooting of an officer of this department, does it?"

Bosch had no answer for that. But he was now coming to a full understanding of what Gilmore was doing. It was important for him and the department to conclude and be able to announce that Brasher was shot during a struggle for control of her gun. It was heroic that way. And it was something the department public relations machine could take advantage of and run with. There was nothing like the shooting of a good cop — a female rookie, no less — in the line of duty to help remind the public of all that was good and noble about their police department and all that was dangerous about the police officer's duty.

The alternative, to announce that Brasher had shot herself accidentally — or even something worse — would be an embarrassment for the department. One more in a long line of public relations fiascos.

Standing in the way of the conclusion Gilmore — and therefore Irving and the department brass — wanted was Stokes, of course, and then Bosch. Stokes was no problem. A convicted felon facing prison time for shooting a cop, whatever he said would be self-serving and unimportant. But Bosch was an eyewitness with a badge. Gilmore had to change his account or failing that, taint it. The first soft spot to attack was Bosch's physical condition — considering what had been thrown in his eyes, could he actually have seen what he claimed to have seen? The second move was to go after Bosch the detective. In order to preserve Stokes as a witness in his murder case, would Bosch go so far as to lie about seeing Stokes shoot a cop?

To Bosch, it was so outlandish as to be bizarre. But

over the years he had seen even worse things happen to cops who had stepped in front of the machinery that produced the image of the department that was delivered to the public.

"Wait a minute, you —" Bosch said, able to hold himself from calling a superior officer an expletive. "If you're trying to say I would lie about Stokes shooting Julia — uh, Officer Brasher — so he would stay in the clear for my case, then you — with all due respect — are out of your fucking mind."

"Detective Bosch, I am exploring all possibilities here. It is my job to do so."

"Well, you can explore them without me."

Bosch stood up and went to the door.

"Where are you going?"

"I'm done with this."

He glanced at the mirror and opened the door, then looked back at Gilmore.

"I got news for you, Lieutenant. Your theory is for shit. Stokes is nothing to my case. A zero. Julia getting shot, it was for nothing."

"But you didn't know that until you got him in here, did you?"

Bosch looked at him and then slowly shook his head.

"Have a good day, Lieutenant."

He turned to go through the door and almost stepped into Irving. The deputy chief stood ramrod straight in the hallway outside the room.

"Step back inside for a moment, Detective," he said calmly. "Please."

Bosch backed into the room. Irving followed him in.

"Lieutenant, give us some space here," the deputy chief said. "And I want everyone out of the viewing room as well."

He pointed at the mirror as he said this.

"Yes, sir," Gilmore said and he left the room, closing the door behind him.

"Take your seat again," Irving said.

Bosch moved back to the seat facing the mirror. Irving remained standing. After a moment he also started pacing, moving back and forth in front of the mirror, a double image for Bosch to track.

"We are going to call the shooting accidental," Irving said, not looking at Bosch. "Officer Brasher apprehended the suspect and while reholstering her weapon inadvertently fired the shot."

"Is that what she said?" Bosch asked.

Irving looked momentarily confused, then shook his head.

"As far as I know, she only spoke to you and you said she didn't say anything specifically in regard to the shooting."

Bosch nodded.

"So that's the end of it?"

"I don't see why it should go any further."

Bosch thought of the photo of the shark on Julia's mantel. About what he knew about her in such a short time with her. Again the images of what he saw in the garage played back in slow motion. And things didn't add up.

"If we can't be honest with ourselves, how can we ever tell the truth to the people out there?"

Irving cleared his throat.

"I am not going to debate things with you, Detective. The decision has been made."

"By you."

"Yes, by me."

"What about Stokes?"

"That will be up to the District Attorney's Office. He could be charged under the felony-murder law. His action

of fleeing ultimately led to the shooting. It will get techni-
cal. If it is determined he was already in custody when the
fatal shot occurred, then he might be able to —"

"Wait a minute, wait a minute," Bosch said, coming out
of his chair. "Felony-*murder* law? Did you say *fatal* shot?"

Irving turned to face him.

"Lieutenant Gilmore did not tell you?"

Bosch dropped back into the chair and put his elbows on
the table. He covered his face with his hands.

"The bullet hit a bone in her shoulder and apparently
ricocheted inside her body. It cut through her chest.
Pierced her heart. And she was dead on arrival."

Bosch lowered his face so that his hands were now on
top of his head. He felt himself get dizzy and he thought he
might fall out of the chair. He tried to breathe deeply until
it passed. After a few moments Irving spoke into the darkness of his mind.

"Detective, there are some officers in this department
they call 'shit magnets.' I am sure you have heard the term.
Personally, I find the phrase distasteful. But its meaning is
that things always seem to happen to these particular officers. Bad things. Repeatedly. Always."

Bosch waited in the dark for what he knew was coming.

"Unfortunately, Detective Bosch, you are one of those
officers."

Bosch unconsciously nodded. He was thinking about
the moment that the paramedic put the breathing mask
over Julia's mouth as she was speaking.

Don't let them —

What did she mean? Don't let them what? He was
beginning to put things together and to know what she was
going to say.

"Detective," Irving said, his strong voice cutting through
Bosch's thoughts. "I have shown tremendous patience with

you over the cases and over the years. But I have grown tired of it. So has this department. I want you to start thinking about retirement. Soon, Detective. Soon."

Bosch kept his head down and didn't respond. After a moment he heard the door open and close.

34

In keeping with the wishes of Julia Brasher's family that she be buried in accordance with her faith, her funeral was late the next morning at Hollywood Memorial Park. Because she had been killed accidentally while in the line of duty, she was accorded the full police burial ceremony, complete with motorcycle procession, honor guard, twenty-one-gun salute and a generous showing of the department's brass at graveside. The department's aero squadron also flew over the cemetery, five helicopters flying in "missing man" formation.

But because the funeral was not even twenty-four hours after her death it was not well attended. Line-of-duty deaths routinely bring at least token representations of officers from departments all over the state and the southwest. It was not to be with Julia Brasher. The quickness of the ceremony and the circumstances of her death added up to it being a relatively small affair — by police burial standards. A death in a gun battle would have crowded the small cemetery from stone to stone with the trappings of the blue religion. A cop killing herself while holstering her weapon did not engender much of the mythology and danger of police work. The funeral simply wasn't a draw.

Bosch watched from the outer edges of the funeral

group. His head was throbbing from a night of drinking and trying to dull the guilt and pain he felt. Bones had come out of the ground and now two people were dead for reasons that made little sense to him. His eyes were badly bloodshot and swollen but he knew he could pass that off, if he had to, to being sprayed with the tire cleaner by Stokes the day before.

He saw Teresa Corazon, for once without her videographer, seated in the front row line of brass and dignitaries, what few of them there were in attendance. She wore sunglasses but Bosch could tell when she had noticed him. Her mouth seemed to settle into a hard, thin line. A perfect funeral smile.

Bosch was the first to look away.

It was a beautiful day for a funeral. Brisk overnight winds from the Pacific had temporarily cleared the smog out of the sky. Even the view of the Valley from Bosch's home had been clear that morning. Cirrus clouds scudded across the upper reaches of the sky along with contrails left by high-flying jets. The air in the cemetery smelled sweet from all the flowers arranged near the grave. From his standpoint, Bosch could see the crooked letters of the Hollywood sign, high up on Mount Lee, presiding over the service.

The chief of police did not deliver the eulogy as was his custom in line-of-duty deaths. Instead, the academy commander spoke, using the moment to talk about how danger in police work always comes from the unexpected corner and how Officer Brasher's death might save other cops by being a reminder never to let down the guard of caution. He never called her anything but Officer Brasher during his ten-minute speech, giving it an embarrassingly impersonal touch.

During the whole thing Bosch kept thinking about photos of sharks with open mouths and volcanoes disgorging their molten flows. He wondered if Julia had finally proven herself to the person she believed she needed to.

Amidst the blue uniforms surrounding the silver casket was a swath of gray. The lawyers. Her father and a large contingent from the firm. In the second row behind Brasher's father Bosch could see the man from the photo on the mantel of the Venice bungalow. For a while Bosch fantasized about going up to him and slapping him or bringing a knee up into his genitals. Doing it right in the middle of the service for all to see, then pointing to the casket and telling the man that he sent her on the path to this.

But he let it go. He knew that explanation and assignment of blame was too simple and wrong. Ultimately, he knew, people chose their own path. They can be pointed and pushed, but they always get the final choice. Everybody's got a cage that keeps out the sharks. Those who open the door and venture out do so at their own risk.

Seven members of Brasher's rookie class were chosen for the salute. They pointed rifles toward the blue sky and fired three rounds of blanks each, the ejected brass jackets arcing through the light and falling to the grass like tears. While the shots were still echoing off the stones, the helicopters made their pass overhead and then the funeral was over.

Bosch slowly made his way toward the grave, passing people heading away. A hand tugged his elbow from behind and he turned around. It was Brasher's partner, Edgewood.

"I, uh, just wanted to apologize about yesterday, about what I did," he said. "It won't happen again."

Bosch waited for him to make eye contact and then just nodded. He had nothing to say to Edgewood.

"I guess you didn't mention it to OIS and I, uh, just want to say I appreciate it."

Bosch just looked at him. Edgewood became uncomfortable, nodded once and walked away. When he was gone Bosch found himself looking at a woman who had been standing right behind the cop. A Latina with silver hair. It took Bosch a moment to recognize her.

"Dr. Hinojos."

"Detective Bosch, how are you?"

It was the hair. Almost seven years earlier, when Bosch had been a regular visitor to Hinojos's office, her hair had been a deep brown without a hint of gray. She was still an attractive woman, gray or brown. But the change was startling.

"I'm doing okay. How're things in the psych shop?"

She smiled.

"They're fine."

"I hear you run the whole show now."

She nodded. Bosch felt himself getting nervous. When he had known her before, he had been on an involuntary stress leave. In twice-a-week sessions he had told her things he had never told anyone before or since. And once he was returned to duty he had never spoken to her again.

Until now.

"Did you know Julia Brasher?" he asked.

It wasn't unusual for a department shrink to attend a line-of-duty funeral; to offer on-the-spot counseling to those close to the deceased.

"No, not really. Not personally. As head of the department I reviewed her academy application and screening interview. I signed off on it."

She waited a moment, studying Bosch for a reaction.

"I understand you were close to her. And that you were there. You were the witness."

Bosch nodded. People leaving the funeral were passing on both sides of them. Hinojos took a step closer to him so that she would not be overheard.

"This is not the time or place but, Harry, I want to talk to you about her."

"What's there to talk about?"

"I want to know what happened. And why."

"It was an accident. Talk to Chief Irving."

"I have and I'm not satisfied. I doubt you are, either."

"Listen, Doctor, she's dead, okay? I'm not going to —"

"I signed off on her. My signature put that badge on her. If we missed something — if I missed something — I want to know. If there were signs, we should have seen them."

Bosch nodded and looked down at the grass between them.

"Don't worry, there were signs I should've seen. But I didn't put it together either."

She took another step closer. Now Bosch could look nowhere but directly at her.

"Then I am right. There is something more to this."

He nodded.

"Nothing overt. It's just that she lived close to the edge. She took risks — she crossed the tube. She was trying to prove something. I don't think she was even sure she wanted to be a cop."

"Prove something to who?"

"I don't know. Maybe herself, maybe somebody else."

"Harry, I knew you as a man of great instincts. What else?"

Bosch shrugged.

"It's just things she did or said. . . . I have a scar on my shoulder from a bullet wound. She asked me about it. The other night. She asked how I got shot and I told her how I had been lucky that it hit me where it did because it was all bone. Then . . . where she shot herself, it's the same spot. Only with her . . . it ricocheted. She didn't expect that."

Hinojos nodded and waited.

"What I've been thinking I can't stand thinking, know what I mean?"

"Tell me, Harry."

"I keep replaying it in my head. What I saw and what I

know. She pointed her gun at him. And I think if I hadn't been there and yelled that maybe she would have shot him. Once he was down she would have wrapped his hands around the gun and fired a shot into the ceiling or maybe a car. Or maybe into him. It wouldn't matter as long as he ended up dead with paraffin on his hands and she could claim he went for her gun."

"What are you suggesting, that she shot herself in order to kill him and make herself look like a hero?"

"I don't know. She talked about the world needing heroes. Especially now. She said she hoped to get a chance to be a hero one day. But I think there was something else in all of this. It was like she wanted the scar, the experience of it."

"And she was willing to kill for it?"

"I don't know. I don't know if I'm even right about any of this. All I know is that she might have been a rookie but she had already reached the point where there was a line between us and them, where everybody without a badge is a scumbag. She saw it happening to herself. She might have been just looking for a way out . . ."

Bosch shook his head and looked off to the side. The cemetery was almost deserted now.

"I don't know. Saying it out loud makes it sound . . . I don't know. It's a crazy world."

He took a step back from Hinojos.

"I guess you never really know anybody, do you?" he asked. "You might think you do. You might be close enough to sleep with somebody but you'll never know what's really going on inside."

"No, you won't. Everybody's got secrets."

Bosch nodded and was about to step away.

"Wait, Harry."

She lifted her purse and opened it. She started digging through it.

"I still want to talk about this," she said as she came out with a business card and handed it to him. "I want you to call me. Completely unofficial, confidential. For the good of the department."

Bosch almost laughed.

"The department doesn't care about it. The department cares about the image, not the truth. And when the truth endangers the image, then fuck the truth."

"Well, I care, Harry. And so do you."

Bosch looked down at the card and nodded and put it in his pocket.

"Okay, I'll call you."

"My cell phone's on there. I carry it with me all the time."

Bosch nodded. She stepped forward and reached out. She grasped his arm and squeezed it.

"What about you, Harry? Are you okay?"

"Well, other than losing her and being told by Irving to start thinking about retiring, I'm doing okay."

Hinojos frowned.

"Hang in there, Harry."

Bosch nodded, thinking about how he had used the same words with Julia at the end.

Hinojos went off and Bosch continued his trek to the grave. He thought he was alone now. He grabbed a handful of dirt from the fill mound and walked over and looked down. A whole bouquet and several single flowers had been dropped on top of the casket. Bosch thought about holding Julia in his bed just two nights before. He wished he had seen what was coming. He wished he had been able to take the hints and put them into a clear picture of what she was doing and where she was going.

Slowly, he raised his hand out and let the dirt slide through his fingers.

"City of bones," he whispered.

He watched the dirt fall into the grave like dreams disappearing.

"I assume you knew her."

Bosch quickly turned. It was her father. Smiling sadly. They were the only two left in the cemetery. Bosch nodded.

"Just recently. I got to know her. I'm sorry for your loss."

"Frederick Brasher."

He put out his hand. Bosch started to take it but then held up.

"My hand's dirty."

"Don't worry. So is mine."

They shook hands.

"Harry Bosch."

Brasher's hand stopped its shaking movement for a moment as the name registered.

"The detective," he said. "You were there yesterday."

"Yes. I tried . . . I did what I could to help her. I . . ."

He stopped. He didn't know what to say.

"I'm sure you did. It must've been an awful thing to be there."

Bosch nodded. A wave of guilt passed through him like an X-ray lighting his bones. He had left her there, thinking she would be all right. Somehow it hurt almost as bad as the fact she had died.

"What I don't understand is how it happened," Brasher said. "A mistake like that, how could it kill her? And then the District Attorney's Office today saying this man Stokes would not face any charge in the shooting. I'm a lawyer but I just don't understand. They are letting him go."

Bosch studied the older man, saw the misery in his eyes.

"I'm sorry, sir. I wish I could tell you. I have the same questions as you."

Brasher nodded and looked into the grave.

"I'm going now," he said after a long moment. "Thank you for coming, Detective Bosch."

Bosch nodded. They shook hands again and Brasher started to walk away.

"Sir?" Bosch asked.

Brasher turned back.

"Do you know when someone from the family will be going to her house?"

"Actually, I was given her keys today. I was going to go now. Take a look at things. Try to get a sense of her, I guess. In recent years we hadn't . . ."

He didn't finish. Bosch stepped closer to him.

"There's something that she had. A picture in a frame. If it's not . . . if it's okay with you, I'd like to keep it."

Brasher nodded.

"Why don't you come now? Meet me there. Show me this picture."

Bosch looked at his watch. Lt. Billets had scheduled a one-thirty meeting to discuss the status of the case. He probably had just enough time to make it to Venice and back to the station. There would be no time for lunch but he couldn't see himself eating anything anyway.

"Okay, I will."

They parted and headed toward their cars. On the way Bosch stopped on the grass where the salute had been fired. Combing the grass with his foot, he looked until he saw the glint of brass and bent down to pick up one of the ejected rifle shells. He held it on his palm and looked at it for a few moments, then closed his hand and dropped it into his coat pocket. He had picked up a shell from every cop funeral he had ever attended. He had a jar full of them.

He turned and walked out of the cemetery.

35

Jerry Edgar had a warrant knock that sounded like no other Bosch had ever heard. Like a gifted athlete who can focus the forces of his whole body into the swinging of a bat or the dunking of a basketball, Edgar could put his whole weight and six-foot-four frame into his knock. It was as though he could call down and concentrate all the power and fury of the righteous into the fist of his large left hand. He'd plant his feet firmly and stand sideways to the door. He'd raise his left arm, bend the elbow to less than thirty degrees and hit the door with the fleshy side of his fist. It was a backhand knock, but he was able to fire the pistons of this muscle assembly so quickly that it sounded like the staccato bark of a machine gun. What it sounded like was Judgment Day.

Samuel Delacroix's aluminum-skinned trailer seemed to shudder from end to end when Edgar hit its door with his fist at 3:30 on Thursday afternoon. Edgar waited a few seconds and then hit it again, this time announcing "POLICE!" and then stepping back off the stoop, which was a stack of unconnected concrete blocks.

They waited. Neither had a weapon out but Bosch had his hand under his jacket and was gripping his gun in its holster. It was his standard procedure when delivering a warrant on a person not believed to be dangerous.

Bosch listened for movements from inside but the hiss from the nearby freeway was too loud. He checked the windows; none of the closed curtains were moving.

"You know," Bosch whispered, "I'm starting to think it comes as a relief when you yell it's just the cops after that knock. At least then they know it's not an earthquake."

Edgar didn't respond. He probably knew it was just nervous banter from Bosch. It wasn't anxiety about the door knock — Bosch fully expected Delacroix to be easy. He was anxious because he knew the case was all coming down to the next few hours with Delacroix. They would search the trailer and then have to make a decision, largely communicated in partners' code, on whether to arrest Delacroix for his son's murder. Somewhere in that process they would need to find the evidence or elicit the confession that would change a case largely built on theory into one built on lawyer-resistant fact.

So in Bosch's mind they were quickly approaching the moment of truth, and that always made him nervous.

Earlier, in the case status meeting with Lt. Billets, it had been decided that it was time to talk to Sam Delacroix. He was the victim's father, he was the chief suspect. What little evidence they had still pointed to him. They spent the next hour typing up a search warrant for Delacroix's trailer and taking it to the downtown criminal courts building to a judge who was normally a soft touch.

But even this judge took some convincing. The problem was the case was old, the evidence directly linking the suspect was thin and the place Bosch and Edgar wanted to search was not where the homicide could have occurred and was not even occupied by the suspect at the time of the death.

What the detectives had in their favor was the emotional impact that came from the list in the warrant of all the injuries that the boy's bones indicated he had sustained over his short life. In the end, it was all those fractures that won the judge over and he signed the warrant.

They had gone to the driving range first but were informed that Delacroix was finished driving the tractor for the day.

"Give him another shot," Bosch told Edgar outside the trailer.

"I think I can hear him coming."

"I don't care. I want him rattled."

Edgar stepped back up onto the stoop and hit the door again. The concrete blocks wobbled and he didn't plant his feet firmly. The resulting knock didn't carry the power and terror of the first two assaults on the door.

Edgar stepped back down.

"That wasn't the police," Bosch whispered. "That was a neighbor complaining about the dog or something."

"Sorry, I —"

The door came open and Edgar shut up. Bosch went into high alert. Trailers were tricky. Unlike most structures, their doors opened outward so that the interior space didn't have to accommodate the swing. Bosch was positioned on the blind side, so that whoever answered was looking at Edgar but couldn't see Bosch. The problem was Bosch couldn't see whoever had opened the door either. If there was trouble Edgar's job was to yell a warning to Bosch and get himself clear. Without hesitation Bosch would empty his gun into the door of the trailer, the bullets tearing through the aluminum and whoever was on the other side like they were paper.

"What?" a man's voice said.

Edgar held up his badge. Bosch studied his partner for any warning sign of trouble.

"Mr. Delacroix, police."

Seeing no sign of alarm, Bosch stepped forward and grabbed the knob and pulled the door all the way open. He kept his jacket flipped back and his hand on the grip of his gun.

The man he had seen on the golf range the day before was standing there. He wore an old pair of plaid shorts and a washed-out maroon T-shirt with permanent stains under the arms.

"We have a warrant allowing us to search these premises," Bosch said. "Can we come in?"

"You guys," Delacroix said. "You guys were at the range yesterday."

"Sir," Bosch said forcefully, "I said that we have a search warrant for this trailer. Can we come in and conduct the search?"

Bosch took the folded warrant out of his pocket and held it up, but not within Delacroix's reach. That was the trick. To get the warrant they had to show all their cards to a judge. But they didn't want to show the same cards to Delacroix. Not just yet. So while Delacroix was entitled to read and study the warrant before granting the detectives entrance, Bosch was hoping to get inside the trailer without that happening. Delacroix would soon know the facts of the case, but Bosch wanted to control the delivery of information to him so that he could take readings and make judgments based on the suspect's reactions.

Bosch started putting the warrant back into his inside coat pocket.

"What's this about?" Delacroix asked in muted protest. "Can I at least see that thing?"

"Are you Samuel Delacroix?" Bosch replied quickly.

"Yes."

"This is your trailer, correct, sir?"

"It's my trailer. I lease the spot. I want to read the —"

"Mr. Delacroix," Edgar said. "We'd rather not stand out here in the view of your neighbors discussing this. I'm sure you don't want that either. Are you going to allow us to lawfully execute the search warrant or not?"

Delacroix looked from Bosch to Edgar and then back to Bosch. He nodded his head.

"I guess so."

Bosch was first onto the stoop. He entered, squeezing by Delacroix on the threshold and picking up the odor of bourbon and bad breath and cat urine.

"Starting early, Mr. Delacroix?"

"Yeah, I've had a drink," Delacroix said with a mixture of so-what and self-loathing in his voice. "I'm done my work. I'm entitled."

Edgar came in then, a much tighter squeeze past Delacroix, and he and Bosch scanned what they could see of the dimly lit trailer. To the right from the doorway was the living room. It was wood paneled and had a green Naugahyde couch and a coffee table with pieces of the wood veneer scraped off, exposing the particleboard beneath. There was a matching lamp table with no lamp on it and a television stand with a TV awkwardly stacked on top of a videocassette recorder. There were several videotapes stacked on top of the television. Across from the coffee table was an old recliner with its shoulders torn open — probably by a cat — and stuffing leaking out. Under the coffee table was a stack of newspapers, most of them gossip tabloids with blaring headlines.

To the left was a galley-style kitchen with sink, cabinets, stove, oven and refrigerator on one side and a four-person dining booth on the right. There was a bottle of Ancient Age bourbon on the table. On the floor under the table were a few crumbs of cat food on a plate and an old plastic margarine tub half full of water. There was no sign of the cat, other than the smell of its urine.

Beyond the kitchen was a narrow hallway leading back to one or two bedrooms and a bathroom.

"Let's leave the door open and open up a few windows," Bosch said. "Mr. Delacroix, why don't you sit down on the couch there?"

Delacroix moved toward the couch and said, "Look, you don't have to search the place. I know why you're here."

Bosch glanced at Edgar and then at Delacroix.

"Yeah?" Edgar said. "Why are we here?"

Delacroix dropped himself heavily into the middle of the couch. The springs were shot. He sank into the mid-section, and the ends of the cushion on either side of him rose into the air like the bows of twin *Titanic*s going down.

"The gas," Delacroix said. "And I hardly used any of it. I don't go anywhere but back and forth from the range. I have a restricted license because of my DUI."

"The gas?" Edgar asked. "What are —"

"Mr. Delacroix, we're not here about you stealing gas," Bosch said.

He picked up one of the videotapes off the stack on the television. There was tape on the spine with writing on it. *First Infantry, episode 46.* He put it back down and glanced at the writing on some of the other tapes. They were all episodes of the television show Delacroix had worked on as an actor more than thirty years before.

"That's not really our gig," he added, without looking at Delacroix.

"Then what? What do you want?"

Now Bosch looked at him.

"We're here about your son."

Delacroix stared at him for a long moment, his mouth slowly coming open and exposing his yellowed teeth.

"Arthur," he finally said.

"Yeah. We found him."

Delacroix's eyes dropped from Bosch's and seemed to

leave the trailer as he studied a far-off memory. In his look was knowledge. Bosch saw it. His instincts told him that what they would tell Delacroix next he would already know. He glanced over at Edgar to see if he had seen it. Edgar gave a single short nod.

Bosch looked back at the man on the couch.

"You don't seem very excited for a father who hasn't seen his son in more than twenty years," he said.

Delacroix looked at him.

"I guess that's because I know he's dead."

Bosch studied him for a long moment, his breath holding in his lungs.

"Why would you say that? What would make you think that?"

"Because I know. I've known all along."

"What have you known?"

"That he wasn't coming back."

This wasn't going the way of any of the scenarios Bosch had imagined. It seemed to him that Delacroix had been waiting for them, expecting them, maybe for years. He decided that they might have to change the strategy and arrest Delacroix and advise him of his rights.

"Am I under arrest?" Delacroix asked, as if he had joined Bosch in his thoughts.

Bosch glanced at Edgar again, wondering if his partner had sensed how their plan was now slipping away from them.

"We thought we might want to talk first. You know, informally."

"You might as well arrest me," Delacroix said quietly.

"You think so? Does that mean you don't want to talk to us?"

Delacroix shook his head slowly and went into the long-distance stare again.

"No, I'll talk to you," he said. "I'll tell you all about it."

"Tell us about what?"

"How it happened."

"How what happened?"

"My son."

"You know how it happened?"

"Sure I know. I did it."

Bosch almost cursed out loud. Their suspect had literally just confessed before they had advised him of his rights, including the right to avoid giving self-incriminating statements.

"Mr. Delacroix, we're going to cut this off right here. I am going to advise you of your rights now."

"I just want to —"

"No, please, sir, don't say anything else. Not yet. Let's get this rights thing taken care of and then we'll be more than happy to listen to anything you want to tell us."

Delacroix waved a hand like it didn't matter to him, like nothing mattered.

"Jerry, where's your recorder? I never got mine back from IAD."

"Uh, in the car. I don't know about the batteries, though."

"Go check."

Edgar left the trailer and Bosch waited in silence. Delacroix put his elbows on his knees and his face in his hands. Bosch studied his posture. It didn't happen often, but it wouldn't be the first time he had scored a confession during his first meeting with a suspect.

Edgar came back in with a tape recorder but shook his head.

"Batteries are dead. I thought you had yours."

"Shit. Then take notes."

Bosch took out his badge case and took out one of his business cards. He'd had them made with the Miranda rights advisory printed on the back, along with a signature line. He read the advisory statement and asked Delacroix if he understood his rights. Delacroix nodded his head.

"Is that a yes?"

"Yes, it's a yes."

"Then sign on the line beneath what I just read to you."

He gave Delacroix the card and a pen. Once it was signed, Bosch returned the card to his badge wallet. He stepped over and sat on the edge of the recliner chair.

"Now, Mr. Delacroix, do you want to repeat what you just said to us a few minutes ago?"

Delacroix shrugged like it was no big deal.

"I killed my son. Arthur. I killed him. I knew you people would show up someday. It took a long time."

Bosch looked over at Edgar. He was writing in a note-book. They would have some record of Delacroix's admission. He looked back at the suspect and waited, hoping the silence would be an invitation for Delacroix to say more. But he didn't. Instead, the suspect buried his face in his hands again. His shoulders soon began shaking as he started to cry.

"God help me . . . I did it."

Bosch looked back at Edgar and raised his eyebrows. His partner gave a quick thumbs-up sign. They had more than enough to move to the next stage; the controlled and recorded setting of an interview room at the police station.

"Mr. Delacroix, do you have a cat?" Bosch asked. "Where's your cat?"

Delacroix peeked his wet eyes through his fingers.

"He's around. Probably sleepin' in the bed. Why?"

"Well, we're going to call Animal Control and they'll come get him to take care of him. You're going to have to come with us. We're going to place you under arrest now. And we'll talk more at the police station."

Delacroix dropped his hands and seemed upset.

"No. Animal Control won't take care of him. They'll gas him the minute they find out I won't be coming back."

"Well, we can't just leave him here."

"Mrs. Kresky will take care of him. She's next door. She can come in and feed him."

Bosch shook his head. The whole thing was foundering because of a cat.

"We can't do that. We have to seal this place until we can search it."

"What do you have to search it for?" Delacroix said, real anger in his voice now. "I'm telling you what you need to know. I killed my son. It was an accident. I hit him too hard, I guess. I . . ."

Delacroix put his face back into his hands and tearfully mumbled, "God . . . what did I do?"

Bosch checked Edgar; he was writing. Bosch stood up. He wanted to get Delacroix to the station and into one of the interview rooms. His anxiety was gone now, replaced by a sense of urgency. Attacks of conscience and guilt were ephemeral. He wanted to get Delacroix locked down on tape — video and audio — before he decided to talk to a lawyer and before he realized that he was talking himself into a 9×6 room for the rest of his life.

"Okay, we'll figure out the cat thing later," he said. "We'll leave enough food for now. Stand up, Mr. Delacroix, we're going to go."

Delacroix stood up.

"Can I change into something nicer? This is just old stuff I was wearing around here."

"No, don't worry about that," Bosch said. "We'll bring you clothes to wear later on."

He didn't bother telling him that those clothes wouldn't be his. What would happen was that he'd be given a county jail–issued jumpsuit with a number across the back. His jumpsuit would be yellow, the color given to custodies on the high-power floor — the murderers.

"Are you going to handcuff me?" Delacroix asked.

"It's department policy," Bosch said. "We have to."

He came around the coffee table and turned Delacroix so he could cuff his hands behind his back.

"I was an actor, you know. I once played a prisoner in an episode of *The Fugitive*. The first series, with David Janssen. It was just a small role. I sat on a bench next to Janssen. That's all I did. I was supposed to be on drugs, I think."

Bosch didn't say anything. He gently pushed Delacroix toward the trailer's narrow door.

"I don't know why I just remembered that," Delacroix said.

"It's all right," Edgar said. "People remember the strangest things at a time like this."

"Just be careful on these steps," Bosch said.

They led him out, Edgar in front and Bosch behind him.

"Is there a key?" Bosch asked.

"On the kitchen counter there," Delacroix said.

Bosch went back inside and found the keys. He then started opening cabinets in the kitchenette until he found the box of cat food. He opened it and dumped it out onto the paper plate under the table. There was not very much food. Bosch knew he would have to do something about the animal later.

When Bosch came out of the trailer Edgar had already put Delacroix into the rear of the slickback. He saw a neighbor watching from the open front door of a nearby trailer. He turned and closed and locked Delacroix's door.

36

Bosch stuck his head into Lt. Billets's office. She was turned sideways at her desk and working on a computer at a side table. Her desk had been cleared. She was about to go home for the day.

"Yes?" she said without looking to see who it was.

"Looks like we got lucky," Bosch said.

She turned from the computer and saw it was Bosch.

"Let me guess. Delacroix invites you in and just sits down and confesses."

Bosch nodded.

"Just about."

Her eyes grew wide in surprise.

"You are fucking kidding me."

"He says he did it. We had to shut him up so we could get him back here on tape. It was like he had been waiting for us to show up."

Billets asked a few more questions and Bosch ended up recapping the entire visit to the trailer, including the problem they had in not having a working tape recorder with which to take Delacroix's confession. Billets grew concerned and annoyed, equally with Bosch and Edgar for not being prepared and Bradley of IAD for not returning Bosch's tape recorder.

"All I can say is that this better not put hair on the cake, Harry," she said, referring to the possibility of a legal challenge to any confession because Delacroix's initial words were not on tape. "If we lose this one because of a screwup on our part . . ."

She didn't finish but didn't need to.

"Look, I think we'll be all right. Edgar got everything he said down verbatim. We stopped as soon as we got enough to hook him up and now we'll lock it all down with sound and video."

Billets seemed barely placated.

"And what about Miranda? You're confident we will not have a Miranda situation," she said, the last part not a question but an order.

"I don't see it. He started spouting off before we had a chance to advise him. Then he kept talking afterward. Sometimes it goes like that. You're ready to go with the battering ram and they just open the door for you. Whoever he gets as a lawyer might have a heart attack and start screaming about it but nothing's going to come of it. We're clean, Lieutenant."

Billets nodded, a sign that Bosch was convincing her.

"I wish they were all this easy," she said. "What about the DA's office?"

"I'm calling them next."

"Okay, which room if I want to take a look?"

"Three."

"Okay, Harry, go wrap him up."

She turned back to her computer. Bosch threw a salute at her and was about to duck out of the doorway when he stopped. She sensed he had not left and turned back to him.

"What is it?"

Bosch shrugged his shoulders.

"I don't know. The whole way in I was thinking about

what could have been avoided if we just went to him instead of dancing around him, gathering string."

"Harry, I know what you're thinking and there's no way in the world you could have known that this guy — after twenty-some years — was just waiting for you to knock on his door. You handled it the right way and if you had it to do again you would still do it the same way. You circle the prey. What happened with Officer Brasher had nothing to do with how you ran this case."

Bosch looked at her for a moment and then nodded. What she said would help ease his conscience.

Billets turned back to her computer.

"Like I said, go wrap him up."

Bosch went back to the homicide table to call the District Attorney's Office to advise that an arrest had been made in a murder case and that a confession was being taken. He talked to a supervisor named O'Brien and told her that either he or his partner would be coming in to file charges by the end of the day. O'Brien, who was familiar with the case only through media reports, said she wanted to send a prosecutor to the station to oversee the handling of the confession and the forward movement of the case at this stage.

Bosch knew that with rush hour traffic out of downtown it would still be a minimum of forty-five minutes before the prosecutor got to the station. He told O'Brien the prosecutor was welcome but that he wasn't going to wait for anyone before taking the suspect's confession. O'Brien suggested he should.

"Look, this guy wants to talk," Bosch said. "In forty-five minutes or an hour it could be a different story. We can't wait. Tell your guy to knock on the door at room three when he gets here. We'll bring him into it as soon as we can."

In a perfect world the prosecutor would be there for an interview but Bosch knew from years working cases that a guilty conscience doesn't always stay guilty. When someone tells you they want to confess to a killing, you don't wait. You turn on the tape recorder and say, "Tell me all about it."

O'Brien reluctantly agreed, citing her own experiences, and they hung up. Bosch immediately picked the phone back up and called Internal Affairs and asked for Carol Bradley. He was transferred.

"This is Bosch, Hollywood Division, where's my damn tape recorder?"

There was silence in response.

"Bradley? Hello? Are you —"

"I'm here. I have your recorder here."

"Why did you take it? I told you to listen to the tape. I didn't say take my machine, I don't need it anymore."

"I wanted to review it and have the tape checked, to make sure it was continuous."

"Then open it up and take the tape. Don't take the machine."

"Detective, sometimes they need the original recorder to authenticate the tape."

Bosch shook his head in frustration.

"Jesus, why are you doing this? You know who the leak is, why are you wasting time?"

Again there was a pause before she answered.

"I needed to cover all bases. Detective, I need to run my investigation the way I see fit."

Now Bosch paused for a moment, wondering if he was missing something, if there was something else going on. He finally decided he couldn't worry about it. He had to keep his eyes on the prize. His case.

"Cover the bases, that's great," he said. "Well, I almost lost a confession today because I didn't have my machine. I would appreciate it if you would get it back to me."

"I'm finished with it and am putting it in inter-office dispatch right now."

"Thank you. Good-bye."

He hung up, just as Edgar showed up at the table with three cups of coffee. It made Bosch think of something they should do.

"Who's got the watch down there?" he asked.

"Mankiewicz was in there," Edgar said. "So was Young."

Bosch poured the coffee from the Styrofoam container into the mug he got out of his drawer. He then picked up the phone and dialed the watch office. Mankiewicz answered.

"You got anybody in the bat cave?"

"Bosch? I thought you might take some time off."

"You thought wrong. What about the cave?"

"No, nobody till about eight today. What do you need?"

"I'm about to take a confession and don't want any lawyer to be able to open the box once I wrap it. My guy smells like Ancient Age but I think he's straight. I'd like to make a record of it, just the same."

"This the bones case?"

"Yeah."

"Bring him down and I'll do it. I'm certified."

"Thanks, Mank."

He hung up and looked at Edgar.

"Let's take him down to the cave and see what he blows. Just to be safe."

"Good idea."

They took their coffees into interview room 3, where they had earlier shackled Delacroix to the table's center ring. They released him from the cuffs and let him take a few gulps of his coffee before walking him down the back hallway to the station's small jail facility. The jail essentially consisted of two large holding cells for drunks and prostitutes. Arrestees of a higher order were usually transported to the main city or county jail. There was a small third cell that was known as the bat cave, as in blood alcohol testing.

They met Mankiewicz in the hallway and followed him to the cave, where he turned on the Breathalyzer and instructed Delacroix to blow into a clear plastic tube attached to the machine. Bosch noticed that Mankiewicz had a black mourning ribbon across his badge for Brasher.

In a few minutes they had the result. Delacroix blew a .003, not even close to the legal limit for driving. There was no standard set for giving a confession to murder.

As they took Delacroix out of the tank Bosch felt Mankiewicz tap his arm from behind. He turned to face him while Edgar headed back up the hallway with Delacroix.

Mankiewicz nodded.

"Harry, I just wanted to say I'm sorry. You know, about what happened out there."

Bosch knew he was talking about Brasher. He nodded back.

"Yeah, thanks. It's a tough one."

"I had to put her out there, you know. I knew she was green but —"

"Hey, Mank, you did the right thing. Don't second-guess anything."

Mankiewicz nodded.

"I gotta go," Bosch said.

While Edgar returned Delacroix to his spot in the interview room Bosch went into the viewing room, focused the video camera through the one-way glass and put in a new cassette he took from the supply cabinet. He then turned on the camera as well as the backup sound recorder. Everything was set. He went back into the interview room to finish wrapping the package.

37

Bosch identified the three occupants of the interview room and announced the date and time, even though both of these would be printed on the lower frame of the video being recorded of the session. He put a rights waiver form on the table and told Delacroix he wanted to advise him one more time of his rights. When he was finished he asked Delacroix to sign the form and then moved it to the side of the table. He took a gulp of coffee and started.

"Mr. Delacroix, earlier today you expressed to me a desire to talk about what happened to your son, Arthur, in nineteen eighty. Do you still wish to speak to us about that?"

"Yes."

"Let's start with the basic questions and then we can go back and cover everything else. Did you cause the death of your son, Arthur Delacroix?"

"Yes, I did."

He said it without hesitation or emotion.

"Did you kill him?"

"Yes, I did. I didn't mean to, but I did. Yes."

"When did this occur?"

"It was in May, I think, of nineteen eighty. I think that's when it was. You people probably know more about it than me."

"Please don't assume that. Please answer each question to the best of your ability and recollection."

"I'll try."

"Where was your son killed?"

"In the house where we lived at the time. In his room."

"How was he killed? Did you strike him?"

"Uh, yes. I . . ."

Delacroix's businesslike approach to the interview suddenly eroded and his face seemed to close in on itself. He used the heels of his palms to wipe tears from the corners of his eyes.

"You struck him?"

"Yes."

"Where?"

"All over, I guess."

"Including the head?"

"Yes."

"This was in his room, you said?"

"Yes, his room."

"What did you hit him with?"

"What do you mean?"

"Did you use your fists or an object of some kind?"

"Yes, both. My hands and an object."

"What was the object you struck your son with?"

"I really can't remember. I'll have to . . . it was just something he had there. In his room. I have to think."

"We can come back to it, Mr. Delacroix. Why on that day did you — first of all, when did it happen? What time of day?"

"It was in the morning. After Sheila — she's my daughter — had gone to school. That's really all I remember, Sheila was gone."

"What about your wife, the boy's mother?"

"Oh, she was long gone. She's the reason I started —"

He stopped. Bosch assumed he was going to lay blame

for his drinking on his wife, which would conveniently blame her for everything that came out of the drinking, including murder.

"When was the last time you talked to your wife?"

"Ex-wife. I haven't talked to her since the day she left. That was . . ."

He didn't finish. He couldn't remember how long.

"What about your daughter? When did you talk to her last?"

Delacroix looked away from Bosch and down at his hands on the table.

"Long time," he said.

"How long?"

"I don't remember. We don't talk. She helped me buy the trailer. That was five or six years ago."

"You didn't talk to her this week?"

Delacroix looked up at him, a curious look on his face.

"This week? No. Why would —"

"Let me ask the questions. What about the news? Did you read any newspapers in the last couple weeks or watch the news on TV?"

Delacroix shook his head.

"I don't like what's on television now. I like to watch tapes."

Bosch realized he had gotten off track. He decided to get back to the basic story. What was important for him to achieve here was a clear and simple confession to Arthur Delacroix's death. It needed to be solid and detailed enough to stand up. Without a doubt Bosch knew that at some point after Delacroix got a lawyer, the confession would be withdrawn. They always were. It would be chal-lenged on all fronts — from the procedures followed to the suspect's state of mind — and Bosch's duty was not only to take the confession but to make sure it survived and could eventually be delivered to twelve jurors.

"Let's get back to your son, Arthur. Do you remember what the object was you struck him with on the day of his death?"

"I'm thinking it was this little bat he had. A miniature baseball bat that was like a souvenir from a Dodgers game."

Bosch nodded. He knew what he was talking about. They sold bats at the souvenir stands that were like the old billy clubs cops carried until they went to metal batons. They could be lethal.

"Why did you hit him?"

Delacroix looked down at his hands. Bosch noticed his fingernails were gone. It looked painful.

"Um, I don't remember. I was probably drunk. I . . ."

Again the tears came in a burst and he hid his face in his tortured hands. Bosch waited until he dropped his hands and continued.

"He . . . he should have been in school. And he wasn't. I came in the room and there he was. I got mad. I paid good money — money I didn't have — for that school. I started to yell. I started to hit and then . . . then I just picked up the little bat and I hit him. I hit him too hard, I guess. I didn't mean to."

Bosch waited again but Delacroix didn't go on.

"He was dead then?"

Delacroix nodded.

"That means yes?"

"Yes. Yes."

There was a soft knock on the door. Bosch nodded to Edgar, who got up and went out. Bosch assumed it was the prosecutor but he wasn't going to interrupt things now to make introductions. He pressed on.

"What did you do next? After Arthur was dead."

"I took him out the back and down the steps to the garage. Nobody saw me. I put him in the trunk of my car. I then went back to his room, I cleaned up and put some of his clothes in a bag."

"What kind of bag?"

"It was his school bag. His backpack."

"What clothes did you put into it?"

"I don't remember. Whatever I grabbed out of the drawer, you know?"

"All right. Can you describe this backpack?"

Delacroix shrugged his shoulders.

"I don't remember. It was just a normal backpack."

"Okay, after you put clothes in it, what did you do?"

"I put it in the trunk. And I closed it."

"What car was that?"

"That was my 'seventy-two Impala."

"You still have it?"

"I wish; it'd be a classic. But I wrecked it. That was my first DUI."

"What do you mean 'wrecked'?"

"I totaled it. I wrapped it around a palm tree in Beverly Hills. It was taken to a junkyard somewhere."

Bosch knew that tracing a thirty-year-old car would be difficult, but news that the vehicle had been totaled ended all hope of finding it and checking the trunk for physical evidence.

"Then let's go back to your story. You had the body in the trunk. When did you dispose of it?"

"That night. Late. When he didn't come home from school that day we started looking for him."

"We?"

"Sheila and me. We drove around and we looked. We went to all the skateboard spots."

"And all the time Arthur's body was in the trunk of the car you were in?"

"That's right. You see, I didn't want her to know what I had done. I was protecting her."

"I understand. Did you make a missing person report with the police?"

Delacroix shook his head.

"No. I went to the Wilshire station and talked to a cop. He was right there where you walk in. At the desk. He told me Arthur probably ran away and he'd be back. To give it a few days. So I didn't make out the report."

Bosch was trying to cover as many markers as he could, going over story facts that could be verified and therefore used to buttress the confession when Delacroix and his lawyer withdrew it and denied it. The best way to do this was with hard evidence or scientific fact. But cross-matching stories was also important. Sheila Delacroix had already told Bosch and Edgar that she and her father had driven to the police station on the night Arthur didn't come home. Her father went in while she waited in the car. But Bosch found no record of a missing person report. It now seemed to fit. He had a marker that would help validate the confession.

"Mr. Delacroix, are you comfortable talking to me?"

"Yeah, sure."

"You are not feeling coerced or threatened in any way?"

"No, I'm fine."

"You are talking freely to me, right?"

"That's right."

"Okay, when did you take your son's body from the trunk?"

"I did that later. After Sheila went to sleep I went back out to the car and I took it to where I could hide the body."

"And where was that?"

"Up in the hills. Laurel Canyon."

"Can you remember more specifically where?"

"Not too much. I went up Lookout Mountain past the school. Up in around there. It was dark and I . . . you know, I was drinking because I felt so bad about the accident, you know."

"Accident?"

"Hitting Arthur too hard like I did."

"Oh. So up past the school, do you remember what road you were on?"

"Wonderland."

"Wonderland? Are you sure?"

"No, but that's what I think it was. I've spent all these years . . . I tried to forget as much about this as I could."

"So you're saying you were intoxicated when you hid the body?"

"I was drunk. Don't you think I'd have to be?"

"It doesn't matter what I think."

Bosch felt the first tremor of danger go through him. While Delacroix was offering a complete confession, Bosch had elicited information that might be damaging to the case as well. Delacroix being drunk could explain why the body had apparently been hurriedly dropped in the hillside woods and quickly covered with loose soil and pine needles. But Bosch recalled his own difficult climb up the hill and couldn't imagine an intoxicated man doing it while carrying or dragging the body of his own son along with him.

Not to mention the backpack. Would it have been carried along with the body or did Delacroix climb back up the hill a second time with the bag, somehow finding the same spot in the dark where he had left the body?

Bosch studied Delacroix, trying to figure out which way to go. He had to be very careful. It would be case suicide to bring out a response that a defense attorney could later exploit for days in court.

"All I remember," Delacroix suddenly said unbidden, "is that it took me a long time. I was gone almost all night. And I remember that I hugged him as tight as I could before I put him down in the hole. It was like I had a funeral for him."

Delacroix nodded and searched Bosch's eyes as if looking for an acknowledgment that he had done the right thing. Bosch returned nothing with his look.

"Let's start with that," he said. "The hole you put him into, how deep was it?"

"It wasn't that deep, maybe a couple feet at the most."

"How did you dig it? Did you have tools with you?"

"No, I didn't think about that. So I had to dig with my hands. I didn't get very far either."

"What about the backpack?"

"Um, I put it there, too. In the hole. But I'm not sure."

Bosch nodded.

"Okay. Do you remember anything else about this place? Was it steep or flat or muddy?"

Delacroix shook his head.

"I can't remember."

"Were there houses there?"

"There was some right nearby, yeah, but nobody saw me, if that's what you mean."

Bosch finally concluded that he was going too far down a path of legal peril. He had to stop and go back and clean up a few details.

"What about your son's skateboard?"

"What about it?"

"What did you do with it?"

Delacroix leaned forward to consider this.

"You know, I don't really remember."

"Did you bury it with him?"

"I can't . . . I don't remember."

Bosch waited a long moment to see if something would come out. Delacroix said nothing.

"Okay, Mr. Delacroix, we're going to take a break here while I go talk to my partner. I want you to think about what we were just talking about. About the place where you took your son. I need you to remember more about it. And about the skateboard, too."

"Okay, I'll try."

"I'll bring you back some more coffee."

"That would be good."

Bosch got up and took the empties from the room. He immediately went to the viewing room and opened the door. Edgar and another man were in there. The man, whom Bosch didn't know, was looking at Delacroix through the one-way glass. Edgar was reaching to the video to turn it off.

"Don't turn it off," Bosch said quickly.

Edgar held back.

"Let it run. If he starts remembering more stuff I don't want anybody to try to say we gave it to him."

Edgar nodded. The other man turned from the window and put out his hand. He looked like he was no more than thirty. He had dark hair that was slicked back and very white skin. He had a broad smile on his face.

"Hi, George Portugal, deputy district attorney."

Bosch put the empty cups down on a table and shook his hand.

"Looks like you've got an interesting case here," Portugal said.

"And getting more so all the time," Bosch said.

"Well, from what I've seen in the last ten minutes, you don't have a worry in the world. This is a slam dunk."

Bosch nodded but didn't return the smile. What he wanted to do was laugh at the inanity of Portugal's statement. He knew better than to trust the instincts of young prosecutors. He thought of all that had happened before they had gotten Delacroix into the room on the other side of the glass. And he knew there was no such thing as a slam dunk.

38

AT 7 P.M. Bosch and Edgar drove Samuel Delacroix downtown to be booked at Parker Center on charges of murdering his son. With Portugal in the interview room taking part in the questioning, they had interrogated Delacroix for almost another hour, gleaning only a few new details about the killing. The father's memory of his son's death and his part in it had been eroded by twenty years of guilt and whiskey.

Portugal left the room still believing the case was a slam dunk. Bosch, on the other hand, was not so sure. He was never as welcoming of voluntary confessions as other detectives and prosecutors were. He believed true remorse was rare in the world. He treated the unanticipated confession with extreme caution, always looking for the play behind the words. To him, every case was like a house under construction. When a confession came into play, it became the concrete slab the house was built upon. If it was mixed wrong or poured wrong, the house might not withstand the jolt of the first earthquake. As he drove Delacroix toward Parker Center, Bosch couldn't help but think there were unseen cracks in this house's foundation. And that the earthquake was coming.

Bosch's thoughts were interrupted by his cell phone chirping. It was Lt. Billets.

"You guys slipped out of here before we had a chance to talk."

"We're taking him down to booking."

"You sound happy about it."

"Well . . . I can't really talk."

"You're in the car with him?"

"Yeah."

"Is it serious or are you just playing mother hen?"

"I don't know yet."

"I've got Irving and Media Relations calling me. I guess word is already out through the DA's press office that charges are coming. How do you want me to handle it?"

Bosch looked at his watch. He figured that after booking Delacroix they could get to Sheila Delacroix's house by eight. The trouble was that an announcement to the media might mean that reporters would get to her before that.

"Tell you what, we want to get to the daughter first. Can you get to the DA's office and see if they can hold it till nine? Same with Media Relations."

"No problem. And look, after you dump the guy, call me when you can talk. At home. If there's a problem, I want to know about it."

"You got it."

He closed the phone and looked over at Edgar.

"First thing Portugal must've done was call his press office."

"Figures. Probably his first big case. He's going to milk it for all he can."

"Yeah."

They drove in silence for a few minutes. Bosch thought about what he had insinuated to Billets. He couldn't quite place his reason for discomfort. The case was now moving

from the realm of the police investigation to the realm of
the court system. There was still a lot of investigative work
to be done, but all cases changed once a suspect was charged
and in custody and the prosecution began. Most times
Bosch felt a sense of relief and fulfillment at the moment he
was taking a killer to be booked. He felt as though he was a
prince of the city, that he had made a difference in some
way. But not this time and he wasn't sure why.

He finally tied off his feelings on his own missteps and
the uncontrollable movements of the case. He decided
he could not celebrate or feel much like a prince of the
city when the case had cost so much. Yes, they had the ad-
mitted killer of a child in the car with them and they were
taking him to jail. But Nicholas Trent and Julia Brasher
were dead. The house he had built of the case would
always have rooms containing their ghosts. They would
always haunt him.

"Was that my daughter you were talking about? You're
going to talk to her?"

Bosch looked up into the rearview mirror. Delacroix
was hunched forward because his hands were cuffed
behind his back. Bosch had to adjust the mirror and turn
on the dome light to see his eyes.

"Yeah. We're going to give her the news."

"Do you have to? Do you have to bring her into this?"

Bosch watched him in the mirror for a moment.
Delacroix's eyes were shifting back and forth.

"We've got no choice," Bosch said. "It's her brother, her
father."

Bosch put the car onto the Los Angeles Street exit. They
would be at the booking entrance at the back of Parker
Center in five minutes.

"What are you going to tell her?"

"What you told us. That you killed Arthur. We want to

tell her before the reporters get to her or she sees it on the news."

He checked the mirror. He saw Delacroix nod his approval. Then the man's eyes came up and looked at Bosch's in the mirror.

"Will you tell her something for me?"

"Tell her what?"

Bosch reached inside his coat pocket for his recorder but then realized he didn't have it with him. He silently cursed Bradley and his own decision to cooperate with IAD.

Delacroix was quiet for a moment. He moved his head as he looked from side to side as if searching for the thing he wanted to say to his daughter. Then he looked back up at the mirror and spoke.

"Just tell her that I'm sorry for everything. Just like that. Sorry for everything. Tell her that."

"You're sorry for everything. I got it. Anything else?"

"No, just that."

Edgar shifted in his seat so he could look back at Delacroix.

"You're sorry, huh?" he said. "Seems kind of late after twenty years, don't you think?"

Bosch turned right onto Los Angeles Street. He couldn't check the mirror for Delacroix's reaction.

"You don't know anything," Delacroix angrily retorted. "I've been crying for twenty years."

"Yeah," Edgar threw back. "Crying in your whiskey. But not enough to do anything about it until we showed up. Not enough to crawl out of your bottle and turn yourself in and get your boy out of the dirt while there was still enough of him for a proper burial. All we have is bones, you know. Bones."

Bosch now checked the mirror. Delacroix shook his head and leaned even further forward, until his head was against the back of the front seat.

"I couldn't," he said. "I didn't even —"

He stopped himself and Bosch watched the mirror as Delacroix's shoulders started to shake. He was crying.

"Didn't even what?" Bosch asked.

Delacroix didn't respond.

"Didn't even what?" Bosch asked louder.

Then he heard Delacroix vomit onto the floor of the back compartment.

"Ah, shit!" Edgar yelled. "I knew this was going to happen."

The car filled with the acrid smell of a drunk tank. Alcohol-based vomit. Bosch lowered his window all the way despite the brisk January air. Edgar did the same. Bosch turned the car into Parker Center.

"It's your turn, I think," Bosch said. "I got the last one. That wit we pulled out of Bar Marmount."

"I know, I know," Edgar said. "Just what I wanna be doing before dinner."

Bosch pulled into one of the spaces near the intake doors that were reserved for vehicles carrying prisoners. A booking officer standing by the door started heading toward the car.

Bosch recalled Julia Brasher's complaint about having to clean vomit out of the back of patrol cars. It was almost like she was jabbing him in the sore ribs again, making him smile despite the pain.

39

SHEILA Delacroix answered the door of the home where she and her brother had lived but only one of them had grown up. She was wearing black leggings and a long T-shirt that went almost to her knees. Her face was scrubbed of makeup and Bosch noticed for the first time that she had a pretty face when it was not hidden by paint and powder. Her eyes grew wide when she recognized Bosch and Edgar.

"Detectives? I wasn't expecting you."

She made no move to invite them in. Bosch spoke.

"Sheila, we have been able to identify the remains from Laurel Canyon as those of your brother, Arthur. We are sorry to have to tell you this. Can we come in for a few minutes?"

She nodded as she received the information and leaned for just a moment on the door frame. Bosch wondered if she would leave the place now that there was no chance of Arthur ever coming back.

She stepped aside and waved them in.

"Please," she said, signaling them to sit down as they moved to the living room.

Everybody took the same seats as they had before. Bosch noticed the box of photos she had retrieved the other day was still on the coffee table. The photos were neatly stacked in rows in the box now. Sheila noticed his glance.

"I kind of put them in order. I had been meaning to get around to it for a long time."

Bosch nodded. He waited until she took her seat before sitting down last and continuing. He and Edgar had worked out how the visit should go on the way over. Sheila Delacroix was going to be an important component of the case. They had her father's confession and the evidence of the bones. But what would pull it all together would be her story. They needed her to tell what it was like growing up in the Delacroix house.

"Uh, there's more, Sheila. We wanted to talk to you before you saw it on the news. Late today your father was charged with Arthur's murder."

"Oh, my God."

She leaned forward and brought her elbows down to her knees. She clasped her hands into fists and held them tight against her mouth. She closed her eyes and her hair fell forward, helping to hide her face.

"He's being held down at Parker Center pending his arraignment tomorrow and a bail hearing. I would say that from the looks of things — his lifestyle, I mean — I don't think he'll be able to make the kind of bail they're going to be talking about."

She opened her eyes.

"There must be some kind of mistake. What about the man, the man across the street? He killed himself, he must be the one."

"We don't think so, Sheila."

"My father couldn't have done this."

"Actually," Edgar said softly, "he confessed to it."

She straightened herself, and Bosch saw the true surprise on her face. And this surprised him. He thought she would have always harbored the idea, the suspicion about her father.

"He told us that he hit him with a baseball bat because he skipped school," Bosch said. "Your father said he was drinking at the time and that he just lost it and he hit him too hard. An accident, according to him."

Sheila stared back at him as she tried to process this information.

"He then put your brother's body in the trunk of the car. He told us that when you two drove around looking for him that night, he was in the trunk all along."

She closed her eyes again.

"Then, later that night," Edgar continued, "while you were sleeping, he snuck out and drove up into the hills and dumped the body."

Sheila started shaking her head like she was trying to fend off the words.

"No, no, he . . ."

"Did you ever see your father strike Arthur?" Bosch asked.

Sheila looked at him, seemingly coming out of her daze.

"No, never."

"Are you sure about that?"

She shook her head.

"Nothing more than a swat on the behind when he was small and being a brat. That's all."

Bosch looked over at Edgar and then back at the woman, who was leaning forward again, looking down at the floor by her feet.

"Sheila, I know we're talking about your father here. But we're also talking about your brother. He didn't get much of a chance at life, did he?"

He waited and after a long moment she shook her head without looking up.

"We have your father's confession and we have evidence. Arthur's bones tell us a story, Sheila. There are injuries. A lot of them. From his whole life."

She nodded.

"What we need is another voice. Someone who can tell us what it was like for Arthur to grow up in this house."

"To try to grow up," Edgar added.

Sheila straightened herself and used her palms to smear tears across her cheeks.

"All I can tell you is that I never saw him hit my brother. Never once."

She wiped more tears away. Her face was becoming shiny and distorted.

"This is unbelievable," she said. "All I did . . . all I wanted was to see if that was Arthur up there. And now . . . I should have never called you people. I should've . . ."

She didn't finish. She pinched the bridge of her nose in an effort to stop the tears.

"Sheila," Edgar said. "If your father didn't do it, why would he tell us he did?"

She sharply shook her head and seemed to grow agitated.

"Why would he tell us to tell you he said he was sorry?"

"I don't know. He's sick. He drinks. Maybe he wants the attention, I don't know. He was an actor, you know. "

Bosch pulled the box of photos across the coffee table and used his finger to go through one of the rows. He saw a photo of Arthur as maybe a five-year-old. He pulled it out and studied it. There was no hint in the picture that the boy was doomed, that the bones beneath the flesh were already damaged.

He slid the photo back into its place and looked up at the woman. Their eyes held.

"Sheila, will you help us?"

She looked away from him.

"I can't."

40

Bosch pulled the car to a stop in front of the drainage culvert and quickly cut the engine. He didn't want to draw any attention from the residents on Wonderland Avenue. Being in a slickback exposed him. But he hoped it was late enough that all the curtains would be drawn across all the windows.

Bosch was alone in the car, his partner having gone home for the night. He reached down and pushed the trunk release button. He leaned to the side window and looked up into the darkness of the hillside. He could tell that the Special Services unit had already been out and removed the network of ramps and staircases that led to the crime scene. This was the way Bosch wanted it. He wanted it to be as close as possible to the way it was when Samuel Delacroix had dragged his son's body up the hillside in the dead of night.

The flashlight came on and momentarily startled Bosch. He hadn't realized he had his thumb on the button. He turned it off and looked out at the quiet houses on the circle. Bosch was following his instincts, returning to the place where it had all begun. He had a guy in lockup for a murder more than twenty years old but it didn't feel good to him. Something wasn't right and he was going to start here.

He reached up and switched the dome light off. He quietly opened the door and got out with the flashlight.

At the back of the car he looked around once more and raised the lid. Lying in the trunk was a test dummy he had borrowed from Jesper at the SID lab. Dummies were used on occasion in the restaging of crimes, particularly suspicious suicide jumps and hit-and-runs. The SID had an assortment ranging in size from infant to adult. The weight of each dummy could be manipulated by adding or removing one-pound sandbags from zippered pockets on the torso and limbs.

The dummy in Bosch's trunk had SID stenciled across the chest. It had no face. In the lab Bosch and Jesper had used sandbags to make it weigh seventy pounds, the estimated weight Golliher had given to Arthur Delacroix based on bone size and the photos of the boy. The dummy wore a store-bought backpack similar to the one recovered during the excavation. It was stuffed with old rags from the trunk of the slickback in an approximation of the clothing found buried with the bones.

Bosch put the flashlight down and grabbed the dummy by its upper arms and pulled it out of the trunk. He hefted it up and over his left shoulder. He stepped back to get his balance and then reached back into the trunk for the flashlight. It was a cheap drugstore light, the kind Samuel Delacroix told them he had used the night he buried his son. Bosch turned it on, stepped over the curb and headed for the hillside.

Bosch started to climb but immediately realized he needed both his hands to grab tree limbs to help pull him up the incline. He shoved the flashlight into one of his front pockets and its beam largely illuminated the upper reaches of the trees and was useless to him.

He fell twice in the first five minutes and quickly exhausted himself before getting thirty feet up the steep slope. Without the flashlight illuminating his path he didn't see a small leafless branch he was passing and it raked across his cheek, cutting it open. Bosch cursed but kept going.

At fifty feet up Bosch took his first break, dropping the dummy next to the trunk of a Monterey pine and then sitting down on its chest. He pulled his T-shirt up out of his pants and used the cloth to help stanch the flow of blood on his cheek. The wound stung from the sweat that was dripping down his face.

"Okay, Sid, let's go," he said when he had caught his breath.

For the next twenty feet he pulled the dummy up the slope. The progress was slower but it was easier than carrying the full weight and it was also the way Delacroix told them he remembered doing it.

After one more break Bosch made it the last thirty feet to the level spot and dragged the dummy into the clearing beneath the acacia trees. He dropped to his knees and sat back on his heels.

"Bullshit," he said while gulping breath. "This is bullshit."

He couldn't see Delacroix doing it. He was maybe ten years older than Delacroix had been when he had supposedly accomplished the same feat but Bosch was in good shape for a man his age. He was also sober, something Delacroix claimed he had not been.

Even though Bosch had been able to get the body to the burial spot, his gut instinct told him Delacroix had lied to them. He had not done it the way he claimed. He either didn't take the body up the hill or he'd had help. And there was a third possibility, that Arthur Delacroix had been alive and climbed up the hill by himself.

His breathing finally returned to normal. Bosch leaned his head back and looked up through the opening in the canopy of the trees. He could see the night sky and a partial piece of the moon behind a cloud. He realized he could smell burning wood from a fireplace in one of the houses on the circle below.

He pulled the flashlight from his pocket and reached down to a strap sewn onto the back of the dummy. Since taking the dummy down the hill was not part of the test, he intended to pull it by the carrying strap. He was about to get up when he heard movement in the ground cover about thirty feet to his left.

Bosch immediately extended the flashlight in the direction of the noise and caught a fleeting glimpse of a coyote moving in the brush. The animal quickly moved out of the light beam and disappeared. Bosch swept the light back and forth but couldn't find it. He got up and started dragging the dummy toward the slope.

The law of gravity made going down easier but just as treacherous. As he carefully and slowly chose his steps, Bosch wondered about the coyote. He wondered how long coyotes lived and if the one he had seen tonight could have watched another man twenty years before as he buried a body in the same spot.

Bosch made it down the hill without falling. When he carried the dummy out to the curb he saw Dr. Guyot and his dog standing next to the slickback. The dog was on a leash. Bosch quickly went to the trunk, dumped in the dummy and then slammed it closed. Guyot came around to the back of his car.

"Detective Bosch."

He seemed to know better than to ask what Bosch was doing.

"Dr. Guyot. How are you?"

"Better than you, I'm afraid. You've hurt yourself again. That looks like a nasty laceration."

Bosch touched his cheek. It still stung.

"It's all right. Just a scratch. You better keep Calamity on the leash. I just saw a coyote up there."

"Yes, I never take her off the leash at night. The hills are full of roaming coyotes. We hear them at night. You better come with me to the house. I can butterfly that. If you don't do it right it will scar."

A memory of Julia Brasher asking about his scars suddenly came into Bosch's mind. He looked at Guyot.

"Okay."

They left the car on the circle and walked down to Guyot's house. In the back office Bosch sat on the desk while the doctor cleaned the cut on his cheek and then used two butterfly bandages to close it.

"I think you'll recover," Guyot said as he closed his first-aid kit. "I don't know if your shirt will, though."

Bosch looked down at his T-shirt. It was stained with his blood at the bottom.

"Thanks for fixing me up, Doc. How long do I have to leave these things on?"

"Few days. If you can stand it."

Bosch gently touched his cheek. It was swelling slightly but the wound was no longer stinging. Guyot turned from his first-aid kit and looked at him and Bosch knew he wanted to say something. He guessed he was going to ask about the dummy.

"What is it, Doctor?"

"The officer that was here that first night. The woman. She was the one who got killed?"

Bosch nodded.

"Yes, that was her."

Guyot shook his head in genuine sadness. He slowly stepped around the desk and sank into the chair.

"It's funny sometimes how things go," he said. "Chain reaction. Mr. Trent across the street. That officer. All because a dog fetched a bone. A most natural thing to do."

All Bosch could do was nod. He started tucking in his shirt to see if it would hide the part with blood stains.

Guyot looked down at his dog, who was lying in the spot next to the desk chair.

"I wish that I'd never taken her off that leash," he said. "I really do."

Bosch slid off the desk and stood up. He looked down at his midsection. The blood stain could not be seen but it didn't matter because the shirt was stained with his sweat.

"I don't know about that, Dr. Guyot," he said. "I think if you start thinking that way, then you'll never be able to come out your door again."

They looked at each other and exchanged nods. Bosch pointed to his cheek.

"Thanks for this," he said. "I can find my way out."

He turned toward the door. Guyot stopped him.

"On television there was a commercial for the news. They said the police announced an arrest in the case. I was going to watch it at eleven."

Bosch looked back at him from the doorway.

"Don't believe everything you see on TV."

41

THE phone rang just as Bosch had finished watching the first session of Samuel Delacroix's confession. He picked up the remote and muted the sound on his television and then answered the call. It was Lieutenant Billets.

"I thought you were going to call me."

Bosch took a pull from the bottle of beer he was holding and put it down on the table next to his television chair.

"Sorry, I forgot."

"Still feeling the same way about things?"

"More so."

"Well, what is it, Harry? I don't think I've ever seen a detective more upset about a confession before."

"It's a lot of things. Something's going on."

"What do you mean?"

"I mean I'm beginning to think that maybe he didn't do it. That maybe he's setting something up and I don't know what."

Billets was quiet a long moment, probably not sure how to respond.

"What does Jerry think?" she finally asked.

"I don't know what he thinks. He's happy to clear the case."

"We all are, Harry. But not if he's not the guy. Do you

have anything concrete? Anything to back up these doubts you are having?"

Bosch gently touched his cheek. The swelling had gone down but the wound itself was sore to the touch. He couldn't stop himself from touching it.

"I went up to the crime scene tonight. With a dummy from SID. Seventy pounds. I got it up there but it was a hell of a fight."

"Okay, so you proved it could be done. Where's the problem?"

"I hauled a dummy up there. This guy was dragging his dead son's body. I was straight; Delacroix says he was looped. I had been up there before; he hadn't. I don't think he could've done it. At least not alone."

"You think he had help? The daughter maybe?"

"Maybe he had help and maybe he was never there. I don't know. We talked to the daughter tonight and she won't come across on the father. Won't say a word. So you start to think, maybe it was the two of them. But then, no. If she was involved, why would she call us and give us the ID on the bones? Doesn't make sense."

Billets didn't respond. Bosch looked at his watch and saw it was eleven o'clock. He wanted to watch the news. He used the remote to turn off the VCR and put the TV on Channel 4.

"You got the news on?" he asked Billets.

"Yes. Four."

It was the lead story — father kills son and then buries the body, arrested twenty-some years later because of a dog. A perfect L.A. story. Bosch watched silently and so did Billets on her end. The report by Judy Surtain had no inaccuracies that Bosch picked up on. He was surprised.

"Not bad," he said when it was over. "They finally get it right."

He muted the television again just as the anchor segued

to the next story. He was silent for a moment as he watched the television. The story was about the human bones found at the La Brea Tar Pits. Golliher was shown at a press conference, standing in front of a cluster of microphones.

"Harry, come on," Billets said. "What else is bugging you? There's got to be more than just your feeling that he couldn't have done it. And as far as the daughter goes, it doesn't bug me that she made the call with the ID. She saw it on the news, right? The story about Trent. Maybe she thought she could just pin it on Trent. After twenty years of worrying, she had a way to put it on somebody else."

Bosch shook his head, though he knew she could not see this. He just didn't think Sheila would call the tip line if she had been involved in her brother's death.

"I don't know," he said. "It doesn't really work for me."

"Then what are you going to do?"

"I'm going through everything now. I'll start over."

"When's the arraignment, tomorrow?"

"Yup."

"You don't have enough time, Harry."

"I know. But I'm doing it. I already picked up a contradiction I didn't see before."

"What?"

"Delacroix said he killed Arthur in the morning after he discovered the boy hadn't gone to school. When we interviewed the daughter the first time, she said Arthur didn't come home from school. There's a difference there."

Billets made a chortling sound in the phone.

"Harry, that's minor. It's been more than twenty years and he's a drunk. I assume you are going to check the school's records?"

"Tomorrow."

"Then you get it ironed out then. But how would the sister know for sure whether he went to school or not? All she knows is that he wasn't home afterward. You're not convincing me of anything."

"I know. I'm not trying to. I'm just telling you about the things I'm looking at."

"Did you guys find anything when you searched his trailer?"

"We didn't search it yet. He started talking almost as soon as we got in there. We're going tomorrow after the arraignment."

"What's the window on the warrant?"

"Forty-eight hours. We're all right."

Talking about the trailer made Bosch suddenly remember Delacroix's cat. They had gotten so involved in the suspect's confession that Bosch had forgotten to make arrangements for the animal.

"Shit."

"What?"

"Nothing. I forgot about the guy's cat. Delacroix has a cat. I said I'd get a neighbor to take care of it."

"Should've called Animal Control."

"He was on to us about that. Hey, you have cats, right?"

"Yeah, but I'm not taking in this guy's."

"No, I don't mean that. I just want to know, like, how long do they last without food and some water?"

"You mean you didn't leave any food for the cat?"

"No, we did, but it's probably gone by now."

"Well, if you fed it today it can probably last until tomorrow. But it won't be too happy about it. Maybe tear the place up a little bit."

"Looked like it already had. Listen, I gotta go. I want to watch the rest of the tape and see how we sit."

"All right, I'll let you go. But, Harry, don't kick a gift horse in the mouth. You know what I mean?"

"I think so."

They hung up then and Bosch started the videotape of the confession again. But almost immediately he turned it back off. The cat was bugging him. He should have made arrangements for it to be taken care of. He decided to go back out.

42

As Bosch approached Delacroix's trailer he saw light behind every curtain of every window. There had been no lights on when they left with Delacroix twelve hours earlier. He drove on by and pulled into the open parking space of a lot several trailers away. He left the box of cat food in the car, walked back to Delacroix's trailer and watched it from the same position where he had stood when Edgar had hit the door with his warrant knock. Despite the late hour the freeway's hiss was ever present and hindered his ability to hear sounds or movement from within the trailer.

He slipped his gun out of its holster and went to the door. He carefully and quietly stepped up onto the cinder blocks and tried the doorknob. It turned. He leaned to the door and listened but still could hear nothing from within. He waited another moment, slowly and silently turned the knob and then pulled the door open while raising his weapon.

The living room was empty. Bosch stepped in and swept the trailer with his eyes. No one. He pulled the door closed without a sound.

He looked through the kitchen and down the hallway to the bedroom. The door was partially closed and he could not see anyone, but he heard banging sounds, like somebody closing drawers. He started moving through the kitchen. The smell of cat urine was horrible. He noticed the plate on the floor under the table was clean, the water bowl almost empty. He moved into the hallway and was six feet from the bedroom door when it opened and a head-down figure came toward him.

Sheila Delacroix screamed when she looked up and saw Bosch. Bosch raised his gun and then immediately lowered it when he recognized who it was. Sheila raised her hand to her chest, her eyes growing wide.

"What are you doing here?" she said.

Bosch holstered his weapon.

"I was going to ask you the same thing."

"It's my father's place. I have a key."

"And?"

She shook her head and shrugged.

"I was . . . I was worried about the cat. I was looking for the cat. What happened to your face?"

Bosch moved past her in the tight space and stepped into the bedroom.

"Had an accident."

He looked around the room and saw no cat or anything else that drew his attention.

"I think he's under the bed."

Bosch looked back at her.

"The cat. I couldn't get him out."

Bosch came back to the door and touched her shoulder, directing her to the living room.

"Let's go sit down."

In the living room she sat down in the recliner while Bosch remained standing.

"What were you looking for?"

"I told you, the cat."

"I heard you opening and closing drawers. The cat like to hide in drawers?"

Sheila shook her head as if to say he was bothering over nothing.

"I was just curious about my father. While I was here I looked around, that's all."

"And where's your car?"

"I parked it by the front office. I didn't know if there'd be any parking here, so I parked there and walked in."

"And you were going to walk the cat back on a leash or something?"

"No, I was going to carry him. Why are you asking me all these questions?"

Bosch studied her. He could tell she was lying but he wasn't sure what he should or could do about it. He decided to throw her a fastball.

"Sheila, listen to me. If you were in any way involved with what happened to your brother, now's the time to tell me and to try to make a deal."

"What are you talking about?"

"Did you help your father that night? Did you help him carry your brother up the hill and bury him?"

She brought her hands up to her face so quickly it was as if Bosch had thrown acid in her eyes. Through her hands she yelled, "Oh my God, oh my God, I can't believe this is happening! What are you —"

She just as abruptly dropped her hands and stared at him with bewildered eyes.

"You think *I* had something to do with it? How could you think that?"

Bosch waited a moment for her to calm down before answering.

"I think you're not telling me the truth about what's going on here. So it makes me suspicious and it means I have to consider all possibilities."

She abruptly stood up.

"Am I under arrest?"

Bosch shook his head.

"No, Sheila, you're not. But I would appreciate it if you'd tell me the —"

"Then I'm leaving."

She stepped around the coffee table and headed for the door with a purposeful stride.

"What about the cat?" Bosch asked.

She didn't stop. She was through the door and into the night. Bosch heard her answer from outside.

"You take care of it."

Bosch stepped to the door and watched her walking down the trailer park's access road, out toward the management building, where her car was parked.

"Yeah," he said to himself.

He leaned against the door frame and breathed some of the untainted air from the outside. He thought about Sheila and what she might have been doing. After a while he checked his watch and looked back over his shoulder at the interior of the trailer. It was after midnight and he was tired. But he decided he was going to stay and look for whatever it was she had been looking for.

He felt something brush up against his leg and looked down to see a black cat rubbing up against him. He gently pushed it away with his leg. He didn't care much for cats.

The animal came back and insisted on rubbing its head against Bosch's leg again. Bosch stepped back into the trailer, causing the cat to make a cautionary retreat of a few feet.

"Wait here," Bosch said. "I've got some food in the car."

43

Downtown arraignment court was always a zoo. When Bosch entered the courtroom at ten minutes before nine on Friday morning, he saw no judge yet on the bench but a flurry of lawyers conferring and moving about the front of the courtroom like ants on a kicked-over hill. It took a seasoned veteran to know and understand what was going on at any given time in arraignment court.

Bosch first scanned the rows of public seating for Sheila Delacroix but didn't see her. He next looked for his partner and Portugal, the prosecutor, but they weren't in the courtroom either. He did notice that two cameramen were setting up equipment next to the bailiff's desk. Their position would give them a clear view of the glass prisoner docket once court was in session.

Bosch moved forward and pushed through the gate. He took out his badge, palmed it and showed it to the bailiff, who had been studying a computer printout of the day's arraignment schedule.

"You got a Samuel Delacroix on there?" he asked.

"Arrested Wednesday or Thursday?"

"Thursday. Yesterday."

The bailiff flipped the top sheet over and ran his finger down a list. He stopped at Delacroix's name.

"Got it."

"When will he come up?"

"We've still got some Wednesdays to finish. When we get to Thursdays it will depend on who his lawyer is. Private or public?"

"It'll be a PD, I think."

"They go in order. You're looking at an hour, at least. That's if the judge starts at nine. Last I heard he wasn't here yet."

"Thanks."

Bosch moved toward the prosecution table, having to weave around two groupings of defense lawyers telling war stories while waiting for the judge to take the bench. In the first position at the table was a woman Bosch didn't recognize. She would be the arraignments deputy assigned to the courtroom. She would routinely handle eighty percent of the arraignments, as most of the cases were minor in nature and had not yet been assigned to prosecutors. In front of her on the table was a stack of files — the morning's cases — half a foot high. Bosch showed her his badge, too.

"Do you know if George Portugal is coming down for the Delacroix arraignment? It's a Thursday."

"Yes, he is," she said, without looking up. "I just talked to him."

She now looked up and Bosch saw her eyes go to the cut on his cheek. He'd taken the butterfly bandages off before his shower that morning but the wound was still quite noticeable.

"It's not going to happen for an hour or so. Delacroix has a public defender. That looks like it hurts."

"Only when I smile. Can I use your phone?"

"Until the judge comes out."

Bosch picked up the phone and called the DA's Office, which was three floors above. He asked for Portugal and was transferred.

"Yeah, it's Bosch. All right if I come up? We've gotta talk."

"I'm here until I'm called down to arraignments."

"See you in five."

On the way out Bosch told the bailiff that if a detective named Edgar checked in he should be sent up to the DA's Office. The bailiff said no problem.

The hallway outside the courtroom was teeming with lawyers and citizens, all with some business with the courts. Everybody seemed to be on a cell phone. The marble floor and high ceiling took all of the voices and multiplied them into a fierce cacophony of white noise. Bosch ducked into the little snack bar and had to wait more than five minutes in line just to buy a coffee. After he was out, he legged it up the fire exit stairs because he didn't want to lose another five minutes waiting for one of the horribly slow elevators.

When he stepped into Portugal's small office Edgar was already there.

"We were beginning to wonder where you were," Portugal said.

"What the hell happened to you?" Edgar added after seeing Bosch's cheek.

"It's a long story. And I'm about to tell it."

He took the other chair in front of Portugal's desk and put his coffee down on the floor next to him. He realized he should have brought cups for Portugal and Edgar, so he decided not to drink in front of them.

He opened his briefcase on his lap and took out a folded section of the *Los Angeles Times*. He closed the briefcase and put it on the floor.

"So what's going on?" Portugal said, clearly anxious about the reason Bosch had called the meeting.

Bosch started unfolding the newspaper.

"What's going on is we charged the wrong guy and we better fix it before he gets arraigned."

"Whoa, shit. I knew you were going to say something like that," Portugal said. "I don't know if I want to hear this. You are messing up a good thing, Bosch."

"I don't care what I'm doing. If the guy didn't do it, he didn't do it."

"But he *told* us he did it. *Several* times."

"Look," Edgar said to Portugal. "Let Harry say what he wants to say. We don't want to fuck this up."

"It may be too late with Mr. Can't-Leave-A-Good-Thing-Alone here."

"Harry, just go on. What's wrong?"

Bosch told them about taking the dummy up to Wonderland Avenue and re-creating Delacroix's supposed trek up the steep hillside.

"I made it — just barely," he said, gently touching his cheek. "But the point is, Del —"

"Yeah, you made it," Portugal said. "You made it, so Delacroix could have made it. What's the problem with that?"

"The problem is that I was sober when I did it and he says he wasn't. I also knew where I was going. I knew it leveled off up there. He didn't."

"This is all minor bullshit."

"No, what's bullshit is Delacroix's story. Nobody dragged that kid's body up there. He was alive when he was up there. Somebody killed him up there."

Portugal shook his head in frustration.

"This is all wild conjecture, Detective Bosch. I'm not going to stop this whole process because —"

"It's conjecture. Not wild conjecture."

Bosch looked over at Edgar but his partner didn't look back at him. He had a glum look on his face. Bosch looked back at Portugal.

"Look, I'm not done. There's more. After I got home last night I remembered Delacroix's cat. We left it in his trailer and told him we'd take care of it but we forgot. So I went back."

Bosch could hear Edgar breathing heavily and he knew what the problem was. Edgar had been left out of the loop by his own partner. It was embarrassing for him to be getting this information at the same time as Portugal. In a perfect world Bosch would have told him what he had before going to the prosecutor. But there hadn't been time for that.

"All I was going to do was feed the cat. But when I got there somebody was already in the trailer. It was his daughter."

"Sheila?" Edgar said. "What was she doing there?"

The news was apparently surprising enough for Edgar to no longer care if Portugal knew he was out of the latest investigative moves.

"She was searching the place. She claimed she was there for the cat, too, but she was searching the place when I got there."

"For what?" Edgar said.

"She wouldn't tell me. She claimed she wasn't looking for anything. But after she left I stayed. I found some things."

Bosch held up the newspaper.

"This is Sunday's Metro section. It has a pretty big story on the case, mostly a generic feature about forensics on cases like this. But there's a lot of detail about our case from an unnamed source. Mostly about the crime scene."

Bosch thought after reading the article the first time in Delacroix's trailer the night before that the source was probably Teresa Corazon, since she was quoted by name in the article in regard to generic information about bone cases. He was aware of the trading that went on between reporters and sources; direct attribution for some information, no attribution for other information. But the identity of the source wasn't important to the present discussion and he didn't bring it up.

"So there was an article," Portugal asked. "What does it mean?"

"Well, it reveals that the bones were in a shallow grave and that it appeared that the body was not buried with the use of any tools. It also says that a knapsack had been buried along with the body. A lot of other details. Also details left out, like no mention of the kid's skateboard."

"Your point being?" Portugal asked with a bored tone in his voice.

"That if you were going to put together a false confession, a lot of what you'd need is right here."

"Oh, come on, Detective. Delacroix gave us much more than the crime scene details. He gave us the killing itself, the driving around with the body, all of that."

"All of that was easy. It can't be proved or disproved. There were no witnesses. We'll never find the car because it's been squashed to the size of a mailbox in some junkyard in the Valley. All we have is his story. And the only place where his story meets the physical evidence is the crime scene. And every marker he gave us he could have gotten from this."

He tossed the newspaper onto Portugal's desk but the prosecutor didn't even look at it. He leaned his elbows on the desk and brought his hands flat against each other and spread his fingers wide. Bosch could see his muscles flexing under his shirtsleeves and realized he was doing some kind of an at-your-desk exercise. Portugal spoke while his hands pushed against each other.

"I work out the tension this way."

He finally stopped, releasing his breath loudly and leaning back in his seat.

"Okay, he had the ability to concoct a confession if he wanted to do it. Why would he want to do it? We're talking about his own son. Why would he say he killed his own son if he didn't?"

"Because of these," Bosch said.

He reached into his inside jacket pocket and took out an envelope that was folded in half. He leaned forward and gently put it down on top of the newspaper on Portugal's desk.

As Portugal picked up the envelope and started to open it, Bosch said, "I think that was what Sheila was looking for in the trailer last night. I found it in the night table next to her father's bed. It was underneath the bottom drawer. A hiding place there. You had to take the drawer out to find it. She didn't do that."

From the envelope Portugal took a stack of Polaroid photos. He started looking through them.

"Oh, God," he said almost immediately. "Is this her? The daughter? I don't want to look at these."

He shuffled through the remaining photos quickly and put them down on the desk. Edgar got up and leaned over the desk. With one finger he spread the photos out on the desk so he could view them. His jaw drew tight but he didn't say anything.

The photos were old. The white borders were yellowed, the colors of the images almost washed out by time. Bosch used Polaroids on the job all the time. He knew by the degradation of the colors that the photos on the desk were far more than a decade old and some of them were older than others. There were fourteen photos in all. The constant in each was a naked girl. Based on physical changes to the girl's body and hair length, he had guessed that the photos spanned at least a five-year-period. The girl innocently smiled in some of the photos. In others there was sadness and maybe even anger evident in her eyes. It had been clear to Bosch from the moment he first looked at them that the girl in the photos was Sheila Delacroix.

Edgar sat back down heavily. Bosch could no longer tell if he was upset by being so far behind on the case or by the content of the photos.

"Yesterday this was a slam dunk," Portugal said. "Today it's a can of worms. I assume you are going to give me your theory on these, Detective Bosch?"

Bosch nodded.

"You start with a family," he said.

As he spoke he leaned forward and collected the photos, squared the edges and put them back in the envelope. He didn't like them being on display. He held the envelope in his hand.

"For one reason or another, the mother's weak," he said. "Too young to marry, too young to have kids. The boy she has is too hard to handle. She sees where her life is going and she decides she doesn't want to go there. She ups and splits and that leaves Sheila . . . to pick up with the boy and to fend for herself with the father."

Bosch glanced from Portugal to Edgar to see how he was playing so far. Both men seemed hooked by the story. Bosch held the envelope with the photos up.

"Obviously, a hellish life. And what could she do about it? She could blame her mother, her father, her brother. But who could she lash out against? Her mother was gone. Her father was big and overpowering. In control. That only left . . . Arthur."

He noticed a subtle shake of Edgar's head.

"What are you saying, that she killed him? That doesn't make sense. She's the one who called us and gave us the ID."

"I know. But her father doesn't know she called us."

Edgar frowned. Portugal leaned forward and started doing his hand exercise again.

"I don't think I am following you, Detective," he said.

"How does this have anything to do with whether or not he killed the son?"

Bosch also leaned forward and became more animated. He held the envelope up again, as if it was the answer to everything.

"Don't you see? The bones. All the injuries. We had it wrong. It wasn't the father who hurt him. It was her. Sheila. She was abused and she turned right around and became the abuser. To Arthur."

Portugal dropped his hands to the desk and shook his head.

"So you *are* saying that she killed the boy and then twenty years later called up and gave you a key clue in the investigation. Don't tell me, you're going to say she has amnesia about killing him, right?"

Bosch let the sarcasm go.

"No, I'm saying she didn't kill him. But her record of abuse led her father to suspect she did. All these years Arthur's been gone, the father thought she did it. And he knew why."

Once more Bosch proffered the envelope of photos.

"And so he carried the guilt of knowing his actions with Sheila caused it all. Then the bones come up, he reads it in the paper and puts two and two together. We show up and he starts confessing before we're three feet in the door."

Portugal raised his hands wide.

"Why?"

Bosch had been turning it over in his mind ever since he had found the photos.

"Redemption."

"Oh, please."

"I'm serious. The guy's getting old, broken down. When you have more to look back at than forward to, you start thinking about the things you've done. You try making up for things. He thinks his daughter killed his son because of his own actions. So now he's willing to take the fall for her. After all, what's he got to lose? He lives in a trailer next to the freeway and works at a driving range. This is a guy who once had a shot at fame and fortune. Now look at him. He could be looking at this as his last shot at making up for everything."

"And he's wrong about her but doesn't know it."

"That's right."

Portugal kicked his chair back from his desk. It was on wheels and he let it bang into the wall behind his desk.

"I got a guy waiting down there I could put in Q with one hand tied to my balls and you come in here and want me to kick him loose."

Bosch nodded.

"If I'm wrong, you could always charge him again. But if I'm right, he's going to try to plead guilty down there. No trial, no lawyer, nothing. He wants to plead and if the judge lets him, then we're done. Whoever really killed Arthur is safe."

Bosch looked over at Edgar.

"What do you think?"

"I think you got your mojo working."

Portugal smiled but not because he found any humor in the situation.

"Two against one. That's not fair."

"There's two things we can do," Bosch said. "To help be sure. He's probably down there in the holding tank by now. We can go down there, tell him it was Sheila who gave us the ID and flat out ask him if he's covering for her."

"And?"

"Ask him to take a polygraph."

"They're worthless. We can't admit them in —"

"I'm not talking about court. I'm talking about bluffing him. If he's lying, he won't take it."

Portugal pulled his chair back to his desk. He picked up the paper and glanced at the story for a moment. His eyes then appeared to take a roving inventory of the desktop while he thought and came to a decision.

"Okay," he finally said. "Go do it. I'm dropping the charge. For now."

44

Bosch and Edgar walked out to the elevator alcove and stood silently after Edgar pushed the down button.

Bosch looked at his blurred image reflected in the stainless steel doors of the elevator. He looked over at Edgar's reflection and then directly at his partner.

"So," he said. "How pissed off are you?"

"Somewhere between very and not too."

Bosch nodded.

"You really left me with my dick in my hand in there, Harry."

"I know. I'm sorry. You want to just take the stairs?"

"Have patience, Harry. What happened to your cell phone last night? You break it or something?"

Bosch shook his head.

"No, I just wanted to — I wasn't sure of what I was thinking and so I wanted to check things out on my own first. Besides, I knew you had the kid on Thursday nights. Then running into Sheila at the trailer, that was out of left field."

"What about when you started searching the place? You coulda called. My kid was back home asleep by then."

"Yeah, I know. I should have, Jed."

Edgar nodded and that was the end of it.

"You know this theory of yours puts us at ground zero now," he said.

"Yeah, ground zero. We're gonna have to start over, look at everything again."

"You going to work it this weekend?"

"Yeah, probably."

"Then call me."

"I will."

Finally, Bosch's impatience got the better of him.

"Fuck it. I'm taking the stairs. I'll see you down there."

He left the alcove and went to the emergency stairwell.

45

THROUGH an assistant in Sheila Delacroix's office Bosch and Edgar learned that she was working out of a temporary production office on the Westside, where she was casting a television pilot called *The Closers*.

Bosch and Edgar parked in a reserved lot full of Jaguars and BMWs and went into a brick warehouse that had been divided into two levels of offices. There were paper signs taped on the wall that said CASTING and showed arrows pointing the way. They went down a long hallway and then up a rear staircase.

When they reached the second floor they came into another long hallway that was lined with men in dark suits that were rumpled and out of style. Some of the men wore raincoats and fedoras. Some were pacing and gesturing and talking quietly to themselves.

Bosch and Edgar followed the arrows and turned into a large room lined with chairs holding more men in bad suits. They all stared as the partners walked to a desk at the far end of the room where a young woman sat, studying the names on a clipboard. There were stacks of 8 × 10 photos on the desk and script pages. From beyond a closed door behind the woman, Bosch could hear the muffled sounds of tense voices.

They waited until the woman looked up from her clip-board.

"We need to see Sheila Delacroix," Bosch said.

"And your names?"

"Detectives Bosch and Edgar."

She started to smile and Bosch took out his badge and let her see it.

"You guys are good," she said. "Did you get the sides already?"

"Excuse me?"

"The sides. And where are your head shots?"

Bosch put it together.

"We're not actors. We're real cops. Would you please tell her we need to see her right away?"

The woman continued to smile.

"Is that real, that cut on your cheek?" she said. "It looks real."

Bosch looked at Edgar and nodded toward the door. Simultaneously they went around both sides of her desk and approached the door.

"Hey! She's taking a reading! You can't —"

Bosch opened the door and stepped into a small room where Sheila Delacroix was sitting behind a desk watching a man seated on a folding chair in the middle of the room. He was reading from a page of script. A young woman was in the corner behind a video camera on a tripod. In another corner two men sat on folding chairs watching the reading.

The man reading the script didn't stop when Bosch and Edgar entered.

"The proof's in your pudding, you mutt!" he said. "You left your DNA all over the scene. Now get up and get against —"

"Okay, okay," Delacroix said. "Stop there, Frank."

She looked up at Bosch and Edgar.

"*What* is this?"

The woman from the desk roughly pushed past Bosch into the room.

"I'm sorry, Sheila, these guys just bullied their way in like they're real cops or something."

"We need to talk to you, Sheila," Bosch said. "Right now."

"I'm in the middle of a reading. Can't you see that I —"

"We're in the middle of a murder investigation. Remember?"

She threw a pen down on the desk and pushed her hands up through her hair. She turned to the woman on the video camera, which was now focused on Bosch and Edgar.

"Okay, Jennifer, turn that off," she said. "Everybody, I need a few minutes. Frank, I am very sorry. You were doing great. Can you stay and wait a few minutes? I promise to take you first, as soon as I am done."

Frank stood up and smiled brilliantly.

"No problem, Sheila. I'll be right outside."

Everybody shuffled out of the room, leaving Bosch and Edgar alone with Sheila.

"Well," she said after the door closed. "With an entrance like that, you really should be actors."

She tried smiling but it didn't work. Bosch came over to the desk. He remained standing. Edgar leaned his back against the door. They had decided on the way over that Bosch would handle her.

She said, "The show I'm casting is about two detectives called 'the closers' because they have a perfect record of closing cases nobody else seems able to. I guess there's no such thing in real life, is there?"

"Nobody's perfect," Bosch said. "Not even close."

"What is so important that you had to come bursting in here, embarrassing me like that?"

"Couple things. I thought you might want to know that I found what you were looking for last night and —"

"I told you, I wasn't —"

"— your father was released from custody about an hour ago."

"What do you mean *released*? You said last night he wouldn't be able to make bail."

"He wouldn't have been able to. But he's not charged with the crime anymore."

"But he confessed. You said he —"

"Well, he de-confessed this morning. That was after we told him we were going to put him on a polygraph machine and mentioned that it was you who called us up and gave us the tip that led to the ID of your brother."

She shook her head slightly.

"I don't understand."

"I think you do, Sheila. Your father thought you killed Arthur. You were the one who hit him all the time, who hurt him, who put him in the hospital that time after hitting him with the bat. When he disappeared your father thought maybe you'd finally gone all the way and killed him, then hidden the body. He even went into Arthur's room and got rid of that little bat in case you had used that again."

Sheila put her elbows on the desk and hid her face in her hands.

"So when we showed up he started confessing. He was willing to take the fall for you to make up for what he did to you. For this."

Bosch reached into his pocket and took out the envelope containing the photos. He dropped it onto the desk between her elbows. She slowly lowered her hands and picked it up. She didn't open the envelope. She didn't have to.

"How's that for a reading, Sheila?"

"You people . . . is this what you do? Invade people's lives like this? I mean, their secrets, everything?"

"We're the closers, Sheila. Sometimes we have to."

Bosch saw a case of water bottles on the floor next to her desk. He reached down and opened a bottle for her. He looked at Edgar, who shook his head. Bosch got another bottle for himself, pulled the chair Frank had used close to her desk and sat down.

"Listen to me, Sheila. You were a victim. You were a kid. He was your father, he was strong and in control. There is no shame for you in being a victim."

She didn't respond.

"Whatever baggage you carry with you, now is the time to lose it. To tell us what happened. Everything. I think there is more than what you told us before. We're back at square one and we need your help. This is your brother we're talking about."

He opened the bottle and took a long draw of water. For the first time he noticed how warm it was in the room. Sheila spoke while he took his second drink from the bottle.

"I understand something now . . ."

"What is that?"

She was staring down at her hands. When she spoke it was like she was speaking to herself. Or to nobody.

"After Arthur was gone, my father never touched me again. I never . . . I thought it was because I had become undesirable in some way. I was overweight, ugly. I think now maybe it was because . . . he was afraid of what he thought I had done or what I might be able to do."

She put the envelope back down on the desk. Bosch leaned forward again.

"Sheila, is there anything else about that time, about that last day, that you didn't tell us before? Anything that can help us?"

She nodded very slightly and then bowed her head, hiding her face behind her raised fists.

"I knew he was running away," she said slowly. "And I didn't do anything to stop him."

Bosch moved forward on the edge of the seat. He spoke gently to her.

"How so, Sheila?"

There was a long pause before she answered.

"When I came home from school that day. He was there. In his room."

"So he did come home?"

"Yes. For a little bit. His door was open a crack and I looked in. He didn't see me. He was putting things into his book bag. Clothes, things like that. I knew what he was doing. He was packing and was going to run. I just . . . I went into my room and closed the door. I wanted him to go. I guess I hated him, I don't know. But I wanted him gone. To me he was the cause of everything. I just wanted him to be gone. I stayed in my room until I heard the front door close."

She raised her face and looked at Bosch. Her eyes were wet but Bosch had often before seen that in a purging of guilt and truth came a strength. He saw it in her eyes now.

"I could have stopped him but I didn't. And that's what I've had to live with. Now that I know what happened to him . . ."

Her eyes went off past Bosch, somewhere over his shoulder, where she could see the wave of guilt coming toward her.

"Thank you, Sheila," Bosch said softly. "Is there anything else you know that could help us?"

She shook her head.

"We'll leave you alone now."

He got up and moved the chair back to the spot in the middle of the room. He then came back to the desk and picked up the envelope containing the Polaroids. He headed toward the office door and Edgar opened it.

"What will happen to him?" she asked.

They turned around and looked back. Edgar closed the door. Bosch knew she was talking about her father.

"Nothing," he said. "What he did to you is long past any statute of limitation. He goes back to his trailer."

She nodded without looking up at Bosch.

"Sheila, he may have been a destroyer at one time. But time has a way of changing things. It's a circle. It takes power away and gives it to those who once had none. Right now your father is the one who is destroyed. Believe me. He can't hurt you anymore. He's nothing."

"What will you do with the photographs?"

Bosch looked down at the envelope in his hand and then back up at her.

"They have to go into the file. Nobody will see them."

"I want to burn them."

"Burn the memories."

She nodded. Bosch was turning to go when he heard her laugh and he looked back at her. She was shaking her head.

"What?"

"Nothing. It's just that I've got to sit here and listen to people trying to talk and sound like you all day. And I know right now nobody will come close. Nobody will get it right."

"That's show business," Bosch said.

As they headed back down the hallway to the stairs Bosch and Edgar passed by all the actors again. In the stairwell the one named Frank was saying his lines out loud. He smiled at the true detectives as they passed.

"Hey, guys, you guys are for real, right? How do you think I was doing in there?"

Bosch didn't answer.

"You were great, Frank," Edgar said. "You're a closer, man. The proof is in the pudding."

46

At two o'clock Friday afternoon Bosch and Edgar made their way through the squad room to the homicide table. They had driven from the Westside to Hollywood in virtual silence. It was the tenth day of the case. They were no closer to the killer of Arthur Delacroix than they had been during all the years that Arthur Delacroix's bones had lain silently on the hillside above Wonderland Avenue. All they had to show for their ten days was a dead cop and the suicide of an apparently reformed pedophile.

As usual there was a stack of pink phone messages left for Bosch at his place. There was also an inter-office dispatch envelope. He picked up the envelope first, guessing he knew what was in it.

"About time," he said.

He opened the envelope and slid his mini-cassette recorder out of it. He pushed the play button to check the battery. He immediately heard his own voice. He lowered the volume and turned off the device. He slipped it into his jacket pocket and dropped the envelope into the trash can by his feet.

He shuffled through the phone messages. Almost all were from reporters. Live by the media, die by the media, he thought. He would leave it to the Media Relations Office to explain to the world how a man who confessed to and was charged with a murder one day was exonerated and released the next.

"You know," Bosch said to Edgar, "in Canada the cops don't have to tell the media jack about a case until it's over. It's like a media blackout on every case."

"Plus, they've got that round bacon up there," Edgar replied. "What're we doing here, Harry?"

There was a message from the family counselor at the medical examiner's office telling Bosch that the remains of Arthur Delacroix had been released to his family for burial on Sunday. Bosch put it aside so he could call back to find out about the funeral arrangements and which member of the family had claimed the remains.

He went back to the messages and came upon a pink slip that immediately gave him pause. He leaned back in his chair and studied it, a tightness coming over his scalp and going down the back of his neck. The message came in at ten-thirty-five and was from a Lieutenant Bollenbach in the Office of Operations — the O-3 as it was more popularly known by the rank and file. The O-3 was where all personnel assignments and transfers were issued. A decade before when Bosch was moved to the Hollywood Division he had gotten the word after a forthwith from the O-3. Same thing with Kiz Rider going to RHD the year before.

Bosch thought about what Irving had said to him in the interview room three days earlier. He guessed that the O-3 was now about to begin an effort to achieve the deputy chief's wish for Bosch's retirement. He took the message as a sign he was being transferred out of Hollywood. His new assignment would likely involve some freeway therapy — a posting far from his home and requiring long drives each day to and from work. It was a frequently used management tool for convincing cops they might be better off turning in the badge and doing something else.

Bosch looked at Edgar. His partner was going through his own collection of phone messages, none of which appeared to have stopped him the way the one in Bosch's hand had. He decided not to return the call yet or to tell Edgar about it. He folded the message and put it in his pocket. He took a look around the squad room, at all the bustling activity of the detectives. He would miss it if the new assignment wasn't a posting with the same kind of ebb and flow of adrenaline. He didn't care about freeway therapy. He could take the best punch they could give and not care. What he did care about was the job, the mission. He knew that without it he was lost.

He went back to the messages. The last one in the stack, meaning it was the first one received, was from Antoine Jesper in SID. He had called at ten that morning.

"Shit," Bosch said.

"What?" Edgar said.

"I'm going to have to go downtown. I still have the dummy I borrowed last night in my trunk. I think Jesper needs it back."

He picked up the phone and was about to call SID when he heard his and Edgar's names called from the far end of the squad room. It was Lieutenant Billets. She signaled them to her office.

"Here we go," Edgar said as he got up. "Harry, you can have the honors. You tell her where we're at on this thing. More like where we aren't at."

Bosch did. In five minutes he brought Billets completely up to date on the case and its latest reversal and lack of progress.

"So where do we go from here?" she asked when he was finished.

"We start over, look at everything we've got, see what

we missed. We go to the kid's school, see what records they have, look at yearbooks, try to contact classmates. Things like that."

Billets nodded. If she knew anything about the call from the O-3, she wasn't letting on.

"I think the most important thing is that spot up there on the hill," Bosch added.

"How so?"

"I think the kid was alive when he got up there. That's where he was killed. We have to figure out what or who brought him up there. We're going to have to go back in time on that whole street. Profile the whole neighborhood. It's going to take time."

She shook her head.

"Well, we don't have time to work it full-time," she said. "You guys just sat out of the rotation for ten days. This isn't RHD. That's the longest I've been able to hold a team out since I got here."

"So we're back in?"

She nodded.

"And right now it's your up — the next case is yours."

Bosch nodded. He had assumed that was coming. In the ten days they'd been working the case, the two other Hollywood homicide teams had both caught cases. It was now their turn. It was rare to get such a long ride on a divisional case anyway. It had been a luxury. Too bad they hadn't turned the case, he thought.

Bosch also knew that by putting them back on the rotation Billets was making a tacit acknowledgment that she wasn't expecting the case to clear. With each day that a case stayed open, the chances of clearing it dropped markedly. It was a given in homicide and it happened to everybody. There were no closers.

"Okay," Billets said. "Anything else anybody wants to talk about?"

She looked at Bosch with a raised eyebrow. He suddenly thought maybe she did know something about the call from the O-3. He hesitated, then shook his head along with Edgar.

"Okay, guys. Thanks."

They went back to the table and Bosch called Jesper.

"The dummy's safe," he said when the criminalist picked up the phone. "I'll bring it down later today."

"Cool, man. But that wasn't why I called. I just wanted to tell you I can make a little refinement on that report I sent you on the skateboard. That is, if it still matters."

Bosch hesitated for a moment.

"Not really, but what do you want to refine, Antoine?"

Bosch opened the murder book in front of him and leafed through it until he found the SID report. He looked at it as Jesper spoke.

"Well, in there I said we could put manufacture of the board between February of 'seventy-eight and June of 'eighty-six, right?"

"Right. I'm looking at it."

"Okay, well, I can now cut more than half of that time period. This particular board was made between 'seventy-eight and 'eighty. Two years. I don't know if that means anything to the case or not."

Bosch scanned the report. Jesper's amendment to the report didn't really matter, since they had dropped Trent as a suspect and the skateboard had never been linked to Arthur Delacroix. But Bosch was curious about it, anyway.

"How'd you cut it down? Says here the same design was manufactured until 'eighty-six."

"It was. But this particular board has a date on it. Nineteen eighty."

Bosch was puzzled.

"Wait a minute. Where? I didn't see any —"

"I took the trucks off — you know, the wheels. I had

344 / MICHAEL CONNELLY

some time here between things and I wanted to see if there were any manufacture markings on the hardware. You know, patent or trademark coding. There weren't. But then I saw that somebody had scratched the date in the wood. Like carved it in on the underside of the board and then it was covered up by the truck assembly."

"You mean like when the board was made?"

"No, I don't think so. It's not a professional job. In fact it was hard to read. I had to put it under glass and angled light. I just think it was the original owner's way of marking his board in a secret way in case there was ever a dispute or something over ownership. Like if somebody stole it from him. Like I said in the report, Boney boards were the choice board for a while there. They were hard to get — might've been easier to steal one than find one in a store. So the kid who had this one took off the back truck — this would have been the original truck, not the current wheels — and carved in the date. Nineteen eighty A.D."

Bosch looked over at Edgar. He was on the phone speaking with his hand cupped over the mouthpiece. A personal call.

"You said A.D.?"

"Yeah, you know, as in anno Domini or however you say it. It's Latin. Means the year of our Lord. I looked it up."

"No, it means Arthur Delacroix."

"What? Who's that?"

"That's the vic, Antoine. Arthur Delacroix. As in A.D."

"Damn! I didn't have the vic's name here, Bosch. You filed all of this evidence while he was still a John Doe and never amended it, man. I didn't even know you had an ID."

Bosch wasn't listening to him. A surge of adrenaline was moving through his body. He knew his pulse was quickening.

"Antoine, don't move. I'm coming down there."

"I'll be here."

47

THE freeway was crowded with people getting an early start on the weekend. Bosch couldn't keep his speed as he headed downtown. He had a feeling of pulsing urgency. He knew it was because of Jesper's discovery and the message from the O-3.

He turned his wrist on the wheel so he could see his watch and check the date. He knew that transfers usually took place at the end of a pay period. There were two pay periods a month — beginning the first and the fifteenth. If the transfer they were going to put on him was immediate, he knew that gave him only three or four days to wrap up the case. He didn't want to be taken off it, to leave it in Edgar's or anybody else's hands. He wanted to finish it.

Bosch reached into his pocket and brought out the phone slip. He unfolded it, driving with the heels of his palms on the wheel. He studied it for a moment and then got out his phone. He punched in the number from the message and waited.

"Office of Operations, Lieutenant Bollenbach speaking."

Bosch clicked the phone off. He felt his face grow hot. He wondered if Bollenbach had caller ID on his phone. He knew that delaying the call was ridiculous because what was done was done whether he called in to get the news or not.

He put the phone and the message aside and tried to concentrate on the case, particularly the latest information Antoine Jesper had provided about the skateboard found in Nicholas Trent's house. Bosch realized that after ten days the case was wholly out of his grasp. A man he had fought with others in the department to clear was now the only suspect — with apparent physical evidence tying him to the victim. The thought that immediately poked through all of this was that maybe Irving was right. It was time for Bosch to go.

His phone chirped and he immediately thought it was Bollenbach. He was not going to answer but then decided his fate was unavoidable. He flipped open the phone. It was Edgar.

"Harry, what are you doing?"

"I told you. I had to go to SID."

He didn't want to tell him about Jesper's latest discovery until he had seen it for himself.

"I could've gone with you."

"Would've been a waste of your time."

"Yeah, well, listen, Harry, Bullets is looking for you and, uh, there's a rumor floatin' around up here that you caught a transfer."

"Don't know anything about it."

"Well, you're going to let me know if something's happening, aren't you? We've been together a long time."

"You'll be the first, Jerry."

When Bosch got to Parker Center he had one of the patrolmen stationed in the lobby help him lug the dummy up to SID, where he returned it to Jesper, who took it and carried it easily to its storage closet.

Jesper led Bosch into a lab where the skateboard was on an examination table. He turned on a light that was mounted on a stand next to the board, then turned off the overhead light. He swung a mounted magnifying glass over the skateboard and invited Bosch to look. The angled light created small shadows in the etchings of the wood, allowing the letters to be clearly seen.

1980 A.D.

Bosch could definitely see why Jesper had jumped to the conclusion he did about the letters, especially since he did not have the case victim's name.

"It looks like somebody sanded it down," Jesper said while Bosch continued to look. "I bet what happened was that the whole board was rehabbed at one point. New trucks and new lacquer."

Bosch nodded.

"All right," he said after straightening up from the magnifying glass. "I'm going to need to take this with me, maybe show it to some people."

"I'm done with it," Jesper said. "It's all yours."

He turned the overhead light back on.

"Did you check under these other wheels?"

"'Course. Nothing there, though. So I put the truck back on."

"You got a box or something?"

"Oh, I thought you were going to ride it out of here, Harry."

Bosch didn't smile.

"That's a joke."

"Yeah, I know."

Jesper left the room and came back with an empty cardboard file box that was long enough to contain the skateboard. He put the skateboard in it along with the detached set of wheels and the screws, which were in a small plastic bag. Bosch thanked him.

"Did I do good, Harry?"

Bosch hesitated and then said, "Yeah, I think so, Antoine."

Jesper pointed to Bosch's cheek.

"Shaving?"

"Something like that."

The drive back to Hollywood was even slower on the freeway. Bosch finally bailed at the Alvarado exit and worked his way over to Sunset. He took it the rest of the way in, not making any better time and knowing it.

As he drove he kept thinking about the skateboard and Nicholas Trent, trying to fit explanations into the framework of time and evidence that they had. He couldn't do it. There was a piece missing from the equation. He knew that at some level and at some place it all made sense. He was confident he would get there, if he had enough time.

At four-thirty Bosch banged through the back door into the station house carrying the file box containing the skateboard. He was heading quickly down the hallway to the squad room, when Mankiewicz ducked his head into the hallway from the watch office.

"Hey, Harry?"

Bosch looked back at him but kept walking.

"What's up?"

"I heard the news. We're gonna miss you around here."

The word traveled fast. Bosch held the box with his right arm and raised his left hand palm down and made a sweeping gesture across the flat surface of an imaginary ocean. It was a gesture usually reserved for drivers of patrol cars passing on the street. It said, Smooth sailing to you, brother. Bosch kept going.

Edgar had a large white board lying flat across his desk and covering most of Bosch's as well. He had drawn what looked like a thermometer on it. It was Wonderland Avenue, the turnaround circle at the end being the bulb at the bottom of the thermometer. From the street there were lines drawn signifying the various homes. Extending from these lines were names printed in green, blue and black marker. There was a red X that marked the spot where the bones had been found.

Bosch stood and stared at the street diagram without asking a question.

"We should've done this from the start," Edgar said.

"How's it work?"

"The green names are residents in nineteen eighty who moved sometime after. The blue names are anybody who came after 'eighty but has already left. The black names are current residents. Anywhere you see just a black name — like Guyot right here — that means they've been there the whole time."

Bosch nodded. There were only two names in black. Dr. Guyot and someone named Al Hutter, who was at the end of the street farthest from the crime scene.

"Good," Bosch said, though he didn't know what use the chart would be now.

"What's in the box?" Edgar asked.

"The skateboard. Jesper found something."

Bosch put the box down on his desk and took off the top. He told and showed Edgar the scratched date and initials.

"We've got to start looking at Trent again. Maybe look at that theory you had about him moving into the neighborhood *because* he had buried the kid up there."

"Jesus, Harry, I was almost joking about that."

"Yeah, well, it's no joke now. We have to go back, put together a whole profile on Trent going all the way back to nineteen eighty, at least."

"And meantime we catch the next case here. That's real sweet."

"I heard on the radio it's supposed to rain this weekend. If we're lucky it will keep everybody inside and quiet."

"Harry, inside is where most of the killing is done."

Bosch looked across the squad room and saw Lt. Billets standing in her office. She was waving him in. He had forgotten that Edgar said she was looking for him. He pointed a finger at Edgar and then back at himself, asking if she wanted to see them both. Billets shook her head and pointed back only at Bosch. He knew what it was about.

"I gotta go see Bullets."

Edgar looked up at him. He knew what it was about, too.

"Good luck, partner."

"Yeah, partner. If that's still the case."

He crossed the squad room to the lieutenant's office. She was now seated behind her desk. She didn't look at him when she spoke.

"Harry, you've got a forthwith from the Oh-Three. Call Lieutenant Bollenbach before you do anything else. That's an order."

Bosch nodded.

"Did you ask him where I'm going?"

"No, Harry, I'm too pissed off about it. I was afraid if I asked I'd get into it with him and it's got nothing to do with him. Bollenbach's just the messenger."

Bosch smiled.

"You're pissed off?"

"That's right. I don't want to lose you. Especially because of some bullshit grudge somebody up top has against you."

He nodded and shrugged.

"Thanks, Lieutenant. Why don't you call him on speakerphone? We'll get this over with."

Now she looked up at him.

"You sure? I could go get a coffee so you can have the office to yourself if you want."

"It's all right. Go ahead and make the call."

She put the phone on speaker and called Bollenbach's office. He answered right away.

"Lieutenant, this is Lieutenant Billets. I have Detective Bosch in my office."

"Very good, Lieutenant. Just let me find the order here."

There was the sound of papers rustling, then Bollenbach cleared his throat.

"Detective High . . . Heronyim . . . is that —"

"Hieronymus," Bosch said. "Rhymes with anonymous."

"Hieronymus then. Detective Hieronymus Bosch, you are ordered to report for duty at Robbery-Homicide Division at oh-eight-hundred January fifteen. That is all. Are these orders clear to you?"

Bosch was stunned. RHD was a promotion. He had been demoted from RHD to Hollywood more than ten years earlier. He looked at Billets, who also had a look of suspicious surprise on her face.

"Did you say RHD?"

"Yes, Detective, Robbery-Homicide Division. Are these orders clear?"

"What's my assignment?"

"I just told you. You report at —"

"No, I mean what do I do at RHD? What's my assignment there?"

"You'll have to get that from your new commanding officer on the morning of the fifteenth. That's all I have for you, Detective Bosch. You have your orders. Have a nice weekend."

He clicked off and a dial tone came from the speaker.

Bosch looked at Billets.

"What do you think? Is this some kind of a joke?"

"If it is, it's a good one. Congratulations."

"But three days ago Irving told me to quit. Then he turns around and sends me downtown?"

"Well, maybe it's because he wants to watch you more closely. They don't call Parker Center the glass house for nothing, Harry. You better be careful."

Bosch nodded.

"On the other hand," she said, "we both know you should be down there. You should've never been taken out of there in the first place. Maybe it's just the circle closing. Whatever it is, we're going to miss you. I'll miss you, Harry. You do good work."

Bosch nodded his thanks. He made a move toward leaving but then looked back up at her and smiled.

"You're not going to believe this, especially in light of what just happened, but we're looking at Trent again. The skateboard. SID found a link to the boy on it."

Billets threw her head back and laughed loudly, loud enough to draw the attention of everyone in the squad room.

"Well," she said, "when Irving hears that, he's definitely going to change RHD to Southeast Division, for sure."

Her reference was to the gang-infested district at the far end of the city. A posting that would be the pure-form example of freeway therapy.

"I wouldn't doubt it," Bosch said.

Billets dropped the smile and got serious. She asked Bosch about the latest turn in the case and listened intently while he outlined the plan to put together what would basically be a full-life profile on the dead set decorator.

"I'll tell you what," she said when he was finished. "I'll take you guys off rotation. No sense in you pulling a new case if you're splitting for RHD. I'm also authorizing weekend OT. So work on Trent and hit it hard and let me know. You've got four days, Harry. Don't leave this one on the table when you go."

Bosch nodded and left the office. On his way back to his space he knew all eyes in the squad room were on him. He gave nothing away. He sat down at his space and kept his eyes down.

"So?" Edgar eventually whispered. "What did you get?"

"RHD."

"RHD?"

He had practically yelled it. It would now be known to all in the squad room. Bosch felt his face getting red. He knew everybody else would be looking at him.

"Jesus Christ," Edgar said. "First Kiz and now you. What am I, fucking chopped liver?"

48

KIND of Blue played on the stereo. Bosch held a bottle of beer and leaned back in the recliner with his eyes closed. It had been a confusing day at the end of a confusing week. He now just wanted to let the music move through him and clear out his insides. He felt sure that what he was looking for he already had in his possession. It was a matter of ordering things and getting rid of the unimportant things that cluttered the view.

He and Edgar had worked until seven before deciding on an early night. Edgar couldn't concentrate. The news of Bosch's transfer had affected him more deeply than it did Bosch. Edgar perceived it as a slight against him because he wasn't chosen to go to RHD. Bosch tried to calm him by assuring him that it was a pit of snakes that Bosch would be entering, but it was no use. Bosch pulled the plug and told his partner to go home, have a drink and get a good night's sleep. They would work through the weekend gathering information on Trent.

Now it was Bosch who was having the drink and falling asleep in his chair. He sensed he was at a threshold of some sort. He was about to begin a new and clearly defined time in his life. A time of higher danger, higher stakes and higher rewards. It made him smile, now that he knew no one was watching him.

The phone rang and Bosch bolted upright. He clicked off the stereo and went into the kitchen. When he answered, a woman's voice told him to hold for Deputy Chief Irving. After a long moment Irving's voice came on the line.

"Detective Bosch?"

"Yes?"

"You received your transfer orders today?"

"Yes, I did."

"Good. I wanted to let you know that I made the decision to bring you back to Robbery-Homicide Division."

"Why is that, Chief?"

"Because I decided after our last conversation to hold out one last chance to you. This assignment is that chance. You will be in a position where I can watch your moves very closely."

"What position is that?"

"You were not told?"

"I was just told to report to RHD next pay period. That was it."

There was silence on the phone and Bosch thought now he would find the sand in the engine oil. He was going back to RHD, but as what? He tried to think, What was the worst assignment within the best assignment?

Irving finally spoke.

"You are getting your old job back. Homicide Special. An opening came up today when Detective Thornton turned in his badge."

"Thornton."

"That is correct."

"I'll be working with Kiz Rider?"

"That will be up to Lieutenant Henriques. But Detective

Rider is currently without a partner and you have an established working relationship with her."

Bosch nodded. The kitchen was dark. He was elated but did not want to transmit his feelings over the phone to Irving.

As if knowing these thoughts, Irving said, "Detective, you may feel as though you fell into the sewer but came out smelling like a rose. Do not think that. Do not make any assumptions. Do not make any mistakes. If you do, I will be there. Am I clear?"

"Crystal clear."

Irving hung up without another word. Bosch stood there in the dark holding the phone to his ear until it started making a loud, annoying tone. He hung up and went back into the living room. He thought about calling Kiz and seeing what she knew but decided he would wait. When he sat back down on the recliner he felt something hard jab into his hip. He knew it wasn't his gun because he had already unclipped it. He reached into his pocket and came up with his mini-cassette recorder.

He turned it on and listened to his verbal exchange with Surtain, the TV reporter outside Trent's house on the night he killed himself. Filtering it through the history of what would happen, Bosch felt guilty and thought that maybe he should have done or said more in an effort to stop the reporter.

After he heard the car door slam on the tape he stopped it and hit the rewind button. He realized that he had not yet heard the whole interview with Trent because he had been out of earshot while searching some parts of the house. He decided he would listen to the interview now. It would be a starting point for the weekend's investigation.

As he listened, Bosch tried to analyze the words and sentences for new meanings, things that would reveal a killer. All the while he was warring with his own instincts. As he listened to Trent speak in almost desperate tones he still felt convinced the man was not the killer, that his protests of innocence had been true. And this of course contradicted what he now knew. The skateboard — found in Trent's house — had the dead boy's initials on it and the year he both got the skateboard and was killed. The skateboard now served as a tombstone of sorts. A marker for Bosch.

He finished the Trent interview, but nothing in it, including the parts he had not previously heard, sparked any ideas in him. He rewound the tape and decided to play it again. And it was early in the second go-through that he picked up on something that made his face suddenly grow hot, almost with a feeling of being feverish. He quickly reversed the tape and replayed the exchange between Edgar and Trent that had drawn his attention. He remembered standing in the hallway in Trent's house and listening to this part of the interview. But he had missed its significance until this moment.

"Did you like watching the kids play up there in the woods, Mr. Trent?"

"No, I couldn't see them if they were up in the woods. On occasion I would be driving up or walking my dog — when he was alive — and I would see the kids climbing up there. The girl across the street. The Fosters next door. All the kids around here. It's a city-owned right-of-way — the only undeveloped land in the neighborhood. So they went up there to play. Some of the neighbors thought the older ones went up there to smoke cigarettes, and the concern was they would set the whole hillside on fire."

He turned off the tape and went back to the kitchen and the phone. Edgar answered after one ring. Bosch could tell he had not been asleep. It was only nine o'clock.

"You didn't bring anything home with you, did you?"

"Like what?"

"The reverse directory lists?"

"No, Harry, they're at the office. What's up?"

"I don't know. Do you remember when you were making that chart on the board today, was there anybody named Foster on Wonderland?"

"Foster. You mean last name of Foster?"

"Yeah, last name."

He waited. Edgar said nothing.

"Jerry, you remember?"

"Harry, take it easy. I'm thinking."

More silence.

"Um," Edgar finally said. "No Foster. None that I can remember."

"How sure are you?"

"Well, Harry, come on. I don't have the board or the lists here. But I think I would've remembered that name. Why is it so important? What's going on?"

"I'll call you back."

Bosch took the phone with him out to the dining room table where he had left his briefcase. He opened it and took out the murder book. He quickly turned to the page that listed the current residents of Wonderland Avenue with their addresses and phone numbers. There were no Fosters on the list. He picked up the phone and punched in a number. After four rings it was answered by a voice he recognized.

"Dr. Guyot, this is Detective Bosch. Am I calling too late?"

"Hello, Detective. No, it's not too late for me. I spent forty years getting phone calls at all hours of the night. Nine o'clock? Nine o'clock is for amateurs. How are your various injuries?"

"They're fine, Doctor. I'm in a bit of a hurry and I need to ask you a couple questions about the neighborhood."

"Well, go right ahead."

"Going way back, nineteen eighty or so, was there ever a family or a couple on the street named Foster?"

There was silence as Guyot thought over the question.

"No, I don't think so," he finally said. "I don't remember anybody named Foster."

"Okay. Then can you tell me if there was anybody on the street that took in foster kids?"

This time Guyot answered without hesitation.

"Uh, yes, there was. That was the Blaylocks. Very nice people. They helped many children over the years, taking them in. I admired them greatly."

Bosch wrote the name down on a blank piece of paper at the front of the murder book. He then flipped to the report on the neighborhood canvas and saw there was no one named Blaylock currently living on the block.

"Do you remember their first names?"

"Don and Audrey."

"What about when they moved from the neighborhood? Do you remember when that was?"

"Oh, that would have been at least ten years ago. After the last child was grown, they didn't need that big house anymore. They sold it and moved."

"Any idea where they moved to? Are they still local?"

Guyot said nothing. Bosch waited.

"I'm trying to remember," Guyot said. "I know I know this."

"Take your time, Doctor," Bosch said, even though it was the last thing he wanted Guyot to do.

"Oh, you know what, Detective?" Guyot said. "Christmas. I saved all the cards I received in a box. So I know who to send cards to next year. My wife always did that. Let me put the phone down and get the box. Audrey still sends me a card every year."

"Go get the box, Doctor. I'll wait."

Bosch heard the phone being put down. He nodded to himself. He was going to get it. He tried to think about what this new information could mean but then decided to wait. He would gather the information and then sift through it after.

It took Guyot several minutes to come back to the phone. The whole time Bosch waited with his pen poised to write the address on the note page.

"Okay, Detective Bosch, I've got it here."

Guyot gave him the address and Bosch almost sighed out loud. Don and Audrey Blaylock had not moved to Alaska or some other far reach of the world. They were still within a car drive. He thanked Guyot and hung up.

49

A T 8 A.M. Saturday morning Bosch was sitting in his slickback watching a small wood-frame house a block off the main drag in the town of Lone Pine three hours north of Los Angeles in the foothills of the Sierra Nevadas. He was sipping cold coffee from a plastic cup and had another one just like it ready to take over when he was finished. His bones ached from the cold and a night spent driving and then trying to sleep in the car. He had made it to the little mountain town too late to find a motel open. He also knew from experience that coming to Lone Pine without a reservation on a weekend was not advisable anyway.

As dawn's light came up he saw the blue-gray mountain rising in the mist behind the town and reducing it to what it was; insignificant in the face of time and the natural pace of things. Bosch looked up at Mt. Whitney, the highest point in California, and knew it had been there long before any human eyes had ever seen it and would be there long after the last set was gone. Somehow it made it easier to know all that he knew.

Bosch was hungry and wanted to go over to one of the diners in town for steak and eggs. But he wouldn't leave his post. If you moved from L.A. to Lone Pine it wasn't just because you hated the crowds, the smog and the pace of the big city. It was because you also loved the mountain. And Bosch wasn't going to risk missing Don and Audrey Blaylock to a morning mountain hike while he was eating breakfast. He settled for turning the car on and running the heater for five minutes. He had been parceling out the heat and the gas that way all night.

Bosch watched the house and waited for a light to come on or someone to pick up the newspaper that had been dropped on the driveway from a passing pickup two hours earlier. It was a thin roll of newspaper. Bosch knew it wasn't the *L.A. Times.* People in Lone Pine didn't care about Los Angeles or its murders or its detectives.

At nine Bosch saw smoke start to curl out of the house's chimney. A few minutes later, a man of about sixty wearing a down vest came out and got the paper. After picking it up he looked a half block down the street to Bosch's car. He then went back inside.

Bosch knew his car stood out on the street. He hadn't been trying to hide himself. He was just waiting. He started the car and drove down to the Blaylocks' house and pulled into the driveway.

When Bosch got to the door the man he had seen earlier opened it before he had to knock.

"Mr. Blaylock?"

"Yeah, that's me."

Bosch showed his badge and ID.

"I was wondering if I could talk to you and your wife for a few minutes. It's about a case I'm working."

"You alone?"

"Yeah."

"How long've you been out there?"

Bosch smiled.

"Since about four. Got here too late to get a room."

"Come in. We have coffee on."

"If it's hot, I'll take it."

He led Bosch in and pointed him toward a seating arrangement of chairs and a couch near the fireplace.

"I'll get my wife and the coffee."

Bosch stepped over to the chair nearest the fireplace. He was about to sit down when he noticed all the framed photographs on the wall behind the couch. He stepped over to study them. They were all of children and young adults. They were of all races. Two had obvious physical or mental handicaps. The foster children. He turned and took the seat closest to the fire and waited.

Soon Blaylock returned with a large mug of steaming coffee. A woman came into the room behind him. She looked a little bit older than her husband. She had eyes still creased by sleep but a kind face.

"This is my wife, Audrey," Blaylock said. "Do you take your coffee black? Every cop I ever knew took it black."

The husband and wife sat next to each other on the couch.

"Black's fine. Did you know a lot of cops?"

"When I was in L.A. I did. I worked thirty years for the city fire department. Quit as a station commander after the 'ninety-two riots. That was enough for me. Came in right before Watts and left after 'ninety-two."

"What is it you want to talk to us about?" Audrey asked, seemingly impatient with her husband's small talk.

Bosch nodded. He had his coffee and the introductions were over.

"I work homicide. Out of Hollywood Division. I'm on a —"

"I worked six years out of fifty-eights," Blaylock said, referring to the fire station that was behind the Hollywood Division station house.

Bosch nodded again.

"Don, let the man tell us why he came all the way up here," Audrey said.

"Sorry, go ahead."

"I'm on a case. A homicide up in Laurel Canyon. Your old neighborhood, actually, and we're contacting people who lived on the street back in nineteen eighty."

"Why then?"

"Because that is when the homicide took place."

They looked at him with puzzled faces.

"Is this one of those cold cases?" Blaylock said. "Because I don't remember anything like that happening in our neighborhood back then."

"In a way it's a cold case. Only the body wasn't discovered until a couple weeks ago. It had been buried up in the woods. In the hills."

Bosch studied their faces. No tells, just shock.

"Oh, my God," Audrey said. "You mean all that time we were living there, somebody was dead up there? Our kids used to play up there. Who was it who was killed?"

"It was a child. A boy twelve years old. His name was Arthur Delacroix. Does that name mean anything to either of you?"

The husband and wife first searched their own memory banks and then looked at each other and confirmed the results, each shaking their head.

"No, not that name," Don Blaylock said.

"Where did he live?" Audrey Blaylock asked. "Not in the neighborhood, I don't think."

"No, he lived down in the Miracle Mile area."

"It sounds awful," Audrey said. "How was he killed?"

"He was beaten to death. If you don't mind — I mean, I know you're curious about it, but I need to ask the questions starting out."

"Oh, I'm sorry," Audrey said. "Please go on. What else can we tell you?"

"Well, we are trying to put together a profile of the

street — Wonderland Avenue — at that time. You know, so we know who was who and who was where. It's really routine."

Bosch smiled and knew right away it didn't come off as sincere.

"And it's been pretty tough so far. The neighborhood has sort of turned over a lot since then. In fact, Dr. Guyot and a man down the street named Hutter are the only residents still there since nineteen eighty."

Audrey smiled warmly.

"Oh, Paul, he is such a nice man. We still get Christmas cards from him, even since his wife passed away."

Bosch nodded.

"Of course, he was too expensive for us. We mostly took our kids to the clinics. But if there was ever an emergency on a weekend or when Paul was home, he never hesitated. Some doctors these days are afraid to do anything because they might get — I'm sorry, I'm going off like my husband, and that's not what you came here to hear."

"It's all right, Mrs. Blaylock. Um, you mentioned your kids. I heard from some of the neighbors that you two had a foster home, is that right?"

"Oh, yes," she said. "Don and I took in children for twenty-five years."

"That's a tremendous, uh, thing you did. I admire that. How many children was it?"

"It was hard to keep track of them. We had some for years, some for only weeks. A lot of it was at the whim of the juvenile courts. It used to break my heart when we were just getting started with a child, you know, making them feel comfortable and at home, and then the child would be ordered home or to the other parent or what have you. I always said that to do foster work you had to have a big heart with a big callus on it."

She looked at her husband and nodded. He nodded back and reached over and took her hand. He looked back at Bosch.

"We counted it up once," he said. "We had a total of thirty-eight kids at one time or another. But realistically, we say we raised seventeen of them. These were kids that were with us long enough for it to have an impact. You know, anywhere from two years to — one child was with us fourteen years."

He turned so he could see the wall over the couch and reached up and pointed to a picture of a boy in a wheel-chair. He was slightly built and had thick glasses. His wrists were bent at sharp angles. His smile was crooked.

"That's Benny," he said.

"Amazing," Bosch said.

He took a notebook out of his pocket and flipped it open to a blank page. He took out a pen. Just then his cell phone started chirping.

"That's me," he said. "Don't worry about it."

"Don't you want to answer it?" Blaylock asked.

"They can leave a message. I didn't even think there'd be clear service this close to the mountain."

"Yeah, we even get TV."

Bosch looked at him and realized he had somehow been insulting.

"Sorry, I didn't mean anything. I was wondering if you could tell me what children you had living in your home in nineteen eighty."

There was a moment when everyone looked at one another and said nothing.

"Is one of our kids involved in this?" Audrey asked.

"I don't know, ma'am. I don't know who was living with you. Like I said, we're trying to put together a profile of that neighborhood. We need to know exactly who was living there. And then we'll go from there."

"Well, I am sure the Division of Youth Services can help you."

Bosch nodded.

"Actually, they changed the name. It's now called the Department of Children's Services. And they're not going to be able to help us until Monday at the earliest, Mrs. Blaylock. This is a homicide. We need this information now."

Again there was a pause as they all looked at one another.

"Well," Don Blaylock finally said, "it's going to be kind of hard to remember exactly who was with us at any given time. There are some obvious ones. Like Benny and Jodi and Frances. But every year we'd have a few kids that, like Audrey said, would be dropped in and then taken out. They're the tough ones. Let's see, nineteen eighty . . ."

He stood up and turned so he could see the breadth of the wall of photos. He pointed to one, a young black boy of about eight.

"William there. He was nineteen eighty. He —"

"No, he wasn't," Audrey said. "He came to us in 'eighty-four. Don't you remember, the Olympics? You made him that torch out of foil."

"Oh, yeah, 'eighty-four."

Bosch leaned forward in his seat. The location near the fire was now getting too warm for him.

"Let's start with the three you mentioned. Benny and the two others. What were their full names?"

He was given their names, and when he asked how they could be contacted he was given phone numbers for two of them but not Benny.

"Benny passed away six years ago," Audrey said. "Multiple sclerosis."

"I'm sorry."

"He was very dear to us."

Bosch nodded and waited for an appropriate silence to go by.

"Um, who else? Didn't you keep records of who came and for how long?"

"We did but we don't have them here," Blaylock said. "They're in storage in L.A."

He suddenly snapped his fingers.

"You know, we have a list of the names of every child we tried to help or did help. It's just not by year. We could probably cut it down a little bit, but would that help you?"

Bosch noticed Audrey give her husband a momentary look of anger. Her husband didn't see it but Bosch did. He knew her instincts would be to protect her children from the threat, real or not, that Bosch represented.

"Yes, that would help a lot."

Blaylock left the room and Bosch looked at Audrey.

"You don't want him to give me that list. Why is that, Mrs. Blaylock?"

"Because I don't think you are being honest with us. You are looking for something. Something that will fit your needs. You don't drive three hours in the middle of the night from Los Angeles for a 'routine questioning,' as you call it. You know these children come from tough back-grounds. They weren't all angels when they came to us. And I don't want any of them blamed for something just because of who they were or where they came from."

Bosch waited to make sure she was done.

"Mrs. Blaylock, have you ever been to the McClaren Youth Hall?"

"Of course. Several of our children came from there."

"I came from there, too. And an assortment of foster homes where I never lasted very long. So I know what these children were like because I was one myself, all right? And I know that some foster homes can be full of love and some can be just as bad as or worse than the place you were taken from. I know that some foster parents are committed to the children and some are committed to the subsistence checks from Children's Services."

She was quiet a long moment before answering.

"It doesn't matter," she said. "You still are looking to finish your puzzle with any piece that fits."

"You're wrong, Mrs. Blaylock. Wrong about that, wrong about me."

Blaylock came back into the room with what looked like a green school folder. He placed it down on the square coffee table and opened it. Its pockets were stuffed with photos and letters. Audrey continued despite his return.

"My husband worked for the city like you do, so he won't want to hear me say this. But, Detective, I don't trust you or the reasons you say you are here. You are not being honest with us."

"Audrey!" Blaylock yelped. "The man is just trying to do his job."

"And he'll say anything to do it. And he'll hurt any of our children to do it."

"Audrey, please."

He turned his attention back to Bosch and offered a sheet of paper. There was a list of handwritten names on it. Before Bosch could read them Blaylock took the page back and put it down on the table. He went to work on it with a pencil, putting check marks next to some of the names. He spoke as he worked.

"We made this list just so we could sort of keep track of everybody. You'd be surprised, you can love somebody to death but when it comes time to remember twenty, thirty birthdays you always forget somebody. The ones I'm checking off here are the kids that came in more recent than nineteen eighty. Audrey will double-check when I'm done."

"No, I won't."

The men ignored her. Bosch's eyes moved ahead of Blaylock's pencil and down the list. Before he was two-thirds to the bottom he reached down and put his finger on a name.

"Tell me about him."

Blaylock looked up at Bosch and then over at his wife.

"Who is it?" she asked.

"Johnny Stokes," Bosch said. "You had him in your home in nineteen eighty, didn't you?"

Audrey stared at him for a moment.

"There, you see?" she said to her husband while looking only at Bosch. "He already knew about Johnny when he came in here. I was right. He's not an honest man."

50

By the time Don Blaylock went to the kitchen to brew a second pot of coffee Bosch had two pages of notes on Johnny Stokes. He had come to the Blaylock house through a DYS referral in January 1980 and was gone the following July, when he was arrested for stealing a car and going on a joyride through Hollywood. It was his second arrest for car theft. He was incarcerated at the Sylmar Juvenile Hall for six months. By the time his period of rehabilitation was completed he was returned by a judge to his parents. Though the Blaylocks heard from him on occasion and even saw him during his infrequent visits to the neighborhood, they had other children still in their care and soon drifted from contact with the boy.

When Blaylock went to make the coffee Bosch settled into what he thought would be an uncomfortable silence with Audrey. But then she spoke to him.

"Twelve of our children graduated from college," she said. "Two have military careers. One followed Don into the fire service. He works in the Valley."

She nodded at Bosch and he nodded back.

"We've never considered ourselves to be one hundred percent successful with our children," she continued. "We did our best with each one. Sometimes the circumstances or the courts or the youth authorities prevented us from helping a child. John was one of those cases. He made a mistake and it was as if we were to blame. He was taken from us . . . before we could help him."

All Bosch could do was nod.

"You seemed to know of him already," she said. "Have you already spoken to him?"

"Yes. Briefly."

"Is he in jail now?"

"No, he's not."

"What has his life been since . . . we knew him?"

Bosch spread his hands apart.

"He hasn't done well. Drugs, a lot of arrests, prison."

She nodded sadly.

"Do you think he killed that boy in our neighborhood? While he was living with us?"

Bosch could tell by her face that if he were to answer truthfully he would knock down everything she had built out of what was good in what they had done. The whole wall of pictures, the graduation gowns and the good jobs would mean nothing next to this.

"I don't really know. But we do know he was a friend of the boy who was killed."

She closed her eyes. Not tightly, just as if she were resting them. She said nothing else until Blaylock came back into the room. He went past Bosch and put another log on the fire.

"Coffee will be up in a minute."

"Thank you," Bosch said.

After Blaylock walked back to the couch, Bosch stood up.

"I have some things I would like you to look at, if you don't mind. They're in my car."

He excused himself and went out to the slickback. He grabbed his briefcase from the front seat and then went to the trunk to get the file box containing the skateboard.

He thought it might be worth a try showing it to the Blaylocks.

His phone chirped just as he closed the trunk and this time he answered it. It was Edgar.

"Harry, where are you?"

"Up in Lone Pine."

"Lone Pine! What the fuck are you doing up there?"

"I don't have time to talk. Where are you?"

"At the table. Like we agreed. I thought you —"

"Listen, I'll call you back in an hour. Meantime, put out a new BOLO on Stokes."

"What?"

Bosch checked the house to make sure the Blaylocks weren't listening or in sight.

"I said put out another BOLO on Stokes. We need him picked up."

"Why?"

"Because he did it. He killed the kid."

"What the fuck, Harry?"

"I'll call you in an hour. Put out the BOLO."

He hung up and this time turned the phone off.

Inside the house Bosch put the file box down on the floor and then opened his briefcase on his lap. He found the envelope containing the family photos borrowed from Sheila Delacroix. He opened it and slid them out. He split the stack in two and gave one-half to each of the Blaylocks.

"Look at the boy in these pictures and tell me if you recognize him, if he ever came to your house. With Johnny or anybody else."

He watched as the couple looked at the photos and then exchanged stacks. When they were finished they both shook their heads and handed the photos back.

"Don't recognize him," Don Blaylock said.

"Okay," Bosch said as he put the photos back into the envelope.

He closed his briefcase and put it on the floor. He then opened the file box and lifted out the skateboard.

"Has either of you —"

"That was John's," Audrey said.

"Are you sure?"

"Yes, I recognize it. When he was . . . taken from us, he left it behind. I told him we had it. I called his house but he never came for it."

"How do you know that this is the one that was his?"

"I just remember. I didn't like the skull and crossbones. I remember those."

Bosch put the skateboard back in the box.

"What happened to it if he never came for it?"

"We sold it," Audrey said. "When Don retired after thirty years and we decided to move up here, we sold all of our junk. We had a gigantic garage sale."

"More like a house sale," her husband added. "We got rid of everything."

"Not everything. You wouldn't sell that stupid fire bell we have in the backyard. Anyway, that was when we sold the skateboard."

"Do you remember who you sold it to?"

"Yes, the man who lived next door. Mr. Trent."

"When was this?"

"Summer of 'ninety-two. Right after we sold the house. We were still in escrow, I remember."

"Why do you remember selling the skateboard to Mr. Trent? 'Ninety-two was a long time ago."

"I remember because he bought half of what we were selling. The junky half. He gathered it all up and offered us one price for everything. He needed it all for his work. He was a set designer."

"Set decorator," her husband corrected. "There is a difference."

"Anyway, he used everything he bought from us on

movie sets. I always hoped I would see something in a movie that I'd know came from our house. But I never did."

Bosch scribbled some notes in his pad. He had just about everything he needed from the Blaylocks. It was almost time to head south, back to the city to put the case together.

"How did you get the skateboard?" Audrey asked him.

Bosch looked up from his notepad.

"Uh, it was in Mr. Trent's possessions."

"He's still on the street?" Don Blaylock asked. "He was a great neighbor. Never a problem at all with him."

"He was until recently," Bosch said. "He passed away, though."

"Oh, my gosh," Audrey proclaimed. "What a shame. And he wasn't that old a man."

"I just have a couple more questions," Bosch said. "Did John Stokes ever tell either of you how he came to have the skateboard?"

"He told me that he had won it during a contest with some other boys at school," Audrey said.

"The Brethren School?"

"Yes, that's where he went. He was going when he first came to us and so we continued it."

Bosch nodded and looked down at his notes. He had everything. He closed the notebook, put it in his coat pocket and stood up to go.

51

Bosch pulled the car into a space in front of the Lone Pine Diner. The booths by all the windows were filled and almost all of the people in them looked out at the LAPD car two hundred miles from home.

He was starved but knew he needed to talk to Edgar before delaying any further. He took out the cell phone and made the call. Edgar answered after half a ring.

"It's me. Did you put the BOLO out?"

"Yeah, it's out. But it's a little hard to do when you don't know what the fuck is going on, *partner.*"

He said the last word as if it was a synonym for asshole. It was their last case together and Bosch felt bad that they were going to end their time this way. He knew it was his fault. He had cut Edgar out of the case for reasons Bosch wasn't even sure about.

"Jerry, you're right," he said. "I fucked up. I just wanted to keep things moving and that meant driving through the night."

"I would've gone with you."

"I know," Bosch lied. "I just didn't think. I just drove. I'm coming back now."

"Well, start at the beginning so I know what the fuck is

going on in our own case. I feel like a moron here, putting out a BOLO and not even knowing why."

"I told you, Stokes is the guy."

"Yeah, you told me that and you didn't tell me anything else."

Bosch spent the next ten minutes watching diners eat their food while he recounted his moves for Edgar and brought him up to date.

"Jesus Christ, and we had him right here," Edgar said when Bosch was finished.

"Yeah, well, it's too late to worry about that. We have to get him back."

"So you're saying that when the kid packed up and ran away, he went to Stokes. Then Stokes leads him up there into the woods and just kills him."

"More or less."

"Why?"

"That's what we have to ask him. I've got a theory, though."

"What, the skateboard?"

"Yeah, he wanted the skateboard."

"He'd kill a kid over a skateboard?"

"We've both seen it done for less and we don't know if he intended to kill him or not. It was a shallow grave, dug by hand. Nothing premeditated about that. Maybe he just pushed him and knocked him down. Maybe he hit him with a rock. Maybe there was something else going on between them we don't even know about."

Edgar didn't say anything for a long moment and Bosch thought maybe they were finished and he could get some food.

"What did the foster parents think about your theory?"

Bosch sighed.

"I didn't really spin it for them. But put it this way, they weren't too surprised when I started asking questions about Stokes."

"You know something, Harry, we've been spinning our wheels is what we've been doing."

"What do you mean?"

"This whole case. It comes down to what?— a thirteen-year-old killing a twelve-year-old over a fucking toy. Stokes was a juvy when this went down. Ain't nobody going to prosecute him now."

Bosch thought about this for a moment.

"They might. Depends on what we get out of him after we pick him up."

"You just said yourself there was no sign of premed. They're not going to file it, partner. I'm telling you. We've been chasing our tail. We close the case but nobody goes away for it."

Bosch knew Edgar was probably right. Under the law, it was rare that adults were prosecuted for crimes committed while they were juveniles as young as thirteen. Even if they pulled a full confession out of Stokes he would probably walk.

"I should have let her shoot him," he whispered.

"What's that, Harry?"

"Nothing. I'm going to grab something to eat and get on the road. You going to be there?"

"Yeah, I'm here. I'll let you know if anything happens."

"All right."

He hung up and got out of the car, thinking about the likelihood of Stokes walking away from his crime. As he entered the warm diner and was hit with the smells of grease and breakfast, he suddenly realized he had lost his appetite.

52

Bosch was just coming down out of the squiggle of treacherous freeway called The Grapevine when his phone chirped. It was Edgar.

"Harry, I've been trying to call you. Where y'at?"

"I was in the mountains. I'm less than an hour out. What's going on?"

"They've got a fix on Stokes. He's squatting in the Usher."

Bosch thought about this. The Usher was a 1930s hotel a block off Hollywood Boulevard. For decades it was a weekly flophouse and prostitution center until redevelopment on the boulevard pushed up against it and suddenly made it a valuable property again. It was sold, closed and readied to go through a major renovation and restoration that would allow it to rejoin the new Hollywood as an elegant grand dame. But the project had been delayed by city planners who held final approval. And in that delay was an opportunity for the denizens of the night.

While the Hotel Usher awaited rebirth, the rooms on its thirteen floors became the homes of squatters who snuck past the fences and plywood barriers to find shelter. In the previous two months Bosch had been inside the Usher twice while searching for suspects. There was no electricity. There was no water, but the squatters used the toilets anyway and the place smelled like an aboveground sewer. There were no doors on any of the rooms and no furniture. People used rolled-up carpets in the rooms as their beds. It was a nightmare to try to search safely. You moved down the hall and every doorway was open and a possible blind for a gunman. You kept your eyes on the openings and you might step on a needle.

Bosch flipped on the car's emergency lights and put his foot hard on the pedal.

"How do we know he's in there?" he asked.

"From last week when we were looking for him. Some guys in narcs were working something in there and got a line on him squatting all the way up on the thirteenth floor. You gotta be scared of something to go all the way to the top in a place with the elevators shut down."

"Okay, what's the plan?"

"We're going to go in big. Four teams from patrol, me and the narcs. We start at the bottom and work our way up."

"When do you go?"

"We're about to go into roll call now and talk it out, then we go. We can't wait for you, Harry. We have to take this guy before he gets out and about."

Bosch wondered for a moment if Edgar's hurry was legitimate or simply an effort to get even with Bosch for his cutting him out of several of the investigative moves on the case.

"I know," he finally said. "You going to have a rover with you?"

"Yeah, we're using channel two."

"Okay, I'll see you there. Put your vest on."

He said the last not because he was concerned about Stokes being armed, but because he knew a heavily armed team of cops in the enclosed confinement of a dark hotel hallway had danger written all over it.

Bosch closed the phone and pushed the pedal down even harder. Soon he crossed the northern perimeter of the city and was in the San Fernando Valley. Saturday traffic was light. He switched freeways twice and was cruising through the Cahuenga Pass into Hollywood a half hour after hanging up with Edgar. As he exited onto Highland he could see the Hotel Usher rising a few blocks to the south. Its windows were uniformly dark, the curtains stripped out in preparation for the work ahead.

Bosch had no rover with him and had forgotten to ask Edgar where the command post for the search would be located. He didn't want to simply drive up to the hotel in his slickback and risk exposing the operation. He took out his phone and called the watch office. Mankiewicz answered.

"Mank, you ever take a day off?"

"Not in January. My kids celebrate Christmas and Chanukah. I need the OT. What's up?"

"Can you get me the CP location on the thing at the Usher?"

"Yeah, it's the parking lot at Hollywood Presbyterian."

"Got it. Thanks."

Two minutes later Bosch pulled into the church parking lot. There were five squad cars parked there along with a slickback and a narc car. The cars were parked up close to the church so that they were shielded from view of the windows of the Usher, which rose into the sky on the other side of the church.

Two officers sat in one of the patrol cars. Bosch parked and walked over to the driver side window. The car was running. Bosch knew it was the pickup car. When the others grabbed Stokes in the Usher, a radio call would go out for the pickup. They would drive over and pick up the prisoner.

"Where are they?"

"Twelfth floor," said the driver. "Nothing yet."

"Let me borrow your rover."

The cop handed his radio out the window to Bosch. Bosch called Edgar on channel two.

"Harry, you here?"

"Yeah, I'm coming up."

"We're almost done."

"I'm still coming up."

He gave the radio back to the driver and started walking out of the parking lot. When he got to the construction fence that surrounded the Usher property he went to the north end, where he knew he would find the seam in the fence the squatters used to get in. It was partially hidden behind a construction sign announcing the arrival soon of historic luxury apartments. He pulled back the loose fence and ducked through.

There were two main staircases at either end of the building. Bosch assumed there would be a team of uniform officers posted at the bottom of each in case Stokes somehow slipped through the search and tried to escape. Bosch took out his badge and held it up and out as he opened the exterior stairwell door on the east side of the building.

As he stepped into the stairwell he was met by two officers who held their weapons out and at their sides. Bosch nodded and the cops nodded back. Bosch started up the stairs.

He tried to pace himself. Each floor had two runners of stairs and a landing for the turn. He had twenty-four to climb. The smell from the overflowing toilets was stifling and all he could think about was what Edgar had told him about all odors being particulate. Sometimes knowledge was an awful thing.

The hallway doors had been removed and with them the floor markings. Though someone had taken it upon himself to paint numbers on the walls of the lower landings, as Bosch got higher the markings disappeared and he lost count and became unsure what floor he was on.

At either the ninth or tenth floor he took a breather. He sat down on a reasonably clean step and waited for his breathing to become more regular. The air was cleaner this high up. Fewer squatters used the upper floors of the building because of the climb.

Bosch listened but he heard no human sounds. He knew the search teams had to be on the top floor by now. He was wondering if the tip on Stokes had been wrong, or if the suspect had slipped out.

Finally, he stood and started up again. A minute later he realized he had counted wrong — but in his favor. He stepped up onto the last landing and the open door of the penthouse — the thirteenth floor.

He blew out his breath and almost smiled at the prospect of not having to climb another set of stairs when he heard shouts coming from the hallway.

"There! Right there!"

"Stokes, no! Police! Free —"

Two quick and brutally loud gunshots sounded and echoed down the hall, obliterating the voices. Bosch drew his gun and quickly moved to the doorway. As he began to peek around the jamb he heard two more shots and pulled back.

The echo prevented him from identifying the origin of the shots. He leaned around the jamb again and looked into the hallway. It was dark with light slashing through it from the doorways of the rooms on the west side. He saw Edgar standing in a combat crouch behind two uniformed officers. Their backs were to Bosch and their weapons were pointed at one of the open doorways. They were fifty feet down the hall from Bosch.

"Clear!" a voice yelled. "We're clear in here!"

The men in the hall raised their weapons up in unison and moved toward the open doorway.

"LAPD in the back!" Bosch yelled and then stepped into the hallway.

Edgar glanced back at him as he followed the two uniforms into the room.

Bosch walked quickly down the hallway and was about to enter the room when he had to step back to let a uniform officer out. He was talking on his rover.

"Central, we need paramedics to forty-one Highland, thirteenth floor. Suspect down, gunshot wounds."

As Bosch entered the room he looked back. The cop on the rover was Edgewood. Their eyes locked for just a moment and then Edgewood disappeared into the shadows of the hallway. Bosch turned back to view the room.

Stokes was sitting in a closet that had no door. He was leaning back against the rear wall. His hands were in his lap, one holding a small gun, a .25 caliber pocket rocket. He wore black jeans and a sleeveless T-shirt that was covered with his own blood. He had entry wounds on his chest and right below his left eye. His eyes were open but he was clearly dead.

Edgar was squatted in front of the body. He didn't touch it. There was no use trying for a pulse and everybody knew it. The smell of burnt cordite invaded Bosch's nose and it was a welcome relief from the smell outside the room.

Bosch turned around to take in the whole room. There were too many people in the small space. There were three uniforms, Edgar, and a plainclothes Bosch assumed was a narc. Two of the uniforms were huddled together at the far wall, studying two bullet holes in the plaster. One raised a finger and was about to probe one of the holes.

"Don't touch that," Bosch barked. "Don't touch anything. I want everybody to back out of here and wait for OIS. Who fired a weapon?"

"Edge did it," said the narc. "The guy was waitin' for us in the closet and we —"

"Excuse me, what's your name?"

"Phillips."

"Okay, Phillips, I don't want to hear your story. Save it for OIS. Go get Edgewood and go back downstairs and wait. When the paramedics get here tell them never mind. Save them a trip up the steps."

The cops reluctantly shuffled out of the room, leaving only Bosch and Edgar. Edgar got up and walked over to the window. Bosch went to the corner farthest from the closet and looked back at the body. He then approached the body and squatted down in the same spot where Edgar had been.

He studied the gun in Stokes's hand. He assumed that when it was removed from the hand OIS investigators would find the serial number had been burned away by acid.

He thought about the shots he had heard while on the stairway landing. Two and two. It was hard to judge them by memory, especially considering his position at the time. But he thought the first two rounds had been louder and heavier than the second two. If that was so it would mean Stokes had fired his little popper after Edgewood had fired his service weapon. It would mean Stokes had gotten off two shots after he had been hit in the face and chest — wounds that appeared instantly fatal to Bosch.

"What do you think?"

Edgar had come up behind him.

"It doesn't matter what I think," Bosch said. "He's dead. It's an OIS case now."

"What it is is a closed case, partner. I guess we didn't have to worry about whether the DA would file the case after all."

Bosch nodded. He knew there would be wrap-up investigation and paperwork, but the case was finished. It would ultimately be classified as "closed by other means," meaning no trial and no conviction but carried in the solved column just the same.

"Guess not," he said.

Edgar swatted him on the shoulder.

"Our last case together, Harry. We go out on top."

"Yeah. Tell me something, did you mention the DA and about it being a juvy case during the briefing in the roll-call room this morning?"

After a long moment Edgar said, "Yeah, I might've mentioned something about it."

"Did you tell them we were spinning our wheels, the way you said it to me? That the DA probably wouldn't even file a case on Stokes?"

"Yeah, I might've said it like that. Why?"

Bosch didn't answer. He stood up and walked over to the room's window. He could see the Capitol Records building and farther past it the Hollywood sign up on the crest of the hill. Painted on the side of a building a few blocks away was an anti-smoking sign showing a cowboy with a drooping cigarette in his mouth accompanied by a warning about cigarettes causing impotence.

He turned back to Edgar.

"You going to hold the scene until OIS gets here?"

"Yeah, sure. They're going to be pissed off about having to hump the thirteen floors."

Bosch headed toward the door.

"Where are you going, Harry?"

Bosch walked out of the room without answering. He used the stairwell at the farthest end of the hallway so that he wouldn't catch up to the others as he was going down.

53

THE living members of what had once been a family stood as points of a hard-edged triangle with the grave in the middle. They stood on a sloping hillside in Forest Lawn, Samuel Delacroix on one side of the coffin while his ex-wife stood across from him. Sheila Delacroix's spot was at the end of the coffin opposite the preacher. The mother and daughter had black umbrellas open against the light drizzle that had been falling since dawn. The father had none. He stood there getting wet, and neither woman made a move to share her protection with him.

The sound of the rain and the freeway hissing nearby drowned out most of what the rented preacher had to say before it got to Bosch. He had no umbrella either and watched from a distance and the protection of an oak tree. He thought that it was somehow appropriate that the boy should be formally buried on a hill and in the rain.

He had called the medical examiner's office to find out which funeral home was handling the service and it had led him to Forest Lawn. He had also learned that it had been the boy's mother who had claimed the remains and planned the service. Bosch came to the funeral for the boy, and because he wanted to see the mother again.

Arthur Delacroix's coffin looked like it had been made

for an adult. It was polished gray with brushed chrome handles. As coffins went it was beautiful, like a newly waxed car. The rain beaded on its surface and then slid down into the hole beneath. But it was still too big for those bones and somehow that bothered Bosch. It was like seeing a child in ill-fitting clothes, obvious hand-me-downs. It always seemed to say something about the child. That they were wanting. That they were second.

When the rain started coming down harder the preacher raised an umbrella from his side and held his prayer book with one hand. A few of his lines managed to drift over to Bosch intact. He was talking about the greater kingdom that had welcomed Arthur. It made Bosch think of Golliher and his unfaltering faith in that kingdom despite the atrocities he studied and documented every day. For Bosch, though, the jury was still out on all of that. He was still a dweller in the lesser kingdom.

Bosch noticed that none of the three family members looked at one another. After the coffin was lowered and the preacher made the final sign of the cross, Sheila turned and started walking down the slope to the parking road. She had never once acknowledged her parents.

Samuel immediately followed and when Sheila looked back and saw him coming after her she picked up speed. Finally, she just dropped the umbrella and started running. She made it to her car and drove away before her father could catch up.

Samuel watched his daughter's car cutting through the vast cemetery until it disappeared through the gate. He then went back and picked up the discarded umbrella. He took it to his own car and left as well.

Bosch looked back at the burial site. The preacher was gone. Bosch looked about and saw the top of a black umbrella disappearing over the crest of the hill. Bosch didn't know where the man was going, unless he had another funeral to officiate on the other side of the hill.

That left Christine Waters at the grave. Bosch watched her say a silent prayer and then walk toward the two remaining cars on the road below. He chose an angle of intersection and headed that way. As he got close she calmly looked at him.

"Detective Bosch, I am surprised to see you here."

"Why is that?"

"Aren't detectives supposed to be aloof, not get emotionally involved? Showing up at a funeral shows emotional attachment, don't you think? Especially rainy-day funerals."

He fell into stride next to her and she gave him half of the umbrella's protection.

"Why did you claim the remains?" he asked. "Why did you do this?"

He gestured back toward the grave on the hill.

"Because I didn't think anybody else would."

They got to the road. Bosch's car was parked in front of hers.

"Good-bye, Detective," she said as she broke from him, walked between the cars and went to the driver's door of hers.

"I have something for you."

She opened the car door and looked back at him.

"What?"

He opened his door and popped the trunk. He walked back between the cars. She closed her umbrella and threw it into her car and then came over.

"Somebody once told me that life was the pursuit of one thing. Redemption. The search for redemption."

"For what?"

"For everything. Anything. We all want to be forgiven."

He raised the trunk lid and took out a cardboard box. He held it out to her.

"Take care of these kids."

She didn't take the box. Instead she lifted the lid and looked inside. There were stacks of envelopes held together by rubber bands. There were loose photos. On top was the photo of the boy from Kosovo who had the thousand-yard stare. She reached into the box.

"Where are they from?" she asked, as she lifted an envelope from one of the charities.

"It doesn't matter," he said. "Somebody has to take care of them."

She nodded and carefully put the lid back on. She took the box from Bosch and walked it back to her car. She put it on the backseat and then went to the open front door. She looked at Bosch before getting in. She looked like she was about to say something but then she stopped. She got in the car and drove away. Bosch closed the trunk of his car and watched her go.

54

THE edict of the chief of police was once again being ignored. Bosch turned on the squad room lights and went to his spot at the homicide table. He put down two empty cardboard boxes.

It was late Sunday, near midnight. He'd decided to come in and clear out his desk and files when no one else would be around to watch. He still had one more day in Hollywood Division but he didn't want to spend it packing boxes and exchanging insincere good-byes with anyone. His plan was to have a clean desk at the start of the day and a three-hour lunch at Musso & Frank's to end it. He'd say a few good-byes to those who mattered and then slip out the back door before anyone even knew he was gone. It was the only way to do it.

He started with his file cabinet, taking the murder books of the open cases that still kept him awake some nights. He wasn't giving up on them just yet. His plan was to work the cases during the downtimes in RHD. Or to work them at home alone.

With one box full he turned to his desk and started emptying the file drawers. When he pulled out the mason jar full of bullet shells, he paused. He had not yet put the shell collected at Julia Brasher's funeral into the jar. Instead he had put that one on a shelf in his home. Next to the picture of the shark he would always keep there as a reminder of the perils of leaving the safety cage. Her father had allowed him to take it.

He carefully put the jar into the corner of the second box and made sure it was held secure by the other contents. He then opened the middle drawer and started collecting all the pens and pads and other office supplies.

Old phone messages and business cards from people he had met on cases were scattered throughout the drawer. Bosch checked each one before deciding whether to keep it or drop it into the trash can. After he had a stack of keepers he put a rubber band around it and dropped it into the box.

When the drawer was almost clear, he pulled out a folded piece of paper and opened it. There was a message on it.

Where are you, tough guy?

Bosch studied it for a long time. Soon it made him think about all that had happened since he had pulled his car to a stop on Wonderland Avenue just thirteen days before. It made him think about what he was doing and where he was going. It made him think of Trent and Stokes and most of all Arthur Delacroix and Julia Brasher. It made him think about what Golliher had said while studying the bones of the murder victims from millenniums ago. And it made him know the answer to the question on the piece of paper.

"Nowhere," he said out loud.

He folded the paper and put it in the box. He looked down at his hands, at the scars across the knuckles. He ran the fingers of one hand across the markings on the other. He thought about the interior scars left from punching all of the brick walls he couldn't see.

He had always known that he would be lost without his job and his badge and his mission. In that moment he came to realize that he could be just as lost with it all. In fact, he could be lost *because* of it. The very thing he thought he needed the most was the thing that drew the shroud of futility around him.

He made a decision.

He reached into his back pocket and took out his badge wallet. He slid the ID card out from behind the plastic window and then unclipped the badge. He ran his thumb along the indentations where it said *Detective*. It felt like the scars on his knuckles.

He put the badge and the ID card in the desk drawer. He then pulled his gun from its holster, looked at it for a long moment and put it in the drawer, too. He closed the drawer and locked it with a key.

He stood up and walked through the squad room to Billets's office. The door was unlocked. He put the key to his desk drawer and the key to his slickback down on her blotter. When he didn't show up in the morning he was sure she would get curious and check out his desk. She'd then understand that he wasn't coming back. Not to Hollywood Division and not to RHD. He was turning in his badge, going Code 7. He was done.

On the walk back through the squad room Bosch looked about and felt a wave of finality move through him. But he didn't hesitate. At his desk he put one box on top of the other and carried them out through the front hallway. He left the lights on behind him. After he passed the front desk he used his back to push open the heavy front door of the station. He called to the officer sitting behind the counter.

"Hey, do me a favor. Call a cab for me."

"You got it. But with the weather it might be a while. You might want to wait in —"

The door closed, cutting off the cop's voice. Bosch walked out to the curb. It was a crisp, wet night. There was no sign of the moon beyond the cloud cover. He held the boxes against his chest and waited in the rain.

AUTHOR'S NOTE: In 1914 the bones of a female homicide victim were recovered from the La Brea Tar Pits in Los Angeles. The bones were nine thousand years old, making the woman the earliest known murder victim in the place now known as Los Angeles. The tar pits continue to churn the past and bring bones to the surface for study. However, the finding of a second homicide victim mentioned in this book is wholly fictional — as of this writing.